Catherine, You Are Not Forgotten
One Woman's Quest for Justice That Evil Will Not Be Left Unanswered

John Rozich

Table of Contents

Dedication

To the honor and eternal memory of Kayla Jean Mueller.
And to Mona, you have been the rock to which I have
clung.

Lacking fame, stature, or importance, I have struggled
knowing the actions of al-Baghdadi. His brutality had
consequences for a beautiful young woman who only wanted
to assist others trapped within the indescribable tragedy of
Syria. May my very limited literary skill and efforts celebrate
her life and bring a justified enduring tribute. My God bless
them and may eternal peaceful rest envelope those who have
perished.

Chapter One

October 26, 2019
The Belly of the Beast

Combat gloves concealed a white-knuckled grip. Yes, she was fearful but determined. The fear was that she might fail in her mission and her right hand tightened even more on the sand-colored nylon loop bolted to the Black Hawk's frame. They were moving rapidly, nearly 145 knots, or almost 167 miles per hour, no more than two hundred feet above the sand. She braced against the sudden unpredictable shuddering of the flying metal beast. One of America's most advanced using "Silent Knight" terrain mapping radar. Sudden adjustments to the desert surface might just toss her out the open side-door killing her instantly. But she held fast, her vice-like grip and taught muscles allowed her to scan the inky black night. She crouched slightly sensing the pressure against her feet as the Black Hawk continuously adjusted its position. In one fluid motion flipped up her night vision, revealing eyes that had often been called "enchanting", but they now revealed something very different. They now held purposeful lethality. Justice for innocent victims. She knew she would kill tonight.

Command had provided three different corridors of entry into this region of Syria, working in close coordination with Kurdish allies. They had scouted carefully to ensure no obstructive elements to very low-level flight. Her destination was a remote stone-enclosed house, or more accurately a walled-off encampment housing one of the world's most wanted men. She had painstakingly assessed and rechecked her equipment. No errors were permissible, at least not foreseeable ones. The rest, she left in God's hands. Her loaded weapon was loosely slung over her shoulder, and hours of practice had ensured it could be in a lethal firing position, ready to discharge its fatal embrace, within 0.64 seconds. An ATPIAL AN/PEQ-15 laser scope modified for the needs of the special operations units in the US military was attached to her M4A1 weapon's rail system, along with an optical AN/PVS-17 night vision package that enabled clear identification of nocturnal operational targets. A rapidly detachable sound suppressor allowing lethal but surprisingly quiet destructive kinetic force was attached to the terminal end of her weapon.

The thudding of the helicopter blades was rhythmic, surprisingly almost pleasant. Yet despite their ultrasecretive design and composition meant to virtually erase the helicopter's characteristic acoustic signature, she intuitively understood the ears of those on the ground would be alerted to their presence—and that this "announcement" would invite a multitude of weapons that could be carried and hand-fired by hostiles on the ground. These shoulder-mounted weapons were derivatives of the famous "stinger" missiles used by the so-called freedom fighters in Afghanistan during the 1980s. These had been almost solely responsible for driving the Soviets out of the country. Almost exactly three decades ago, Russian helicopters had been ripe targets, and the Mujahideen were fearless in confronting the Russians. The end result was that the great Soviet military, with all of its advanced weaponry and technology, had been forced out of the country by a gathering of peasant tribes rooted in a culture reflecting social values prevalent in 1250 AD.

The Americans had replaced the Russians just over twenty years later, at the turn of the new millennium. It was an irony not lost on the woman or her team members. Use of such a weapon, now upgraded third-generation models, on her flying machine would destroy it, killing her and everyone flying with her. But this was not her primary fear.

No, her nagging fear, still percolating within her subconscious as she focused on reviewing each phase of her mission parameters, was that she would fail to conduct herself in a manner that would meet the norm for special operations personnel. That under combat conditions she would suffer an ignominious end, either in being killed or, more worrisome to her, getting her teammates killed because of some personal failure attributable to her sex. For deeply buried within this woman's psyche was the simple acknowledgement that she was alone–the first of her gender to be afforded a truly unique opportunity. She often ruefully smiled at the inherent irony of this concept, even the use of the word "opportunity," as she very likely would end up killed or horribly disfigured after partaking in this "opportunity." But Virginia Lois Mahoney knew she was the first female special operations team member. And her performance, this outcome, would terminate the hard-fought and often bitter experiment of allowing a woman to enter such a sequestered operational theater previously reserved exclusively for and populated solely by men.

They were forcefully descending now. She could feel the metal hulk slowing, the sensation of pressure in the soles of her feet slightly diminishing, and then the dust was kicking up, but the surrounding environment was still black-ink dark. Yet her vision and that of her team was not compromised, as her nocturnal optics had been flipped into position and provided a green illumination of both the background and any objects, a surreal emerald-colored landscape. She was soon out the door, crouching low to provide less of a target for "unfriendlies," but also to avoid becoming headless should unexpected wind gusts pull on the helicopter blades. Such a momentary imbalance in each blade's rotational height would, in effect, momentarily move each closer to the ground, a de facto deadly rotating guillotine for anyone within their whirling touch.

She was now twenty-five yards away from the "bird," moving fast to the first mission checkpoint. Taking her position, she crouched at the front of the five-member team exiting her craft and waited to hear the next set of orders coming through the blackened wire earbuds she wore. Her throat microphone was securely placed and active. Its frequency had been preset at their base camp, and there were backup frequencies that she and the rest of her team had memorized. She scanned the sector immediately in front and to the right using her night scope. The emerald landscape was in itself beautiful, but she was uninterested in aesthetics as she switched to her classified infrared optical probe that would light up anything warm with its white phosphorus signature. If she spotted any of these white phantoms moving over the terrain, betraying a human silhouette, her orders were "Eliminate immediately." She had little doubt that she would comply.

A gentle tap on her shoulder was the communication from the team leader, Jacob Roth, to move to the second preset location. Virginia had been waiting for the sign, and in spite of the circumstances, his action calmed her even within her zoned-in concentration. But then Jacob's conduct usually had that effect on her. Usually, but not always.

Jacob Noah Roth had almost been pulled from the mission and its intense training three months ago, as Command was worried about the impact of his wife's recent perfidious activity. These thoughts tugged at her consciousness but instantly disappeared as she lifted from her position. Her left knee rising and allowing her to scurry rapidly while squatting, she used her night vision to examine the surroundings and held the butt of her weapon firmly against her right shoulder. As a small clump of gravel and dirt fell from her black left kneepad, the air smelled of dry but thinly flowered earth. The wild rue gave a slight woody aroma. There were no identified targets—yet.

Repositioning, Virginia again methodically scanned her surroundings, and again thoughts of Jacob surfaced ever so briefly. Perhaps it was the tension. A correction was in order and, in fact, as she scanned the area to her immediate right, she corrected herself: the thoughts revolved around Jacob's now ex-wife, Jessica. The story was unpleasant and of course had not been provided by Jacob himself, but the narrative had taken on a life of its own within the tightly interwoven special operations community, and it had been told in its multiple derivative versions more often than Virginia felt necessary.

The problem for Virginia was that despite the embellishment or the alleged "factual" content of this particular raconteur, Jacob had ultimately been the recipient of this fraudulent woman and her vacuous morality. Two of the younger team members had provided a snarky assessment that he didn't take care of business at home—specifically in the bedroom—prompting one of the more senior members who heard their speculations to nod slightly. Slowly staring off into the distance, this grizzled veteran, himself twenty-nine years old, ultimately provided his sagely advice, stating that perhaps Jacob himself had been a war casualty. Roth's injury was not physical, but the senior team member thought that perhaps it was psychological; his wounds were hidden, silent, but Roth was a casualty nonetheless. It was Roth's strict devotion to duty, his code of honor, that prevented him from cutting any corners. It evidently had also prevented him from initially seeing the depravity of his now ex-wife.

But this same more senior member of their team, Joe Stallings, had also told the two younger guys to "zip it." He would not tolerate any negative statements about Roth, the conduct of his ex-wife, or their marriage. All were out of bounds and beyond their interest, pay grade, and security clearance. It didn't take much convincing, for the two youngsters actually looked up to Roth and certainly were intimidated by him, his reputation, and his presence. But beyond intimidation, in reality they revered him, almost loved him for the example of courage and leadership that emanated from every pore of Roth's being. He was the personification of a combat leader.

A trained officer who, although very low in the chain of command, was in fact adept in dealing with that most atypical environment encountered by human beings: combat. It was odd, but those who were skilled in such areas often were rapidly advanced through military rank, leaving behind the very origins of their talent and finding themselves in unfamiliar territory as "desk jockeys," where they could potentially be complete failures in strategic planning and personnel management. Roth had stayed in special operations and resisted the pull up the chain of command. There, again, he was different. He was much less interested in his career aspirations than the welfare of his troops and the outcome of the mission. For Roth, this was real. This was his commitment—in fact, his true mistress—and his subordinates knew it. And while these two had quietly discussed Roth's failed marriage, if anyone else outside of the team had even hinted at the sad state of Roth's now dissolved union, these same two youngsters would have ensured a premature end to any outsiders' discussion. Roth was their leader, and he kept them alive.

For many subordinates, any team leader demonstrating such martinet adherence to the details of or the goal of the mission would result in an internal revolt. Command would be notified that this leadership was disingenuous, dangerous, perhaps even fraudulent. But this was not possible with Jacob Noah Roth. Such descriptors did not apply to him. No, he was the first to take often life-threatening risks to protect his teammates, to shield them from danger, and to improvise within orders to ensure safety for his team. His decisions were not irrational or based on an unfounded hubris—they were trenchantly enacted and coherent choices intended to protect his teammates. And thus, the reputation that he carried was that of a dangerous man, devoted to his duty and country and exceptional in his performance of these elements. No one dared "bitch" about him because they didn't want anyone else giving orders. Their lives in highly hazardous environments were dependent upon instant, seasoned, deliberate choices. All knew it was this penetrating insight, his deus ex machina, that was inherent to Jacob's character. They wanted him, and only him, in that position.

He was simplistic in his philosophy. Roth never asked anyone to do any job, assignment, or task that he would not do himself, and if there was some concern in his mind that whatever was being asked was indeed more fluid than he was comfortable with, he did it himself. In fact, more than once his teammates had been forced to emergently respond and rescue this man because he put himself in extreme danger to protect other comrades. Wounded twice and nearly killed in the second incident, he had stunned his superiors into silence in his subsequent after-action review (AAR) conducted by Command of the involved circumstances.

Roth had forcefully responded to a prickly lieutenant commander sitting on the review board that he would not have been able to live with himself, with what he perceived as cowardice, if he had left events as they were—an occurrence that put his troops in danger. The more senior members of the reviewing body, those who themselves had once faced the environment of combat, smiled inwardly at the flummoxed response of the younger officer questioning Roth. They knew the unforgiving circumstances, where split-second decisions are either correct cr they are not, where men are protected or exposed and die in response to such time-sensitive choices. The minor hectoring of Roth was allowed to continue for seventeen seconds more when a senior naval captain cut short the pointed questions by this lieutenant commander and asked Jacob a direct question.

"Lt. Roth, would you make the same decision now given you have had time to review your actions?"

"Yes, sir, I believe I would." This was Jacob's thoughtful, understated answer as he looked into the distance, searching his memories of that specific day. A day he had almost joined God's hereafter.

The collective officialdom had suspended proceedings within 120 seconds and then retired to discuss their findings behind closed doors.

The senior officers experienced in the horror of combat understood that Roth had been daring, but not reckless. Some had shaken their heads at the level of audacity from this younger man, secretly wondering if they themselves had possessed the talent and fortitude of their younger colleague. Collectively, with perhaps the exception of the ersatz warrior —the lieutenant commander who had been asking provocative questions to lay the groundwork for a narrative of Roth's recklessness—these senior scared warriors were almost mesmerized by Jacob's decisions. They found that while his logic and tactics were not infrequently "outside the box," this did not mean they were flawed. Not unless one would call Di Vinci or Michelangelo defective in their advancement of art as a thematic communication sacred to all.

Thus, the review board found no evidence of any violation of military protocols or faulty leadership. In fact, to a person, they had endorsed with rather direct and understated but powerful compliments the actions taken that day. The young and previously critical, if not disparaging, lieutenant commander was "encouraged" to rethink his conclusions, being reminded by that same senior naval officer that memories are long in the service. Further, in a single phrase from this combat-scarred Naval Captain, the "near-shameful interrogation" was an unneeded confrontation with a pure warrior. Such activity might be identical to a cattle brand of "suspected counterfeit" on the lieutenant commander's ass! The findings of the board were thus unanimous.

No, this man was the real deal. Modest, but not without an iron will and supreme confidence in his abilities. Humble, but not with an "aw, shucks" type of bullshit. He simply let the scars on his back, abdomen, and two near his left eye speak for his belief, his commitment to the mission. No one, not even Command, had ever once questioned his effectiveness. They simply worried who would take his place when his time ran out and the Lord called him home during some heroic action taken to shelter or protect his troops.

But of course, this commitment came at a price. His now ex-wife had never understood his concept of honor and duty, that it was not predicated on a Hollywood weekend dress-up role to be worn for show and discarded when there might be some hint of discomfort. Jessica had been instantly attracted to Jacob's masculinity, his confidence, and his unadorned but perceptive analytical mind, set within dark-brown curly hair and a classic chiseled face that not only looked good at twenty-three but would age even better, if he lived to enjoy old age. His soft light-brown eyes hid their near-predatory assessment and categorization of all visual surroundings. His medium frame was muscled, a touch wiry but strong and well-proportioned. He was a natural athlete with exceptional hand-eye coordination and the capability to improvise with an uncanny ability to choose correctly in real-time among seemingly closely related options. Somehow, his choices were nearly always optimal in their discretionary outcomes.

He also loved to read, to learn, and to listen to intelligent discussion from individuals who had studied or were scholarly. It didn't matter if it was Islamic culture in the fourteenth century or Argentinian tolerance, if not outright acceptance, of fleeing Nazis from their lost cause at the end of the Second World War—Jacob wanted to understand as much as he could about nearly everything. He also possessed a near eidetic memory. But those who knew him intimately— not within a physical or carnal liaison, but those who shared a more impactful emotional tethering with the man—were surprised by his seemingly willful blindness to his ex-wife's despicable conduct.

Those who worked closely with Roth had asked themselves if this exceptional individual might be more vulnerable, if not ignorant, to her form of hollow, snarky elitism and its foreseeable treachery. Did it even register in him, they wondered? Did he even understand or recognize such squalid duplicity? For his teammates saw in Jacob a being who constantly grappled with the rarefied air of honorable choices, comparing his conduct to those in history who had proven value. The current crop of shiny parrots, possessing a veneer of cleverness but ill-informed soundbite knowledge, absent scholarly understanding or insight, were thus almost alien beings to Jacob. Such people almost seemed to undress him, leaving him standing naked in front of a shocked crowd in a theater. He would immediately pull deeply inward, attempting to understand their flawed perspective, but it was more than this—it was a momentary sting that he never seemed able to inoculate himself against. To those who knew his talents, they wanted him simply to roll his eyes and dismiss this most common form of twenty-first-century ignorance.

But he could not, and the reasons were complex and deeply embedded in an otherwise perfect warrior, for Roth did understand the more nuanced thematics, narratives, and intricately woven variables that had often pushed history along to its ever-fascinating outcome. Roth always did recover from the malodorous vapors of such people, and quickly. But to those who knew his gravity and skill, and grew both to respect if not love him, it seemed almost absurd that such weightless individuals had any impact upon this man. Yet they did, even if only transiently.

And thus, those who harbored Jacob as a man of significance could not understand his inability or initial unwillingness to apply his remarkable, near-legendary analytical mind and summary judgment to her conduct. She was trash, pure and simple, by anyone's rational metrics. A person with an inability to look beyond the perpetual selfie in the bathroom mirror, beyond the desire to expose her breasts to male strangers and witness the shock, desire, and emotive lust to touch her soft but eternally superficial exterior. She made the concept of self-absorption appear a form of altruism; she adored if not idolized her own exhaled carbon dioxide.

Those few whom Jacob had let into this inner circle realized his vulnerability, his loss of grounding in this most visceral partition of life. But it was more than that. It was as if Jacob seemed to have a sense of disproportionate sensitivity for those who spewed unwarranted criticism of his value. To those who knew him—and possessed rational thought—such criticism was beyond unfounded, for it exposed a malignant deficit within the propagator, calling into immediate question their judgment, intelligence, and indeed their basic human decency. But for Jacob, more often than appropriate, meaning even once, he simply "tried harder to show them his value." This, too, was beyond reasonable. Such a response was totally unnecessary, and to the rational purveyor of human interaction, it angered the soul for someone of such abundant courage to feel the need to demonstrate his "requisite" worth. But in time, Jacob had been duly injured by his ex, harmed to the point of painfully slicing the cord that legally bound them together.

This severance for Roth was as if a channel buoy was suddenly cut loose from its signal location, a guiding marker allowed to float free from its tethered position. But instead of aimless wandering, the floating marker of channel safety had been redirected, as if an internal guidance had instantly activated. And the outcome was good, the serenity found once more, the purpose rediscovered. His teammates, subordinates, and superiors breathed easily and genuinely celebrated in silence.

As to the reasons behind this, a skilled psychologist might mumble words that identified some descriptive personality theories. But to those few Roth trusted, those individuals who shared his career of deadly consequences, they understood that unilateral faithfulness to a cause, to a concept of righteousness, to a self-imposed unforgiving discipline—such commitment could transiently blind one to pedestrian moral duplicity. In inhabiting such an arena, where ideological commitment supplanted natural fear or instinctive self-protection, a predictable consequence was to render oneself open and perhaps even vulnerable to comments, opinions, or attitudes that questioned or denigrated the very fabric upon which Roth had dedicated his life to uphold, for it simply surprised Roth and perhaps briefly startled him and his true believers. They simply were perplexed that such dedication could be mocked or thought useless.

To Roth and those who chose to follow this most unforgiving vocation, the privilege granted to serve his nation and his fellow soldiers was the purest form of empathy. For such a choice stripped away any superficiality and asked the fundamental question: "Are you willing to sacrifice your life to protect your teammate, to shield those who are vulnerable, or for justice?"

Roth operated daily within an environment of death. Thus, he shuddered to think that individuals could obligate their souls to the pursuit of money and need for acceptance by the preening crowd, the elite, the "knowers" of "proper" and indecent entitlement. And in doing so, could these same people not understand the gravity of the fundamental questions governing Roth and those like him?

In this, he found such a moral vacuum beyond his understanding. That people were willing to wander for the duration of their lives, governed by the latest form of groupthink spewed from "trend-setters" or the media. That they plodded endlessly, absent questions or awareness as to life's value. Such a prospect actually repelled him. Intellectually, cognitively, he immediately comprehended that of course this was true; reality, after all, is a cauldron of competing forces, and not everyone seeks understanding. Not everyone even believes it is advisable to engage in such activity as to seek answers to the eternally ambivalent. But Roth reflected on what the ancients had known about the human species: that few among us sought understanding as to our existence. Why were we here? And the exploration of such fundamentals almost certainly were segregationally implicit, forces directing those of potential consequence versus those obsessed with their vacant, self-absorbed drifting between birth and death.

For Roth, he bore a personal disappointment, almost a personal insecurity, when interacting with these sanctimonious, hyperimportant individuals. Perhaps he was aware of how little distance existed between these mindless spiritual vagabonds and those he revered, those who contemplated the unknown but acted to improve it. Perhaps Roth realized how little difference there was between those who were absent critical analysis, those elitists collectively self-absorbed in their proper perspectives, versus those who strove to protect the vulnerable. Those prepared to sacrifice everything. Perhaps ultimately Roth knew that a choice, a split-second decision "properly" conducted, still might ignobly end a life's effort that otherwise exemplified pursuit of an existence founded on purity of purpose. The context of today's decisions may not excuse tomorrow's judgment. Sometimes life just happens that way.

Such recollections instantly flashed within Virginia's mind. She had allowed her thoughts to wander into the emotional link to Roth and its inherent connection to the woman whose life and subsequent death underpinned their mission. Almost simultaneously, she felt herself become calmer but paradoxically more alert. The value of her life was now defined by the mission. And by her performance within its potentially unforgiving, if not unforeseen, exigencies.

The silence of the night was now almost complete, save for the nocturnal calls of wildlife, a wolf's call in the distance, and jerboas moving among the bushes, jumping away from any human presence. Virginia scanned the sectors to her left and saw no movement. These thoughts about Roth had taken on a new dimension for Virginia mirroring much of what her teammates had experienced. They found his presence reassuring, almost comforting. Such was Roth's effect on his subordinates. There was one slight disparity, however, in the impact Roth had on her that was not shared by her other teammates.

She was in love with Roth.

Chapter Two

"She is the only man in my cabinet."
—David Ben-Gurion (PM of Israel)
on Golda Meir (Future PM of Israel)

Virginia Lois Mahoney: A Woman Among Men

Virginia Lois Mahoney was an astute observer of human beings. Such a trait was a gift but also a burden. While it allowed her to readily assess the deficiencies present in those she encountered, as a woman, she was frequently told she lacked any credibility to influence opinion. Not that Virginia intended to influence anyone; she simply was accurate in her assessment and knew it to be so. But because she was a woman, her shrewd observational skills were frequently not applauded. Rather, for many men, and surprisingly many of her female associates, her confidence and trenchant analytical skills were threatening.

In this, she was similar to Roth. Both could read people judiciously, precisely, and rapidly. Men found this irritating, if not intimidating, as they experienced the uncomfortable realization that Virginia's intellectual powers or cognitive workings were superior. Their thinly veiled patronizing, ego-driven quips as to their exceptional talents evaporated within seconds of her immediate perspicacity. She knew them quickly for who they really were. It was as if a prominent label glowed on the forehead of the wannabe, advertising hidden but defective core values. Insecure, vindictive, veneer of honor but a heart of treachery—these were labels that she and Roth each accurately and immediately identified, and then the inflated ham-fisted proprietor suddenly knew they had stumbled into trouble. Often, Virginia allowed them to slither away unscathed but knowing that they had come within millimeters of being exposed.

Thus, it was her prescient view, focused on Roth himself, where she correctly saw an inner conflict within Jacob. One waged emotionally and spiritually in his attempt to understand and protect himself, and others, from those who offered mendacious feedback, pronouncements, or summations.

But Mahoney, unlike Roth, was somewhat less inclined to let these idiots flood her self-belief or self-esteem with pernicious waste. While not immune, she simply realized that it was the uncommon individual who might view her objectively. And once viewed in this light, absent preconceived pejorative muck, she would be valued. Yet this was so rare that she had grown a very resilient shell to combat the bias, prejudice, or dismissive interactions that were commonplace. Ironically, it was Roth who had proven to be one of these singular individuals who just treated her as a member of the team, surprisingly absent preconceived notions reflecting gender or gender-based deficiencies. And it was Roth who had seen the talent, wisdom, and honor within this courageous, vibrant young woman.

What Mahoney couldn't fathom, as she grew to know and then to value Roth, was why he allowed any interactions with sanctimonious high-brow leaders or self-appointed experts to influence his equanimity. In fact, it surprised her. He should have been above it, should have smiled while simultaneously dismissing their shallow understandings, for surely he instantly understood their perfidy and correctly gauged their hollow intellectual and moral infrastructure. But he often couldn't completely avoid the toll.

As the only female within the ultratight-woven fabric of special operations, she was always surrounded by men, the male ego, the defense stratagems, and verbal jousting that pervaded the male sanctum of special ops. It struck her as slightly odd for a man such as Roth, who effortlessly commanded men in war, to be stung or injured by this group of foppish dilatants. In her eyes, his slight hesitancy with these ersatz warriors was almost absurd. Here was a man near flawless in combat, when people were attempting to kill one another, and who epitomized leadership, lightning-fast correct decisions, and a career that had been almost too good. Roth's vulnerability was subtle, but at many levels interesting, if not baffling. Virginia was completely unaware of how accurate she was in her summary observations. She was also ignorant of the consequences these truths would later spawn.

And it must be said that Jessica, his ex-wife—well, she was nearly emblematic within Virginia's perspective of the sad, self-deflating narcissism found within American culture at the end of the twentieth century. Thus, Jacob's growing discontent and budding intolerance to her shallow, nonexistent life's purpose ultimately ensured the dissolution of the marriage. But the end result was characterized by her self-directed injury in the form of promiscuity. She had availed herself to random individuals as long as they possessed a male organ and were willing to enter her after she had consumed enough alcohol at her favorite watering hole to convince herself that she deserved their desire. What she never grasped was the thin masking of near disgust that these testosterone-laden "admirers" felt toward her within seconds of emptying their seed into this alcohol-soaked receptacle. She did, however, comprehend the depth of revulsion, now self-directed and neither thin nor fleeting, as she attempted to resurface from the depths of her depraved vanity the next morning.

It took Jacob longer than one would have predicted to understand or act upon what most readily saw in his unfortunate choice for a bride, but the marital contract was eventually dissolved without any discernable impact upon Roth's professional competency or commitment. What most didn't know was that Virginia Mahoney could see Roth's emotional and spiritual preparation for the finality of the union's dissolution long before three months ago. His focus toward mission goals had seemingly become even more intense and specific, if that were humanly possible. His demeanor, equanimity, and judgment never belied any personal upheaval, although she knew this was occurring. He was perhaps more distant from the normal daily banter between team members, but never enough for anyone else to sense his emotional pain.

And what most also didn't know was that Virginia had been in love with this man for even longer. This development along with her slow recognition of it had been hard for her to initially understand, harder still to admit to herself, but there it was—a testament to stripping away her defenses and ambiguities. That he never made a comment about her sex unless he felt it relevant within the parameters of mission success was another reason Virginia so valued his input. He was honest, lacked any negativity, and explored the possibilities of how her contributions could be maximized not despite, but because of her being female. But only when both of them decided this fact was a relevant element to an optimal mission outcome.

He was the brother she had never had. He was the husband she may never have. But he was also the lover she desperately sought. As their feet hit the Syrian Desert, searching to kill the world's most wanted terrorist, Virginia found the need to communicate her desire to this man as she never had before. She realized her emotional needs were entirely out of place in a combat zone. Yet she absolutely knew that she was not the first human to be in love and going off to war, to combat, to horrific primal encounters with other people, each trying to kill the other. She smiled a tight knowing smirk. She would also not be the last.

Jacob tapped her left shoulder, again providing hand signals that told her the next rise would be the last before opening into a shallow valley. This valley housed the compound that their Kurdish allies had confirmed was the location of a man she hoped to find and kill. To bring a righteous end to his miserable existence. To pay off a debt she felt she carried for her entire sex: to kill Abu Bakr al Al Hassan Abbas.

Chapter Three

Jacob Noah Roth
Twelve Weeks Earlier

Preparing for this latest mission was quite atypical for Roth in that he had to effectively convince his commanders that he would not be a liability to its success. On the surface, their concerns seemed illogical. Yet, perhaps in retrospect, their prescient hesitation spoke of a collective acknowledgment as to the potential pernicious effects of one of life's more mundane setbacks: a recently failed marriage. The illogical component was that Roth was a veteran of three previous missions of high target acquisition or termination and had been a pivotal player in each. This, in addition to twelve additional less dramatic yet still significant missions, made the case that Jacob was not only able to participate, but that in some manner, he might be an important element to the prospect of a successful mission outcome.

Command's concern, however, was grounded in the fact that the disruptive influence of a recently dissolved marriage might degrade the divorcé's ability to fully concentrate on the meticulous preparation that is a critical factor in any undertaking. Further, it might also erode his otherwise sound judgment. Theories exist as to why at least two flights in recent history have crashed at the hands of their pilots, killing all aboard, such as the one piloting Egyptair Flight 990, who actively sought a Shakespearian end to their existence after having suffered severe depression that went either undetected or ignored. And regarding the disappearance of Malaysia

Flight 370 piloted by a Captain Shah, who apparently had a disintegrating relationship with his wife and perhaps also with his apparent mistress, his disillusionment led to a flight-related suicide that unfortunately also cost the lives of his passengers. This probably had been at the forefront of Roth's commanders' thoughts as they spoke to him regarding his suitability as a participant in this mission.

But Roth took this in stride and simply carefully articulated to his commanders his understanding of their reasonable concerns, noting his ongoing preparation. In retrospect, he contemplated what possibly changed their minds was his expressed willingness, if they were hesitant, to gladly continue training as an alternate in readiness in case another of the team leaders was incapacitated or injured, ensuring he would be ready to fill in if needed. Roth didn't take offense, as he understood their concerns. Less than twenty-four hours later, Jacob Noah Roth was back in his role as the highest-ranking team leader and told to be ready within four to six weeks. It turned out to be twelve weeks, but this fact was irrelevant.

There was one part of this mission, however, that was going to be historic, and he was careful in his plans to address this with the appropriate solemnity linked with a prioritization on outcome success. This was to be the first mission wherein a woman had a primary combat role in the Special Operations Team #6 (SP6) and Jacob needed to ensure that she was ready. He was convinced that her role was important, but Roth strove to have his teammates and the entire body of the special operations community so used to her as to be bored with the fact that she was a woman joining the heretofore exclusive fraternity of special operations participants.

The early sun-drenched afternoon of October twenty-sixth, Roth was called from his quarters to Command HQ at Erbil in Iraq and, along with six other team leaders, received a briefing on operational parameters for a quick "capture or kill" penetration into several locations, including Barisha, Syria. Their target was Abu Bakr al Al Hassan Abbas, the self-proclaimed leader of ISIS who only three years previously had swept through large swaths of Syria and Iraq, capturing towns and terrorizing then murdering anyone whom he and his surrogates proclaimed expendable. This included civilians who would not actively support them, husbands of the women who were then enslaved for sex and domestic work, and any residual non-Muslim civilians, such as the Yazidi, an ancient religious minority residing in Northern Iraq. al Al Hassan Abbas wanted to cleanse Iraq of all "infidels," meaning those not adherent to his brand of Islam, and this certainly included Christians or minority sects such as the Yezidis.

But this fanatic also used his followers to kidnap a young woman. Some in the press argued that she had put herself in danger since she was an American aid worker and deliberately placed herself in harm's way. Both beautiful and resolute, this young woman had been captured as she attempted to assist refugees running from the trauma of the Syrian civil war. While some might have quietly criticized her as naïve, to a person, the SP6 personnel thought of her as courageous and determined. Apparently, she had been taken captive in Aleppo after leaving a Doctors Without Borders hospital. Enjoying her company by repeatedly torturing her and raping her until she became a liability, al Al Hassan Abbas then had her killed but blamed her death on Jordanian airstrikes meant for him. For those of the elite Special Forces group now being tasked to find and either capture or kill this poor excuse for a man, their hard-earned veneer of training and professionalism could not quite eliminate a sense of impending righteous justice.

Roth knew he couldn't formally speak in detail for his commanders, but he could relate with absolute assurance that each individual within their group intended to get this guy and bring him back, dead or alive. The focus among the entire fifty-eight-person group was almost supernatural, as it should have been. Roth had made his peace with God. If this was the time for this American's life to be ultimately sacrificed, then he would smile at his end coming in an attempt to deliver a divine retribution for acts so cowardly and barbaric that even other terrorists cringed at their depravity.

In the end, his failed marriage had provided him with a bit of perspective on the desires and shortcomings of human beings. And while Roth could not in any manner be counted among the intellectual elite, he nevertheless has made it his goal to understand human beings, to read them, to rapidly evaluate them and deduce their intentions, as such skills could save his life or those around him. Thus, the events of that October afternoon and his briefing in building 7B had now become relevant.

Inside of this low-profile building, with curved walls reinforced by sandbags up to almost six feet, the air moved in accordance with the ceiling fans, but the aroma was that of an unclean high school gymnasium locker room. The pong of male sweat mixed with a not quite dissipated ground fog of anxiety still hung in the air despite the best effort of these rotating metal blades. Cool air was being pumped in by portable thermal units via six-inch polyvinyl ribbed tan hoses hooked up to vents spaced evenly along the walls, but the room was still too warm.

The outside of the building was similar in shape to a longitudinal piece of cut sausage. A semicircle extended along its long axis to both ends, where its these vertical ends housed double swinging doors and allowed easy entry or exit. The roof was curved along the natural arc of the half circle constructed specifically to deflect mortar or light artillery rounds away from the structure, preventing their embedding into a flat roof. Unfortunately, a direct hit by a missile or air-to-ground ordnance would still penetrate the structure; the design could not offer any protection from these modern airborne arrows of death. The dark green and brown sand-filled bags lined the sides of the building stacked upon one another. Pine logs were interposed every five to seven feet, bracketing the columns of these dense shock-absorbing sacks along the ochre-colored gravel surface. The bags followed the curving contour of the steel-slated outer walls, shielding the side walls of the structure from close-in detonation of enemy ordnance.

After the briefing and the following question interval, Roth was asked to remain. Lt. Commander Gill approached Roth and as he stood to salute, Gill waved him off, motioning for him to sit. As people departed, the methodical hum of the fans continued, but the room otherwise grew eerily silent. His adjuvant, a young second lieutenant one grade beneath Roth's who looked similar to a sixteen-year-old, exited via the opposite set of doors, leaving the two men alone. As Gill sat, Roth wondered if he was now going to be told that he was not going to participate in this mission.

The chairs were plastic and metal, folding seats similar to the mid-priced models at IKEA. As Roth sat, he watched his superior's body language, his knees not twelve inches from Roth's. The lieutenant commander was troubled about something, and in this particular setting it could only be about the mission. Roth had an inclination as to the subject matter, but he was wrong. As is usual with human beings, their recurrent expenditure of energy revolves around the self, and in keeping with the "usual," Roth had mistakenly assumed this was about him and that he was about to be scrubbed from the mission.

Gill was just over six feet in height, heavily muscled with a completely hairless head, dark-brown, almost black eyebrows, slightly hooded light-blue eyes, and no glasses. His neck was thick, his ears slightly larger than normal, but not in the league of Lyndon Johnson's Dumbo-sized windsails. His conversational tone was even but direct, and he wasted no time in relating the following.

"The parameters of the mission are now set. We have alternates and minimal but some redundancy. Do I substitute for Virginia Mahoney?"

His eyes were pools of concern, conveying questions as to eliminating any influence that could contribute to task failure.

Roth answered, "No."

"Care to elaborate?" Gill posited.

"No, sir, no need."

Gill's eyes were locked onto his, and Jacob registered no ambiguity or pause. Their eyes now reflected acceptance built on trust as both looked to the other. Gill's expression was of concern, Roth's a penetrating focus.

Roth had made a decision as to what best served his team's needs, and Virginia Mahoney was required.

Gill started to sigh, then stopped. He looked from Roth, then to the ceiling, and while not smiling exactly, he imparted a finality to his acceptance and stated simply, "OK."

That was it.

He rose, and Jacob followed with a crisp salute and watched him turn and retrace his steps to the small dark-brown speaker's stand in front of the empty assembly room. Gill lifted his three-ring notebook and opened it, turning back to Roth. He exposed the pages to him as he spread the notebook wide, holding each end with a separate hand to show the inner transparent plastic sheaths ready to receive paper and documents. The entire notebook was empty.

Lt. Commander Gill had just delivered the entire briefing—containing classified radio frequencies, numeric identifier codes, everything—entirely by memory. He smiled at Roth, a brief window into his tightly controlled ego, and then closed the book. Message delivered.

Jacob saluted a second time. Message received: no sloppiness, no errors, no room for failure. As he left, Roth turned and proceeded in the opposite direction, pushing out the doors to enter onto a gravel pathway in front of building 7B. Jacob walked while thinking of V. Mahoney.

He actually had known surprisingly little about her until reading her file. Personal information obtained through communication with her had been limited to background and security clearance confirmation and mission-related input. In this last point, she was remarkable. Thorough to the point of near perfection, and she was unique in that she didn't get lost in the details but identified serious flaws and discarded irrelevant or extraneous data rapidly. But in all of these exchanges, Roth saw an extremely intelligent driven individual who brokered none of the typical male condescension directed toward her at times. Nor was she delicate with the repetitive jocular expressions of a sexual nature, especially when she was the object of said interest.

She was the preverbal "ballbuster" to those idiots who tried to inappropriately test the waters or intended to derisively use her as the butt of a joke during mission-related review or critique sessions. Her response would be to roll her eyes, turn to the guy sitting next to her, and ask if he wanted to play with whomever had unwisely mocked her or perhaps commented on her physical beauty inappropriately. While tasseled-loafered attorneys walking the power halls of DC might accurately conclude such communication contained all of the requisite elements to allege sexual harassment, Mahoney didn't comport with victimhood. She was a trained warrior, and in these settings her training and personality surfaced. The knuckle-dragging innuendo-generating gorilla commenting vacuously on Virginia's gender had unfortunately strayed onto thin ice.

And those present at such moments knew what was to follow—that the perpetrator was about to lose his most prized physical attribute, perhaps the source of his limited cognitive powers. She returned the conversation by turning to that nearest colleague and saying, "You want this guy's very tiny little flower?" The perpetrator's often lupine smile would instantly disappear, often with his mouth open but no sound coming out. The man sitting to her side would be invariably respectful, suddenly to an extreme degree, while the rest of the operational team could barely contain their rapidly germinating smiles. After such a display, it was improbable that future banter would be directed at her.

After seeing such exchanges occur in the past several weeks, Jacob once had to clap his hand over his mouth to prevent a guttural laugh from erupting. However, in his role as team leader and ranking officer, Jacob never felt that she needed help or assistance to defend herself; thus, he simply didn't want to step in and, in effect, make a statement that she needed "daddy" to rescue her. So, Roth kept his mouth shut, but he was ready and willing to assist if the occasion presented itself and called for his intervention.

But despite his continual interaction with Mahoney, Jacob never really knew who she was. And this was acceptable as long as she performed. With Virginia there was no talk of family, missing the wife or, in her case, the husband, or concerns over the fidelity of said girlfriend. The normal snippets of male anxiety and expression were absent, and silence occupied that time and space. Hell, more than a couple of the guys thought she was gay, probably a result of her unceremonious but focused verbal castration of them in response to their ill-considered one-liners. Roth couldn't have cared less either way as long as she provided value to the mission. As harsh and uncompromising as this perspective was and continued to be, realpolitik ruled. What little Jacob did know about her thus had been gleaned from proficiency reports and direct observation.

The military is often one of the most misunderstood organizations by average nonmilitary citizens within the constitutional republic. It constitutes a semiclosed society but reflects the inherent values of our nation, as it is composed of a cross section of its inhabitants. They collectively are neither Neanderthals nor Einsteins, but for the most part simply average American people utilizing the talents or overcoming the shortcomings found within a multitude of different individuals.

They follow orders but are encouraged, if not educated, to challenge orders that are ineffectual, have lost time-sensitive relevance, or are simply wrong. They are taught to refuse orders that are illegal or immoral. And finally, they may pause in their obligatory adherence to orders that constitute policy pronouncements from Washington, DC, that may be prescient but are often commonly shortsighted, politically expedient, or just plain stupid. The practical summation is to understand the often nuanced adjustments that military members exercise to satisfy their orders.

They are just normal people, trained in a large and highly disciplined organization to address or solve problems in the most unforgiving environment on the planet: war. Thus, Roth's insight and indeed interest in Virginia Mahoney was limited to her ability to contribute to mission success.

Side interest, romantic entanglement, or special relationships were as unnecessary as they were imprudent.

Chapter Four

Jacob Noah Roth
Ten Weeks Earlier

And then it happened one afternoon a couple of weeks later, on a hot sunlit day not dissimilar to almost all twenty-four-hour intervals within the Iraqi landscape. Roth's superior —a different lieutenant commander, one Richard Greene— ordered Roth to his office. Roth had been busy reviewing different assault strategies and the need for prioritizing personnel that he would employ to enter a compound denoted by classified satellite imagery. The images were displayed on an oversized 110-inch proprietary Korean-sourced microLED screen that allowed direct interaction with the ability to magnify and outline subsets of formatted imagery. Roth was working with a secure and uniquely programed iPad, enabling direct interaction with the larger screen, but he still made hand-written notes spread on the unvarnished but sturdy plywood table before him. He would memorize these notes and then hand them off to the security team for disposal.

Roth's present location was building #5, indistinguishable from others but designated for those with high-level security clearance and a time-sensitive need to know. Inside the first set of doors were guards and a five-member team that rotated within the day to ensure that the computers, maps, or electronic gadgets did not leave the facility. Most importantly, of course, was the need to secure the information from unwanted prying eyes. A series of conflicts within the Middle East and Southwestern Asia had awakened the Americans to the reality that while the cultural norms of their adversaries may have been rooted in the late Middle Ages, such did not conflate with a lack of ingenious military tactical potential. And Roth refused to underestimate individuals who aspired to die serving spiritual concepts that entailed killing Americans.

Roth now was aware that this was one of several prudent destinations for his team, given the increased volume of focused imagery and intelligence. Rumors combined with objective mission-directed evidence of a directed future mission had convinced Jacob that he would soon be targeting either this compound or another within Syria. Command had begun to share very detailed ground-contour-relief data, including drainage formations representing dry riverbeds, footpaths, and of course manmade facilities, including sheds or lean-tos, in the surrounding area of the white stone and cement compound now spread on the screen before him. Jacob knew this was the preparatory interval, and thus twice daily now he sat with his team and reviewed their operational plans and data. They were getting ready for another historic mission, and Jacob was looking for any hidden impediments. He knew the object of their preparation, the identity of their target.

As to Lt. Commander Greene, he personified the bespectacled mouse within a warrior's facade. Jacob strangely was alert to his summons and his routine of thirty or so cigarettes a day. Jacob sensed a problem, and it was almost as if he was on an intel mission as his sensors became fully active and his adrenaline level increased. It was not that

Greene was physically threatening; in fact, there was a thick layer of blue particulate matter that seemed to perpetually surround his rather large and oleaginous head. During briefings, his uniform hung from his drooping shoulders, and only the somewhat generous protuberance of his mid-abdomen pulled at his ill-fitting pixelated desert-camouflaged livery. Standing next to him evoked the smell of an old airport ashtray if one had a sensitive nose, and Jacob did. Roth had long ago considered the costs of tobacco use—not only the fiscal, but he could sense a fatigue associated with cigarette use, and similar to a professional athlete, he demanded that nothing interfere with his performance. For the athlete, it was the difference between winning and losing, reputation and prize money; for Roth, it was simply life or death.

Jacob vaguely distrusted this higher-ranking officer. The reasons were numerous, but amorphous. Roth instinctively knew that Greene was a fraud, a paper warrior unable or unwilling to place himself in real danger, and yet his need to be in a "combat zone" gave him authenticity, at least to the reflection in the mirror. Roth also worried about Rich Hansept, a newer member of the team who appeared to naturally gravitate toward Greene. Both men could be frequently found together, sipping coffee and talking before and after briefings or meetings. Their body language often suggested their conversation was nearly intimate, if not reserved for their ears only without invitation to other team members.

After Roth had seen this pairing three or four times, he had experienced a vague sense of apprehension. He could not quite articulate why, but deep within, foreboding had replaced observation. It tickled Roth's consciousness, creating a sense of discomfort or perhaps unease over his newest addition to the team. These mixed puddles of Roth's emotions centered on the fact that Greene was an administrator, despite his assumed role as a warrior. Greene had done his utmost to remain distant from imminent danger while also striving to soak up the glow of enhanced status reserved for these special operations combatants. Roth found the recurrent pairing of these two odd, if not somehow nearly inappropriate.

But Rich Hansept had performed well in his screening aptitude testing and recorded a solid performance at the Basic Underwater Demolition/Seal (BUD/S) school. He received no standout or superior rating, but he had passed. This in itself was remarkable, given the arduous nearly year-long formal training that all applicants to special operations were required to undergo. The navy wanted only the best, and there was absolutely no exception provided to any wannabe SEALs (Sea Air and Land Team). If you couldn't embrace, accept, and pass the multifaceted training blocks, you were judged not fit for the special operations theater.

Psychological evaluations had been performed on Hansept, as they were to every applicant hopeful to join the navy's most favored class of elite warriors. These were largely personal interviews linked to subsequent analysis of responses from both Hansept and various authority figures from his youth. Typically, these were standardized questions regarding impressions of his character accomplished through interviews of high school and even grade school teachers.

Sometimes Cub Scout or Boy Scout leaders were sought. In Hansept's case, there were areas of interest, but the summary judgment of those conducting the interviews found no "hot flags" that were automatic disqualifications for special operations.

They had, however, unearthed a degree of a semiconcealed intense rivalry directed toward an older and only sibling—a sister who was tangentially found to be remarkably talented. The interviewers had deemed the rivalry at the limits of normal, but not pathological. One comment was telling in that Hansept seemed to reserve an artificially constructed set of statements anytime his sister or her accomplishments were discussed in detail. It was a tell that seasoned investigators found strange, suggesting deeper emotional currents were present, but within the entire context of the interviews, this was a minor blip in an otherwise fairly bland and acceptable review of Hansept's character.

Of tangential interest to a female investigator was that Hansept's sister was now a lawyer making a name for herself in cases involving gender discrimination, including illegal acts directed at lesbians and gays. The sister, Jenna, had herself come out in her second year of law school, much to the shock of her mother and horror of her father and younger brother. But investigators, while not directly interested in his sister's sexual preference, found Hansept's articulated but tightly controlled responses regarding the proclivities of his sister deliberately sterile. And despite the prescient concerns of the female interviewing officer, these deliberate preset comments repeated by Hansept somewhat too often in her view were passed over as unimportant. In truth, these talking points from Hansept barely concealed profound layers of unspeakable rage directed toward his only sibling.

For Rich Hansept mirrored the deep fury of his father, a self-taught rural pastor who railed against the unnatural choices of the deviant class only to learn the truth of and subsequently disown his own daughter. Hansept's mother had initially been confused but recoiled in anger against her husband's proclamation that her lovely little girl who had always excelled, who had always been a source of pride for her parents, was now declared an immoral leper. She found the sanctimony from her husband untenable, he who had nearly destroyed himself with alcohol before finding God and her. Both had rescued his soul, not to mention his physical life! She took a much more measured view of her daughter's choice and, in fact, expressed a degree of happiness in her child's ability to find her true self and identify and then serve her chosen purpose, which included those vulnerable and often outcast by society.

But the recurrent tension between husband and wife over their prodigal daughter was to ultimately result in an acrimonious divorce wherein the daughter and wife threatened the "man of God" with criminal prosecution if he ever again physically assaulted his now ex-wife. This had happened too frequently to continue a self-imposed moratorium on addressing the man's behavior. The mother eventually found meaning and a surprising degree of happiness working as an executive secretary of sorts in the daughter's now nationally recognized law firm. The daughter, Jenna Hansept, was committed personally to and in love with a female US Naval JAG officer who was perhaps even more aggressive in her pursuit of what each woman viewed as justice. Both women lived quietly productive and remarkably satisfying lives within their growing joint reputation for legal excellence.

What had never really surfaced, what had remained hidden during Hansept's interviews, background evaluations, and psychological testing, was the shadow of incongruity felt by the perceptive female interviewer. Hansept's manufactured comments belied an inconsistency that was inextricably linked to a bottomless hatred of his older sibling. The reasons were too numerous to count in his mind, but a single overarching element besides jealousy toward a more talented sibling was that Jenna had simply betrayed him when she voiced her desirous passion for a member of her own gender. That she could have hidden something so basic to her nature from him was evidence, in his mind, of her perfidy. She had not trusted him enough to share such vital information. Objective review of his sister's confidential maintenance of her most private proclivities turned out to be similar to many of her other life's choices: prudent and thoughtful. But to her envious and peculiar younger sibling, her decisions were an unequivocal dismissal of his value, his worth as a male. In ways not reasonable to an outsider, his sister's most intimate desires had shamed Rich Hansept, leaving within him a feeling as though he himself was abnormal or fouled. It was as if his maleness was somehow unimportant. It was certainly not, in Rich's view, because Jenna couldn't land a man. That couldn't have been the reason.

For although Rich was a handsome blue-eyed, somewhat angular-featured male, Jenna, well, she was nothing short of gorgeous. His horror at the discovery that his gifted, multitalented sister was gay had disassembled his understanding of life's foreseeability and screamed of her lack of trust in him, her younger brother. It was too much of a shock. He had assumed she was to marry well, and if he had been honest with himself, he had hoped that through her, perhaps there were benefits that might be sprinkled on him, ripples in the pond of life's opportunities. Instead, she was one of those, a newly freed subculture previously labeled deviant. And instead of any benefit of her prodigious intellect, his ability to brag to anyone willing to listen about her remarkable talent, he now had to hide her proclivities. He felt he had to hide any discussion of her in nearly all of his daily encounters.

That Jenna was pretty was an understatement. She was strikingly beautiful; she was gorgeous. In fact, her beauty was so captivating that one of her teachers had cautiously approached their parents and suggested that perhaps she might dabble in modeling to make some money. Her father thought this was reasonable, quickly aware of additional funds being produced and directed to him. Her mother contemplated the impact of this choice for their daughter, worried that excessive emphasis on physical attributes might somehow redirect her from developing what was universally agreed upon as her incredible intellect. However, it was ultimately a moot point; Jenna said no, wanting no part of what she felt was a disparaging culture fixated on a woman's physical attributes instead of her mental acuity.

Their mother had, of course, carried the genetic template; her Nordic features ensured that if even a faint resemblance to her existed, both children would be quite attractive individuals. And for all their father's psychologic baggage, he was not an unappealing man. In fact, it is precisely because he was rather striking in his youth that he veered off the path of normalcy and embraced a recurrent drunken state, an easier pursuit only to be saved through the tender mercies of his now ex-wife and his discovery of the Creator's power. Unfortunately, all members of his family, especially the women, felt that David Hansept too often weaponized the spiritual messages that he found rather easy to understand and communicate to those seeking pious assistance. Even Rich saw the ulterior motives within his father's sharp-eyed, almost predatory gaze manifest during a Saturday evening or Sunday morning sermon. The natural magnetism of the man was made more potent while delivering the message, allowing him to pull vulnerable divorcées and single women into his sphere of influence.

What ultimately became of the influential force emanating from his father, Rich never bothered to confirm. He had mentally shrugged it off, thinking that these servile women had gotten what they deserved. But Jenna's pronouncement had destabilized both Rich and his father. How could this be true, he wondered? Not from his seed! A modicum of self-reflection from the self-anointed pastor might have grasped that his daughter's view of the male persona might have been irrevocably warped as a consequence of her father's past invitations to explore mutual intimacy between them. Revulsion coupled with the anger of betrayal had suffused within the maturing beauty, but it was her ever-perceptive mother who sensed trouble as her young adult daughter grew into a breathtaking beauty and never ever allowed daughter and father to be alone together.

And with Jenna's pronouncement, in spite of incessant angry shouting and condemnation by the man of Christian understanding and forgiveness, both mother and daughter held fast, weathering the blatant anger from both men. Foreseeably, the need to shelter against the tyrants appeared to draw each of the women closer together. But still Rich hoped that Jenna would get hers. He secretly waited for what he thought was the very predictable fall from grace, the destruction of her life and life's purpose. It had not yet occurred, however.

That Hansept did not quite fit within the smooth, nearly seamless team that Roth oversaw was similar to a small filament or splinter present in a calloused hand. Unless the hand gripped the object a certain way with a specific tension, the small needle of wood remained undetectable. But if the hand tightened just a certain way, and indeed it might at a critical moment, then the needle would announce its presence, causing the hand to reflexively loosen and drop the object in its grasp.

Roth, if asked, would have admitted that he couldn't identify what or why he was uneasy with Hansept. But if objectively reviewing the circumstances, Roth would have simply said that he had not seen Hansept perform in any high-pressure or volatile settings. Settings where all pretense or cosmetic layering was stripped away. Combat, unlike any other environment, publicly and uniquely "undresses" an individual, revealing their core attributes or failings until a residual essential is all that remains. And it is this most basic, most granular set of elements, residual ashes after the fire, that is shown to fellow combatants. Most of the remnants are common to all—fear, dread, but a willingness to engage if only to survive or protect a nearby buddy. Yet some wilt, unable to move, terrified of harm or death, and are either cut down or cause others to die since they are unable to perform their assigned tasks, that which is called "duty." And yet some find within themselves unknown or hidden strengths, reserves of such unique quality that their activity to command in this most unforgiving of environments astonishes all who bear witness. Perhaps in the end, those most truly surprised are themselves, those who have climbed this most sharply defined peak of heroic action when all around them have conceded to fate.

It is often years later, when the arms of conflict are confined to dusty museums, that those survivors first hear the voices of their opposite numbers, those on the other side who remember the actions of this one individual. They, too, remain in awe, for they also were but mortal yet for a few seconds of this one individual's existence, he became immortal in their collective memories.

If asked, Roth would have posited that as an administrator, Greene was attempting to achieve an ersatz combat warrior status. By being in the region or location of war and attending to those who actually physically lived and died within the dangerous missions, he was stealing his portion of valor. Roth would readily admit that each individual serving in combat-related or hostile territories must be provided their due quantum of courage. Yet an important distinction exists between disparate roles for each person. While there is an abundance of danger in any zone and for anyone serving, when they are exposed to the asymmetric warfare that typifies the modern hostile battlefield environment, a subtle but very powerful barrier delineates those who ride a desk from those who enter the belly of the beast. Greene had sought shelter behind the four corners of a desk, yet claimed the status of one who has faced the darkness of combat.

It is almost a universal truism that for those who genuinely partake in the darkness of combat, given the loss of morality that accompanies each instantaneous decision enabling survival, such participants do not trivialize or embellish the experience. How does one communicate such an event, the immersion into combat wherein an individual is instantly stripped of the collective goodness of normal humanity and decency? What is there to say? Mere seconds have passed, but young men who once attended church, temple, or synagogue and who held doors open for aging neighbors or elderly widows suddenly become animal distortions within a rabid, unforgiving domain. But even animals, where survival is not guaranteed and where predation is the norm, have rules, hard rules, to follow. Animals do not kill without intent, without need, or without a subtle overarching balance within the ecological system they inhabit. Only human beings kill absent rules.

These young men who only recently were nervous regarding a Friday night high school dance were now being forced to commit such horrible acts, often only to ensure their own survival, but at the cost of their innocence, their beauty, their soul. For it is within seconds of experiencing the intimacy of violence that they are fundamentally and irrevocably transformed, wrapped in a rasping tool's coarse embrace and scraped raw as the bristly steel wool removes the varnish from old furniture.

In seconds, they become efficient and effective killers of other human beings. And although legally permissible as defined in some lawyer's mind, a rule written codifying that combat makes it permissible to savagely destroy someone else's life, for many, all innocence instantly evaporates. It will never reappear. Life's goodness and beauty are disassembled, left behind in the erosive force of a river's churning rapids. Their souls suffer and may not recover.

Identical to furniture, its surface, once coated and protected, is subsequently exposed. The combatant's original texture is forever changed, laden with residual scars representing permanent damage, abrasions that are not removable. Learning to cope with the guilt of what has been done permeates the consciousness. These requisite actions are done in order to live, to survive, but each erode portions of the soul. Human beings damaged by one's own hand must be forgotten—a lifelong pursuit that some never achieve.

For many, a redemption is sought, but a price is to be paid. A bill is due. Each tries to address the elements needed for full payment in their own way. For some, they will not be successful. For others, the contents of the self-directed judgment must be tucked away in a locked box, secured within the furthest recesses of the mind. Yet even this may not be enough, as the keeper of such concerns quietly, reluctantly waits for the ghosts of the past to revisit.

Thus, subsequent officious, loud, slap-happy descriptive narratives comparing the metrics of bravery identify the ersatz warrior. Such behavior is incompatible, if not discordant, with those whom have entered the terror of life-threatening violence. Such showy forms of courage do not exist in the searing, often troubled memories where the horror of killing another human being is never completely erased. Those who have seen the ugly intimacy of survival only because of another's forfeiture often spend their lives attempting to cleanse their beings of this indelible stain. Often a profound humility and sadness grows to replace the exuberant bravery of youth—the sorrow expressed for those killed in order to survive. How often in history have former adversaries embraced decades after the hostilities ceased, each trying to absolve the other of the burden of what was necessary to survive?

It is the starkest expression of a zero-sum game, there are no winners. And it is not in any fashion or manner a game. It is the eternal plague within our species, the willingness and even eagerness to enter into violent conflict to solve disagreements. Only later as life predictably ebbs, giving way to age, do the participants often wonder if any of it was ever necessary.

Roth was a survivor of such brutal intimacy. He would not hesitate to absolve himself of past actions. And his absolution was thus complete . . . almost, for Jacob was also aware of the duty owed to the souls he had taken. To remember, if not embrace their cost, even for those who wanted and fought for his departure rather than theirs, he reminded himself both souls inhabited a singular habitat. To find oneself standing over the lifeless form of what was only seconds before a living human being is to understand finality in a manner unique among our species. You cannot reverse your actions. What you have done is absolute. God will demand that you one day stand in judgment for your actions, for you have destroyed one of His creations. Whether in defense of self or not, whether to survive or not, you have ruined an example of God's divine work, and in order to maintain sanity, one must accept that this is the price that war extracts from the souls of its participants.

This man, Lt. Commander Greene, thus struck Roth as a bit too enthusiastic, too interested in the ambiance of combat-related accoutrements absent actual physical strife. Wanting the survivor's stature absent the genuine participant's ambiguity, uncertainty, and fear. The prototypical Pentagon briefer: crisp, detailed, and oozing with self-importance and experience, but lacking inherent value of any kind . . . a fraud. And the near magnetic pull between Hansept and Greene was odd, but beyond that, it was troubling to Roth.

Roth traversed the compound to where Greene was located and reluctantly pushed open the doors to the smaller but almost identical sausage-shaped fortified bunker buildings. Greene rose from behind his metal-legged plywood-surfaced desk as he entered and lazily returned Roth's salute. The lieutenant's midsection did, in truth, bulge over the webbed belt, his loose-fitting desert-brown camouflage outer shirt tight at his waist. His cheeks appeared almost ashen and unhealthy, and his respiratory status would clearly last thirty seconds in actual combat. His greasy thinning strands of dark hair were combed over his shiny pate, and thick square plastic lenses within issued black frames made his eyes appear as tiny ball bearings under glass. The man's teeth were a hazel-colored light brown nestled within his mouth emanating breath likened to a malodorous, almost putrid fog. Delicate fingers held a ballpoint pen, and his gold Rolex on his thin left wrist dangled. Even in the rather dim light of the office it lit up as an exploding supernova, not for wear in combat. Cigarette ash smudges provided small islands of gray mixed in with the desert tan and brown of his pants. He stood at nearly five feet nine inches but his shoulders awkwardly rolled forward, bending his upper back forward as well, diminishing his already somewhat small stature. Roth briefly considered how he must appear when he tried to come to "attention" in the presence of a senior officer.

A single battered brown metal gooseneck lamp was to his immediate left. The partially exposed bulb hung out over a series of papers that appeared to have been tossed haphazardly onto the unfinished plywood surface of his desk, spread unevenly into a tan heavy manila-papered file. Across the upper lip of the file were red block letters that read "CONFIDENTIAL." As Roth stood there, his eyes drifted to Greene's desk and saw the fragment of a name for the file: ". . . ONEY." Roth assumed the lieutenant commander was reviewing personnel and matching skills to needs, but this was a guess.

Greene wasted no time before saying, "We need you to review her file."

The "her" rather significantly narrowed the possibilities. Roth responded, "Sir, I have looked at her file as recently as three days ago, as we needed to assess marksmanship scores."

"This is not about her proficiency, Lt. Roth. I am requesting you review her entire file."

Jacob shuddered to a near full stop. What the hell was this? Why on Earth did he have to see such personal material about any of his folks? This was not standard or normal.

Was he being set up? Was this an excuse for a soldier using Roth to displace or evade sole responsibility? Jacob's alarms were now lit up bright red, all of them actively blinking.

Everything that could impact a mission was Roth's area of responsibility, and if needed, he knew that he would go toe to toe with senior leadership or the friggin' admiral, for that matter, to ensure that mission success remained viable. But reading background on someone's family histories, failed relationships, and sexual preferences—that was part of the routine screening for highly classified and confidential mission eligibility and was NONE of Jacob's business, at least in his mind. Not unless it might register in combat!

"Permission to ask a question or two, sir?"

"Yeah, go ahead, Jacob." Greene's patience was clearly not holding out very well this afternoon.

"Am I allowed to do that?"

"Yes, I am requesting you review her entire file."

Again, Roth paused, uncertain how to proceed here. "Second question?"

He nodded.

"May I defer?"

"What?!" Greene sneered as he glowered at Roth. "Are you challenging my order, Roth? You are a presumptuous prick!"

Now Roth knew that something in this was terribly wrong. This was not the way to address a junior officer who felt uncomfortable with seeing classified information almost certainly adding little to his mission success other than fodder for gossip. Actually, this was not an appropriate manner of response to anyone.

What most individuals outside of the military don't know is that the system is actually rather carefully constructed, with checks and balances at multiple levels to ensure fairness and reasonable behavior. Lives are at stake, and only during times of extreme stress such as war or immediate conflict do these multiple safety instruments get bypassed. And even then, the lawyers within the military would not let illegal orders given or acted upon go without an investigative effort and conclusive analysis.

This is not to suggest that mistakes and harm do not occur. It is one of history's most recurrent lessons that the more formidable the force, the greater in degree is the good or harm that may result from such action. Great nations and great governments may make mistakes, and history may judge something that was believed to be correct at the time to be injudicious from the perspective of history, with time serving as the ultimate detergent for extraneous details, for political noise.

But when in doubt, sensible individuals have maintained their perspective and argued for the change or modification of rules, tactics, or strategic perspective. Officers at all levels are taught to balance the validity of an order against its outcome. In combat, this is seldom realistic, but make no mistake—the weighing of the order given against its outcome will indeed be reviewed, argued, and litigated if the order is an outlier, even if given during combat.

Roth was now at a pivotal intersection of being given an order that he felt was inappropriate, and perhaps even illegal. Playing peek-a-boo with an individual's confidential professional material outside of the authorized chain of command was simply not done.

He needed someone higher than this malodorous desk rat to approve his viewing Mahoney's file. Roth knew it had already cost him his relationship with Greene, and Jacob's review/rating from him would almost undoubtedly suck—but thankfully Greene's opinion meant little, and Roth's conduct during actual combat would address any perceived administrative deficiencies that this clown wanted to raise.

Jacob held his ground and stated, "May we ask Commander Hayes to weigh in on this, sir?"

If looks could kill, Roth's life would have been terminated forthwith. This Greene character was pissed, but now he was also trapped.

Greene's stare held his, but Jacob was in no hurry to let him think that some blubber-butt could intimidate him. Roth knew that if he lost his temper, it would have taken less than twenty-two seconds to end Greene's life. So, he continued to hold his stare until Greene folded and looked down to his desk, meaninglessly pushing some papers around before putting the various documents back into the folder.

Roth then began to quickly surmise the possible reasons as to why he wanted Jacob to assess Virginia's folder. Why? What did he want Roth to see?

Jacob stood there with these thoughts running in his mind when Greene stated, "Ok, let's go to Hayes's office, Lieutenant."

This was going to be interesting. Roth was actually anticipating the interaction.

"Yes, sir," he answered.

They walked out of the smaller elongated half-sausage structure, passing through the steel-reinforced steel doors. Roth followed Greene as he walked on the narrow pathway away from the building and traversed a single lane of packed dirt and gravel, a small center road, before heading to building #4.

The layout of the base reflected the evolution of architectural concepts gained via hard and often tragic consequences of modern asymmetric combat. Satellite pictures routinely identified American outposts in Iraq and Syria, even in shared facilities in Jordan or Kuwait, to be uniform, typically symmetrical if not predictable constructive efforts. Often buildings were too close together, even when reinforced against explosive ordnance, precision strikes, or just lucky targeting, and being too close could disproportionately damage assets. Thus, slowly—too slowly, according to critics—planners had learned to position command or operational centers randomly, locations haphazardly spaced by design in an effort to reduce collateral damage.

Commander Hayes, the SP operational commander, was thus located fifty yards from Greene's office, set in the ground and surrounded by an earthen wall three feet in both height and breadth. The operational center had no markings other than a misnomer designating the building as kitchen facilities. In truth, it was anything but that. The structure linked the special operations forward post to Central Command by a series of satellite-encrypted phones and open radio channels as well as live feed video communications. Hidden as groupings of tubular "chimneys" emanating from the surface of the reinforced steel corrugated roof, these cylinders were compressed within tightly bundled groupings of sandbags and surrounded by packaged deflecting explosive charges. EOD engineers had posited that in order to dissipate the downward force of impact by rockets or mortars, these rooftop explosives—next-generation mines similar to claymores, or rectangular boxes containing charges —were to detonate instantly. The thinking was that their eruption of kinetic force pushing up and away from the roof would diminish the destructive concussive force of any targeted attacks meant to direct a blast down into the building. The cylindrical three-foot exhaust ports were sophisticated antennae, often wrapped in braded wire and cable, yet remarkably difficult to identify. Again, the thought was to minimize or at least make the targeting of the command and control center more difficult for the Iranian-backed proxies hoping to harm Americans.

Hayes himself had a reputation—a good one. A SEAL graduate, he had completed the BUD/S and qualification training and went on to more advanced and increasingly classified training to serve with distinction during several covert missions. But it was Hayes being a member of the DEVGRU team—SEAL Team 6, also known as the United States Naval Special Warfare Development Group—that solidified his near legendary status in the tightly held special operations community. He had been involved in Operation Neptune Spear, the covert mission that killed Osama bin Laden in Abbottabad, Pakistan, on May 2, 2011.

Unlike several members of the actual SP team that partook in Neptune Spear—some who went on to openly state and then publicly argue as to theirs being the specific shot that killed Bin Laden—Hayes was emblematic of the authentic SP team member. He said nothing. He answered the post-mission debrief and review, but never said another word. What may be of slight interest to those who actually read the highly classified summary of the mission was that Hayes's position as point man when the team accessed Bin Laden's compound put him in the lead as they traversed up the stairs into the private living quarters on the third floor of bin Laden's cinderblock and concrete compound, a compound not dissimilar to the one that Roth now felt was being targeted for al Al Hassan Abbas. Hayes had had to acknowledge to Department of Defense lawyers that he had killed five men during the raid, three compound guards and two of bin Laden's personal bodyguards. He did not claim that he killed bin Laden, but he deliberately underestimated his role.

The formal press release heard throughout the world from the White House on the second of May noted the rather sterile narrative of entering and attempting to capture the world's most wanted fugitive. There was some drama as the then-commander in chief publicly reinforced the message as he announced to his fellow Americans and to the world that bin Laden was dead. The expanded written press release provided later did not confirm what any sensible law enforcement agent throughout the world knew: that bin Laden had held no chance of being captured and brought back alive.

The mission was a kill mission: "eliminate with extreme prejudice." There was no chance at capture or abduction; they were simply to eliminate him. The American government was not going to take the chance that this intelligent, well-educated, articulate and thoughtful revolutionary in the hands of well-trained, albeit American citizen lawyers would ever be able to provide the world with a credible argument as to why he had chosen to take actions that destroyed a large section of downtown New York City and claimed upwards of three thousand American lives. What was unknown to the Americans, however, was that bin Laden was nearly an invalid, suffering the ravages of chronic kidney failure at the time of his death. He had almost certainly had less than twelve months to live, but it was an important symbolic venture that the government of the United States of America ended his life and did so deliberately and violently.

The aforementioned government was not going to pay money for a potential spectacle. They were not going to provide any assistance in developing a cult of personality for a man who had caused such injury to America, its people, or its veil of invulnerability. Holding a trial, keeping bin Laden alive, or providing medical care were all simply out of the question. He had caused the most profound and numerically significant loss of American civilian lives from a single manmade source—a history that included terror, violence, and war—ever. His actions had killed more than any other singular event, save those occasions wherein earthquakes, typhoons, or hurricanes claimed more, and there were only three times such events outnumbered this Saudi's outcome. The narrative given to the public also noted that this man had been shot twice in the chest while he stood at the head of the stairs, transiently attempting to "bravely" shield himself with one of his children before suddenly moving, in effect exposing himself and receiving the two fatal bullets. This, however, was not quite accurate.

What was not reported publicly was that Hayes had split his team as he followed a curving passageway branching out from the main staircase and sent the larger part of his team up the geometrically precise staircase, three floors up from their starting point. Just he and one other man had wound around a narrow circuitous hallway, moving quickly but checking rooms and doors along the way, mounting one hidden staircase until Hayes was directly under bin Laden's upper floor landing that was adjacent to the terror leader's bedroom and main living quarters. Hayes ultimately found himself immediately one floor below bin Laden.

Most of the house's exterior and its huge surrounding walls were made of a crude cinderblock construction topped by barbed wire. These defensive walls were left unpainted, but the compound's buildings, especially the main building, had a simple whitewash but without a stucco texture. All were reinforced with steel bars running inside of the cinderblock, an internal rebar construction for maximum strength and impenetrability. There were very few windows, but there was a seven-foot-high privacy wall along the outermost external boundary of the third-floor balcony. This minimized any public exposure to someone sitting outside in the open air yet allowed them to enjoy the radiant warmth of the sun.

Sophisticated US satellite imagery, on more than one occasion, had captured images of a robed figure with long legs wearing sunglasses and comfortably lounging while reading a newspaper within the enclosed terrace. Most atypically, a large straw hat of the kind seen in the Southern United States or the Italian island of Sicily shielded the individual's face. That the figure wanted to conceal his identity was not unusual, but using a straw hat that precluded any facial features from being identified was thought by analysts to be a tell that was, in fact, strangely revealing. As if its owner was challenging those he knew were looking at him from miles above the Earth's surface.

After the raid, some interest among the public was found in the cluttered but modest furnishings housing the highly sequestered existence of bin Laden. Yet he had several satellite hookups on the premises linked to advanced satellite phones, but no local phones or internet wiring running into the compound. The distinguishing feature of what the locals called the Waziristan Haveli, Waziristan—the locality and haveli, meaning "mansion"—was its immense surrounding twelve-foot-, sometimes even eighteen-foot-high solid cinderblock rebar reinforced walls with only three external gates. The entire compound was walled in, and certain protective inner walls also sprouted curved spooled barbed wire over the top of the barriers. The layout of the grounds required that any attempt to efficiently enter the main house required passage through a single gate that opened to a narrow seventy-five-yard high-concrete-walled corridor. This gauntletlike channel with twelve-foot-high sidewalls offered no protection to anyone traversing its length, and the intent of its design was to ensure maximum exposure to anyone within its confines.

Identical to an American bank, there were two sets of entry doors set five feet apart so that a person could not hold both open while entering or exiting the space. Entering the first set of doors to get to the second, they would find themselves temporarily within a sealed chamber and the bank would then unlock the second door, denoted by the characteristic buzz. Many inexperienced individuals attempting to forcefully procure funds without permission, otherwise known as robbing a bank, found themselves suddenly confined within the closed space as they attempted to flee, stuck between both sets of doors that now were locked. The design enabled them to involuntarily wait for the police to arrive.

Such was the design and intent of the gauntlet. It was sealed at its innermost end by an additional gate, composed of reinforced paneled nine-foot steel double doors, and this mirrored the heavy nine-foot welded steel doors at the other end of the long enclosed channel driveway. The innermost gate opened into the main yard with direct access to the three-story structure of the living quarters. To any reasonable inspection of the compound, the near military-grade gates with large protected hinges were enough to announce to any outsider that this haveli was something different.

The inside of the house was a compilation of finished and partially completed construction, with the third floor having been added last to what was originally a two-story structure. This most recent addition of the uppermost structure was built in late 2005 and was illegal construction, having never been registered in the Pakistan building code approval process. Subsequent investigation by both journalists and the American and Pakistani governments noted that the building was lavishly funded, raising suspicion among at least one contractor that the quarters completed were for some important figure wishing to remain hidden. However, the contractor never said anything, assuming that the Pakistani government fully knew about and had approved the construction. The American government shared the contractor's conclusion.

The staircase was solid wood, with whitewashed textured or stucco-walled surfaces absent the pictures or normal decorative embellishments found in other comparably sized residences. The landing or balcony just outside the large third-floor master bedroom also had sturdy wood framing, and medium-gauge particleboard composed its adequate wooden joist-supported floor covered by a tightly woven Berber-wool patterned surface.

As Hayes and his companion immediately behind him rounded this last separate hallway curve, they entered a lower landing, now on the second level, that then opened into the ascending staircase connected to the third floor. Hearing bin Laden's voice, memorized from top secret tapings of the leader, Hayes could tangentially see his lead team member on this ascending stairwell. The lead SEAL was about to expose himself to bin Laden as the man rounded a final curve before turning to ascend the last ten steps.

Hayes moved quickly and, with hand signals, caught his attention and signaled that bin Laden was directly above Hayes on this third-story landing. Hayes also warned his point man that Bin Laden was probably armed. Both of the Americans had their night vision optics in use, but without hesitation and with the perpetrator of 9/11 standing five feet directly above him, Hayes reacted. He immediately fired straight up seven times, not eight and a half feet from the six-foot, three-inch terrorist's abdomen and chest. In fact, the official and extremely confidential rapid autopsy conducted to morphometrically and genetically confirm the body was bin Laden's noted that he had been shot multiple times, with two diffuse and ragged entry wounds in both his upper thighs and two similar wounds in his central perineum or skin surrounding and interposed between the anus and genitals. Portions of these projectiles dissipated their kinetic force, tearing while partially vaporizing delicate soft tissue as they traveled upward from his groin into his abdomen, slicing through his common iliac artery with one round entering his liver.

As the Parabellum rounds exited Hayes's M4A1 carbine, the first two or three created explosive spiked holes in the wood of the floor, slowing but allowing fragmented heavy metal to continue upwards at diminished yet lethal speed. An uncounted majority of the subsequent rounds were not impeded as to their velocity as they enjoyed the plow-clearing efficiency of the earlier rounds, instantly passing through the damaged wood and the holes created. Their kinetic force was thus near full force as they tore into bin Laden.

Thus, those participating in the after-action review concluded that the cause of Bin Laden's erratic lunge, suddenly exposing himself to those in front of him in the ascending stairwell, was the force of Hayes's rounds entering the man's body. But the net effect was that bin Laden instantly became unceremoniously unshielded as he reflexively jerked to his left and immediately received the terminal round in the forehead, falling back into the bedroom. Two SP teammates immediately entered the bedroom and, upon finding Bin Laden twitching involuntarily on the floor, lying in a growing pool of his own blood, emptied another five rounds into his chest until the twitching ceased.

What also was not reported was the subsequent placement of a 9mm M9 Beretta barrel against bin Laden's temple before discharging a single shot from point-blank distance into his head. This, Hayes did himself within thirty seconds of the now-still body's loss of movement so as to protect his team members from any unjustified criticism. But it was also a mortal confirmation to ensure that the mastermind behind the tragedy that enveloped New York City was now officially terminated. The malleable lead hollow tip 9x19mm Parabellum round entered his right temple, creating immediate soft tissue bruising, bleeding, and swelling in response to the traumatic force of entry. Bin Laden's face was therefore almost unrecognizable, with a sizable plum-sized swelling in response to the bullet's entry that distorted the entire right frontal area of his skull.

This, along with the first shot fired from the advancing SEALs mounting the stairs that entered his forehead slightly over his left eye, had savagely cratered his face. An exit wound on the back of his skull formed in response to Hayes's barrel-to-skin executionlike discharge, a mass of bone, brains, and hair that blew back and formed a jagged baseball-sized exit cavity that necessitated bin Laden's head be wrapped in gauze and towels as he was placed in a body bag. Carried out of the haveli by two SEALs, one of them sat on his chest as he lay in the body bag in the returning helicopter, as space was scarce in the steel flying machine.

The man responsible for over three thousand civilian deaths in the largest act of terror on American soil was then rapidly transported back to an American base in Afghanistan, forensically identified using standard morphometrics but also genetically using his relative's DNA. His last destination was a US carrier group, his remains being flown for the body's disposal into the ocean.

The prior actions of this particular naval commander now in charge of his elite team was thus known and respected by all, especially Roth. The only issue for Commander Hayes, at least from his perspective, was that he had been ordered to command the group from the relative safety of a desktop computer and its screen monitors. He had asked but was forbidden to "kinetically participate" in the actual upcoming mission—militaryspeak for the confirmation that he could not accompany his cherished subordinates on the imminent undertaking.

As Jacob and Greene entered his office, he was just laying a paper map out on the desk and comparing its markings to the satellite imagery seen on the flickering screen, a recently emailed set of images sent by encrypted Pentagon linkage. With both arms stretched out in front of him as he leaned on the desk, his palms flattened against the particleboard surface, he looked up and frowned slightly as the two men entered his tiny office.

"Gentleman, I am predisposed to hope this is important. I have to ensure that our forthcoming mission is still viable." Hayes had a thin veneer of professional military manners, but the man did not suffer fools well, if at all.

Greene spoke first and attempted to color the water.

"Sir, Roth here is having trouble with one of my mission-related orders."

Normally, this might have been enough for a senior commander to look at the junior officer and simply tell him to comply and get the hell out of his office. But Hayes knew Roth, his reputation, and his universally acknowledged status among the special operations community.

In fact, Roth might have been the one member of the team who Hayes himself respected as a near equal. Not in rank, but in mission responsibilities, as a soldier, as a combatant, and as a man. Hayes was older, but the current active and dangerous environment of covert mission success belonged to Roth. And there was something else. Hayes personally liked, perhaps even admired Roth. Roth certainly revered Hayes. But beyond a mutual respect, both men were rather similar in their outward appearances; they showed the same humility, the same attention to fellow team members, and were taciturn in their self-promotion. Neither indulged in this latter practice, as others were quick to provide a positive narrative as to their individual attributes.

Between the two, Hayes relied upon intuition often more than Roth who, in many ways, was the more cerebral of the two men. Hayes was grounded more to his experiences melded to his training, while Roth continually and systematically provided an analytical framework within each second of his real-time actions. There were other subtle differences between these two men, but each were appreciated by those who worked with them.

Hayes might be expected to knock on a door, wait, and then fire through it, aiming high and low within the rectangle to ensure adequate coverage in order to kill an armed adversary, whereas Roth might stealthily gain entrance to the other side of the door via some route, surprising and eliminating this same adversary along with the potential of harm to anyone knocking at the door.

Both men understood the other's mindset, their individual trenchant perspectives, and together they could have been a formidable team. Roth often consulted Hayes and had done so in the past as well, casually discussing various mission parameters with Hayes while each sat sipping coffee in the officer's canteen. This was the excuse for a combined beverage and dining facility, a small enclosed building with a generous open single room populated by beat-up tables and chairs. This smaller building abutted the larger mess hall used by enlisted soldiers. "Spartan" would have been embellishing the room's accoutrements, as it literally had only small round plywood-topped tables resting on four-legged rusted cast-iron stands, surrounded by the same IKEA chairs as were dispersed throughout the camp. The ceiling was unfinished, with electrical conduit draped between the evenly spaced wooden joists connecting naked bulbs in their white glazed porcelain fixtures.

The similarity to a barn or workshop was obvious, and in fact, the officers' canteen had become known as "the garage" to the enlisted personnel, a categorical but respectful insult meant to highlight the slightly more "luxurious" accommodations enjoyed by these same enlisted members as opposed to the officers. Their mess, unlike the officers' tiny hovel, had paper table coverings, changed occasionally, and some jokester had placed a small frosted glass flower vase containing a plastic damaged leafy structure on the largest table to remind all that ambiance was important! Both Hayes and Roth wanted this disparity. It was good for morale.

Roth remained quiet as he stood in Hayes's office, locking eyes with his commander. Hayes held his gaze and then shifted slowly toward Greene.

"Say that again, Commander Greene."

In the moment between his first and now second response, Greene sensed what each of the three now felt: that he had stepped off a plank into a black void.

But he attempted, "Lt. Roth has a concern with one of my orders, sir."

Hayes waited, then finally stated, "Are you going to tell me what you gave as the order, Commander?"

"I told him he was to review Mahoney's file."

Hayes looked at Roth. Jacob could tell momentary confusion had been supplanted by suspicion, then immediately by confirmation.

He stated flatly, "Ok, Commander Greene, thank you. May I have the record? You are free to leave, Commander."

Greene hesitated just a fraction too long, reluctant but realizing he had no alternative. A checkmate had occurred. He stepped forward and handed the file to Hayes. Stepping back, his salute was absent confidence; he had been severed from the process. Moving toward the door, Greene paused for only a moment and then forcefully pulled it open.

Roth stood erect, unmoving, but his breathing was controlled, regular and comfortable.

As Greene exited and closed the door, Hayes waited and then did something Roth had not anticipated. He silently moved around to the front of his desk, and within a second he had the door to his office open, moving quickly through it. Roth saw from the corner of his eye that Greene had belatedly begun to walk down the hallway toward the building exit.

Greene had evidently hesitated by the door, pausing to listen, but he never had a chance. Hayes moved too rapidly for him.

Hayes re-entered his office, and almost hidden in his entrance was a subtle rolling of his eyes to the heavens as he silently expressed his assessment of Lt. Commander Greene.

He turned to Jacob and stated, "You had a problem with evaluating her?"

"Absolutely not, sir."

"Then . . . ?"

"I didn't think I needed to see her personal history and background information, sir."

"You are correct, you didn't. However, now you do need to see it if you are to understand what is happening."

Roth looked hard at Hayes. The same misgivings that had originally surfaced in Hayes's eyes now were crowding into Jacob's, and Hayes read them immediately. Hayes held up his hand, the traffic stop sign, and paused, searching for the correct words.

"Greene doesn't know this, as it transpired less than six hours ago and he has no contact with the decision-makers. So, I don't know what his angle is, but mine is rather direct: Command wants you to review her entire record, as she is the first female that we are thinking of deploying on special operations for a live mission. Apparently, they are asking you and me to review everything to ensure that she has 'what it takes.'"

Jacob continued to look directly into Hayes's ice-blue eyes. Roth did not blink, waiting.

"Jacob, they are looking for anything to shit-can her participation. It's up to you and me to find the variables that are problematic and report back to have her recalled or reassigned to somewhere in Central Command or back to Germany. They do not want her to go along with us. They are afraid she might get killed, and then it will be a woman who was lost getting the target."

"So I am to assume we are going after al Al Hassan Abbas."

He smiled ruefully. "You are perceptive, my young friend, aren't you?"

"Sir, this is not rocket science. We have been looking for this man for fourteen months, and now we have the Kurds as our allies and ISIS on the run. We should be ready to zero in on him with their help, right? And now we have Command having fits because we have a woman who is going to serve with us on a mission. So, that signals that we are close, if not getting ready now—I don't know, but it suggests we are close."

Hayes responded with a smile and slight forward nod. "Yep," he concluded.

Jacob spoke carefully, but he was not going to play politically correct. "So, I am being asked to look at her file to ensure that they have an excuse to kick her off the team, at least for this mission?"

"Yes."

"And if we—or, more succinctly, I—don't?"

Hayes smiled, but this time it was aggressive, almost a snarl but still friendly, representing the bond between both.

"If neither of us feel she needs to come off the team, both of us would almost certainly be replaced."

Roth asked directly, "Do you want me to do this, sir?"

Very softly, Hayes proffered, "Jacob, what sort of individual do you think I am?"

Roth did not answer, but simply smiled and asked for the file.

Hayes moved to hand Roth the same file Greene had placed on his desk. But before Roth took it from Hayes, Jacob placed his right hand over Hayes's, locking his grip around the hand of the senior officer.

Roth looked at Hayes, still holding on to his right hand.

71

Both still held the file and its material.

A bit more melodramatically than Roth intended, as he was suffused with a new anger that had risen within him to an uncomfortable level, he spoke, "I, Jacob Roth, swear under penalty of perjury, prosecution, or court-martial to uphold the Constitution of the United States, to be truthful, and to comply with the demeanor and actions expected of a United States Military officer."

He then released his senior officer's hand, stepped back six inches, and saluted.

Locking eyes with Hayes, he said, "If you now want to dismiss me from the team, feel free, sir, but I am not going to sabotage the efforts of V. Mahoney. She is ready. She has earned her spot."

Hayes was now standing, and with a crooked smile he placed his large left paw on Jacob's right shoulder. "Excellent. I knew you were the right man for this. Now, if you don't mind, would you read her folder? And don't attempt to hold my hand again. I'm beginning to worry about you!" he teased as an older brother would to a beloved younger sibling. "Read all of it, and then let's move on, Jacob. It is necessary. I read it this morning, and I want to state to Command that you and I individually have read, reviewed, and evaluated the file and feel V. Mahoney is adequate for the mission." This was stated less emphatically, but it was no less an order. "I don't make up stories, Jacob Roth, so please sit in that corner." Hayes pointed to a small stand with a stool next to it.

Roth spotted a dull green metal stool with a round dark-brown disc seat, its worn leather surface adjustable by spinning the seat. The threading along its supporting long metal vertical axel acted similarly to a reverse screw, permitting its adaptive height. Next to it was a stand that appeared to be a relic of the last great war, that being World War II, as it had faded brown metal legs and a wooden top flat surface, about twenty-eight inches from the floor. "Battered" would have been a complimentary term, as the chipped paint and rust at the edges of the painted metal interfaces were numerous. Its scared wooden surface was a flat discolored disc the size of a small car's tire. Solidly anchored to the metal legs, the smooth ancient wood had multiple divots but also had room for a brown gooseneck light with a naked bulb. Roth switched it on. Despite the room's relatively bright surroundings, the corner was masked in shadow. The single unprotected bulb, almost a flare demarcating a roadside accident, was not sufficient to make reading comfortable, but it was all that existed. Roth settled on the stool and flipped open the file.

Roth's reluctant accessing of her personal records, beyond her proficiency reports and graded responses, was only occurring because he had been ordered. But Roth briefly considered if Virginia would have let him view her record, as otherwise, absent a direct order, Jacob would have never considered asking for this intimate privilege or, more accurately, the additional "burden" to be viewed without her consent.

Somewhat less important but still relevant in Jacob's mind was that he would not have asked to read her file. There were dozens of more senior officers and enlisted who were paid within the structure of the military to handle just this sort of data and be prepared to share appropriate portions of its contents with the press, family, or loved ones if tragedy struck. And tragedy was something that all special operations team members routinely encountered.

Hayes deliberately walked up to Roth's stool and stated, "Given that you are her team leader, that there are no other females in this operational command, and that she has no family . . . well, you are it, along with me, to assess her skills. As noted, they are looking for anything that can be used to reassign her."

"With all due respect, sir, don't you think whomever these people are, this is their call?" Jacob paused and searched for the correct words. "Their need?"

"Yes, Jacob, but I need you to see this. The issue is whether there is a potential area of interest regarding performance in combat."

Roth searched his face, carefully examining the clear pools of unrippled thoughtfulness that were in turn looking at Jacob.

"Yes, sir" was Roth's almost inaudible reply.

He was still uncomfortable, a residual effect of his actual need to see potentially very personal information that he felt had little to do with Virginia's combat readiness. Roth felt that he was invading her most private concerns. He could see in the reflection from the studied eyes of Hayes that the senior man instantly understood Roth's misgivings. And perhaps that was the reason this lingering hesitancy existed.

The "Now what?" was evident in Hayes's face. He was ordering that Roth read it, because he was going to tell the truth to the senior commanders and note that both of them had actually accessed the file.

Hayes picked up his coffee cup, a battered metal travel mug with a Naval Academy emblem, and sipped while not lowering his gaze. His eyes motioned for Roth to get on with it.

As Jacob began to read, he initially found himself wondering if there was anything that might exist that Hayes really was troubled over. Had Hayes seen something that disturbed him or caught his attention? Or did Hayes just want to have Jacob share the burden of opening Virginia's private life, what little she had experienced, with someone he trusted?

But by his actions, Jacob had entered an unspoken honor-bound contract to ensure that Virginia's life, her desires, her dreams, and goals, would not disappear from the Earth.

But did such a promise require a sacrifice?

Roth repositioned, smoothed the folder's cover with his left hand, and began to read.

Virginia Mahoney was a soldier, a teammate on the special operations team focused on mission success. But as Jacob read, he immediately saw a different individual—the real Virginia Lois Mahoney, in fact. He had never even known her middle name, but this individual appeared to rise out of the pages of reports as a unique, almost gifted individual with motivation linked to an unwillingness to accept defeat. But as Roth took in the official document, he was not simply impressed—he found himself in near awe of her. The sterile but candid, almost naked narrative summarizing her life and what she had overcome tightened his stomach.

Virginia had matriculated through the same rigorous testing, mental, emotional, and physical, that all had similarly passed. Along the way, her high school teachers, her Presbyterian minister, and her coach in varsity tennis were all interviewed, who each provided a small window of understanding into this complex individual. Jacob read each of the interview summaries and found himself smiling at times and grimacing at others, as her life was not reflective of a typical sheltered American teenager.

Then Roth froze, and his heart accelerated.

Virginia had been born to an unwed teenage girl, apparently raped in the backseat of a car at homecoming in the suburbs of Chicago. This rather unadorned statement was a summary conclusion based on interviews with Virginia and her adoptive mother. There was also a note attached from a social worker at the time of Virginia's birth and arranged adoption. Finding herself pregnant, Virginia's mother had considered abortion but decided against it, as her sister convinced her to put the baby up for adoption. Her biological mother had wanted nothing to do with the child and was killed four years later in an automobile head-on collision with the concrete abutment of an overpass. Her blood alcohol was .32 at the time, and the trauma to her skull and neck caused the county coroner to grimace and comment that if the impact had somehow been insufficient, she might have expired nonetheless from alcohol poisoning.

Virginia had been adopted by working-class parents before she was two weeks old even though another married couple, far wealthier and with genuine stature and political pull, also wanted this baby girl. But Virginia's destiny was to be adopted by the Mahoneys and given one ingredient essential to a child's future: love, unlimited, unquestioned, and unconditional.

Her early years were those of a young woman working to "help" her mom and dad. She cut grass, babysat, and washed cars, this latter task often the unspoken purvey of the young men her age. But she did this routinely, apparently providing her neighborhood with the cleanest grouping of old Dodges, Chevys, and Fords that could be found on Chicago's Near West Side. Life was pleasant, but money was never plentiful throughout most of her youth. She had described her years as wonderful, but this omitted a couple of rather important events.

Different police reports were found along with three separate summaries of one incident that occurred near her eleventh birthday. Apparently, one of her friends—an attractive, very beautiful young girl of Italian descent—had been pinned against the wall in her mother's apartment by her mother's boyfriend. The forty-six-year-old man was apparently intoxicated and later claimed he thought that this twelve-year-old friend of Virginia's was the girl's mother.

The report by the police was dripping with sarcasm even in the professional, rather sterile summary of events provided, as the young girl had dark, almost black hair and her mother's hair was "bottle blonde." This paired with the fact that the report described the twelve-year-old's appearance, including her rather premature breast development, suggested that her mom's boyfriend knew who and what he was doing when he decided to prey on this child.

The police received a very emotional call—angry, tearful, but not crying—from this same young Italian girl to come "real fast" to her mom's apartment. The young girl was aware enough to provide an accurate address.

Upon arrival, what they found was the young girl talking angrily with the man and one Virginia Mahoney sitting on the back of this same guy, the mother's boyfriend. His arm was unceremoniously twisted behind him, touching his spine, and his hand was forced upward to the occipital region of his head, a position producing significant pain and rendering him immobile. What made the scene less than comical was the seven-inch blade from a kitchen knife that Virginia had resting along the side of his neck, specifically in the region of his carotid artery, and our future soldier yelling along with her friend into the reprobate's ear that she would cut his "fucking head off and then his cock!" if he so much as twitched.

Of the trio of cops who arrived to find this gathering, two of them broke into sarcastic grins. But the older man, the individual with a daughter about Virginia's age, rapidly became focused and his tone serious as he unemotionally but cautiously instructed Virginia to withdraw the knife from the man's neck.

He later put in his report that what he saw in this young girl's eyes conveyed to him that she was close to actually separating lecher's head from his body and might have done the same for his male organ.

Charges were filed against the man, but none against Virginia. In fact, the reports had been heavily redacted, and the court ordered them sealed. It almost suggested that someone had been interested in protecting her, or perhaps her future. Neither Jacob nor Hayes could know that this same older police officer, the one with a daughter almost Virginia's age, had assiduously worked to call in all outstanding political favors owed him to wash away the potential of a personal court appearance for Virginia. Her actions were thus buried for years, but in the course of her security clearance review, all relevant material was reopened to the military investigators. This had required her consent, which she rapidly provided.

Roth read this and part of him smiled while part of him shrugged, as this was anything but a problem for Virginia. The smile was to accept that he was proud of her and her sense of justice; the shrug was an attempt to find this "private" tidbit innocuous, but he hoped deep within his consciousness that nothing else noteworthy existed. Such was not to be the case.

There was another much less tepid occurrence, a second police report. As Roth read it, he found his heart rate again picking up and its force augmented.

Just short of her seventeenth birthday, she had visited a friend. While sitting in her backyard sharing opinions about their classmates, idiot boys, and their immature attempts to impress members of the opposite sex, a sudden disruption to the lazy summer afternoon occurred. According to the report, V. Mahoney and her friend abruptly heard muffled yells from an adjacent house. The report provided some background, stating that the home's owner, a single mother, was at work. Her oldest daughter, who was often in trouble with the law due to drug-related charges, such as minor possession violations in the past, visited the home frequently when her mother was at work to pilfer food and drink—in effect feeding her boyfriend on mom's dime. Both of these individuals were not working, nor did they feel the need to work unless it was to cash in on selling contraband in the form of recreational marijuana. The single mother worked tirelessly to feed herself and her youngest daughter, her thirteen-year-old, but was unable to control the activities of her oldest child, the twenty-two-year-old daughter.

But the report noted that Virginia had distinctly heard irregular and partially muffled cries for help coming from the kitchen located at the back of the gray-and-white shingle-style house. Its large glass windows facing the backyard were open but showed partially torn and stained plastic roller shades that had been pulled down and obscured any view inside. Loosely fitted summer screens to keep out insects were attached to the window frames but did little to entrap or diminish sound coming from inside of the house. The house itself was dilapidated, the wooden siding partially rotted and damaged, old paint peeling off the sides, and the hinges of the front screen door rusted and pulling away from the wooden frame.

The report suggested that Virginia's friend had advised her to ignore the sounds, as the older girl—the "slut," according to Virginia's friend—was home with her boyfriend, and from the gathering of the four motorcycles in front of the residence, three friends were with him.

Virginia hesitantly complied after hearing the first cry for assistance, although her friend subsequently reported to police that Virginia was fidgeting nervously, continually looking toward origin of the sound at the back of the house. But when a second muffled scream from someone sounding younger was followed by what sounded like a slap that abruptly terminated the shriek for assistance, Virginia was up running to the back of the house. She tried the back door that led directly into the kitchen and, finding it locked, raised her right foot and shattered the wooden frame, dislodging the lock and popping the door open.

The scene inside the kitchen caused Virginia to slow to a near stop as she immediately processed the setting, but the sum duration of 500 milliseconds was all that was needed before she was again moving, and rapidly. In fact, reports noted that according to the younger sister's statements, she became a blur of motion.

For what Virginia saw was an unclothed twenty-two-year-old woman standing but bent forward ninety degrees at her waist, the front of her naked torso partially flattened against the kitchen table, her arms outstretched in front of her and tightly held by an unkempt, unshaven man of about twenty-five with greasy hair positioned on the opposite side of the table. The woman's pants and panties were still around her right ankle, but her shoes were off and her bare legs and buttocks were spread as another man from behind grabbed a handful of her rich blonde hair and held her head down, using his left hand to cup and massage her naked left breast. His movement was repetitive, actually rhythmic as he ground his pelvis and his appendage deep into her. His pants were also at his ankles. The woman struggled slightly but apparently had reluctantly accepted the imbalance of his strength against hers, the forced intercourse in front of her kid sister causing her eyes to fill with tears.

On Virginia's immediate right, not five feet from her shoulder, two people stood. One was the younger thirteen-year-old sister, tears running down her face, her eyes already puffy and red and her left cheek reddened with the outline of a hand imprinted on her skin. Her bloodless lips tightly sealed as she grimaced. Her plain white blouse had been torn open, her bra askew, as a different twenty-five-year-old man held her from behind, fondling her bare left breast while he held her tight. His right hand was full of her thick light-brown hair, forcing her head upright and whispering for her to watch her sister entertain them. The young girl was no match for the strength of the man, and behind the tears her eyes registered the terror that she would soon be joining her sister in satisfying these men.

To Virginia's immediate left was the last member of the foursome. She had not seen him when she kicked in the door, and he grabbed her left arm just above the elbow as she came into the kitchen. The other three men looked at her, and the one holding the older sister's arms smiled a wicked leering gesture. The younger woman looked toward Virginia, startled but registering confusion; her sister spread out on the kitchen table could not readily move her head to see who had burst through the door.

The report did not relate what was said between Virginia and the man who grabbed her arm, only that Virginia moved too rapidly for him to immobilize her and tore her arm from his grasp. She crossed the space between the kitchen back door and the table in less than a second. Raising her right foot up to her waist, she brought it down and unleashed the force of her bent leg, almost as a snake releases from a coil to viciously strike. The side of the immobile, slightly bent knee of the man enjoying the act of unwanted penetrance was the target. There was an immediate popping sound and his knee buckled, the ligaments and cartilage instantly shredded. Within seconds of her foot's impact, the knee itself expanded to the size of a grapefruit. The man fell backwards, involuntarily disengaging from the forcefully restrained woman, and screamed as he crumpled to the kitchen floor, rolling onto his back clutching his knee. The wave of pain was so great that he vomited.

The report briefly summarized that Virginia had whipped around and, using her right foot again, harnessed the circumferential force of her leg like the end of a whip, cutting through the air to land in the groin of her ineffective arm-grabber. He immediately genuflected forward, registering explosive pain, searing discomfort, and nausea, only to have his face, moving downward, meet Virginia's left knee and be forcefully raised upward. Her effort was maximal, a hopping motion allowing her to drive her knee up into his face, fracturing his nose, dislodging two front teeth, and rendering him instantly unconscious. But she was not done.

She then whirled around and grabbed the closest item sitting on the side of the kitchen sink, which happened to be a Mr. Coffee glass coffeepot, and brought it down toward the head of the man who, by this time, had defensively pushed the thirteen-year-old girl at Virginia. Virginia sidestepped the young woman as she went flying across the kitchen, stumbling, falling, and then landing next to the unconscious man whose bleeding nose now had grown to the size of a summer squash. Virginia's aim was true, and she decisively shattered the glass coffeepot on the assailant's head. Still holding the pot's handle, she used its jagged remnants as a cutting tool and raked it across his face, opening a deep laceration across his right cheek. The cut nearly separated the distal portion of his nose from his face before ultimately gouging out a four-inch furrow of skin reaching the bone of his skull above his left eye.

Blood erupted from his facial wounds, and he registered intense flooding heat and then pain. Yelling as he fell backwards into the waist-high wooden cabinets filled with bowls and pans, he landed awkwardly on his left elbow, bent forward with his head over his thighs. His bellow was partially distorted as he sputtered, spraying copious droplets of his own body's red liquid over his filthy denim jeans. Within seconds, his face was the color of a stop sign minus any lettering. The front of his shirt was almost completely saturated. His hands now holding his face trembled, eyes wide in shock as he registered the rich ruby-red color coating his fingers and palms.

Turning toward the last man who had been holding the older sister's hands, immobilizing her during the forced sex, he was already running toward the front of the house. Within seconds, she heard his motorcycle's engine kick to life before he sped off.

Virginia had been arrested along with the three men. But only hours after her incarceration, the report documented that she was freed and no charges were filed against her. There was little direct articulation of what had specifically been said or what had been discussed at the time of this event in the summary Roth was reading. However, it was clear that one or both of the victims had provided police with enough evidence for the police to put together what had transpired and to act in accordance with a just and reasonable response. The men stayed behind bars. One man received forty-seven stiches in his face, and the other would go on to visit a prison orthopedic physician while awaiting trial. He would walk with a limp for the rest of his life.

The young thirteen-year-old sister later attempted to visit Virginia, coming to her home. Virginia's mother had answered the door, as her husband was at work, and the young girl asked to speak to the person who rescued her and her sister. The young woman was to live her life in awe of this beautiful avenging angel who had burst through her dwelling's door and washed her family's kitchen of the filth her older sister had unwisely permitted to enter.

But the visit apparently confused Virginia's mother, as she and her husband had no knowledge of any of these events. Virginia had pleaded for it to be so, and the older officer—the same man with his own daughter who responded to the first event, now more senior within the department—had once again moved rapidly to protect Virginia and honor her request. Her parents were not called or informed. Apparently, the actions, subsequent arrest, and release of her daughter were totally unknown to them. Her daughter's heroics had never been discussed. Probably not even to this day, thought Roth.

As Roth read on, his thoughts wandered. He began to ask himself a question that was impossible to answer yet vital to ask, one he could not ignore. Who was Virginia Mahoney? That she would take on four men who were unmistakably stronger than she and not only overpower them but neutralize each one more efficiently than at least 90 percent of any men off the street was indeed heroic, but . . . well, it was potentially a bit irresponsible. There were numerous other scenarios that could have unfolded for young Virginia, and none of the alternative endings were attractive. He had to admire her, however, and if not outright admiration, then there was certainly respect. Most often an individual does not get to choose the confrontation that they encounter; they simply must decide whether to respond or to turn the other way and avoid it entirely. Virginia Mahoney had been under absolutely no obligation at any level to respond to the younger sister's yell for help. But Virginia had responded, and the rest, well—the rest was irrelevant, in Roth's mind. The decision to get involved had been pivotal, and the outcome was fortunate.

Despite himself, he shook his head and smiled. Roth pondered if he himself would have been successful in this confrontation. Almost certainly yes, but he was a member of one of the world's elite "kill squads." Let's call it what it is, thought Roth. But would he have responded without any foreknowledge as to the events transpiring? He honestly hoped so, but just as honestly, he was not certain. How could anyone be certain? But what would make a person—a young, not even seventeen-year-old woman, no less—bust into a house and take on four of society's less honorable, a collection of dregs, and inarguably rescue two women?

Bravery? Anger and then a loss of control? Was she held captive by raw emotional needs? He wondered. Superheroes exist in comics and on movie screens, not in real life. Virginia had put herself at extreme risk of injury, rape, or even murder. But she was not only successful—she was definitive. As the law officer overseeing the entire matter had commented, the three injured males were fortunate that she had decided not to finish the job. She might have killed each of them. According to the seasoned judgment of a certain newly minted detective lieutenant who summarized his interviews with Virginia, there had been a real potential of this occurring.

This man had seen this look in her eyes years earlier with a steel blade resting on a man's neck, and again he saw within her the same emotive force: not fear, but a nearly preternatural focus. And later, during her interview with this same seasoned officer, an almost eerie tranquility in her demeanor suggested equanimity regarding her actions. There was no bravado, but an acceptance of purpose. Even for this weathered veteran and guardian of the law, he had reflected as to its unsettling effect.

He had seen the kitchen. The copious blood and the mangled face, knee, and nose of the respective male recipients spoke to the unbridled violent force of her intervention. This level of justifiable aggression was unusual for anyone, but he had never witnessed anything like it from a teenage girl. By the end of his forty-year career, years into the future, this fact remained unchanged; it was a singular event. Yet the officer had edited his remarks and respectfully inserted "young lady" throughout his narrative, eliminating other monikers such as female, girl, or kid. As a military veteran, he had recognized the soul of a warrior when he encountered one. She was the disinclined hero, an individual who displayed a quiet selflessness and rock-solid sense of duty to care for her sister, her neighbor, her friend. She was not the loud-mouthed "watch me" sort of extrovert hero, but the authentic version who went forward when everyone else headed the other direction. She would not abandon someone in need. She might fail, might succumb to forces that would take her life, but she would not turn and run.

It was her sense of supreme focus that the veteran detective found so riveting, so beyond normal. It caused him to write a bit more in the report than was usual and emphasize his personal foreboding over Virginia's future, for this hardened and typically cynical law officer sensed in her serenity, exemplified in her summary of events, a fearlessness, a clarion call to righteousness that would characterize her future. A combat veteran of Viet Nam, he had seen this type of response rarely in men he had fought alongside of, and often they were the ones who never returned home. At least not alive. In the end, their sense of duty and commitment to comrades superseded the normal human response of self-preservation. Their need to protect their friends, to accomplish the mission could not be trained, and it could not be ignored. It was fundamentally different than the norm.

Unknown to Roth, Hayes, or anyone else was the fact that this same detective had followed Virginia's life from a distant vantage point. When he discovered that she had joined the military within two years of his incident report, he smiled. And that same workday, as this knowledge of Virginia's enlistment occurred, he went to the large stone-and-brick Church of Rome occupying almost half of a complete city block located less than a mile from the police station. There, climbing the stone steps, he pulled back the heavy oak front door and entered a structure that he seldom visited. On a Wednesday evening, few parishioners were present, the cathedral's semidark cavernous surroundings were quiet, and the odor of incense enveloped the shadows. Near seven p.m., third pew from the front, the detective humbly got on his knees.

The wooden figure before him, almost life-size, was of a man with his head bent forward, chin resting on his chest, and his hands and feet impaled with representations of iron spikes. These were driven into the cross. The sculpted figure and cross hung from the front wall of the church above the pulpit. The detective desperately sought to again believe that this figure represented the actual Son of God. That there was a God, and that His Son blessed the inhabitants of this planet, were distant memories for the officer of the law. Long ago in a flooded rice field soaked by monsoon rains, he had abandoned such beliefs as the sorrowful cries from fellow soldiers and civilians mangled by war had stripped him of what little belief had existed in him. He now asked God for permission to renew his faith. He now asked that God provide this young woman a degree of special safety, to guide, guard, and shepherd her. To watch over her. This detective knew Virginia would place herself in harm's way.

That she would deliberately, but not rashly place herself in the path of evil to demonstrate that goodness would demand rectification. This was inarguable; the detective knew this as sure as he knew his own name. Thus, he needed to call back a long dormant faith lost thirty-four years previously in those fields of Viet Nam. He needed to ask his Creator to forgive his lack of faith, but now he asked with humility, but purposefully, for God to protect this young individual. He looked at the figure on the cross. He proposed to God that his faith would again be reborn if God promised to protect this woman. The detective knew this was childish —one couldn't bargain with God—but the officer of the law went even further. "Her life for mine!" There, he said it—and meant it. He knew that he was being juvenile. This was not a celestial swap meet! And yet, he made the request anyway. And he immediately knew his request was pure, correct, and somehow, he knew beyond reason or understanding that God would honor this plea.

She was another version of him, but better. She was a person possessing courage. Quiet, soft-spoken courage, unadulterated courage. His supplication caused him to become quiet and realize the enormity of his bargain, but he knew it was proper. Upon returning to his residence, sitting at the dining room table he was quiet, reflective but alert.

His wife of thirty-two years looked at him and recognized his haunted eyes, the fragments of memories that still scalded his soul. Their children had seldom, if ever, seen this in their father, but his wife had been his companion and witness to this remnant sorrow previously. It had been worse immediately after he returned from the war, but she knew him better than she knew anyone else alive. She asked him if he was going to be ok. He looked up at her, and with large tears cascading down both cheeks, he told her he had been to church to pray for a soldier. She understandably but incorrectly assumed that, inexplicably, something had triggered a sliver of grief in her spouse, that he was praying for a man he had seen killed in those distant fields of Viet Nam. She would have been unable to audibly register her surprise if she had been told that he was actually praying for a vibrant young woman who had herself chosen a path that only God could foresee and direct.

While reading this detective's professional narrative on V. Mahoney, Roth let his mind drift into old papers, essays written on bravery, on exceptional actions taken by now legendary men on the field of battle in WWII, Korea, and Viet Nam. Both historical accounts and classified military analysis of what drove human beings to perform life-saving heroics. He was a willing audience to the scores of military investigators who had probed the depths of human activities seen during combat. Some of the research was in an attempt to weed out the oddballs, the sadists, the sociopaths who enjoyed killing. But other more nuanced and thoughtful essays were examinations of the interactions between culture, home environment, and those felt to be the reluctant heroes.

The human psyche is infinitely complex, a journey down a mist-shrouded river at the break of dawn slowly winding through an endless canyon. It is interminably subtle, opaque, and amorphous, with resulting actions or decisions not clearly predicated on variables or elements that can be touched or seen. It is an often chaotic compilation of memories, emotion, and need. Why some exhibit remarkable bravery when most cannot, will not, or are unable remains as impermeable today as when Aristotle, in The Nicomachean Ethics, listed courage as an ill-defined midpoint between rashness and cowardice. But few people could have shown what Mahoney had already manifested.

Roth read further, and a distant sadness enveloped him.

Unfortunately, her adoptive father suffered a massive heart attack near his forty-sixth birthday as she was preparing for her college entrance examinations. Her distraught mother cascaded into a dark depression, and with little savings and no way to continue paying the mortgage on her small bungalow on Chicago's Northwest Side, her mother nearly had to be institutionalized. But Virginia began to think outside of the box. Looking at a tour or two in the military, she realized she could send a significant amount of her voluntary navy pay back to her mother while accruing the modern version of the GI Bill that would allow her to attend college. Virginia figured she could do anything for three years, and she might have to start college three or four years late at the most, but then she would have the funds via the navy.

What no one expected, anticipated, or could have foretold, however, was that Virginia loved the military. The discipline, the structure, and the mission were newfound discoveries in an arena of purposeful existence, and she wanted desperately to contribute. She had not understood much about her genetics, and in truth only her father, now dead, had ever really examined her biological mother and her purported biological father. But here, as Roth read, he actually looked up and wondered if he was actually meant to see this material. It was very private, and he was concerned that it should not be in her file at all, let alone laid out for some single silver bar lieutenant reading its narrative.

Mr. William Mahoney, the loving and gentle adoptive father to Virginia, had understood that his daughter's young teenage mother, Stacy Alam, was actually something of a gifted child herself. Able to speak a second language by age four, her grandmother's native German, the child had begun to read and ultimately write in both English and German by age five. As she entered her mid-elementary school years, she was not satisfied with being able to read translations of Japanese anime. Stacy wanted to experience firsthand what the Japanese cartoonists were communicating and understand the subtleties of the expressed humor. Thus, without tutoring or classes, Stacy became proficient in speaking and understanding spoken Japanese. This was unsettling to her mother, but by the time Stacy was fifteen, she was receiving recruitment letters for national universities such as Cornell and Brown.

But Stacy had a problem, and unfortunately it involved her anatomy. At about age eleven she began to "fill out," and by age fourteen had a twenty-four-year old's breasts that were, in a word, abundant. As such, they drew male attention as honey draws bears in the spring. She wasn't unaware of the impact of her bountiful mammary tissue on men. The age of the males registering interest didn't seem to matter, but she miscalculated the extent of aggressiveness that some would invoke to see or touch her. And in one of the untold tragedies in life, she found herself attending her high school prom with a varsity football player whose sole focus was to get his hands on her.

This unfortunately ended sadly, as he forcefully raped her in the back of his parents white Ford LTD. Stacy found it unimaginable and then unacceptable that no one would believe that she had neither consented to his forceful entry or to the harm that this event subsequently had on her reputation. She had understood that she had consented to be his date, but not to be pinned on her back on the rear seat of his family's car, for her panties to be ripped off, and then to be violated. Why was this concept so foreign to those who she had counted as friends and confidants? From that moment forward, she found their near universal acceptance of her assumed guilt "for putting herself in the situation." For Stacy, this was heart-wrenching and difficult, if not impossible, to understand. Foreseeably, self-medication through alcohol and drugs to numb the sense of shame and isolation became the norm.

Roth read this and silently shook his head. And now, we are about to ask her daughter to enter into combat where the odds of her getting killed are not zero. Would Virginia have approved of him or anyone of his rank reading her entire file, including where she came from and who she was? Roth obviously had a file, and his chapters were off-limits to anyone but those who truly had a "need to know." He felt this same way about what he was seeing; he felt that he had violated her confidential information. But Roth also began to have a slight tickle in the hair on his neck, a response that reflected his growing understanding of her character. He realized in ways that he could not fully articulate that he was looking at a female version of himself. This took him by surprise and seemed to emphasize that the information on Virginia was not for casual consumption.

While Roth was humble by nature, he was aware of his analytical gifts and, as most agreed, very perceptive. He did not revel in the idea that his knowledge about Virginia Mahoney might be used for any other purpose than necessary military mission-related data. He felt similarly about his own data. But more than this was the realization that he was looking in the mirror, and what he saw was almost an identical image of himself—but the gender had changed! He again shook his head at the irony of this reality. Roth also realized that within days to weeks, he would be going into combat with the mirror image of himself.

As he was thinking and to some extent feeling these thoughts, the telltale sound of a coffee cup being placed down on a plywood surface caught his attention. Roth was almost at the end of the file and turned to look at Hayes. Roth thought that perhaps it was time he left the military; he didn't find pleasure in certain aspects of the missions that were, in fact, some of the most famous actions taken by his nation. This involved killing other people, evil individuals who did indeed deserve to die, but Roth took no pleasure in this. It was his duty, his obligation to his oath, and he would comply up to the point of his death. But perhaps he was beginning to have too much philosophical background noise to be as effective as he once was?

He felt a strange need to talk with her, but he kept reading. Virginia's aptitude testing was quite literally nearly off the charts. Roth wondered why she had chosen the military and began to compare his own history and choices. What would he have said if someone had been reading his file?

Roth himself had done extremely well at the academy, graduating ranked eighth in a class of individuals wherein the meticulous grading of every aspect of the midshipman's life was not only condoned, but also expected. The evolving academic trend to eliminate grades and test scores due to their inherent "racial bias" and judged proclivity to disadvantage one group as opposed to another—well, the United States Naval Academy and all of the funded service academies rejected this unproven academic "flavor of the month" in favor of good-old uniform testing. If one was to succeed in the navy, then said individual needed to excel in the material that the navy held important. There were no victims, no identity-based political considerations. This would change, at least for a brief interval, during one president's administration but revert quickly back to the norm, as this president was viewed among the worst—if not the singular largest bottom-dweller—of those who were elected to the office. His policies had been unsound, and while some might argue that he did some good, even his name was now a moniker for "absurd corruption."

Roth had been the highest-ranking graduate who also had a demerit marked against him, received in his first year in the navy as a plebe. The summer between his first and second years, Roth was assigned to a summer tour, receiving six weeks on two separate cruisers berthed in Hawaii. During one of the weekends in port, he was attending a party composed of his classmates but became worried about a more senior midshipman who had illegally purchased enough distilled liquor in the form of vodka to float one of the battlegroup carriers. Apparently, the kid had consumed an enormous amount of this alcohol and was lying nearly unresponsive in a bathtub during the party in the visiting officer's quarters. Roth became concerned, as the music, cacophony of voices, and background laughter from the partygoers diverted attention from anyone noticing the near fatal anesthetic level of intoxication manifest in this twenty-year-old academy upperclassman.

Roth was unwilling to leave him when the gathering started to break up, and in fact, he placed a call to his high school friend's father, an internal medicine physician. Apologizing to the physician for the untimely interruption, Roth related by phone his concerns: a rather detailed description of the inebriated individual's breathing rate, the coolness and bluish color of his extremities, and his slowed, at times pausing respiratory rate. This caused the physician listening to become instantly awake, for it was 4:30 a.m. He paused in his response, as he could not help but be impressed by this young man's rather complete assessment of the young drunken midshipman. The detailed assessment allowed the physician to make some very specific recommendations.

But Roth candidly shared with the physician that if the inebriated "Middy" was delivered to the hospital by Roth, the drunken sailor would be reported to his commander and disciplined. Trouble with that was, Roth would be reported too—and disciplined. This might have resulted in Roth getting kicked off the ship, his summer tour being terminated, and a formal hearing wherein Roth could have even been terminated from the academy.

The physician simply stated that Roth needed to "make a decision." If there was a chance that the student was seriously intoxicated to the point of alcohol poisoning, he might suffer pulmonary aspiration, sucking his stomach contents into his lung, or even die from such acute self-induced alcohol overdosing. Roth had to choose between watching over him to ensure he was going to recover or taking him into the hospital. Unspoken was the fact that Roth's career would be put at immediate risk and his standing in the school would suffer, but this was irrelevant. The physician knew that Roth understood this and never even brought it up. A human being's life was at risk. Roth expressed his appreciation to his friend's father and hung up the phone. He then walked into the main area of the party with the residual revelers and told two of them to help him get Parker, the drunk, out of the bathtub and to the hospital. They initially refused, but Roth stated that he alone would be responsible for ensuring that Parker was seen by the hospital staff.

It wasn't until two years later that the physician, through his son, found out that Roth had been immediately reported to naval superiors by hospital personnel after taking the upperclassman into the emergency room. He had been disciplined, and that same year, at the beginning of the fall semester for Roth's second year at the Naval Academy, brought before the entire assembled student body. Standing alone in front of seven senior officers with the assembled 4,262 midshipmen behind him, gathered in the large fieldhouse used for Naval Academy basketball, Roth received his rather public sentence. He was quite dramatically and, according to some reports, harshly verbally criticized for being part of a group of underage drinkers of alcohol. He was confined to quarters for two weeks, allowed only to attend class, and restricted from any leave for five months.

The senior commanders wanted to know who else had been at the party, but Roth gave them nothing. One of the younger naval captains, the equivalent to an army colonel, wanted Roth immediately terminated from the academy, but the two supervising admirals, including the Naval Academy Commandant, smiled and refused to even consider this. The admirals deliberately pronounced their sentence on Roth in front of his peers with the entire collective knowing, to a person, that each and every one of the midshipmen had imbibed alcohol illegally at some point in their life. Roth actually had not even had a drink—something that the hospital physician had noted in his report when he described the friend who had accompanied the dangerously intoxicated patient. The senior Naval Academy leadership had already confirmed that Roth had indeed not consumed any alcohol.

The upshot of this theatrical consecrated lesson in humility—a young man chastened in front of the entire student body who refused to cooperate with senior leadership to rat out anyone else, had knowingly placed himself in jeopardy to safeguard his classmate (an individual he didn't even consider a friend!), and had not even consumed alcohol himself—was interesting. The upperclassman immediately rallied to Roth, aggressively petitioned their leadership and faculty, and then demanded that the participants in attendance at the party come forward and self-report. And they did!

The admiral overseeing the academy recognized a unifying force when it presented itself. He conferred with his subordinates and used the episode to mold the entire group of matriculating midshipmen, all four years, into a single coalescing corpus. There was a palpable enhanced crispness in the salutes, the drills, the language, and the general conduct of the midshipmen as they united in their support of Roth. In this, Admiral Cretch was grateful to Roth. But more than grateful, he was impressed by Roth's intransigent protection and consideration of classmates. Rather than terminate Roth's academy appointment, Cretch wrote a two-page narrative detailing the entire episode and placed it in his academic file, specifically ensuring that Roth would have first choice of whatever career field he requested upon graduation. He also forbid any negative or punitive narrative from entering Roth's file regarding this incident, but did not remove his demerit. "Let the mark of a 'rebel' be preserved," he stated, "and wear it proudly."

Thus, upon graduation Roth was ranked eighth out of 1,348 graduates and the only one with a demerit—likely costing him two to three ranking positions, perhaps even four —but with an endorsement by the two-star admiral commandant of the US Naval Academy. Furthermore, he was someone who possessed a veiled but very bright shroud coloring him as among the "chosen" within the military fraternity. This meant that the navy would watch him carefully over the course of his career, but had begun to consider him for senior leadership if he continued his development along approved pathways. Roth felt more than knew something had marked him, but he was uninterested in status or adulation; he simply wanted to meet his own expectations of personal achievement.

Roth continued reading Virginia's file, realizing that as he completed the last pages, he had a growing sense of respect mixed with a tinge of wonder that someone so obviously promising had risen identical to a phoenix from the brutality of a rape in the backseat of a Ford LTD. But then life does not demand the best of circumstances either for its creation or its termination. Her biological mother had wanted nothing to do with her, the residual reminder of the nonconsensual procreation, and would have terminated her life in an abortion but for the hand of God in the form of her sister who begged her younger sister to carry the child to term.

The working-class family, the Mahoneys, had been married seven years without children. Young Jean Mahoney had suffered a botched gynecological operation in her seventeenth year that resulted in both of her ovaries being removed, as she had nearly exsanguinated due to inadvertent tearing of tissue during a routine invasive assessment of endometriosis. Jean had desperately wanted children but resigned herself to the reality that it was simply not to be. And then God stepped in, and Virginia demanded a mother.

Jean found herself on her knees in her bedroom before her simple dark wooden crucifix carefully placed on her nightstand. She had prayed, thanking the Creator, asking herself over and over how it was possible that this beautiful healthy baby was now her child. Virginia's mother related that she had wept staring at the crucifix, her sight distorted by salty tears filling her eyes, her shoulders bouncing almost uncontrollably as her sobs roiled her body and her consciousness. There, in her rather spartan bedroom consisting of a traditional white-painted metal framed double bed, a dresser, and her nightstand, she attempted to understand how her prayers had been answered. She accepted immediately that it was divine intervention. Jean then promised the Almighty her life at any time in return, if ever necessary, in order to always protect and watch over her new daughter. It was a promised exchange she found joyous. Those conducting this interview related that the woman had begun to weep recalling the arrival of Virginia.

Roth felt a growing unease paired with apprehension. This material was now very private, if not actually intimate! He was not comfortable looking into or viewing these very private events in a person's life. Roth felt as though he was almost in a dream and had unwittingly stumbled into a girl's dressing room. Suddenly seeing the women in various stages of undress, without awareness of his presence, he was embarrassed as he viewed their bodies, having no right to be on the premises or viewing their discreet activity. Within the snippets of this dreamlike scene, he felt that he had to rapidly look for an exit. He was an intruder.

If a woman had invited him in, he was a normal male and almost certainly would have been excited by the offer. But peeping around at the cloistered actions of a woman, or women, unaware of his presence did not bring him comfort, satisfaction, or arousal. It actually engendered a sense of dishonor, if not shame. But he was not in a dream, and he sensed that the information he was reading was raw, too candid for a stranger to read, and even wondered why any of this information was in her file. This was not some exhibit at a museum, where patrons could look at nudes as imagined in some artist's creative mind. No, this was an individual who he knew and was about to lead into combat. He indeed felt he had been almost indiscreet, even knowing he had been asked to read the file's contents.

But there was another emotion percolating in Roth. Remarkably, it was one of commonality, almost companionship. He acknowledged that he admired the person he was reading about, but beyond that, he almost felt the tightening of deep affinity with her, for both Roth and Mahoney had come from nowhere to build a life of purpose. Again, a symbolic mirror image was surfacing. The journey that this woman had undertaken, its details were very different from those in his life, yet thematically there were rather striking similarities, almost duplicate elements. Roth was almost stunned at her pivotal decisions, the prescient moral framework that suggested Roth, not Virginia, had written this personal history. Virginia had established an underpinning of courage to meet life's challenges head-on, refusing to surrender to despair or defeat. She had willed herself to an internal slow-burning but persistent flame that would continue to glow despite of and perhaps in response to all external clues attempting to convince her she was unworthy or doomed to fail. Like him, she would rather be dead than give up her chosen life's journey—its dreams, hopes, and pursuit of purposefulness.

Roth had already surmised that there was a profound and clear reservoir of quality, a desire within Virginia Mahoney to excel. He had been allowed to step upon its shoreline and peer into its depths. In part, he was looking at the same reflection of his own most private inspiration and resolve. This not only excited him, but also awakened within him a need to understand the gravity of Virginia's most intimate thoughts, her faith, her fears. For the first time, Roth wanted to go beyond the sterile professional relationship and understand the totality of who Virginia was. She had not asked this of him, but he now saw this as his personal need.

He finished the file, neatly arranged the different-sized official documents, and clipped them to the inner surface of the front cover, closing the heavy manila folder with its red block-letter "CONFIDENTIAL" external label. Roth turned back toward Hayes's desk and saw him standing there with his eyes locked onto him.

"Interesting reading?" Hayes asked.

Roth said nothing, but his eyes didn't move from Hayes's.

"Does this change your willingness to have her on your team?"

Roth looked hard into the other man's questioning gaze. An uncertainty, perhaps even surprise, was reflected in the younger officer's eyes.

"No, sir."

The commander's right eyebrow elevated slightly. He wanted more, but Roth's face was stone. His chin pulled forward and both his eyebrows now were raised, his mouth registering almost a reluctant pout—acceptance as to the paucity of returned communication.

An absent need to please.

Roth's loyalty already forming toward Virginia Mahoney, however, did not belittle or diminish his loyalty to Hayes.

Hayes smiled a satisfied acceptance. "Good. Dismissed, Lieutenant."

Chapter Five

Reflections

The next several hours for Roth were spent carefully reviewing thoughts that concerned both the contents of Virginia Mahoney's file and, more importantly, what had been "unspoken." Roth had learned a significant amount, but this was dwarfed in magnitude by how this had impacted him. He felt as though he had glimpsed within these pages the very soul of another individual, and what he saw spoke to a beauty and courage he had seldom thought existed. She had no idea that he knew any of the information about her very personal history. Strangely, this fact itself might have upset Roth more than he anticipated, but it was offset by her remarkable inherent decency. He felt it appropriate that he communicate that he had read the entire file and that he had done so because he was ordered to do so.

Why bring it up at all? Well, he needed to ask her permission; although after the fact, he still wanted to openly state that he needed her permission. He legally did not, yet he certainly had the professional right to know about her. He was in charge of taking her into combat with the team and her performance was critical to ensure that the mission was not compromised, and team members were not to be put at risk. But Roth knew that she was not the issue. He, Roth, was the issue! In fact, now his feelings were the issue. Up until two hours before reading the file, his concerns regarding her had been sterile, but now he admitted to himself that he felt protective, and this was potentially lethal. It was not only potentially fatal for him, but for her and any number of his subordinates.

Professionalism must be absolute during a mission involving split-second decision-making wherein the mission always supersedes the men, and now a single woman. Distorting priorities during a mission was potentially ruinous. He knew it, and he pondered what he might tell a colleague who presented this dilemma to him. He would almost certainly tell him to recuse himself from the mission. Roth felt he needed to do this, but not before he talked to V. Mahoney. If she wanted out, then he could complete the mission. Yet if she wanted to continue in her role, which was her moral and ethical right, then he needed to withdraw. It was that simple.

He almost laughed, although this was in part a bitter gesture. Roth's response and future relationship with the woman was now clouded with emotion. He couldn't believe it! He had never really looked at Mahoney as a woman previously, but had meticulously examined her role as a team member tasked with successfully completing several critical undertakings. It had not been an error to conduct himself in this manner; if anything, it was entirely appropriate, and it had been easy. From the first time he had met her and reviewed her contribution, he had assessed the quality of her cognition, judgement, and competence. In this, he found her among the very best that he worked with and several times, independent of any of what he had just been privy to, he had asked for her input linked to her seemingly remarkable analytical talent.

He had established that her comments were limited, but valuable. Her answers and observations were lacking the all-too-familiar jocularity of other males in the team, the need to impress, the need to subtlety infer "look at me"—what Roth privately called the "peacock syndrome"—the "it's really all about me" statements. She was direct, at times surprisingly unvarnished, but she possessed a detailed, expansive vocabulary that might actually have been considered surprising for any individual who thus far lacked higher education or scholarly experience. But she, similar to Roth himself, was known for her almost insatiable desire to read and study on her own. Virginia nearly always had a book or an iPad in her hand whenever she was off active status in her quarters or the enlisted mess.

She had joked with her teammates when they commented on her studious nature that she rather enjoyed the "cloistered academic atmosphere" provided by special operations. This not-so-subtle retort amplified the collective perceptive irony shared among those tasked to defend America's geopolitical priorities, if not its fundamental security. They often lived a spartan existence with few creature comforts in comparison to their civilian counterparts. They were routinely exposed to foreseeable but unpredictable life-threatening attacks in the form of missile or drone incursions, each day wondering when, where, and how the next attempt to end their lives would occur. They had long accepted the iron hand of discipline needed to exist within the modern theater of asymmetric warfare. They had witnessed the death of buddies or the irreparable maiming of friends who only moments before were young, whole, and filled with future promise. Yet they reluctantly accepted but were cogently aware that their peers, those children of money attending exclusive universities, possessed a near exclusive naïve blindness to reality or the realpolitik and its consequences permeating the world inhabited by America's enemies.

Virginia had observed that her peers, these children of affluence, were more disturbed by the choices of clothes, jewelry, and perfume to be worn while attending college lectures or extracurricular seminars. These sessions with their cherry-picked factual legitimacy demonstrating the oppression of the masses by Euro-American policies were all the rage among the freshman and sophomore students within these most expensive universities. Yet they remained blissfully unaware of the jealousy that such coddled, indulgent, and decadent lifestyles spawned. Intractably blind to their own extravagant lives of comfort and pamper, they were not infrequently the basis of the ideological hatred of all that America represented. But these *vacuous* elites took as their birthright a life that had been built upon the sacrifices of countless Americans, most lost to history. Those now buried, objects of transient fragmented memories of loved ones, who had searched and often died yearning for a better future. They had little significance within a mindset of assumed privilege.

Virginia's good-natured sarcasm as to the cloistered academic ambiance within special operations belied a commonly held elitist view of the military. She understood that sheltered yet outspoken adult wannabes found nothing incongruent in their ill-informed, if not blatantly ignorant condemnation of the military. Viewed as dangerous redneck

Southerners who liked guns or uneducated predators seeking a legal mechanism to inflict harm, the military and its culture of service was as foreign to these elites as thoughtful commitment from salamanders inhabiting a shallow pond. Yet their snarky illiteracy was not confined to those safeguarding the very country they inhabited; it was eventually to wash over into a general sanctimony regarding history and political acceptability, for they had assimilated the "correct" viewpoints absent factual evidence or scholarly investigative effort while labeling anyone in disagreement with their moral highbrow opinions as Neanderthal, even evil. Not five years later, possessing a unified unbridled anger directed toward the actions of Israel's regional policies, the lemming mentality of the self-anointed elites at Harvard, MIT, and other American campuses led to indiscriminate actions of violence against students of Hebrew origin.

Such activities were to horrify the American public. There was no shortage of irony in the fact that the supposedly "best and brightest" attending near legendary centers of learning could both demonstrate such typical mob behavior and such robotic mindsets underpinning this behavior. It was as though arguable or debatable perspectives regarding Palestinian autonomy or Israeli military response were void. Only one view was acceptable, allowable, or endorsable. This political advocacy by Harvard students, ratifying the current ivory tower "flavor of the month" manifest as anti-Semitic behavior, was perhaps the most distressing element to those wise to the perils of history. For many, now children of those survivors of the Holocaust, America suddenly resembled Berlin in the 1930s.

Roth listened, impressed to the point of near-speechless admiration, as Virginia discussed that it was the lack of intellectual discipline and interest in seeking truth among such a select group of excelling academic enrollees that harbored real concern. Forgotten by the mainstream press and the pandering politicians was the reality that the epicenter of cultural advancement, home to then cutting-edge science, literature, and even art, were the academic intuitions of Berlin at the turn of the twentieth century. To forget is to relive.

Virginia's pointed question to Roth was to query if there was no "appreciation by any of these 'Harvard automatons'" that history was never simple, and that "two things could be correct." An acceptance that two perspectives might have remarkably solid foundations but result in diametrically opposed outcomes. Roth's respectful summation to this incongruence was simple: These elite students were remarkably adroit at parroting a single viewpoint, but were either too lazy or lacked proper training to study and analyze history. This was the shameful failure of Harvard's "celebrated faculty," leaving such promising minds devoid of investigative methodology or curiosity.

That secure in their properness, their single viewpoint, unknown to both Roth and Virginia, would eventually facilitate enthusiastic endorsement of Hamas and within five years accept as "understandable" its preemptive strike on Israeli civilians. Somehow, stunning to many, these same students pardoned the barbaric killing of 1,400 innocent civilians, the kidnapping of over 200 hostages, and the systematic rape, assault, and murder by beheading women, children, and infants. Such moral ignorance of the true nature of Hamas and their Iranian masters would ensure that they, these Harvard elites, could justify physical confrontations with Jewish students while their university administrations did nothing.

Sitting with Roth, Virginia had almost laughed holding back her tears of frustration for these children of privilege, blind to the world and its evil. Lost in their dismissive condensation, in the legacy press's sanctimony was a dark future reality. But for people like Roth and Virginia, the eventual barbarism that was to be inflicted on innocent Israelis would also wash up on the shores of the US homeland. The energy and sacrifice required to secure America's geopolitical priorities, if not her fundamental security, remained within the domain of those willing to die for the abstract concept of country. For these snarky, youthful, cognitively empty vassals, they lacked the ability to fathom that they, too, would be an afterthought in the world Hamas contemplated.

But Virginia had also told Jacob that the future would harbor pain and even horror for those who understood the potential for human wickedness. She was looking over his left shoulder, peering out into the infinite distance. She noted that anyone with an ounce of foresight knew that a day of reckoning was coming. That once again, as in the events of September 11, America was heading toward yet another moment of harm, a momentum damni. Innocents would perish, lives would be cut short, and once again, history would later judge it all avoidable but for the willful ennui of leaders self-absorbed in their hold on power instead of their commitment to those they represented.

As Roth had looked deeply into Virginia's eyes, he saw pools of beautiful mystery, magnetic in their attractiveness and growing wisdom. He also saw that she would protect those illiterate elites while hoping for their eventual maturation. He had begun to realize that she was special. He had begun to care about this woman; his professional concerns had become personal. And a growing sense of worry over her future began to germinate. He liked her.

And thus, on subsequent days, he was more aware of Virginia sitting and reading. She would be sitting with a cup of coffee or a runner's thermally insulated water dispenser, deeply engrossed in some topic. Various males initially tried to strike up degrees of conversation to test the potential of establishing some form of relationship but were invariably, either politely or curtly, dissuaded from such action. Thus, she was often alone in the communal gathering place, the mess hall, sipping coffee sitting at one of the four-by-eight-foot particleboard structures. These sturdy wooden stands had been laid over and then bolted to two to three empty dull black fifty-gallon aviation fuel drums, serving as tables. The requisite IKEA plastic chairs that could be stacked quickly, creating floor space, usually surrounded the tables. This magnificent ambiance was complete with white rolled paper sheets covering each table, topped by centerpieces of chipped cream-colored Walmart vases holding faded plastic floral gatherings. To those inhabiting the environment of asymmetric chaotic warfare, such deliberate sarcasm to the highbrow atmospheres of the eateries in Paris, DC, and

Rome, brought smiles to the young warriors. That the rarified ambiance "superseded Monte Carlo's finest" was the quip heard one morning.

Objectively, anyone could reasonably understand the attraction by the plentiful groups of males who saw her sitting alone. The veritable dangling worm on a hook lowered into a school of hungry piranhas. Roth had not previously appreciated any of this, because he just was not actually analyzing this aspect of Virginia's qualities. But slowly, he was, in fact, becoming more conscious that she was strikingly attractive and remarkably beautiful woman. Sharply defined cheekbones framed a sensual feminine aquiline nose that rested between piercing blue eyes, each bordered superiorly by thick deep-brown eyebrows. Her slightly high forehead showed very early traces of permanent horizontal creases, soon to be actual wrinkles, but in near-perfect soft exposed tanned skin. A telltale diminutive V-shaped crease between her symmetrically attractive eyebrows appeared when in thought or angry.

Roth's lack of attention regarding her beauty might have caused concern as to his being sightless! It had initially caused Virginia herself to wonder if Roth was putting on some weird act of ignoring her physical presentation. Was he playing some game? While not in the least narcissistic—she was rather refreshingly humble—she could not detect that Roth had ever responded to her in any of the typical manners that nearly every other guy registered upon first seeing her. It didn't matter if they were seven or seventy-seven years old; men enjoyed looking at her, as she was . . . well, she was stunning. But she had concluded that Roth genuinely addressed her as he did his other team members, focusing upon the mission requirements and not on her physical beauty. She appreciated this in part, but in truth was disappointed that he seemed not to react to her—at all!

Yet he had been married, and perhaps this explained his complete lack of recognition of her female contours, her voice, her femininity. Or was it that he had been married but now she had realized he was not? Somewhere within the calendar span of ongoing mission preparation, the rumor and then confirmation occurred that the "unworthy bitch" he had been bound to had finally pushed him beyond his rather uncharacteristic liberal tolerances. He had reluctantly terminated the union. To a person, Roth's teammates had breathed a collective sigh of relief that he had finally definitively ended his association with the woman. All felt he deserved better.

Virginia couldn't help but shake her head in self-admonition as to fragments of daydreams passing through her mind. Almost as the torn irregular edges of a flag perpetually whipped by the wind, uneven elements of imagery populated her consciousness: sitting at a table with Roth, sharing a cup of coffee in a real home kitchen, or ordering food while he asked her about her choices in perfume. She had asked herself what he would be like on a date. What would his presence in her life cause? It was absurd to dote on such imaginings. But she could not lie to herself, for she found that he was attractive, even more so as a single male, void of the typical boisterous and self-aggrandizement so often found in men of all ages. She actually found Roth humble, but driven to achieve his veiled dreams. Would she ever be provided a hint as to their composition? She trusted that his aspirations and desires were just.

She almost regretted her time-honored practice of minimizing her feminine presence, especially when it involved Roth. She had purposefully nearly perfected the ability to limit her impact, at least to some immeasurable degree, by de-emphasizing the gifts that had been genetically bestowed upon her. This took the form of wearing absolutely no makeup and severely drawing back her thick luscious light-brown, almost sandy-blonde hair, forming a short bun at the nape of her neck. She usually wore her military-issued plastic eye protection, a sleek wraparound Oakley-style set of matte black eyeglasses. These did not have prescription lenses, as she did not yet need corrective optics, but they served to cut glare, as they were polarized and improved vision in sunny, dusty conditions. They also masked those remarkably sensuous deep blue eyes, thoughtfully spaced and split by her slender but defined aquiline nose. The glasses also added a slightly austere, even formidable hauteur. Without the eyewear, her eyes and midface belied a Nordic beauty with statuesque high cheekbones and sensual lips covering nearly perfect white teeth, save a single small chip in her lower left incisor.

She took three minutes every morning to deliberately but loosely wrap her chest along with her breasts in an elastic bandage, identical to those used for supporting an injured ankle or thigh, in an effort to reduce their profile. The bandage was not overly tight, but along with a sports bra added first, this served to enable movement without encumbrance. In combination with her loose desert-brown and tan camouflage top, her profile was nearly flat. Such preparation also had reduced unwanted attention, part of what she believed males had intrinsically hardwired into their brains regarding visual detection of her or any woman's generous breasts. Said males were incapable of ignoring them.

And for better or worse, without these preparations she would indeed attract significant interest, for identical to her biological mother, she was born to develop rather significant mammary tissue. Her breasts were quite large and, in the medical lexicon, pendulous. Virginia grew to be taller than her absent mother, for she was five feet seven inches in height, bordering on being tall for a woman. But she was not gangly; her shapely hips were also masked within the loose pixilated desert camouflage pants issued by the military and she wore the same boots as the typical man, only smaller. These were sandy-brown suede tops with tightly woven synthetic nylon joined to rubber outsoles and were anything but stylish. None of it really hid her beauty, however. Anyone looking for more than three seconds saw the sharply defined elegant features of a regal face, the classic Northern European characteristics that turned heads. She had a brown matte metal watch with a nylon strap and a covered plastic crystal to eliminate reflection unless being directly viewed. Her small tactical gloves were also camouflage with brown tacky surfaces on the palms, and her kneepads had elastic backing with their semihardened exposed ground contact areas.

Her portable weapons numbered two and were identical to most of the men. She carried a M9A1 Beretta with a fifteen-round 9mm magazine and had added the green dot ArmaLaser and become beyond proficient. She was deadly. Virginia had tried several rifles, as she wanted to balance weight against the actual firepower, understanding that fractions of a second required to reposition her weapon could mean life or death. She settled on a shortened version, a CQBR carbine with a rail system that allowed her to have advanced optical and laser capabilities, increasing both the accuracy and efficiency for her acquisition of targets. In simple terms, these advancements ensured a better kill rate. She placed an acoustic dampener on the end of the weapon not for some Hollywood stealth fictional drama, but so she could hear better, providing another advantage to staying alive. This dampener—or silencer, as it was commonly known—used to be a forbidden asset, as it had negatively impacted accuracy and ballistic force, but the modern version of this instrument actually improved both. Her accuracy and proficiency testing was in the top 7 percent in the larger special operations group.

Finally, she carried a sheathed Ontario Mark 3 Navy combat knife, its 6.5-inch blade a fixed steel metal stabbing, slashing, and cutting tool. It was sheathed in her right boot, and a second was on her left calf. She wore a tactical vest allowing three loaded magazines for each of her two weapons along with her requisite accoutrements of war, including communications gear and detonator devices. Her helmet was dull pea-soup green but could be fitted with night vision optics, a variety of camouflage covers, or ghillie surfaces with irregular contours composed of earthen-colored rags that blended to the point of invisibility within woods or jungles, if appropriate.

When Virginia was fully outfitted, few would have looked to enjoy the curves of her athletic but—some might suggest—generously endowed figure. She was a trained soldier and thus a professional killer of enemy combatants as allowed under US and international law. Roth was equipped in almost an identical fashion other than a different sidearm; he used the P226 9mm with ten rounds. Although Roth had experimented with customized aftermarket magazines holding more rounds, he always came back to the ten-round magazine. He also carried identical knives, though only one was in his left boot and the other, his primary knife, was sheathed on the left front of his chest, handle pointing down for easy access with his right hand.

As fate would have it, Roth now chuckled to himself as he walked back to his officer's quarters thinking how a date with Virginia would look. Even the roughest neighborhoods in his hometown of Chicago would provide them plenty of room. But he was not really thinking of her as a date—at least this was not in the forefront of his mind. Rather, he was wondering if he should even mention that he had read her file, her entire file, and simply leave the conversation at that. If she found this intrusive, he would ask her to bring it up with Hayes and leave it to his commander to justify this event.

Roth wanted her to know that he was now aware of the rather intimate circumstances of her life and that, out of respect, he felt she was owed this knowledge. But he felt she was also owed something else: that he truly respected what he had read. He needed to tell her this. A niggling irritant was surfacing within his mind, refusing to stay submerged but fighting to the surface as pockets of air rise from the water's depths. Roth wanted to be familiar with this remarkable person. He wanted to talk about the events, her reactions, and past responses to these challenges. He was respectful, but he had to admit that he wanted to spend time with her to understand her more completely. He justified this by reasoning it could make a difference in the arena of combat.

He also knew this was bullshit.

He simply wanted to get to know her. Out of the inky darkness of his own personal despair, he sought this woman's presence.

Shit, he thought, must be the divorce crap.

That admission suddenly took root in his mind, and he frowned. He turned to cut between two buildings heading for his quarters, lost in these thoughts. The variable crunchy sound of his weight on the gravel mixed with a gentle zephyr stirring the faint herbal odor of the Syrian Desert.

And at that moment, one Virginia Lois Mahoney rounded the corner of building #11 and shuttered to a complete stop, saluting him. He returned the salute and for a second was at a loss of how he should respond. Then he just said internally, Bullshit!

"Petty Officer Mahoney," Roth intoned.

"Lt. Roth."

"I was asked to review your file."

There was an almost imperceptible widening of her eyes, and then her face closed.

"Yes, sir." A mechanical response.

"I have completed this request," Roth responded gently, quieter in volume than his normal command exchange with his team members. "I want to be clear, I read your entire file."

She stood motionless.

He met her gaze. His eyes, normally sharp, almost predatory, were now softer and waiting.

"They are looking to boot you from the team."

Her eyes narrowed, lips pressed so that almost all of their rich red color was now gone and pale pink ribbons of tissue remained.

Roth stated simply, "I will not do that. I will not comply with any such suggestion or demand. You have earned your spot."

And he started again, saluted, and began to move past her.

Her eyes flickered—anger mixed with questions, even confusion.

"Sir?"

"We are going into combat. They do not want you KIA, captured, or injured, 'they' being the nameless faceless bureaucracy. I disagree and probably will be removed as team leader."

"Then you are asking me to withdraw voluntarily."

"I am asking no such thing and will be very disappointed if you so much as consider anything of the sort."

She looked directly at him, her striking blue eyes becoming deep pools reflecting satisfaction, gratefulness, and then something far more tender.

Chapter Six

How Does One Constitute Love?

Virginia Mahoney knew immediately that Roth was her ally, her protector within a massive bureaucracy that now wanted her off the team for fear of her experiencing harm. What enraged Virginia was not that there was worry that team members of special operations units might come to injury; it was that they were concerned because and only because she was a woman. To Virginia, this was another way of saying she was unworthy. A subtle message that she was to receive special treatment that in itself was the mark of weakness and an inability to meet the rigorous standards of combat.

She was furious for two reasons. One was that she was certain that her training had prepared her for the eventuality of combat, even with its unforeseeable potential for personal injury. The other reason, she admitted to herself, was that she was uncertain she was prepared or that she or any woman could meet the requisite preparedness for life's ultimate challenge. Are the bastards correct? Here, there was no last-minute shot that won the game. There was no "We'll get them next year, and you gave it all you could. Great effort!" Here, defeat meant death.

Was she ready for that? How was she to know? How was anyone to judge before combat whether they were ready?

She needed to confront Roth and ask him what he thought. But had he not already told her that he refused to take her off the team? That she had "earned her spot"?

Could she ask Roth what she should do? Deep within her, Virginia sensed that her need to ask Roth came from the fact that, of course, it was Roth who was involved! What a mess!

The very man she was incredibly attracted to was who she was about to ask if she should be removed from the team because she was a woman! He had already told her the answer, but she needed more from this man. Why? Because she wanted to understand what Roth thought and if he could meet her standard of being Mr. Right.

How utterly ridiculous! Here she was, in the middle of a mission to kill the world's most wanted terrorist, and she wanted to know whether her imaginary lover was a good fit for her. She was being juvenile. Perhaps, she bitterly thought, that if such thoughts occupied her mind and sat within her emotional horizon, perhaps she was not a "good fit" for this mission?

Bullshit! her mind screamed.

She had earned her spot!

But she wanted to understand Roth, and his opinion suddenly mattered to her as much as her own certainty that she had justified her membership through work and sacrifice to become a team member within the elite status of special operations.

Sitting in her small room, shared with a female assigned to an administrative position within Command, Virginia fidgeted with the strap of her automatic rifle. The room itself consisted of two single beds against opposite walls, with two small desks composed of cheap particleboard aligned between the beds along the wall opposite the door to the quarters. Virginia's desk surface was uncluttered, a single battered brown metal gooseneck lamp occupying the space. She gently laid her helmet with its night vision optical package on the surface of her desk and grabbed her cap. If anyone could have seen her, they would have recognized in her face the same emotions she had reserved for her first date in high school: anticipation and curiosity.

She suddenly rose from sitting on her bed, left her room, and made a straight path for Roth's room. As she walked, her resolve did not fade. Paradoxically, it grew stronger; she knew she needed Roth's input, but more than that, she needed to hear his perspectives. He didn't know that he was being tested as to "suitability," but she almost smiled to herself, as such is the repetitive dynamic exchange between men and women as to the infinite sorting of variables underpinning mating. Arriving at his quarters, she took a calming breath as she knocked on Roth's door softly but loud enough for any occupant to hear.

"Enter" came the partially muffled response.

As she depressed the handle of the door and pulled it outwards, Roth was sitting at his desk, nearly identical to Virginia's, in his pea-green undershirt and regulation pixilated uniform pants. His boots were off, sitting at the foot of the steel-framed bed in the unadorned room. His feet were covered by the same thick green cotton-and-spandex weave socks. His thick arms, absent tattoos so popular again in their generation, were actually rather white to the wrists, where the back of his hands were deeply tanned. His dog tags were hanging loosely from his neck, exposed. Roth's roommate was stateside for the birth of his first son. As an administrative officer for the command structure, he had been classified as noncritical to mission success that otherwise might demand instant activation and deployment from "mission essential" personnel. Roth looked up, and for once Virginia saw genuine surprise fill his searching gaze as he pushed back his chair and fumbled just for a second, searching for the appropriate response.

"Petty Officer Mahoney, I apologize—I wasn't expecting anyone, or I would have been properly dressed."

He was already reaching for his camouflage top and eyeing his boots as he hesitantly decided against rushing to pull them back on. So, as he pulled his top on, he motioned for her to sit in the only other chair, hoping that she did not mistake his gesture as an invitation to sit on Peterson's bed.

"You can leave the door open," he cautioned.

"Lieutenant, what I have to discuss is of confidential—no, actually, it is private, and I would appreciate being able to briefly shut the door. Don't worry, I'm not going to tell anyone you tried to rape me."

She knew regulations required that the doors were to remain open if two members of the opposite sex were gathered, especially if they were of disparate rank.

"Are you always so . . ." He searched for the words. "Deliberate?"

"Only with people I trust, so the answer is virtually never." And she held his gaze.

"Oh, so that's how it is going to be," he gently responded, his voice losing any authoritative tone as a genuine smile replaced the perplexed but anticipatory set of his jaw.

"If that is acceptable to you, Lieutenant?"

"It's fine. How may I help you?"

She stared at him, searching for any trace of dismissive impatience, and saw none.

"What do you want me to do?" she asked.

His voice was cautious, his mannerisms very soft with a gentle expression, and she could tell he was searching, trying to reach a midpoint between honesty and support. The former was required for her own benefit, the latter his attempt to buttress any disappointment or bitterness. Then suddenly his shoulders relaxed, and he looked intently into her eyes. She saw reflective pools of concern conveying a genuine empathy and careful measure of her potential.

Almost imperceptibly, he ventured, "I want you to pursue your dreams and your goals, Virginia, as I want and need to pursue mine."

"Mine may interfere with yours, it appears."

"Temporarily. And not of your doing, so don't think along those lines—think of what you need to accomplish."

She started to speak, "Permission to—" but he raised his hand to signal a halt, palm facing her, and then shook his head.

"Please, say what you need to say," Roth stated kindly.

"I was going to ask . . . Jacob, I need you to give me advice as a friend, not as an officer. Ok?"

The use of his Christian name caught his attention, not because he was insulted but because he enjoyed the way it sounded coming out of her mouth, the movement of her lips. He suddenly realized that she was incredibly beautiful, and he was shocked that he had not really quantified this previously. While he reacted to this sudden realization, he smiled at his past foolishness. He was supposed to be one of the rare breed, someone who immediately took in almost all there was to absorb from the environment. This was what kept him and his troops alive.

But he had missed this very essential and now glaring issue: that Virginia Mahoney was gorgeous. She was really a beautiful woman. Wow, he thought. He must have been blind to not process this previously.

But he had been married then, and she was a team member under his leadership. So, yes, he had missed this, and he immediately understood that the months of pain with his ex-wife had opacified if not transiently obscured any clarity toward the opposite sex. The funny thing, however, was that this was a real-time realization of her beauty, and he actually found his sudden awareness of her physical attributes enjoyable. No—more accurately, he found them satisfying. An odd sense for him, but actually he suddenly felt as though he had somehow immediately emotionally connected to her and that she was open to this unspoken comprehension. But there was something else, something that felt freeing. He felt alive again. His life was suddenly moving. Almost instantly, he was being propelled forward. He was seeing a future again.

A remarkable change from the weeks of buried anger that he had suffered in trying to compartmentalize the betrayals of Jessica.

Virginia saw the flicker of self-awareness in Roth, and although she didn't know its origins, somehow she sensed that acceptance. An inner peace had suddenly ceased to be elusive but had again taken up residence within this man. In return she smiled, her eyes sparkling, and her body's tension began to ease, her shoulders relaxing ever so slightly.

"I am happy to assist," Roth ventured and then corrected himself, "Actually, I would feel privileged to provide anything you need."

She was looking at him, intently focused on his response, and saw in his eyes something that made her relax even more. "Lieutenant—Jacob, I need you to tell me what you want me to do. Tell me what is best for me to do from your perspective."

"I want you to . . ." The words stopped in mid-sentence. His face was unmasked, open and unguarded. "Are you aware of how beautiful you are?" His gaze was transfixed, and his words hung in the air, balloons filled with heated gas, lingering, floating. His cheeks began to flush, and he stammered slightly.

"I . . . apologize, Petty Officer Mahoney, that . . . was uncalled for. I really am sorry." He moved to get up but she extended her arm, touching his to slow and then stop him from rising.

"I was hoping you might finally notice! That at least I'm ok to look at!" She said this with mock surprise and then a seriousness that accompanied a young girl's grin, perhaps her grin from when she was twelve.

He sat back down and again looked at her, removing any retreat into social convention. "In truth, I just actually noticed, and that is why that ill-timed statement came out. Ill-timed does not mean false or incorrect, however, just that I probably shouldn't have said it."

"Can we agree your statement is ok, Lt. Roth—Jacob? From my humble perspective, perhaps it is even a bit, if not really long, overdue. So, shall we move on?" she queried. Again, there was the wisp of a grin.

He raised his eyebrows, his forehead wrinkling in surrender and acceptance, and smiled. "Then I must genuinely apologize for being sort of a dumbass for not seeing the obvious." He grinned.

"Ok, enough of the apology stuff. Please talk to me about what I need to do here."

She was serious again, and he instantly responded, "I don't know, Virginia. I feel strongly that you have absolutely earned your spot and that no one has the right to ask you to step down or kick you off the team under the grounds that you are a female and somehow are unworthy. I can't accept that premise."

She was watching him carefully, and what he stated and the manner of his communication removed any doubt in her that he was performing for a politically correct perspective. He genuinely felt she was qualified, the work she had done was excellent, and the rest was irrelevant.

"So you are good with me staying."

"As stated, yes."

"Ok. Unless there is a change, I will not broach the subject again. Ok?"

"Sure."

As she moved to the door, she realized that she was going to go into combat soon. And she likely would never meet or feel the embrace of a man she actually wanted to physically share intimacy with. She just might not survive the first mission—some didn't. And she wondered ever so fleetingly if she would die before she had felt the thrill of intimacy with that special someone.

She had experienced sex—one a rather inebriated event, both after high school, and both were less than fulfilling. But then she had never intended them to be anything other than exploratory. She had wanted to ensure that she was attractive, and she also was curious about how it would physically feel. They guys were overjoyed, they were safe, and she controlled the encounters. She had been excited, but the experiences were not unpleasant, just not that memorable. The last of the two men—several months, almost a year apart—had kept calling her until she changed her permanent duty station and then tried to continue long-distance. She liked him, but it was just that: nothing special.

Virginia knew immediately that Jacob Noah Roth was different. He was someone who might just work his way into her life, even her soul, and this scared her a little. It also thrilled her that someone might actually exist who could fulfill this role. But the timing couldn't have been worse; they were about ready to go into combat. But then when in God's plan would there be a proper time? She was deployed with special operations and tasked by her nation to eliminate threats to her nation and her nation's people.

As she stood and crossed to the door, she turned back toward Jacob. Oh, hell, I could be dead next month or horribly injured. Looking at Roth, he met her gaze. His soft brown eyes registered deep pools of uncertainty, of questions.

She said softly, "This next mission might be tough. People could get killed."

"It is always that way, Virginia. If that is a problem, then perhaps—"

"You misunderstand. I . . . I . . . oh, shit . . . it's just that I have never been with a man I really desired and, well, this may not ever get a chance to happen, and you are it. You are this man, Lieutenant . . . Jacob."

Roth's jaw went slack. His mouth fell open slightly as his pupils dilated.

"Jacob, I realize that you probably are working out the issues with your recent divorce, and I get that . . ."

He rose, went to her, and wrapped his arms around her, pulling her into him.

"It's the pressure of this stuff that is making me insane, right?"

"You can't expect me to answer that, Virginia."

"This isn't a sympathy issue, Jacob . . . is it?"

"Are you nuts? Have you looked in the mirror?"

And then the desert flowers suddenly were more vibrant, their fragrance sweeter, and the blazing sun a bit softer, if only slightly, within this ancient arid land. But time slowed for two souls within its confines, and one of God's infinite joys became a reality.

And almost at that instant, at another location in the middle of the Syrian Desert, the world's most wanted criminal was finishing his late afternoon meal, sipping tea from a chipped Chinese porcelain cup. He was reflecting on the vagaries of fortune, the ebb and flow of life's path. Of kingdoms won and lost. He could not know that the soulmate of one Catherine Morgan, a woman not different in age or beauty, was at this very minute embracing her final preparations needed to provide justice for Catherine.

This woman, however, was distinct from Catherine, and this distasteful excuse for a man was unaware that she was readying herself to kill this man still tasting his sweetened tea. He might have scoffed at the notion that a woman could be so determined, let alone successful. He, who at this moment was placing the half-filled cup on a small wooden side table, could not know his life was now measured in hours. For this woman was indeed unwavering, and she asked God to forgive her, as she knew along with her Creator that her destiny was to be fulfilled.

Chapter Seven

The Father of Hate

Ibrahim Awwad Ibrahim Ali al-Badri al-Samaras was born the third of four sons to a family known by their tribal group, the al-Bu Badri tribe. This is an insignificant tribe save the Quraysh, who are traced to a mercantile Arab group historically tied to Mecca and Ka'aba. The Quraysh's true consequence is that the Islamic prophet Muhammad was born into the Hashemite clan of this tribe. In fact, al Al Hassan Abbas later claimed that he was a descendent of the Quraysh tribe and thus directly tied to Muhammad. This was another one of his many lies, if not delusions.

The intelligence compiled regarding this man was inherently limited, a fact utilized by al Al Hassan Abbas himself, as he crafted a persona of mystery and intrigue. He realized this was fascinating to many of the young, impressionable, and naïve willing to believe whatever sophistry he claimed. He also used the internet to publicize his absolute brutality and debauchery. The recorded beheadings of innocents or immolation of a Jordanian pilot were but a few of the many hidden atrocities he directed and apparently enjoyed.

And while he employed the internet extensively and intertwined the objective paucity of information regarding his early life, there were objective reasons for his seemingly enigmatic origins. In the plain lexicon of a Missouri farmer from the "Show-Me State," al Al Hassan Abbas hadn't really done anything important or significant with his life up until the time he decided to begin killing, raping, and mutilating innocent human beings.

Official education records from Samarra High School revealed that our self-described "caliph" had to retake his high school certificate in 1991 and scored 481 out of 600 possible points, or 80 percent, which translates to perhaps "just above" if not well within "average." He was unfit for military service, as judged by the Iraqi military establishment, and his grades did not qualify him for his preferred subjects of law, education, science, or languages. Similar to Hitler, who was a failed architect and artist, al Al Hassan Abbas perhaps had the convenience of a mysterious history because he was indeed of average intelligence, skill, talent, and prospect, traits perfect for anonymity. Competing with others of his generation for constructive and purposeful lives, he was destined for obscurity.

This summation was only reinforced by those who actually knew him and described him as "shy, unimpressive." He attended the Islamic University and Ahmed al-Dabash, the leader of the Islamic Army of Iraq, found that he was "quiet and retiring" to the point that even those in such close proximity to al Al Hassan Abbas found him to be "insignificant where no one really noticed him."

Roth had read what intelligence existed on this murderer and was impressed only in the ability of certain personalities to become leaders of a movement at odds with sustainable human conduct. He knew, as did anyone with any prescient understanding of history, that al Al Hassan Abbas espoused a philosophy within Islam that would end his life prematurely. As long as there were forces within the human species who desired a future for their children, individuals pledged to protect the innocent, so-called men like this delusional preacher would be eliminated.

Roth himself had wondered what elements constituted the defining formula that ultimately produced such a person, one straying so far from the path of normal human conduct as to take pleasure in the pain, suffering, and misery of others. He personally had concluded that al Al Hassan Abbas was yet another in a long line of resentful "also-rans" who found a willing, vulnerable audience within the ultraconservative religious groups of Iraq, eerily similar to Jim Jones, a bizarre and comparable predatory preacher born in Indiana. The way this entertainer wannabe had deliberately murdered 918 commune members, 304 of them children, as they were all forced to consume a cyanide-poisoned flavored drink spoke of the twisted outcomes of a failed personality desperate for recognition.

al Al Hassan Abbas's stage was bigger, however, in that he used the instability within the regions of Syria and Iraq to opportunistically advance his "religious" message. In truth, his message was meant to propel a personal need for acknowledgment, a self-absorbed proof of his own worth. To Roth, he was a "nobody" who had long been ignored—the ticket collector in a theater or the man hauling away trash in a neighborhood. Faceless, unimportant, and unremarkable in any demonstrable manner. But he dreamed of notoriety and fame and unforeseeably, once he had been given the "microphone," he would not relinquish the audience or the benefits of his newfound stature. That he was a serial rapist, kept women as sex slaves, and mutilated opposing males, filming their horrific deaths by fire or decapitation, enhanced his self-perceived position within a world that was mesmerized by such brutality. It was the fascination of watching a car wreck on the freeway to many internet viewers. Roth found him emblematic of a culture that spawned a jealousy of position and rank. al Al Hassan Abbas was a nobody desperately seeking to be a somebody. Void of constructive talent, he thus reverted to an ageless yet brutal commonality: murdering innocent human beings.

But that was the human explanation for him, for his origins, and those like him. His story was as old as time. For specific Roman generals, battlefield commanders of the Hittites or Sumerians, and the early French and English pioneers who valued scalps as a form of payment, cruelty was not a novel trait. But it could not last, as the human species would eventually rise to replace the seminal violence with other forms of pivotal human behavior: justice and love. Roth felt that this was the natural history of his species, as eventually all came to understand that such barbarism was simply not sustainable or profitable. The net outcome was to relive the same triggered consequences on the perpetrators as they had inflicted on their victims.

And Roth reflected with growing satisfaction that his country was now mounting a call for justice and the end to not just al Al Hassan Abbas's ersatz caliphate, but to eliminate the fraudulent, immoral, and feckless coward who claimed to be its caliph. His time was limited, and all knew it. Deep within his grandiose delusional creation, a tiny sliver of fear had festered. al Al Hassan Abbas had pushed humanity beyond reasonable tolerance, and resources of the most powerful nation on the globe sought his death. Perhaps this was the operational justice for such depraved human beings.

That for whatever time left, such individuals understood with certainty that they were now hunted. And for their remaining time, however long it lasted, their present and future existence would be encased within the withering, perhaps crushing knowledge they were to die by the same forces they had unleashed. Even those who, in their arrogance and sanctimony, felt they would outlast such forces of retribution and justice had to contend with a troubling sleep, dreams populated by the last images of Muammar Gaddafi. Captured in a storm sewer, held down, face in rancid water, as a bayonet was used to viciously and repeatedly open wounds in his anus. This once charismatic, handsome egomaniac had his life terminated from a head wound inflicted from a handgun, his body then mutilated as a sign of the pent-up rage regarding his four-decade rule over Libya.

Roth wondered, and not for the first time, whether even within their hubris of denial such individuals eventually realized their end was preordained. Once convinced of their unique and purposeful existence, they might still belatedly experience the horror of their folly in the seconds before their life's flame was deliberately extinguished. Roth presciently grasped that this was to very likely be the same ignominious end to al Al Hassan Abbas. Did it offset his insurmountable atrocities? No, but then the memories of his victims would be nobly etched within the global consciousness wherein his historic stature was as a meaningless but transient cutaneous boil that needed lancing.

The problem for Roth was not al Al Hassan Abbas, but his son, Hudhayfah al-Badri. Roth almost sympathized for this nineteen-year-old young man. How could one be normal with a father dedicated to hatred of all but those within the perverse al Al Hassan Abbas cult of personality? Yet the highly classified intelligence supported that this man was, in fact, different from his father in several important ways.

By all accounts—mainly from local Syrian allies, the Kurds—Hudhayfah was different from his father in that the younger man was gifted with rather remarkable intelligence. Having attended local Iraqi schools while his father was finishing his scholarly work at the Islamic University in Baghdad, the youngster astonished his teachers with nearly perfect recitations from the Koran by the age of four. But this was only the beginning of his demonstrable intelligence, as he was almost a polyglot, speaking the various dialects within the Arabic world in addition to English and French. His true love was mathematics, and had he been provided a less toxic culture, he might have been a theoretical physicist. But his mathematical proclivities were not wasted, as he was guided toward computer science, exhibiting such insight into the language of machines that his father's associates harnessed his abilities to further their collective goals.

By age fourteen, he had developed or modified existing computer applications and enabled his father's organization to breach the internet-based security at several European banks and steal millions in several different currencies. His father was so proud of his son's efforts that he doted on the young man incessantly, causing a degree of friction between the elder man and his other wives and their young families.

But still, Hudhayfah wanted to prove himself in the field of combat. He wanted that singular honor reserved for those who had killed the enemy, and especially to those few who had killed Americans. This was the ultimate proof of valor and courage, establishing a status second only to the caliph himself: the taking of an American life. A close second was any British or Russian. It did not matter if these were soldiers within the rules of armed conflict or civilians; a dead American, Brit, or Russian was a sure means toward distinction within the ISIL combat-related culture. But unfortunately for Hudhayfah, al Al Hassan Abbas himself forbade any activities that placed his son in harm's way. In fact, he went so far as to confide in the young man that such engagement with the enemies of the caliphate were reserved for those who could not contribute much of value other than their efforts and ultimately their lives. al Al Hassan Abbas had no difficulty seeing his family and those nearest to him as the elite within the culture of the caliphate and those who made his rule possible as mere servants to him, as this was Allah's will. His son bristled at his father's dismissal of the warriors who enabled his rule.

But this did not diminish the love or loyalty of the son for the father, despite the slowly growing realization by Hudhayfah of al Al Hassan Abbas's hypocrisy, sanctimony, and viciousness. Hudhayfah loved his father as sons throughout the vast expanses of time have similarly embraced the first male to hold them and whisper a sought destiny for their newborn. Their birth is immortality, a check on the vagaries of an unfair existence. How many men have looked into the curious questioning eyes of the innocent babe and ordained their knowledge and faith that despite their own failures, their sought destiny may yet still manifest? Every father begins as a de facto giant in their young son's lives. It was similar for Hudhayfah.

For many, it is only later that the process, a slow evaporation of the emotional bond, gives way to a rational understanding of a father's many flaws, if not outright delusions. Again, it was similar for Hudhayfah. But his love for the man who had favored him and protected him would never completely be extinguished. His father had spent hours sitting with Hudhayfah discussing the "rational" behind the need for horrific executions of perceived enemies. Sitting on comfortable but worn cushions, the tight intricacy of geometric patterns woven into a red-and-silver rug between them, cups of sweet tea alongside copies of the Koran and loose sheets of al Al Hassan Abbas's own writings, the two men absorbed each other. Here, the older man—dressed in black, his similarly colored shemagh covering his graying hair, his eyes focused, almost luminous—lectured his son.

Even though Hudhayfah knew these victims were often tribal members clustered in small forgotten towns in the Syrian or Iranian desert, absent any malicious intent other than to eke out their existence through farming or trade, or women and their children savagely butchered by machine gun fire while young ISIS troops applauded and cheered as though they were at a futbol game in Aleppo's 53,000-capacity stadium. But then the stadium, identical to the bodies torn by automatic gunfire, was in absolute ruins, as was the entire city of Aleppo.

But his father had explained his own "remarkable epiphanies" that came to him through "erudite study" of the Koran and interpretation of past great Islamic religious scholars. His thoughts, as he explained to Hudhayfah, were suddenly so clear in that al Al Hassan Abbas was chosen to cleanse the land of infidels and retake their land, as did their historic countryman An-Nasir Salah ad-Din Yusuf ibn Ayyub, or Saladin. Conceptualizing a narrative that equated al Al Hassan Abbas with Saladin was only possible if one ignored reality, dismissed factual evidence established by historians, and soiled the turbulent but remarkable history of Saladin, but such was al Al Hassan Abbas's perspective.

Such savage revenge upon infidels became an ever-more orchestrated series of theatrical outcomes featuring unspeakable violence perpetrated by al Al Hassan Abbas's followers, who themselves had been traumatized by the Iraq War. The surge in testosterone coupled with the neurochemical satiety achieved from oxytocin release underpinned their barbarity. Scholars understood and had described that changes in brain chemistry underwrote the human brain's simultaneous need to quell primal fear and engender endearment to a group, a tribe. This duality in the bathing of neurons with endogenous or pre-existing biologically generated chemicals would be recognized by many neuropsychologists who tied its endogenous release to the horrific atrocities as young ISIL-ISIS men captured large swaths of Syria and Iraq. Global leaders sought explanation for such barbarism, incorrectly concluding that the level of such brutality was almost unique in the annals of history. Unfortunately, most political leaders are not scholars of history; such inhumane proclivities more routinely populate the timeline of the human species than presumed.

Such horrors and the neural biochemistry that underpinned it were anything but unique within war. Often, as each side seeks membership and stature within their group/tribe, they are rewarded with the oxytocin surge with acts that grow increasingly violent, if not barbaric. Whether the war was between Iraq and Iran, Viet Nam, or within the Bible's Old Testament, butchering the losing side was a remarkably consistent outcome facilitated and often typified within the quest for neurochemical satiety. Such acts were thus a mechanism for ordination, membership, and acceptance. These outcomes had not changed in ten thousand years; it was simply that the "tribe" was now ISIL-ISIS.

Hudhayfah had frequently listened to his father and found his emotions traversing the emotional expanse between incredulity and disgust, yet bound he was to the man who had raised him and provided him with the only life he knew. Simultaneously, he realized that his father's destiny was to be different from his own but his fate would also be intense and, similar to his father's, at times manifest brilliance, but probably ever short. And in all likelihood, it would parallel his father's destiny in that Hudhayfah's also would end violently.

Roth could not have known, nor could Virginia Mahoney, that the arcs of their collective futures would intersect with Hudhayfah's. But it would not be in the old world, the cradle of civilization lying between the Euphrates and Tigris Rivers or its nearby plains encompassing Tell Halaf. No, neither soldier of the United States of America could have predicted that it would be in the new world—it would be in their home.

Chapter Eight

Love Begins in the Desert

Neither Virginia Mahoney nor Jacob Noah Roth could have expected or rationalized the remarkable intimacy that flowered between them in the Syrian Desert. Objectively, albeit humorously, both considered that the initial phase of their relationship was underwritten to a substantive degree by mutual lust, for each found the other extremely striking in physical appearance and, to some unspoken degree, a desire long sought. As a result, they discussed their frequent brief physical intimacy, often stolen minutes in his quarters. Thanks to his absent roommate still at home with a newborn daughter, Jacob could finally express his interest in Virginia, part of a long-withheld emotional unguent. She would knock on his door and deliberately leave it open as they talked quietly, their heads not six inches apart, each taking in the other's scent and feeling the warm radiating as the kinetic energy swirled between them.

They laughed softly, as they both knew that their lives had taken a turn toward the bizarre when they kissed each other as she was preparing to leave his room. There were remarkedly candid with each other, Virginia telling him that she had to "get him out of her system" and groping him shamelessly for fractions of different minutes just before leaving his room.

Such actions left Roth speechless, and without embarrassment. It also left him erect!

On one such encounter, after honestly admitting to each other the "rather unusual" foundations of their relationship, each expressed that a future between them was desired. Both had agreed and smiled warmly, heads briefly touching, recognizing that they truly wanted the other for the semipermanence of a life's union.

Virginia kissed Jacob deeply as she stood behind the partially open door to his quarters. She reached out with her right hand and pushed her flattened fingers and palm against his muscled abdomen and down into his pants, feeling his soft skin, and grasped his maleness. His eyes popped open and he gasped, but did not remove his lips from hers.

Instead, he instantly stopped breathing. His member became erect and she, looking into his now wide-open eyes, radiated a twinkling playfulness in her returned gaze.

"The peter-meter doesn't lie, Lieutenant." She smiled, her lips millimeters from his.

Flustered but happy, and terribly aroused, Roth couldn't speak but just nodded in the affirmative.

She laughed a happy, soft, deeply satisfying chuckle before holding his sex firmly and kissing him deeply again.

It was all he could do not to erupt, he was so aroused. She could tell, as his facial expression was new to her, yet she immediately understood its message. Satisfied, she kissed him a final time and slipped out of his room.

He had to sit, as he felt unsteady. His legs were weak for the next several seconds.

And so, the relationship grew rapidly in depth and feeling but also in comfort and candor. Both individuals within the pressure cooker of combat preparation, in a land characterized by violence and ongoing strife, Virginia and Jacob were nearly instantaneously annealed into a single entity. Forbidden by rules to embrace or show their affection, Roth tried to stay away from her outside of mission directives, but he found every second he was in her presence a welcome interval of being with someone he valued. Someone he was beginning to love.

For her part, Virginia respected the burden of command that Roth wore and wondered if their entire newly formed but unpredictable relationship was to be a catastrophic mistake. Would it harm their mission, their individual or collective performance? This pushed into her mind, but she quickly locked it away, as paradoxically, she found her ability to concentrate on mission parameters, demands, and innovations easier and clearer than ever. Her comments during briefings and planning sessions and the near continuous review of operational elements somehow was almost prescient in their requisite adjustments.

She surprised herself and caused stunned silence as she interrupted a lieutenant colonel from Command during an early morning operational presentation. This meeting was outlining the boundaries of the compound thought to be one of the locations used infrequently by al Al Hassan Abbas. As this desk jockey intoned on the necessities of quick and decisive penetration, Virginia interrupted and asked him about the potential of mines being placed outside the walled compound thought to be a refuge by the ISIS leader.

"I'm sorry, you are who?" Lieutenant Colonel Bydin queried.

"Petty Officer Mahoney, sir."

"Are you a required member of this special team?" he stated, a hint of sarcasm rising slightly to the surface.

"I am," she responded evenly.

"I apologize, but I meant, are you going to be one of the team members actually on the ground entering the location?" He smiled, a knowing dismissive curl to the corner of his mouth appearing and then just as quickly disappearing. The colonel rather concretely believed that since a woman was asking this question, she was, by gender, disqualified from such an unwelcomed intrusion into his virtuoso briefing performance.

The smile disappeared completely only to be replaced by a frown, wrinkled forehead, and eyebrows closing together, his eyes narrowing as her answer almost slapped him in the face.

"I will be on the ground at the point of entry, Colonel, sir."

There was a ruffling of papers, the sheets containing the outline of the brief that had been ceremoniously passed at the start of the lecture.

It was then that Roth, in his most casual voice, stood and stated, "Colonel, this is V. Mahoney, a valued member of #6. She almost certainly will be at the tip of our entry efforts, sir."

Clearly flummoxed, Bydin actually stuttered, "Well, I . . . I mean . . . well, but Mahoney, you are a woman!"

A brief chuckle oscillated through the group, and a barely audible comment of "Well at least the dude is not blind!" was heard.

Again Roth, still standing, attempted to dissipate as much of the gathering adversarial breeze as possible. "Sir, she is our first female team member, approved by Command and a respected member of the team, sir."

Bydin, still confused, recovered as fast as possible. "Ok, great, and welcome?" he stated, although the inflection of his remark was more of a question than declarative.

"Back to my question, sir. Are there mines surrounding the outer walls?" Virginia could finally repeat.

"Ahem . . . well, we don't know," he ventured. Clearly, he had not thoroughly examined or analyzed this possibility or made the efforts to address this potential lethal risk. His embarrassment was evident, as if it foretold a paucity of competence that had so unceremoniously been unmasked.

"Might I make a suggestion, sir?" Mahoney was still focused on the problem, not the political correctness of asking.

Bydin could not disguise his insecurity; it was manifesting as irritation. "And what might that be?"

"Our Kurdish allies have drones that we have provided with infrared thermal detectors. Might they be used to provide a heat signature of the surrounding area?" Mahoney asked.

This was a novel use of the technology that Roth immediately recognized as ingenious. He also humbly accepted that this individual, this woman, had understood something that he should have already recognized or considered. But Roth did not suffer from insecurities much; he simply wanted the optimal outcome.

It was only Rich Hansept sitting near the door, his head tilted in reflection as he processed what the young woman had proposed, who secretly wanted Mahoney to keep quiet and hoped her question would expose her as inept. He was, of course, to be bitterly disappointed.

Roth stepped into the discussion, providing cover for the increasingly irrelevant lieutenant colonel again by asking, "Petty Officer Mahoney, explain how you want to use the drones."

Without hesitating, she began, "Our recent advancements in the digital processing of static infrared drone-acquired images allow the possibility of differential heat signatures being detectable from altitudes of five hundred to fifteen hundred feet for small objects that are embedded in the soil. This would, of course, apply to mines or other antipersonnel devices, since their rate of cooling is distinct from the surrounding soil. Thus, flying the drones over the selected regions outside and inside the walls might be able to demonstrate almost a polka-dot thermal signature, suggesting ordnance existing in and around the walled compound."

There was silence in the room. Roth smiled internally but also was thinking carefully about the remarkable proposal, and yet he fought against the suggestion that it was all that more amazing because a woman had uttered it. Damn it, it was remarkable as a standalone comment from a fish!

Bydin stood speechless, processing what he had just heard as though someone had told him the Earth was indeed flat and the universe circled around this flat environment.

He then cautiously stated, "But we don't want to tip them off as to our investigative efforts, now do we?" The tone of his sentence changed as he was near completion, suggesting that he might have unmasked a fatal flaw in Mahoney's rationale. At least this was his hope!

But she was very prepared. "Well, sir, conducting this drone surveillance at night would allow us the advantage of the differential cooling of heated ordnance different from the ground ambient thermal signature. Yes, there is a risk of drone detection, but it is probably much less at night than in the day and would be valuable, if our technogeeks think it a reasonable application of the technology."

Now Isaiah James stood up in the back row, seated two chairs away from Hansept.

"Sir, this is a remarkable suggestion, and I will be calling my guys in Germany to ask if we have the resolution capable of picking up small antipersonnel devices." James was a newer member to the team of Korean and Irish ancestry and considered brilliant. He had taken to Virginia Mahoney immediately as a younger brother might enjoy the company of a challenging older sister. Challenging, yet also demanding!

Bydin had lost control of his performance and scrambled for reassertion of his influence, but it was too late.

Another member of the team stood up from the back row of the two lines of chairs. "Sir, has anyone run the list of other 'nasties' we are potentially going to be exposed to? I mean, Command sends down orders, sir, but have they used their resources to protect us as we enter what may be a heavily defended area?" he implored. This was Adam Dow, another member with computer skills and EOD training (explosive ordnance disposal). The question was almost a directed accusation that the pencil pushers in Command needed to think outside of the box, but Adam was quick on his feet and followed with, "Perhaps we preempted you, sir. You were going to discuss this, right?"

Bydin actually looked to the ground, unable to summon the courage to admit that such interest or perspicacity in understanding the possibilities of harm to troops entering the compound was incomplete. While the man remained silent, his gaze a vacant stare sliding from his boots to the back wall of the cramped briefing room, Roth moved to assist the mounting discredit beginning to wash over the lieutenant colonel.

Hansept's eyes were now intently focused on Bydin, and to anyone looking at his narrowed visual fields there would have been the obvious conclusion that Hansept was questioning the competency of Bydin or his team—but they would have been wrong. Hansept was internally processing his anger directed at Virginia Mahoney for once again demonstrating her aptitude, her intelligence. The all-too-familiar emotions washed over Hansept at the gorgeous, brilliant woman showing up the guys as he silently watched the unfolding embarrassment for Bydin.

"Folks." Roth turned to his teammates in an effort further attempting to blunt the growing hostility directed toward this ersatz warrior. "I'm going to assign a couple of you as subgroups to investigate and request additional data for our entry and exit tactics. We have spent enormous time on the process of tactical exit, but we need some additional time spent in the unknown ordnance or unfriendly material that might await us." Roth turned back to the lieutenant colonel and nodded not unkindly toward him. "This may assist everyone and provide some insight into what we may prioritize differently than Command. Ok?"

A knowing expression combining disgust directed toward the ranking officer and focused admiration for Roth progressively registered among the members of the special operations team.

"Petty Officer Mahoney, would you lead the exploration into the potential use of the infrared technology that you proposed? You are to inform the group here in, let's say, forty-eight hours. Is that acceptable?"

"That would be fine, sir," Virginia responded, her face void of emotion, but the hint of a twinkle in her eyes flooded Roth with warmth.

Turning back to Bydin, Roth made certain that his last request was public. "Sir, this exchange has been very helpful, and we collectively appreciate your input. May we anticipate that all resources at Command will be open and available to us to enhance mission success?"

Bydin had not expected the open compliment from the junior officer in front of individuals who he himself had perceived were appropriate in their suspicion of his gravitas. His head came up, and he looked directly at Roth to ensure an absence of sarcasm. "Well . . . yeah. Yes, thank you, Lieutenant. And of course, I will assist in ensuring that all resources are available."

"Thank you, sir," Roth concluded.

As the members were leaving the building housing the cramped briefing room, Roth and Mahoney found themselves nearly shoulder to shoulder at the sand-colored double doors exiting the building.

"That was impressive," Roth stated.

"Surprised?" Mahoney countered.

Roth slowed and then stopped just before the doors. "Is that what you really think?"

She smiled and then slightly dipped her chin, looking down toward the floor. "I think our light colonel was, but no, I didn't and don't suppose you were. Believe it or not, I saw your face Jacob. I felt your expression was almost one of . . ." She pensively searched for the words. "Pride, I guess."

"That would be an accurate summation." Roth's eyes had been smiling, revealing his pleasure in watching her provide a unique and creative application of the technology needed to ensure safety for the teams tasked to enter al Al Hassan Abbas's compound.

Suddenly, Virginia turned toward Roth, her face not eighteen inches from his body. He was now three feet from the doors leading to the outside of the building. "We are close now, aren't we?"

The question was only a remnant query; both knew the answer.

Roth nodded, affirmative but silent.

She hesitated and then looked directly into his eyes. The metal blades of the ceiling fans could be heard ruffling the air in the room, but Jacob and Virginia were alone. A strange emptiness had descended upon the room so recently packed with soldiers. She wore no makeup. Her brown eyebrows were thick, but perfectly symmetrical. She spent little time in front of a mirror. It didn't matter; she did not need a mirror, as her beauty was undeniable, almost regal.

Her eyes wandered from his face, searching to connect a thought to action to appropriateness. Then she smiled tentatively, looking up from some undefined space, and again locked her eyes onto his.

"Jacob, there may be no tomorrow or no future for us. Realistically, one of us may not return, or both of us." This was not a question, but a simple admission of the potential that every soldier knows when going into combat.

He was silent, but almost imperceptibly his head moved, a subtle confirmation.

Then she quietly ushered, "Would you mind . . . ?"

His breathing changed as he sucked in a gulp of air and reached out, both hands clasping her shoulders, and pulled her gently into him. He held her.

Roth absorbed her scent, a faint wisp of lavender, and moved his head to kiss her. "Would I mind what?"

She looked up into his face, the warmth from her breath gently touching Jacob. He shivered despite the heat of the room and the warmth from her body as he recognized that he had crossed an emotional, if not spiritual bridge. "Before God, Virginia, I love you. You promise to marry me?"

"I guess I have to agree, don't I?" she playfully danced.

"Yes, you do." His voice was quiet but strong, a pseudo-command.

And then he kissed her.

Stan Ostrowski, like Roth, had been born in Chicago. His parents were the first born in America, his grandmother, his mother's mother, being the single remnant of the family who had survived WWII and the Nazi invasion of their homeland, Poland. The entire family were devout Roman Catholics. Stan's mother, Hania, or the Americanized Ann, had been a single child born two months after arriving in Chicago from Britain. Hania's mother had left the British relocation camps set up by the victors trying to cope with the millions of displaced peoples after the war. She wanted to be as far away from the killing fields of Europe as possible and give her child a new life in a new land. The men in green uniforms with tired faces but ready smiles welcomed her to their homeland. She was with child and they, as men do, were protective of this husbandless expectant mother.

Her daughter, Hania, was thus born in Chicago, and mother and daughter lived together in a modest single-bedroom apartment on the West Side of that expansive metropolis. Hania had met Peter Ostrowski, the only child of an army major within the free Polish forces fighting with the Allies embedded in Poland against the Nazis. Engaged in guerilla warfare, his father, also Peter—a leader in the Armia Krajowa, the "home army"—had perished in Western Poland, but not before having a Catholic priest marry him to Basia, Peter's mother and Stan's paternal grandmother.

Stan's grandfather was not widely known to the Americans outside of the OSS, the forerunners of the CIA. But to these clandestine warriors and his countrymen, this blond blue-eyed man standing just under six feet was indeed a well-known and celebrated national hero. To those who fought in the war, this soft-spoken former boiler mechanic had been transformed into one of Poland's most effective and lethal combatants. His exploits were not to be forgotten to those left in Poland after the war.

A kind man, intelligent with an iron will, he had spent the war waging a savage response to the Nazis, who he felt represented the embodiment of pure evil. Time and time again, Peter—or Piotr, in his native Polish—inflicted injury to Hitler's forces sabotaging trains and military supply depots and killing German soldiers. It was a shadow war, always in darkness and never close to full entanglement, as he lacked any modicum of equality in strength or resources. Yet he became incredibly effective and was credited in part with the poor German response to the deteriorating conditions on the Eastern Front in the Soviet Union. The resources being allocated to hunt and attempt to kill these native Polish fighters drained the Wehrmacht and prevented a robust response needed for deployment further east.

At times, the repercussions of his activities were devastating for his native Poles forced into inhuman, unbearable servitude to the Reich. As Ostrowski inflicted more damage to the Reich's military efforts, the reprisals became unspeakably savage to those living under their boot. Yet almost to a person, they were willing to endure the suffering if the Armia Krajowa remained vigilant in attacking the invaders from the West. The unknown and largely uncelebrated history of Poland was reflected in a majestic people who were willing to die rather than surrender. Thus, the uprising in the Warsaw ghetto was not an atypical or unique event, but one of countless sacrifices by a proud and determined nation caught between two empires founded on fear, lies, and intimidation.

Few also knew that it was during the Jewish Passover that Stan's very Catholic family held a solemn memorial service conducted annually. His father, Piotr, had passed this very personal family ceremony down to his son. Stan's memories reaching back to his childhood evoked their gathering around the deep-brown mahogany table, covered with a delicate hand-crocheted linen tablecloth, in their modest dining room. In the center of the table, a single candle burned. There they would stand and silently hold hands, praying. Their homage was offered to the children of Abraham lost in the Shoah, to those colleagues who fought and died with Stan's grandfather, and to those innocents butchered by the Nazis and the Russians.

For hidden in the more modern American history of the Ostrowski family was an almost mythical recognition within the forests of Poland regarding their family's legacy, of his warrior grandfather's total dedication to rescue those neighbors and countrymen from the "purification" preached by Hitler. Piotr Ostrowski, the grandfather, was responsible for over 3,500 Jewish lives saved among more than 10,000 attempts. Yet Piotr's failures had deeply troubled, almost haunted him—the loss of so many innocents. During the war, each night when possible his men watched him bend to his knees in silent prayer for several minutes, often witnessing tears running down his cheeks. Until his untimely and violent death, his efforts nevertheless unquestionably endeared him to his Zionist neighbors, colleagues, and fellow soldiers. All understood that this stubborn, quiet, and intelligent Pole was a servant to God and answered only to His calling. He could not allow the murder of innocents; their faith was irrelevant. He would have sacrificed his life to defeat evil, and in the end he did.

But the meeting of Stan's grandparents had been fortuitous. His grandmother was hidden in a barn cellar under bales of hay, found starving and dehydrated. But Piotr saw only her maiden beauty that had been the reason for her being concealed from the Nazis. The Catholic priest who married Stan's grandfather and grandmother had proclaimed that he was too busy to marry two people so obviously interested in the physical act of fornication rather than the spiritual blessings and sacraments of marriage. But Piotr's riveting stare, his locked eyes, communicated the opposite.

His sky-blue eyes burned with the message of his pure appeal to sacredly join with this woman. A man self-trained to extirpate evil who lived within a landscape of violence and death almost certainly foresaw the end to his brief existence. And as his time dissipated somehow, he knew his seed would continue and prosper with this young woman he had found starving, hidden beneath the barn floor.

After receiving water and hard dried bread, she had looked into those orbs of pure blue, his face and those eyes containing a gentle acceptance of his eventual fate, and she had known instantly this was her man. Her parents were dead, her brother taken out in the back of the barn and shot once through the head by an officer of the Reich. Whatever the priest saw in Piotr's eyes, it caused this man of God to shudder with fear. It caused the priest to reconsider.

Piotr's second-in-command also put a Nagant M1895 revolver to the priest's head in the cloistered sacristy and told him he was to join God prematurely if he did not perform the marriage of his commander to this beautiful village maiden. Thus, in a brief ceremony, Basia became Piotr's soulmate for eternity and in a single four-day span conceived a son: Stan's father. His grandfather never returned after having fallen in combat, sacrificing himself in the calling of his faith and as he saw God's purpose for him. But Basia bore his son, named after the love of her life, three months after she arrived in Chicago. She never remarried, and Stan's father often would hear his mother "communicating" in her native tongue with her husband as though he had just returned from work or entered the kitchen from mowing the grass.

Thus, it was Stan's father, an only child from a widowed young woman of Polish ancestry, who met Hania within the tightly knit Chicago Polish community. Both children of the war, both absent fathers, they brought their families together, determined to honor the sacrifices of those who had allowed them to live. Basia, Stan's grandmother, was still alive and frequently told her grandson that he was the carbon copy of her beloved Piotr. That she had known his grandfather for a total of ninety-seven hours before he had returned to the war that killed him never seemed odd, strange, or sad. But it had reinforced in Stan that life could be unbearably harsh and, similar to his grandfather, courage and strength were necessities.

For like Piotr, Stan was also a warrior, with the same commitment to innocents and to his commander. He was certain of very little in life, as he had witnessed horrors on the battlefield that challenged his faith and his spiritual strength. But at age thirty-one, he believed in Jacob Roth and believed God had placed him in the proximity of Roth to watch over this man from his hometown and protect him. Stan admired Roth, his hesitant acceptance of the darker elements of man's actions, his attempts to salvage the goodness when possible and to protect the innocents, the vulnerable. The atrocities committed in war are never novel. They define and illuminate the flawed character of human beings: killing not to survive, but to punish.

Roth similarly admired Stan, his quiet thoughtfulness, his ability to instantly spring into decisive action knowing without being told what requisites were vital as opposed to those that were not. The second time Roth had been injured, near fatally, it was Stan who ensured he was pulled from danger and treated in a timely manner to save his life and to extend Roth's service to the nation that both men revered. But Roth might not have realized that Stan was even more perceptive than he credited him. It was not that Roth discounted Stan—far from it. It was that Stan somehow knew Roth almost as well as Roth knew himself.

And thus, it was obvious to Stan Ostrowski that Jacob Noah Roth was in love. It was as evident as it was understandable, for Stan had seen Roth in the months prior to his divorce: the quiet focus, the haunted eyes, and the subtle yet telltale slumped shoulders at the end of the day. He now witnessed the Jacob Noah Roth he loved as an older brother. A man who exuded confidence through a quiet determination, leading by example, and careful perceptive assessment of his surroundings and anticipation of the future. The sparkle was back in Roth's eyes, and Stan was happy for him and, of course, the object of his love: Virginia Lois Mahoney.

Stan carefully but covertly observed both individuals and knew the relationship was alive and clearly on fire. He actually had to admonish himself in that he had become a bit of a joyful voyeur in that he almost looked forward to seeing these two interact. The subtle but demonstrative gentleness Roth communicated to Mahoney was noteworthy, and Stan thought how he would like to copy such behavior in any future relationship with the woman of his interest. Mahoney almost lit up the room when the two were within ten feet of one another. Stan could feel the energy of her happiness. But like the two principals, he contemplated the wisdom of their obvious budding love in the middle of the Syrian Desert days, if not hours, before a determinative combat mission.

But Stan almost certainly would have shocked any of his colleagues if asked to judge the couple, as he would have simply shrugged his shoulders and stated that "life happens." Under God's stars and universe, Stan was certain that individuals have remarkably little control over events and their delusions suggesting otherwise were foolish, if not dangerous. Roth and Mahoney were not the only two individuals finding love in the worst of all settings: ongoing combat. Stan's own lineage had begun in exactly the same manner. He looked to the heavens and more than once imagined he saw the happy smiling and knowing face of his long-deceased grandfather, a man he had never met but knew lived within him.

Stan's philosophical outlook of "plan for the worst and hope for the best" could not entirely protect from the vagaries of fortune found within the collective human experience. He had no doubt that many would be extremely critical of the couple, suggesting—and not without some evidence—that their liaison might influence the outcome of any mission. But Stan might have been the only one who thought that this might just be God's plan. To place growing love and affection in the middle of evil, to extirpate the terror with the anticipation of passion and the union of souls. Stan felt certain that this relationship would not jeopardize any mission nor put fellow team members' lives at risk. Perhaps God wanted to remind them, all of them, what they were fighting for, just as He had for Stan's grandparents. So perhaps only Ostrowski, the pillar of strength within #6, would roll his eyes at the manufactured outrage of Command if they discovered the liaison between Roth and Mahoney. That is, other than the Broderick Pickney.

Broderick could not have come from more different a background that Stan Ostrowski, and yet the two men were as philosophically similar as they were physically different. One with skin that had to have sunscreen thickly layered on it to prevent sunburn in the high plains of the Syrian Desert, the other with a rich, deep chocolate-brown skin that accepted the sun's rays with joy. Their disparate backgrounds and appearances masked an almost template menu of identical moral groundings and personal values. Other than Roth, Broderick was the sole individual who Stan Ostrowski felt responsible for within the closely knit group of special ops personnel. And Broderick felt the same about Stan.

Broderick Luther Pickney grew up in his beloved South Carolina, the sixth generation of his traceable lineage, five generations removed from the slavery of his distant grandfather with several "great" monikers attached to the label "grandfather." He loved the South Carolina of his upbringing but had felt the need to take in the rest of his country and perhaps the world. He was one of six children, a first son, second oldest. Standing nearly six feet four inches and heavily muscled with lightning-fast reflexes, his eyes caught almost everything. His face was rounded but with a heavy brow and slightly bushy eyebrows over an attractive broad nose that led to lips much thinner than his older sister's. As a child, she had teased him about his lips, saying they were "too white" and suggested he was destined for "badness"! His sister, one of his greatest admirers, had long since stopped the ribbing, as she found her younger sibling intense, talented, and driven. She was neither surprised at his decision to join the military nor his rapid and natural acclimation to the lifestyle, and she approved. She, like her sibling, had intuitively understood that remaining in their hometown of Manning in the Midlands of South Carolina was an invitation for settling and procuring a less than purposeful life. She had been satisfied with the realization that at least her brother would get out.

Broderick had a burning desire to achieve in the form of bettering himself and his circumstances. In this, he was again identical to Ostrowski, as both men wanted to more comprehensively understand the world each of them inhabited. Without being told or subjected to manufactured lectures, the young man understood the key to success often was founded upon education and the ability to see the world as it was, not necessarily as it should be. Broderick grounded his perceptions in a reality-based vision of existence; he was an individual who viewed his surroundings through the prism of a gentle soul often operating in a vacuum of morality. He had witnessed the headless corpses lining the entry into small Iraqi and Syrian villages after ISIS had withdrawn. The teenage boys not yet able to grow their facial hair now robbed of their future, hanging lifeless, mutilated, decapitated. Their bodies had been used to display the power and inevitability of ISIS as corpses hung from traffic lights.

He had stared at Roth and seen the flash of unfathomable anger streak across his eyes as he, too, viewed the carnage of ISIS. In understanding Roth's response, Broderick was unlike any of his former peers at his local small community high school. He looked to understand, to seek reason within reality. When there was no reason to be found, he understood that perhaps this in itself was thematic: at times, human beings orchestrate events without thought or reason.

The cruelty emanating from these "true believers" had stunned this South Carolinian native. But Broderick did not recoil or flinch. There was no visual or telltale response from those who might have been present and would have cast a cursory glance, nor did he allow a verbal summation of horror or disgust. Instead, Broderick contemplated and sought clarity as to why. He did look to Roth and saw a measure of bewilderment, almost confusion, at the level of carnage human beings could bestow. He knew Roth was following the same thought processes, asking the same questions. But gradually, over minutes of their entry into one remote Syrian village adorned with lifeless trophies from

ISIS, Pickney began to feel and then see Roth's unmasked rage. It matched Stan's quiet fury, their collective reactions melding into the other.

Pickney immediately understood that one cannot experience the boundaries of human depravity manifest as purposeless unspeakable malice absent a trace, a telltale stain of its impact. Broderick's high school friends called him the "quiet giant," but that did not mean Broderick was unthinking or unaware. It did not mean he was unfeeling. In fact, Roth and Stan knew him to be almost philosophical in his depth of understanding and acceptance of the existence he lived. Both Roth and Stan knew that Pickney had been profoundly shaken by the near unspeakable desecration of other human beings they had collectively witnessed, young men not quite of age. Such events were the real legacies of war, the stains that permeated the soul as a fouled oil dirties pure white linen. Roth and Stan knew that their nights would be forever interrupted by the images of these lifeless beings hung as trophies from lampposts and traffic lights. Some headless, some without hands or feet. Blood-soaked tattered cloths testament to recent efforts to harm and injure while alive. Mangled remnants of God's perfect creation.

And both Stan and Roth knew that Pickney would also never again experience completely restful sleep. A witch's brew had come to life, some imaginary vision, some nightmare haunting the subconscious that had struggled to the surface. Only this dream would not dissipate upon waking, for it was real, and the souls taken as ornaments by a depraved leader had once been young vibrant beings.

As a youth, Broderick had wanted to know the world, to be educated within the realm of understanding, seeking a scholarship of being. And then September 11, 2001, happened, and he saw evil. It took the form of smoking rubble and twisted steel, remnants of the Twin Towers in downtown Manhattan. It took the form of human body parts found within these concrete fragments. Wire-bound hands attached to severed forearms from a stewardess on one of the flights used to impact the towers. DNA samples identified the hands, their owner a single mother of two teenage boys who had recently returned to work to augment her eldest son's chances to afford college. There was a deep visceral anger for the innocents harmed, mutilated, and killed, yet it was a confirmation of his budding life's perspective. Men and women were called to answer evil, and to invoke a righteous response.

Within weeks he was in the military, and despite the misgivings of his family—the exception being his older sister —Broderick found the structured order and the commitment to values greater than the individual refreshing and oddly liberating. He took immediately to the comradery and found, perhaps for the first time, that his skin color neither hurt nor helped him. He was a clever, intelligent young man and rapidly distinguished himself with his work effort and his analytical skills. His aptitude test was stunningly prognostic of his future abilities to think on the fly, and within weeks his commanders had designated him for future entry into special operations. He eventually landed in San Diego with SEAL Team 6 and met both Roth and Ostrowski.

Roth's reputation was well-known and to many, including Broderick, a touch intimidating, but Roth himself was not. He was respectful and wanted to understand Broderick beyond the sterile data found in the new teammate's file. Several times Roth sought him out joining him and his buddies in the chow line, sitting with them at the flimsy plywood tables serviced on both sides with rapidly constructed pine benches. Roth sat with the men and broke the ice between an officer and his enlisted troops by sharing his mishaps during training in addition to even more serious errors he had made during actual missions. In fact, he was rather candid about his poor judgment regarding one of the circumstances that had nearly caused his death. This level of forthrightness was so unusual in officers burdened by the false belief that any admittance of failure was an invitation to loss of "command respect." This quite frequently led to an awkward peroration of innate skills as the young officer attempted to demonstrate his superior status with his team. This was exactly the opposite of what was required and what worked.

Roth's willingness to discuss his past missions, to share information with his team, brought him not infrequently to the edge of violating privileged information or classified material. But Roth seemed to believe that the members of a team who were tasked to risk their lives for their nation were, in fact, entitled to know everything regarding mission failures and successes that he knew. He would editorialize at times and tell them that certain aspects he could not share in case individuals within the team were captured, but this was rare.

Roth knew that the enemy was not stupid, so much of what was labeled "secret" was unneeded.

But Broderick had watched Roth carefully over the weeks of close, almost cramped coexistence and had assessed the officer's character. Broderick looked for the hidden signs of deeply embedded, almost invisible racial oversensitivity in Roth. This was a modern expression of overcompensation, the so-called "white man's guilt," that would pervade corporate boardrooms and underpins identity politics. It was not hostility—no, it was perhaps even worse, in Broderick's eyes. He looked for this officer to have a heightened desire to compliment Broderick, to elevate him as first among equals within the team before or absent reasonable merit, thereby cementing the pseudotokenism of Broderick's status. This false empathy alone would harm this man of African heritage as a small tumor perniciously grows in the body. For more than being singled out in anger, hostility, or more overt racism, this would forever undermine Broderick's status with his team members, as it is the favored status of the nominal member that begins the descent into the role of the circus freak. Special, but not one to be trusted, admired, emulated, or respected. This was what Broderick looked for and feared he would find in Roth's treatment of him.

But he had been wrong.

Roth treated Broderick no differently than any other member of the team—well, except Mahoney, who Broderick, along with Stan, was convinced that Roth was "boinking," or at least they both hoped he was! But Roth had this remarkable tendency to value people as he saw them and treated everyone with an easy but definitive respect. He took interest in his people, often reading their general background information and asking individuals about their sisters, parents, or brothers by name. It was not for show, but team members realized that Roth was often probing their emotional state and the overall philosophical health of his team with such questions.

Broderick also knew that Roth limited his review of team members' data to operational relevance, avoiding or prohibiting assessment of intimate psychological histories or past traumas. Roth had commented once to Stan that such matters were "the purview of those tasked to supply the material to build the team," and his was to sharpen its effectiveness. Thus, Roth didn't spread gossip or demonstrate favoritism; he believed that leaders assumed responsibilities for their team, but his actions often took form in remarkable moments of tender understanding. Knowing about a member's sibling with cerebral palsy might be important upon encountering such a child during a mission. Hidden vulnerabilities may compromise efficiency. Thus, a seemingly offhand query into this sibling's use of Botox to assist in excessive drooling demonstrated Roth's inherent interest and compassion for those under his command. Broderick had subsequently smiled, a deep inward satisfaction, when that particular teammate was heard telling another that he had called his mother to ask if his sister had received this latest treatment suggested by his commander. It was the firm locking in place of a relationship; Roth could now tell this soldier to run through fire, and it would occur with joy!

Seemingly spontaneous comments could unmask but also provide a healing salve to subsurface issues within the psychological health of a particular special ops soldier. This could—and Broderick thought often did—make subtle differences in performance, loyalty, and cohesiveness under conditions of extreme stress associated with mission operations. All knew it was being done to maximize the team's effectiveness, but it occurred because Roth cared about his subordinates.

Broderick also realized that this did not mean that Roth accepted anything less than the very best effort from each individual. And when Broderick had asked, he was told that Roth had sent back two people, releasing them to rotate with another version of a DEVGRU team because of unsatisfactory performance. It was rumored that one of the individuals sent back was, in fact, very skilled but a likely source of rogue activity, and Roth would not tolerate indiscriminate violation of orders. When and if orders from senior leadership were "shit-canned," there had to be a valid reason, and Roth would "go to the mat" for his teammates in support of their decisions, even if they were wrong. But he would not tolerate the violation of orders for show, only for valid intent or effect.

The result was that Roth's team was a highly talented and effective squad mirroring the inherent confidence they found in their commander. They had built trust in him and looked forward to serving under him, but Roth explicitly and symbolically denounced the cult of personalities for a commander. While Roth had enjoyed the movie Patton, he felt the actual message of the movie centered less, much less on Patton's quirky personality rather than his remarkable ability as a commander. His desire to push his troops to their single and collective limits unparalleled in the great conflict was Patton's legacy. But in this, Patton was no different than any of history's other great warrior leaders. For they, similar to Patton, were hated and loved but also obeyed, and thus successful. Roth demanded that their mission was the preeminent goal. In that, he mirrored old "blood and guts."

Command operated almost as civilian lawyers in their desire to minimize risk at every opportunity. The joke among corporate officers was that a lawyer's good day started when everyone came to work and then promptly got under their desk, only to exit this position when the clock suggested it was time to end the workday. Strangely, although the military educational institutions emphasized fluidity and decisiveness, practical application of such qualities seen in commanders was largely absent. Politics, legacy, and pride were the deadly combination that reduced many theater commanders as well as the American chief executive to incremental strategies that were mundane, easily countered, and often sophomoric. But such a perspective was not one based on realism in the theater of human conflict.

Risk was everywhere, and successful commanders assessed and then deemed what was acceptable, separating it from calamitous. What most students of history truly understand is that history's most successful leaders almost universally embodied these qualities, but there was often something more. Sometimes it was simply chance that turned the catastrophic disaster into an unforeseeable success. The unexplainable pause of the Nazi advance on Dunkirk that enabled almost full evacuation of the entire British Army instead of its very likely annihilation Rommel's trip home to celebrate his wife's birthday, thus accounting for his absence from Normandy on the very day the Allies struck and successfully carried out their European invasion. General Lee's worsening angina upon his entry into Gettysburg that many felt sapped his abilities, stamina, and possibly impacted his judgement, resulting in Pickett's ill-advised charge that marked the beginning of the end of the Confederacy's war effort. Sometimes life just intervened.

Roth understood this, embraced it, and planned his team's operations within his capacious mindset of accepting that all plans are but poor offerings for subsequent reality. His willingness to share his failures, misjudgments, and errors was instructive, but it was also something else. It was the glue, the adhesive between those who are tasked to give orders and those that have chosen to respond to them. As the men listened, his easy manners and narrative were welcomed, as evidenced by the slight crowding toward him, shoulders of the men often touching, heads turned, necks craned and lowered for a better view as Roth began to speak. On one occasion Roth had waited through several minutes of mindless banter by several of the younger teammates, and during a natural lull in the conversation he posed a question.

"Who here thinks that Command really has a clue of what they are asking us to do?"

The "us" was deliberate and telling. The men at the table —five others but also four additional men from the adjoining table abutting the end closest to Roth—now focused their attention on their unusual but respected leader.

He did not wait for an answer but noted, "We learn most from the mistakes we make, but gentleman, in our profession, mistakes mean dead friends."

Now the area was quiet. In fact, two additional listeners were now standing nearby, having left their tables to be able to hear better.

Gone were the classic complaints about the food and spartan living conditions. An intensity marked their young faces.

"Two years ago, our mission was to kill Qasim al-Raymi, the al-Qaeda leader who was in Yemen and claimed to be responsible for killing three of our US Navy people in Florida. During that mission, I rounded the corner of one of their brown baked clay brick buildings and saw a rifle partially exposed and vectored toward my two forward scouts who had entered the narrow alley in front of me. Now here is where I made my mistake.

"We were under orders to silently penetrate the area of interest and eliminate with prejudice al-Raymi. The thought was that letting anyone know we were there with noise of any level might jeopardize the mission, as it might give us away and provide time for this guy to escape. As a result, I covered the ground probably five or seven yards to the closest guy, Petty Officer Christian Webbs, and pushed hard from behind and said in a hard whisper to the guy furthest from me, Carson, 'Down now,' which he did immediately. Both men moved per training to immediately hug the walls that lined the alley, but because of my forward momentum, I had gone to my knees and was getting back up when I received the hidden sniper's greeting.

"Single shot hit me in the left pectoral region. Fortunately, I was turning, so it actually did not enter my chest cavity but tore up the muscle, and suddenly I was bleeding significantly. I guess you could say I was bleeding to death. So, what should I have done?" Roth asked, looking at their now transfixed faces.

The table was slow to respond, but Roth's intent was successful. Within forty seconds there was a lively debate among the men as to what he should have done or what actions were warranted.

After a reasonable interval, Roth looked around the wooden flat picnic table and stated, "I don't know what I should have done, but it has given me food for thought for months. When it comes to saving lives, or to preventing harm to teammates, in my mind this priority supersedes bullshit orders from Command. These orders, those formulated at Command, are made in a sterile room far away in both time and place from the activities on the ground that each of us must deal with. Again, I have learned more from my mistakes than from my successes."

"Sir." It was Broderick. He intoned, "Was your action a mistake? I mean, well—I mean, you acted in a manner that you thought was best, and someone got hit. It happens, right?"

"That is the point, yes. My emphasis is that each one of us must decide our subsequent activity based on the data at hand, and this overrides most of the stuff that comes from our orders or briefings. Now, each of us must make that call, and sometimes it will be correct and other times it may not, but that is the issue at hand," Roth responded in a relaxed, softly worded manner. He truly enjoyed talking with his team, hearing their input and their concerns.

Several of the members were nodding their heads, affirming this most basic point.

Roth excused himself from the meal, stating, "Folks, I need to get some tactical planning reviewed. May I ask some of you for your input if I need to check on issues?"

A nearly universal and spontaneous "Yes, sir!" met his ears and he smiled inwardly. Standing and placing his hand on the shoulder of the nearest team member, he gave a slight squeeze and left his hand a moment. The gentle squeeze was of confidence for and intimacy regarding the men at the table, and then he turned and exited the building. The normally cacophonous ambient noise from the room was eerily missing as he pushed through the doors. But as he was three strides from the doors, he heard the first of the team begin what was to be a fruitful and at times highly animated discussion. As the sound built, Roth again smiled. It was just as he had intended.

His movement was deliberate, rhythmic, and purposeful, his habitual intake of his surrounding environment constant. Hearing the rough gravel mixed with sand crunch beneath his rubber composition soles reminded him of the need for deliberately tuning his auditory senses to detect movement when visible exposure was absent. Sound is an improperly undervalued element in the theater of combat. The growing volume within the mess hall ebbed as he continued his pathway back to his quarters, but his finely tuned hearing did detect something. Roth heard her approach.

His smile was a bit too quick, too genuine, too intimate not to be noticed by those who watched him carefully, and his troops to a person did just that. But almost all were happy for both of the lovebirds, although everyone wanted to ensure that mission readiness and effectiveness was enhanced, not compromised because of the flowering romance between their leader and Virginia Mahoney. This, of course, was crowding into the minds of all who were astute enough to discern the relationship between the two individuals. Command, had they known, would have altered the team immediately and more than likely shipped Mahoney and possibly also Roth home to separate billets. But they did not know and were not going to find out, as the tacit understanding among those aware of their budding relationship was to protect both of their teammates. The cohesiveness of the group was rapidly becoming even tighter, an extremely close family unit.

"Lt. Roth, I have some questions regarding our potential upcoming mission."

He could tell from the inflection of her voice that she was indeed grappling with an issue, and he wondered what she had spotted that he had missed.

"Sure. What is the best environment for you to discuss these concerns, Miss Mahoney?"

"Your choice, sir, but I have a map from Triple C. Public, not classified." She hesitated a moment and then looked at him. "Could we lay it out to look at it?"

"Yeah, of course." He was frowning now, curious as to her concerns. Roth wanted to know what she had gleaned from the map from Central Combat Command, inclusive of Iraq, Syria, and Kuwait.

"Could we get a couple of the guys to go over this with us just to ensure that my statements are properly contexed?"

"Pick whomever you think will assist, Miss Mahoney." Now, he was becoming almost agitated; he had missed something. She nodded and Roth stated, "Could you folks meet me in my quarters? I have the table and we have room to sit. My roommate is not back yet."

"Back in five, sir." And then she was gone.

Chapter Nine

Forbidden Consummation

The meeting began almost eleven minutes after Mahoney had informed Roth of the need to discuss matters regarding their planned mission to kill al Al Hassan Abbas. It was not surprising that she had grabbed Stan Ostrowski as he exited the makeshift mess hall voicing his misgivings about eating the soggy burrito that he was convinced had been dipped in 5W-30 synthetic motor oil. He already had noted his bowels were not so gently informing him of impending disaster! He turned to his larger companion, saying, "Brod, this may be a long night, buddy. I think I have poisoned myself with the shit they call food."

Broderick smiled and turned not without sympathy to his friend. "Stan, I suggested that you needed to limit your intake of this crap they try and feed us and eat what I eat."

"Brod, I need meat and calories! Not just vegetables and dried fruit," Ostrowski lamented.

"Stan, my man, let's see how you feel about the subject tomorrow morning!" Broderick Pickney placed his large paw on his friend's shoulder and squeezed it affectionately.

Mahoney had then asked Stan and Broderick to join her with Roth in his quarters for an impromptu reassessment of plans for the al Al Hassan Abbas mission.

They immediately agreed, and although Stan was still focused on his abdominal rumblings, he knew that this meeting would probably be determinative in setting out goals and concerns for their upcoming task.

Mahoney left them, moving quickly in the direction of Roth's quarters while Broderick waited, giving Stan the needed time to attend to his digestive concerns.

As Broderick scanned the horizon, he took in the gentle warm breeze, the hint of the desert fragrance. The robin's-egg-blue sky was almost without interruption save a few high traces of cirrus clouds.

Both men were moving toward Roth's billet within three minutes.

As the men turned off the gravel pathway, they came to the officer's quarters and Stan, followed by Broderick, tucked his chin into his chest as they moved through the door. His head was covered with a patented ceramic helmet, its actual composition secret. Broderick had to stoop slightly more to avoid the upper doorframe of reinforced steel. Command had demanded that thoracic protection, and helmets were to be worn 24/7 due to unpredictable rocket fire from unfriendlies. Weapons were carried at all times; an instantaneous transition from emptying one's bowels to targeting an attempted breaching of their camp was understood by all as a real and constant possibility. No signs or markings designated the heavily fortified half-sausage structure as officers' quarters, and officers and enlisted were spread randomly within each of the living quarters.

Sandbags lined these already narrow dimly lit barracks. The entryway that emptied into a longer opening, forming a T-shaped structure, smelled of stale heavy air mixed with a distinctive locker-room pong. Both men turned to the right, and Roth's quarters were at the end of this longer aisle on the left. They knocked on the open door and both peered into it, seeing Mahoney leaning over a table and Roth nowhere in sight. She looked up and with her right hand silently waved them in.

They then heard a door shut at the distant end of the opposite hallway, and Roth entered the room seconds later wearing an expression of troubled anticipation. It was Mahoney who spoke first.

Looking directly at her two peers, she began, "Hey, guys, our tactical mission resource list has been finalized, and I am troubled by our ongoing discussion of mines that almost certainly line the perimeter and probably also are placed around the more proximal areas leading to the main physical dwelling."

"So you said. What has changed?" It was Broderick who spoke. "What is concerning you?"

This was said not as a challenge nor as a dismissive taunt, but as a colleague with genuine interest in the response.

"Well, here. Look at the list." Mahoney gave a copy to both Stand and Broderick and kept one for herself, then thoughtfully said, "Lieutenant, here, take a look at this. I don't have but three copies." She provided her list to Roth, whose forehead was wrinkled in concentration as he tried to understand where she was going with her concerns.

It was Broderick who looked up suddenly and said, "No dogs!"

And Mahoney, almost proudly nodding to her friend and colleague, confirmed, "No dogs."

Stan looked at Roth and with a trace of anger stated, "What the fuck are these folks thinking, not providing us with our dogs?"

Roth was similarly angered. "Yeah, what are these idiots thinking? Are we sure that the list wasn't updated?"

"I checked forty-five—no, forty-seven minutes ago," Mahoney stated.

"Ok, let's go through our list to see what else we have or don't have and may need," Roth ordered.

For the next two hours, these four individuals carefully reconstructed each phase of the mission, from preflight to touchdown after completion. Between them, the detailed assessment might have been graded remarkable if this were a drill, but it was not, and each member was concerned as to what else might be missing or malapportioned. In the end, it was evident that these four members of the team were the de facto leaders. They knew mission details to the level of minutia. Broderick even suggested they bring a small hatchet in case they needed the hand of al Al Hassan Abbas removed from his body for genetic confirmation and fingerprinting. Stan grinned while Virginia rolled her eyes.

Roth needed to call Command.

Using the encrypted satellite phone, Roth initiated the call and asked to speak to the leader of resource allocation for active missions concerning his team, named through use of its coded identifier.

The same Lt. Col. Bydin who had previously nearly been driven from the briefing after exposure as an armchair dilatant was on the phone and about to upbraid Roth for grandstanding over Command decisions. Instead, he became uncomfortably silent when asked about use of special operations' dogs. He took too long to respond that the determination of need had been reviewed and that the dogs would be of minimal contribution. When Roth asked if his team had been asked for input regarding this decision, there was a telltale hesitation before the individual on the other end of the line asserted his rank, and Roth formally thanked him for the information.

The message from Lt. Col. Bydin was that this was a Command decision and thus had been "competently assessed." The reciprocal response from Roth was, This was a Command decision and thus is idiotic, sophomoric in its appreciation of conditions on the ground, and reflective of a slowly ossifying group of armchair warriors.

This was communicated by Roth with a crisp "Sir," which again was translated into Fuck you, sir!

Roth had communicated to his superiors moving outside of his quarters to provide some degree of privacy to the conversation. Despite this, the three team members heard every word and their inherent tone. To a person, there was a satisfied grin that appeared before Roth rejoined them.

The meeting broke up, as other duties were now requisite of each, and Stan and Broderick were the first to go. They wanted to ensure that several of the items that they knew might be needed were indeed not only on the list, but were being prepared for loading onto the UH-60 Black Hawks.

Virginia was now alone with Roth.

"You're worried," she probed.

"I always am worried before a mission. That is what I am paid to do. That is my nature. That . . ." He stopped and looked at her, her eyes reflecting beautiful pools of empathy and knowledge.

He reached for her hand and she took it, tenderly squeezing.

Roth stated, "I'm sorry. I fall into the routine of compartmentalizing my feelings a bit too easily, I'm afraid."

"I understand." Virginia reached out and gently touched his temple just behind his left eye, communicating tenderness. The touch of her skin caused an electric shock of passion in Roth. He reached for her and puller her into him, kissing her deeply.

Within seconds, the sterile space of Roth's quarters swirled with the electric kinetic energy of passion between two individuals who sought sanctuary within the other. Individually, they understood that days, perhaps hours into the future, each might breathe their final requisite aliquot of Earth's atmosphere before surrendering their life's spark. Such realization made the passion nearly surreal.

Broderick and Stan had stopped seven feet from the entrance to Roth's quarters. The main entrance outside of where they had previously entered was void of activity, but both stood slowly taking in the surroundings before looking at each other and smiling.

"Ten minutes," Stan stated. "I'm giving them ten minutes, and then I'm opening the door and yelling at Roth!"

Broderick grinned, and with care he slowly and quietly commented, "Stan, I give this ninety-two seconds before

Nirvana is reached. We can give them five minutes, which is more than enough."

Stan looked at his friend, the chocolate-brown facial features both handsome yet hard. His friend had witnessed what Stan and the others had seen: the carnage left by ISIS in the villages. The ageless plague of our species, to wantonly maim and harm based on conceptual distinctions that God, Allah, or Jehovah would find unworthy and wrong. This was the embodiment of evil in the modern world. A form of barbarism so base that hardened warriors shed tears of shame and incredulity upon witnessing the outcomes that ISIS ordained as its purposeful cleansing.

Stan reflected upon the origins of his friend's thoughts and revisited his own personal and recurrent interest in this young man that he cared so deeply for, the brother he'd never had. He also found it almost comical that such distinctions as the melanin content of Broderick's skin or that of any individual could be used to foster such political divisiveness in their own country. He wondered not for the first time if those pushing such identity-driven divisions might harvest a whirlwind of unspeakable tragic consequences.

Broderick stood, feeling his friend's gaze, and felt the warmth of the bond between the two men. He understood as few of his generation could that love, the expression of ultimate caring, the willingness to sacrifice one's life for another, could be formed between men without the physical expression of passion. Broderick would do anything for Stan, and he knew, without a moment's hesitation, that Stan would reciprocate in kind. But Broderick was near certain Stan would try to accomplish whatever was needed first, as Stan was the ultimate competitor. This made Broderick smile, and Stan saw the subtle change in his expression.

"What?" Stan inquired.

"Nothing."

"Oh, you visualizing the real-time events inside Roth's quarters as we speak?" Stan concluded.

"Somewhat, yeah . . ." And Broderick again smiled, although this was not quite true.

The events in Roth's quarters took longer than the ninety-two seconds that Broderick had forecast, but not be more than twenty-two seconds beyond the prediction. As both Mahoney and Roth quickly pulled up their underwear and their camouflage pants, they looked at each other, searching for acceptance and approval in what had just transpired.

Mahoney smiled and teasingly said, "Perhaps we can work on a bit of foreplay next time?"

Roth grimaced, drawing in a deep breath, and responded, "I will work on it continuously if that meets with your approval."

"It does."

"I am in love with you," Roth said softly.

Mahoney froze. Her breathing halted as her eyes refocused, having been momentarily dilated, in shock at such a naked and raw admission from this man.

"Jacob?"

"I know this is way too fast, but . . . I am. I am."

He reached over and gently kissed her on the lips, then kissed her forehead.

As he pulled back, he reached cut touched the outline of her jaw.

Her smile was radiant, yet a perceptible mist of concern floated to its surface.

They stood silently facing each other, absorbing the afterglow of intimacy. Only the portable window-mounted air coolers humming in the background gave ambient familiarity, for now everything had changed. They had confirmed their mutual love. They had affirmed their vows before God. All that was left to do was share their commitment with their colleagues and friends.

But this would have to wait. Ard would they ever be provided the opportunity?

They were suddenly startled, quickly returning to reabsorb their surroundings as Stan's loud voice stated, "Lt. Roth! Let's meet in two hours to review our joint plans, ok?"

Roth and Mahoney knew immediately that Stan and perhaps Broderick as well had been standing guard outside of Roth's building, shielding and protecting them from any unwanted interruptions. Roth felt a sudden near overwhelming humility in the face of such commitment.

He responded, speaking with force, "Yes, good idea. Thanks."

Looking at his watch, he relayed the scheduled time and confirmed it with Stan through a final command. But it was Broderick who stated, "Ok, Lieutenant. See you in two hours."

Broderick and Stan walked away from Roth's quarters smiling, looking strangely similar to two kids who had just siphoned forbidden gasoline from their father's car.

Roth's eyes brimmed with tears of grateful acknowledgement for his two ultraloyal human guard dogs. They were beyond teammates; they were his brothers.

Chapter 10

The Desert Serpent and His Handler

Hudhayfah al-Badri, the son of the world's most wanted terrorist, sat looking down into the delicate, almost translucent porcelain cup. His slender fingers flexed and extended as he swirled the white kaolin-feldspar creation, the remnant particulate dregs gaining and then losing their centripetal motion. He frowned. Hudhayfah had just sipped the last of the sweetened tea. The dissipation of the sugary tang that he so enjoyed in this particular brew was near complete. His thoughts returned to the current problem and the potential decision he had embraced. Not seventy kilometers from his remote white-washed brick farmhouse, an American forward basecamp, Al Asad Airbase, existed. His abode was one of several clustered together and nestled within gentle rolling hills of the sparsely populated arid surroundings. It was smaller and less conspicuous than that of his father, located much further north. And whereas his father's temporary shelter was near the Turkish border, Hudhayfah's current location was near Syria's southern border adjoining Iraq. He had obtained information from one of his scouts, a remarkably observant and intuitive nineteen-year-old, that there was a heightened focus among individual security personnel, if not collectively among the American troops visible to the young man at Al Asad.

But young Farid Khaled, the lone surviving male of his family, had witnessed an astonishing sight on day nine of his three-week vigil observing the operational proceedings at the

American base. Dressed as a goat herder—a not entirely fabricated role, as two of his uncles had indeed, in their younger days, been shepherds for their family's flocks. But for Farid Khaled, while walking past the southern boundary of the American base, his careful systematic mental inventories had paid off. And unlike his uncles, Farid was almost as gifted as Hudhayfah in use of the seminal technology of their generation: laptop computers. He had maneuvered within fifty yards from the furthest barbed wire barriers, carefully moving closer and then the next day moving back away from his previous path so as not to arouse suspicion. It was his calculated second pass during his daily walk through the area, pushing a small flock of goats along with his loyal Kangal shepherd dog, that a strange image caught his eye. Something previously unseen, something not foreseen.

He had seen five individuals all in special operations uniforms involved in target practice. The target practice was conducted using suppressors, or what most would call silencers. It was difficult to get a complete assessment of their activities, as he was walking nearly 125 yards from their location and had only transient corridors of limited visual access since the buildings blocked a comprehensive view of the military endeavors. These five individuals, in a choreographed routine, had shown patterns of systematically advancing within the open area at the far end of the base, an area reserved for target practice. Apparently, there were additional groups, but they were practicing in teams of five and moving in tightly preset coordinated drills. He could hear almost no verbal exchange between these individuals, as they were fairly distant from him, and they were also predominantly using hand signals.

Farid knew how the base's main buildings were arranged, and while there were many gaps as to which building served what purpose, he understood the reserved area currently accommodating this drill. This was occurring in an area reserved for refining target acquisition and clearing of ordnance. Simply stated, it was used to increase the Americans' ability to kill their adversaries. This was the same area that Farid knew was infrequently used. He wondered whether there was a correlation between this sudden increased frequency of its use and any planned American special operations missions. Farid could not know any details, or even if any mission was planned, but simply that the registered use of the facility seemed to mean they were practicing for something. Was it linked to some planned activity?

Farid could not loiter as he passed the outskirts of the perimeter barbed wire that demarcated the furthest reaches of the base. Yet he slowed his pace and deliberately dropped his water bottle, giving him precious additional seconds to linger. What Farid accomplished but could not confirm surmised correctly that the teams were indeed beginning last-minute rehearsals for coordinated movement immediately after exiting their specially designed and acoustically silenced helicopters. It was during his calibrated observational stroll last Tuesday that he witnessed the anomalous event. The unforeseeable surprise, however, was that he was almost certain one of the five individuals participating on this particular day was a woman!

The clue despite the heavily uniformed personnel, all wearing some form of plastic eye protection, was the delicate use of a left hand to brush a strand of hair away from the participant's face. It was the same nearly identical motion that his sister employed to control her beautiful but unruly locks as they slipped from beneath her hijab. Men simply didn't have the same feminine motion or delicacy of action. Farid almost missed the actual motion and then nearly did not register its potential importance. This tell, indeed, was unusual, but he nevertheless momentarily questioned his eyesight, if not his judgment, regarding his identification of the feminine gender in this individual. But he had witnessed this motion within his household innumerable times—it was a feminine tell. There was a woman practicing with the men in this American base known to house special operations personnel.

He would relate this to his commanders. They respected Farid's ability to pick up subtle, seemingly unimportant grains of data that might then be woven into an understanding of actions to be taken or plans that had been formulated. This might be one such piece of evidence.

It was eerily similar to the "pizza index" in Washington, DC, long known to foreshadow the potential of American military events. In the 1980s and 90s, it had become apparent that preceding imminent covert military actions, there were abnormal spikes in the orders of pizzas being sent to the Pentagon and the White House, the central hubs of American military decision-making. A simple observation was that requisite White House or Pentagon personnel who were needed to fulfill their duties within assigned roles also needed to eat. But within the multiple layers of logistical support from the gigantic American military infrastructure, many people, far beyond the norm, were suddenly staying late to "ensure success." The problem was that such personnel, in their requisite caloric consumption, drove fast food orders off the charts. The resultant dramatic spike in the early and late evening pizza orders from various local fast food establishments enabled enemy observation of this pizza index to be used as a telltale sign that something was up in the White House and Pentagon. It was so reliable an index of looming activity within the Pentagon that planners had to ban the practice.

Farid smiled, as he, too, knew of the pizza index and now was contemplating the appearance of the weaponized choreography, wondering if it foreshadowed imminent activity. Perceptive future commanders would understand that any indigenous enemy could not be dismissed as unobservant. Indeed, they were often subtle, nuanced, and deadly adversaries. Viet Nam should have authenticated such lessons, yet it is unfortunate that so many of these practical martial teachings must be continually relearned by subsequent generations.

Thus, Farid had communicated his perceptions of the heightened preparations evident at Al Asad along with the odd but interesting additional nugget of information regarding a woman within their personnel. Passed up the fluid ISIS chain of command, this material had reached Hudhayfah.

As the son of the world's most wanted man sat watching the slowing swirls of tea leaves in the bottom of his teacup, he began to wonder if he could use such information. It would be God's will if this woman was either killed or captured, and all the world would see that the infidels were subjecting women to unholy activities within roles of killers. How would this play within the Islamic world, where the conservative clerics of Saudi Arabia were still "slow-walking" any loosening of traditional constraints on the suffocating restrictions placed on Saudi women? Yet Hudhayfah and these same clerics accepted that women could serve as effective shields, sacrificing their lives to protect the men if this was deemed reasonable. He briefly looked to the heavens and again thanked Allah that he had not been born a woman.

He must warn his father, he thought, through a complex web of couriers that there may be something afoot with the Americans, although Hudhayfah was not really concerned that these enemy infidels had identified the location of his father. His father, al Al Hassan Abbas, was simply too mobile, always shifting locations and even changing rooms within the same house each night. He seldom stayed in a house or location for more than three nights, often only one. He had told Hudhayfah that it was the price of immortality in pursuit of their caliphate. He also never used modern forms of communication, knowing that the American drones and satellites were remarkably effective in their monitoring of cell phone and computer internet traffic.

Remarkably, a centuries-old form of communication was employed: carrier pigeons that took tiny rolls of rice paper with a changing code that Hudhayfah had demanded all who communicated with senior ISIS leadership use. It was a rotating code and thus, with the help of Hudhayfah's computer algorithms, one day's matching key would provide the text, and the next or past day's key would provide gibberish. It was, after all, the Americans' proclivity for finding, capturing, and arresting couriers and then mining the data that they possessed in order to identify locations of valued targets. Hudhayfah knew that was the persistent weak link in the chain of the caliphate's communication network. And the Americans would not torture the couriers—no, they would leave that to the Kurds or the multiple other groups that ISIS had terrorized. There was an abundance of willing participants to carve up the unlucky detained ISIS messenger. That was how the Americans had finally traced, found, and killed bin Laden.

It worried Hudhayfah because several of his father's wives and members of his extended family had fallen into American hands. Any information possessed by these wives or relatives was dated and could not be used to trace his father's current whereabouts, but Hudhayfah worried still. It was always the unintended or unforeseeable grain of information that could be used by those trained to see it. To those perceptive enough to expand upon seemingly valueless material, disaster could unfold for the unwitting. And Hudhayfah was different than his father: less of a religious zealot, more meticulous, and although he was reluctant to even usher in such thoughts, perhaps just more intelligent and nuanced in his mental dexterity.

While his father was used to bludgeoning, either physically or psychologically, Hudhayfah was simply not comfortable with this approach. Although in many ways the younger man was more sinister and pernicious, for Hudhayfah wanted to injure beyond physical pain to cause lasting anguish in those who survived or were outside of his immediate reach. Thus, he orchestrated and was the co-originator of the consideration that morphed into action—to abduct that silly American woman who had been trying to assist civilians caught in Syria's civil war. He took a perverse satisfaction in the discomfort, the heartbroken sadness and anguish that not only her immediate family experienced, but also the true target of his action: the American president.

But the real mastermind behind the kidnapping of the American volunteer was a seldom-seen shadowy figure known only to the inner circle of al Al Hassan Abbas's ISIS: Ehsan Karimi, a native Iranian born in Rasht, the capital city of Gilan Province. His family was of mixed Russian-Persian descent, a historic vestige of the 1826–28 Russo-Persian War. Educated and technically inclined, his grandfather, father, and uncles had been assimilated into the modern Iranian state after the Second World War. Serving within the growing military industrial complex under the former Shah, they had no qualms about maintaining identical roles under the mullahs. As an extended family, they were survivors. Few of their friends knew of the family's Russian heritage, and it was only as Ehsan grew into his teen years that his mother and father shared the full extent of his heritage with their second oldest son. To a person, the family felt their Russian lineage was a secret best kept from outsiders, but also shared a collective hidden pride within their tight clan. Their links to Iran's northern leviathan bubbled just under the surface of this proud and accomplished family.

Historically, the city of Rasht was a major transport and business center that even today served to connect Iran to Russia and was the largest urban center on the Caspian Sea coast. Known as the City of Rain, the ethnic diversity paralleled an intellectual vibrancy particular to the metropolis. The family had been active within the market-driven prosperity of this ancient city with roots in the thirteenth century, but the current members of Ehsan's extended relatives were employed within highly technical endeavors rooted in Iran's obsession with developing nuclear weapons. Ehsan's mother and father had each demanded that their children excel in school, and the payoff was the awarding of entry into Iran's most prestigious universities. Ehsan's oldest sibling, his brother, had been the true magnet of both parents' love and near continuous adulation. In fact, Ehsan's grandmother, his father's mother, had admonished his father as to the relative neglect of their other children reflected in a near idolization of the eldest, Hashem. In truth, both parents were more than adequate in their roles of raising their children, but it was clear that Ehsan's father was enraptured with his eldest male offspring.

Yet this did not mean practically or emotionally that Ehsan or his two younger siblings had been ignored, nor was Ehsan even slightly jealous of his older brother. Like his grandmother, parents, and nearly everyone who met Hashem, Ehsan loved his older brother. Ehsan idolized his brother's intellectual gifts, including a remarkable linguistic ability approaching that of a polyglot who, by fourteen, spoke Russian, English, and German along with his native Gilaki and the official Persian Farsi. English had come quickly to

Hashem, as he was fascinated by the development of computer programming and the American innovation called by various terms but known to Hashem as "the internet." English was necessary, he felt, to identify the technological and industrial-driven market nuances within the cultural environment of America. By the time Hashem was sixteen, his teachers had identified him as a special talent, and the government came calling.

The fall of the ruling Pahlavi family in Iran had put the conservative clerics, the mullahs, in control and in direct conflict with America. The siege of the American embassy along with the American hostages taken on November 4, 1979, and held until hours after Reagan took office on January 20, 1981, announced to the world that any reconciliation between Iran's newest leaders and the Americans was impossible. The Supreme Leader, Khamenei, had been the leader of the servants of Astan Quds Razavi since April 14, 1979. After the death of Khomeini—the leader of the Iranian revolution, a radical cleric who ousted the Shah—Khamenei became the most powerful political authority in the Islamic Republic. He was also virulently anti-American.

Thus, it was entirely foreseeable, if not plainly obvious to any who were willing to look, that Iran was to embark on a decades-long quest for nuclear weapons, in part to offset the American hegemony. Their actual quest, at first quietly whispered within diplomatic-intelligence circles but later to become the focus of strident speeches by the Iranian leadership, was ideological. To reinforce that procurement of nuclear weapons was essential to protect the Iranian nation was tantamount to a silent declaration of coming conflict with America. Hashem and other gifted young men, and even some remarkably talented women, were exposed to this national obsession to develop weapons in "defense" of their nation. Hashem was happy, his parents and family immensely proud of his participation in the military curriculum in which he participated. The advanced technological training was free, and his family's stature rose considerably.

In truth, the mullahs reflected upon the tiny, unimportant, almost throwaway nation called North Korea and marveled at their skillful multipurpose use of nuclear ambitions. This small wasteland of ultrarepression and recurrent famine slowly transformed such ambition to actual advanced weapons technology. It did not matter to Korean leadership that most of the population starved and lived within a desolate environment of disease and unimaginable suffering. What monetary or capital was procured by the North's Kim family was used to prop up his military, and specifically to underwrite his weapons development program. It was used as a cudgel against America and her allies. The Kims had realized early, the mullahs later, that the Americans viewed the possession of nuclear weapons as an exclusive club, and new members had to be vetted and considered stable, reasonable, and most optimistically possessing Western values.

The Supreme Leader, Khamenei, was initially stunned by the obvious successful blackmail routinely practiced by the North Koreans against the inept containment strategy of the Americans. Successive American administrations sought to buy off the Koreans, only to voice disappointment and belated surprise at the pernicious duplicity routinely displayed by Kim and his surrogates. The rest of the world, and especially the Iranians, learned these lessons well. If such an inconsequential land of fourteenth-century living standards, the Peoples Republic of North Korea, could achieve ersatz parity with the Americans, at least in the attention paid by this superpower to this mountainous feudal kingdom, well . . . imagine what Iran could achieve.

Hashem was thus one of hundreds of the "best and brightest" of their generation to be swept up within the military-industrial government-run efforts to accelerate nuclear weapons development. But in 1988, at the age of twenty-eight years old, things went horribly wrong for Hashem and indeed for his family. The events left a deep scar within Ehsan, forever changing his view of the West and specifically the Americans. Such events would also attempt to shape future history.

As Hashem rapidly climbed the ranks within Iran's intelligence service, he was pulled into identification of weaknesses in the Iraq stratagem. There, he found that America was carefully selling weapons, often through intermediaries, to Iraq. The Americans' purpose was simple: to hamstring any potential for a decisive victory for the Persian Empire over its archenemy, Iraq under Saddam Hussein. The world knew that Iran was positioning itself to become the dominant power in the Middle East. Within their population, academic and intellectual potential was being unleashed to usher in a new era of Persian geopolitical dominance. But the Americans and Iraq's Hussein, Tehran's western neighbor, did not want expanded Iranian influence.

Thus, the Americans practiced the simple yet effective strategy of letting two troublesome countries destroy each other. This took the form of money, loans, and direct weapons procurements sent via third countries or channeled discretely into Iraq. The United States was only too comforted in witnessing Iranian incremental defeats over Iraq. Grinding down each other's military left little time for intrusion by the mullahs into other regions of the Middle East. Unfortunately, it also meant that for many within Hashem's generation, the Americans' cold-blooded strategy supplanted any tiny modicum of previous support for reconciliation with Washington with pure hatred.

Hashem was somewhat less judgmental, for Hashem, like his younger brother, had been a purveyor of facts and novel interpretive conclusions. He did not partake in or join the thousands demonstrating in the streets, often for the benefit of the Western news media, shouting, "Death to America!" Such images were replayed on the evening television broadcasts in America and formed the bedrock logic for the American strategic perspective of Iranian containment in the form of curtailing their geopolitical influence. Hashem had formulated a more granular view of these curious but ever-talented peoples. He was repetitively impressed by their innovations and their seemingly endless fluid embracement of ideas and technologies that benefited people. His view was tempered by his own admission that the Americans were very dangerous when aroused and possessed military capabilities that he considered decades ahead of his own country's efforts.

But he also resented the duplicity by the Americans and indeed their hypocrisy. He did not view his own government's actions uncritically, but quietly, if not silently, he viewed their ill-conceived conflict with Iraq as terribly wasteful both in blood and treasure. Originally, the war had begun for a multitude of reasons—some strategic, some based on the egos of respective leadership. But Saddam Hussein was worried that the original revolution in 1979 that had toppled the Shah might just come for him as well, as Iran might stir up segments of the large Shia majority in Iraq, effectively supplanting the minority Sunni-led Ba'athist leadership. This, in addition to the desire to supplant the Iranian state as the dominant Persian Gulf power along with the prestige it would bring to Hussein, encapsulated the source of the conflict.

The problem was that once the war was in its second year, 1982, Iraqi ground forces were in retreat from their previous early gains and the Western allies stepped with their previously noted multipronged aid, extending the war, the misery, and the pointless sacrifice on both sides. In fact, so long did the stalemate drag on that it is estimated that each side suffered one million or more deaths. A fact known to the Iranians was that they might have actually been victorious by 1984 but for the continual aid being showered on the Iraqis that began as loans but soon escalated to dual-use technology and then actual direct arms sales. Thus, the slaughter of an entire generation of Iranian and Iraqi young people had commenced. It continued and was propagated by none other than the great beacon of democracy and peace: the United States of America, along with her closest allies. Even the

Soviets were active in selling weapons, although they were less particular in that they serviced both sides simultaneously.

And on July 12, 1988, during a night reconnaissance flight over the contested Iranian-Iraqi border that now both sides had hardened and fortified, an Iraqi pilot picked up the pinging and flashing lights on his plane's radar homing and warning system (RHWS). The war's last dogfight between an Iranian F-14 and Iraqi Soviet-made MiGs was mere days away, but this pilot immediately began evasive procedures in accordance with his training. Such flights had grown increasingly rare, as repetitive past probing of each country's defenses resulted in the same outcomes as achieved in the rolling hills of Eastern France during the first global conflict of the twentieth century: money and blood expended with little to show. Iranian intelligence knew that the French were supplying the Iraqis and that the Americans were pressuring the French to arm the Mirage F1 fighter with the latest avionics to inflict the maximum injury to Iranian assets. Still, by this time in the war, both sides were timid in their probing. Iraqi flights were even less frequent, as there was believed to be little advantage to risking elite and expensive weapons platforms, special military language for "planes," when ground assaults had proven so futile.

But this pilot, a skilled and experienced Iraqi, took immediate and pivotal countermeasures, as the launched Iranian surface-to-air missile (SAM) was already climbing past 12,000 feet. The uncharacteristic novelty of this flight for the pilot was that he was flying the newest French Mirage F1 fighter in a reconnaissance mission, but with state-of-the-art avionics and weaponry. This technology allowed him to lock and store the original coordinates of the fired ground missiles independent of the subsequent missile-contained active radar tracking. The pilot could thus identify the exact surface location of the SAM's launch, but the ground-based aggressive tracking had now been extinguished because it might have been identified and then followed, leading to the hunters becoming a ripe target of the hunted.

To avoid this, the ground-assisting radar tracking was routinely turned off by the Iranians who had launched the missile, even though such coordinated radar tracking by the launch site attackers traditionally had been used to assist the climbing missile find its target. But they had ceased their ground-based tracking, relying instead on the more limited if not primitive system in the rocket's nose. The HQ-1 Chinese-produced SAM was among the latest in the Iranian arsenal and was successfully pinging with its nose-positioned radar homing in on the French-made jet, but it also had a thermal detector in its nose to seek the intense heat of the jet's exhaust. Developed and improved during the Viet Nam conflict, this was almost the latest version produced, absent some additional software that was considered classified by the Chinese, and was not for sale to foreign governments.

The Iraqi pilot, of course, did not know this, but he feared the worst and responded as if his life depended upon the summation that the Iranians had the most technically advanced SAMs. In fact, both thoughts were dispositive. As the pilot sharply banked the Mirage, he briefly touched the controls for afterburner acceleration. His experience and discipline were evident. Although his pulse had now begun pounding, he dispassionately mentally calculated the time interval before he would release his flares and chaff. He believed the craft's warning system gave him about twelve seconds before terminal outcomes transitioned from possible to historical fait accompli. The problem: the upgraded RHWS system reliably identified when the SAM was launched but could not accurately detect the rate of climb or the intrinsic acceleration of the lethal rocket-propelled explosive device; thus, it could not identify the rate of closure on the Mirage. The pilot knew this, of course, and thus was giving himself the best options.

The rocket's acceleration was almost identical to that assumed by the Iraqi pilot. The ground crew waited with heightened anticipation. They wanted this to be their ticket to rapid advancement and perhaps even hero status among the Iranian people. If they shot down this intruder, the tributes and accolades were sure to follow, including a cash bonus. But additionally, the four men comprising the SAM ground grew had important visitors that night. While not overly auspicious in terms of governmental stature, they nonetheless were known to be prominent. Only the youngest member of the three men was insignificant, as judged by the senior officer of the ground station SAM battery. He was simply too young to have any meaningful role or impact.

What was unknown to the ground crew was that Hashem Karimi was among the three visitors, and he was not only the most gifted intellectually—he indeed outranked the other older men. But this became rapidly apparent to the men assigned to forward SAM battery W-324. Even though this recognition was somewhat unsettling to the ground crew, all witnessed that the two older visitors were rather obvious in their respect directed to this younger man. It went beyond a normal polite distinction, as there was a degree of tension exhibited by these older officers during the minimal dialogue involving the handsome, clean-cut Hashem. But Hashem's presence was, in fact, per chance, as he was present to interview a Soviet soldier who had apparently deserted from the Russian Army stationed in Afghanistan. The Iranians were routinely interviewing Russian deserters who had once been rare, but now consisted of a steady trickle crossing over from their common eastern border shared with Afghanistan. This deserter was thought potentially special, as he was reported to have been in Soviet military intelligence. Iran's espionage collegium wanted his full measure.

Hashem's apparent stature was a combination of diligence and luck, so often the heady twins of future notoriety or substantive position. He had been on duty when a senior officer in Iran's intelligence service sent word that an agent with fluency in Russian was needed for a special "debriefing," a euphuism for an interrogation including various forms of physical persuasion. The man was Russian intelligence, and it was hoped that he would be forthcoming, but all options were on the table.

Hashem had paid little attention to the request. He knew that Russian language fluency was not uncommon in the intelligence fraternity and that there were other layers of more senior officers happy to take the assignment and hopefully the potential of success translating into advancement. But upon entering a cluttered five-desk subdivided office, the senior officer who had sent the request, a Colonel Reza, found only Hashem alone at the younger man's desk.

"Where the hell is everyone?" Reza demanded in Farsi.

Hashem's head immediately snapped up. Directing his gaze to the voice, he evenly stated, "I believe they are currently engaged, sir. I am more than happy to help you."

Hashem was walking that very fine line between inferring and exposing his colleagues as incompetent, or worse, covering for illicit substandard employees not fully committed to the Ayatollah's vision regarding Iran. Either way, he was balancing upon this taut boundary as he stood to fully expose himself to the senior officer.

"I was told that the linguists who are part of our organization are housed in this excuse for a workplace." Reza nearly spat the last part.

"They are, sir," Hashem replied but instantly knew something was amiss. There were multiple other offices where more senior linguists with more experience within the organization resided.

"Damn it, I need someone with Russian fluency!" the intelligence colonel nearly barked.

For reasons that Hashem would later find hard to justify, he responded to the older man in fluent Russian with a St. Petersburg intonation and accent, effectively stating, "Although I am certain to be inadequate, I will, of course, serve you as best I can."

Reza, a senior colonel in the VEVAK (Vezarat-e Ettela'at va Amniyat-e Keshvar), suddenly stopped moving. His gaze became two laser beams became focused on the face and expression of Hashem. This officer spoke rudimentary

Russian, but he also knew when he was hearing native dialect spoken; flawless Russian was entering his ears.

Hashem remained still and continued facing the older man, but in a pose that was subservient and not defiant.

"Where did you learn your Russian?" Reza asked in a somewhat softer tone.

"School, the marketplace, and at home, sir." Hashem had briefly toyed with eliminating this last location, as he didn't want any excuse for his family being targeted by Iranian cleansing activities that were common after the fall of the Shah. But he chose to tell the truth, and this, in fact, was one of several little bits that would ultimately cement him as being the correct choice for the mission.

Hashem continued to stand and look at the older man. Ehsan's older brother could almost hear the wheels churning inside the official's head before the senior officer said almost inaudibly, "Please come with me. Come now."

Hashem complied, and thus he began his rapid ascension within the intelligence community of Iran. Reza protected his assets as one would covet pieces still operational on the chess board. He would use these to strike at the enemy when appropriate, and the enemy could either be the dreaded Americans or rivals with Iran's growing revolutionary forces.

The younger man could not have known, but Reza, the man requesting his presence, was a rival of Saeed Emami, a senior official in the Ministry of Intelligence and Security. And so here Hashem was, waiting for these older but less influential donkeys to hang around, trying to impress and intimidate the rocket ground crew. He had almost said something to hurry these people along, but Hashem knew that any overt demonstration of his superior status would be met with hidden attempts to injure him in the eyes of Colonel Reza. But oddly, he felt that they needed to get going, and for some reason, he sensed that they needed to move more quickly than any objective metrics indicated. Sources would later communicate to Colonel Reza that Hashem was indeed the exact and correct choice to interview the Soviet deserter. For Hashem was loyal to his mentor and would keep valuable information away from Reza's rivals within Iranian intelligence, thereby allowing the colonel to share delicious, strategically important data with the most senior leadership. This would undoubtedly enhance the value of Reza and thus drip like precious clear water in a desert onto Hashem and his future. And as it turned out, if Allah had willed it, Hashem would have been one of the youngest and most powerful intelligence officers, potentially wielding surprising force within the byzantine layers of Iran's revolutionary forces. But it was not to be.

The fateful evening as Hashem mulled over his planned interview of the Soviet defector and his two comrades waited for the SAM to strike or miss the Iraqi Mirage F1, the Iraqi pilot was in a delicate reciprocating dance. Using his instincts, experience, and these state-of the-art French avionics, he guided the fighter jet into a nose-up acceleration with his starboard wing pointing directly at the ground some 48,000 feet below. He looked back and saw the telltale white flame rising quickly to meet him, and he waited. Two and a half seconds later, he almost simultaneously released his flares and chaff while violently pushing the Mirage nose down and making a tight loop back into the vector of the ascending missile. Abruptly, seven-tenths of a second from intersecting with the path of the climbing SAM, the Iraqi pulled the nose down and away, but the missile continued toward the last known position of the Mirage.

This was textbook but risky, as the SAM might have locked on to the new position of the Mirage F1. But then the pilot did something that was unforeseen by those on the ground who had released the deadly SAM: He dialed up the coordinates stored in his onboard computer, setting his two air-to-ground armaments to the original SAM launch location. He leveled the Mirage knowing that at least for this SAM site, they were now defenseless. He checked his screen, confirmed that both weapons were armed, and then flipped up the red metal toggle on the front console and depressed the glowing red button.

The coordinates were locked in, and six seconds later, the Iraqi pilot headed home to his base. Four seconds later, Hashem's world turned white as the temperature instantly soared to 1,000 degrees and then went black. One of the ground crew lived; he had been in a bathroom at the far end of a hall when the missiles simultaneously struck. He was dug out three hours later but died two days after with third-degree burns over 70 percent of his body. Hashem, however, was killed instantly.

The Iranian government ensured that families were aware of the heroism of its "martyrs" for the revolution, and for most this meant a form of compensation. This included a certificate or plaque in addition to a death payment for the surviving spouse or parents. The war had grown increasingly unpopular, but there was little chance that popular sentiment would divest leadership from its need to win, or perhaps simply bleed out Saddam Hussein to a stalemate. The propaganda opportunities contained within the tragedies suffered by the Iranians were simply too rich to ignore. In fact, the consolidation of influence and control by the ultraradical Muslim clerics over their country might not have been nearly successful but for the largely ineffective war initiated by the personal fear and vanity of the Iraqi leader, Saddam Hussein.

The conflict allowed the initiation of policies that translated rapidly into an effective execution of ironclad control over the populace. This took the practical form of rooting out spies or sympathizers with the Iraqi regime, but in reality, it conflated to removal of whomever the Iranian leaders thought dangerous. And of course, this applied to anyone who did not embrace and support their version of conservative Shi'a, with almost all of these from the Twelver sect. Thus, war was a gift to this relative neophyte bearded council of clerics attempting to nationalize their policies. A group of hardened, merciless men were able to consolidate their power over what had been one of the most Western-flavored and educated cultures within the Islamic sphere.

And thus, the government informed Hashem's family that he had been killed in a lawless attack on a forward operation base near the Iranian-Iraqi border. What was never stated was that the Iranians had fired the SAM at an Iraqi reconnaissance flight without provocation but within the fluid boundaries of armed conflict. But none of this mattered to Hashem's younger brother, Ehsan, who had grown up adoring his eldest sibling. A deep constricting anger instantly erupted in him toward the Iraqis and their French weapons suppliers. But his almost incalculable rage was directed toward the Americans, for it was they who had pressured the French to up the deliveries of weapons to the hated Iraqi dictator Saddam Hussein. It was the Americans who had refused to provide replacement parts to the Iranian air force for their fighters consisting of F-14 Tomcats and the aging Phantom fighters, both now nearly relics of the Viet Nam war. On the black market, these replacement parts were sold at gouging prices to the Iranian buyers, yet the aircraft themselves were almost two generations behind in the upgraded avionics that were the "brains" of the modern fighter.

And it was the Americans who had secretly notified the country's Shi'a leadership within hours of Reagan taking office of a simple message. That they themselves—the clerics trying to hold onto their massive new prize, Iran's ruling government—would be held personally responsible if the American embassy hostages were harmed. One of history's most guarded secrets had been communicated via Swiss intermediaries and delivered in Bern to Iranian diplomats: a letter from President-Elect Ronald Reagan stating that any harm coming to American hostages would trigger a definitive response. The message was effective as it was simple: an eye for an eye, the systematic elimination of each of the individuals governing Iran. Reagan communicated that he would kill each and every one of them.

It took the Iranian intelligence service nearly three hours to understand what had been attached to this letter, some odd code from a computer printout that was slightly crumpled and frayed along its edges. But when the attachment was deciphered and linked to the letter, it gave pause to even the most hardened Iranian military leaders who had so recently aligned themselves to the new Iranian regime. It was a recent but outdated computer printout of the nuclear launch codes for several ballistic submarines with their locations, then outdated. Each of the four "boomers" were situated within close striking distance to Iran. Message delivered; message received.

The imprisoned American citizens within the former United States embassy were on a plane homeward bound within hours.

Such power and the apparent willingness to use it had shocked Tehran. And thus, Ehsan hated the Americans with a passion that matched the grief he felt for his murdered elder sibling. They had been the major force behind the initial isolation of his nation and its suffering during the Iran-Iraq War as Iranian oil output was catastrophically reduced due to multiple variables, including renewed sanctions against Iranian oil sales in 1987. But more than this was the former President Carter's 1977 toast to the Shah of Iran regarding the Shahs making Iran "an island of stability" and for "the admiration and love which your people give you." Historians would later debate whether there was any other proclamation by any other president that strayed further from the truth or reality. Carter had miscalculated on each of these premised assumptions, and the results were to bear a calamity for both nations.

In January of 1979, the Shah had to flee Iran due to life-threatening security risks, and as American diplomatic personnel scrambled to re-establish relations with the new incoming Iranian leadership, Ambassador William H. Sullivan surmised that sentiment against the Shah was so heated in Iran that any support provided to him by the US might be a tipping point for untoward violence directed at America or its people. He warned that such support "would almost certainly result in an immediate and violent reaction" that Khomeini would prove unwilling or unable to contain. His words demonstrated a remarkable prescience, as days after the Shah was admitted into the US for cancer therapy, extremists overran the embassy and American personnel were held in captivity for over 444 days.

That the Americans wanted to punish Iran for what Ehsan saw as the provocative actions of a bunch of university students and radical Islamic fundamentalists was difficult to take seriously at first. But these individuals had created a firestorm in holding the American embassy personnel hostage, tripping the wire of an international incident that portended war. And the actions of the new Iranian leadership, caught off guard by this unplanned but perhaps not unforeseen event, fumbled its response fueled by rival factions within its own leadership. Some wanted to embarrass the Americans because of their past support for the Shah and especially the idiot Carter. Some within the inner Iranian circle warned that inflaming tensions with the Americans, however, would come to no reasonable endpoint.

But Iranian leaders needed this external crisis, and the faction that won the argument noted that this incident could be used as an opportunity to rid the Islamic Republic of the nonbelievers. This, after all, was the real threat. It was not the Shah. It was not the Americans. It was a counterrevolution that could decapitate the recently installed ruling clerics. But the subsequent events that polarized the West against Iran created incredible hardship upon the average Iranian citizen. Prices for necessities skyrocketed; food, medicine, and basic commodities became scarce. But it provided the corrupt leadership not only the ability to consolidate power, but to externalize their own shortcomings regarding national economic management by blaming the US. Ehsan was wise enough and cynical enough to ascertain that his own government's leaders were culpable, but there was no question as to the pivotal role the Americans played. And now, with the death of Hashem, Ehsan was to live through this era, this most bitter reality.

Thus, as is too frequently the case, individuals were injured, their souls irreparably scared as national policies played out. The chess match between competing superpowers attempting Iranian containment or countering it set in motion countless miniature choreographies for individuals who suffered or were adversely impacted by such titanic national aspirations and goals. Ehsan, for all of his considerable intellect, seethed with hatred for almost everything American. The bitter truth for him, beyond the anger and sorrow over the loss of his brother, was the incipient jealousy for the opportunities available to individual Americans and that they were in large part limiting his future options by their national and global strategies against his nation. In speaking with elder family members and those of his Iranian community who had traveled to the United States—and there were many during the era of the Shah—the stories of near infinite bounty were as dreams. And in the Iran that he inhabited during the 1980s and beyond, the excesses of the "throw-away" culture enjoyed by the Americans simply could not be intellectually or emotionally endured.

And thus, when Iran's intelligence assets confirmed that a single American woman working as a genuine volunteer to assist and care for victims of the Syrian conflict was unguarded and often straying into dangerous geography, he put forth a recommendation: take her.

What almost uniformly characterizes bureaucracies, or any large multilayered organization, is a paucity of dynamic, fluid and efficient interagency communication, and response. Systems representing all governments become tessellated structures of matching overlapping redundancy, unable to react, and through time a near-functional ossification sets in. Whether considering Langley, Yasenevo raion, Moscow, or Haidian District, Beijing, all share this most common pernicious variable. And thus, a most common bias regarding senior intel leadership in Tehran was that the rise of ISIS during the Obama administration was a unique common enemy for both Washington and Tehran, caused in part by Obama's own decision to abandon any calibrated withdrawal, opting for rapid near desertion of its previous tactical and geostrategic gains in Iraq. The result was as foreseeable as it was catastrophic, and ISIS was only one of the elements caused by this ill-planned departure planned by what conflated to a feckless American administration consumed with domestic political expediency rather than genuine international stewardship.

The Iranians, who nearly exclusively represent the Shia form of Islam, were thought to uniformly despise ISIS and their Sunni-Wahhabi ideological branch of Islam. For the young clerics on each side of the philosophical divide, emotive arguments learned early in their lives reinforced the inherent valueless status of the other: they were apostate. Beginning in mosques followed by training in tafsir (Quranic exegesis) and then fiqh (Islamic jurisprudence), the best and brightest minds were subjected to a uniform message that manifested as hostility in strident sermons, monitored and approved by authorities and routinely washed over young minds not ready, able, or willing to discriminate among their often flimsy rhetorical foundations. Each side within this Islamic divide despised the other; nuanced interpretive religious doctrine had spawned unspeakable cruelty. The hardened Iranian clerics who shared power among the ultrabyzantine Tehran-based court of like-minded ossified men would not consider the theological validity of ISIS. But they, too, demanded butchery of innocents—Allah's purpose must be served.

But intellectually more nimble Iranians dared to examine the unforgiving topography of churning geopolitical fluidity within the Levant, or the more expansive Fertile Crescent. This included, among the earliest sites of formative human behavior, the "land between two rivers," what the Greeks called Mesopotamia. This land has a remarkably rich history. And while the ancients might have rolled their eyes at the continuous barbarism encompassed by ISIS, more likely they would have understood and sought advantage; violence within the species seemed to be an integral element, but how to harness it was difficult. And so, perhaps in the same fashion as his relatives living three thousand years ago, Ehsan explored potential uses of the ISIS butchers. Deriving a novel and markedly different examination of the "opportunities" possible in comparison to mainstream Iranian imprimatur dismissal of any value, he sought a manipulative advantage. But in doing so, as opposed to his religious colleagues and even some of his true childhood friends, Ehsan's views were almost identical in mindset to a very select group of senior members of Iran's intelligence community. Predictably, as he put forth a well-written ultrasecret proposal to his immediate supervisors, very senior upper-echelon Iranian leadership immediately responded. Ehsan's proposal was as straightforward as it was deceptively candid. He wanted to foster encouragement to al Al Hassan Abbas and his ragtag group of sadistic criminals to kidnap this American woman who was a volunteer in assisting those decimated by the Syrian civil war. Any willingness by Tehran to assist al Al Hassan Abbas would be noted by ISIS, and yet it provided the plausible deniability of using proxies, a strategy so coveted by Tehran.

And eerily similar to events surrounding his deceased older brother, the plan brought almost immediate favorable attention to Ehsan. He was soon asked to attend more senior-level strategy sessions, and sitting among these vicious older puppet masters of the Iranian populace, Ehsan's intellectual gravitas as well as loyalty was probed. These elder survivors of Iran's new power elite recognized a unique talent in the young man, for Ehsan was able to combine the astute observations of the many but offer the seminal distillations of a precious few. That combination of rapid assimilation of data linked to insights unmasked an intangible mixture of novelty and creativity that captured the enthusiasm of Tehran's suspicious religious leaders. But all saw within this young man a naked truth that in many ways comforted these cynical soulless religious zealots.

In him, they saw what Ehsan's family knew—that there is nothing more toxic than the illicit brew of jealousy mixed with tragic loss. It will devour a soul as certainly as the shark, an apex predator, responds to blood in water. It will corrupt even the most logical and capacious of minds. Ehsan's longing for the daily bountiful opportunities misting so many Americans coupled with the unfathomable loss of his elder sibling created a festering necrotic wound within his young being. Destiny was to witness its pernicious impact on Ehsan and his view of America. It was to influence every one of his actions regarding the "beacon of freedom" for the remainder of his life.

Chapter 11

"Let us render justice."

Zero-Hour

Roth and Virginia took slightly different paths back to the ready room, walking along separate gravel paths. Each deliberately headed back to the common destination wherein confirmation of final operations was completed and, if necessary, amended. Hayes, their commander, insisted on a last final session wherein strategy, mission objectives, and resource utilization could be reviewed quickly within the context that "this was it"—these were the final preparations. But this was different, and everyone knew it. Members were now gathered to finalize the preparations for immediate mission activation. There would be no more meetings to operationally plan and argue about methodology, resources, or practicalities. Perhaps the next time they gathered, it would be for a debriefing with several of the team members absent, having been killed or seriously injured.

As time before the mission rapidly dissipated, the emotions became more focused. Senses sharpened as the moment of activation became nearer. In such intervals preceding each mission, those countdown minutes immediately before, anticipation grew with time seeming to slow for the selected participants. Sunlight was brighter, the gentle desert breeze was more apparent, and the arid land's fragrance, while subtle, was nonetheless somehow more embracing. These were professional combatants, with many of the team having partaken in multiple missions. And because of this, all knew that they were involved in an inherently dangerous profession. Some might not return. It was conceivable that many, even all, might perish. Operation Red Wings had lost multiple SEALs along with an entire crew of a Chinook helicopter. One simply could not accurately predict the outcome of events once combat began.

But each member felt grounded in the "normality" of these emotionally tightening responses within their conscious and subconscious realms. They understood this growing readiness. Yet, there was a perceptible disparity noted for many that distinguished this mission, especially for those who knew the real reason for this activity.

A young American woman had been kidnapped and brutalized before being executed, murdered, eliminated. Now, the score was to be settled, and the individual responsible was to be wiped from the living. Roth felt it, as did Stan, Broderick, and Virginia. And this significance had consequential forms of preparation in several of them.

Roth's mind wandered over the ironies of finding such love within the context of special operations for their nation and the justice that had finally been deemed appropriate. He had watched Virginia's measured but deep fury surfacing as she spoke of the imagined horror of the parents of Catherine finding out that she was the captive of al Al Hassan Abbas. Their helpless frustration with the knowledge that she had been raped, perhaps repeatedly, by this "devout" Muslim. Virginia was willing to die to bring justice for this young woman; she was willing to sacrifice all of her tomorrows so that this woman's soul would be able to rest. A woman who

Virginia didn't know personally but had connected with emotionally as a survivor of life's bitter challenges, even catastrophic defeats. Virginia Mahoney was going to perform her duty and end the individual's life who had so harmed and deflowered this woman, this young aid worker.

Her forehead wrinkled and her speech tightened sitting with Roth and Stan in the makeshift cafeteria in the Syrian Desert as Roth suggested, "Finally, under the current president, unlike the former, efforts are going to be conclusive for eliminating al Al Hassan Abbas."

Roth softened his semi-editorial comment by injecting that Obama's efforts—or lack thereof—while suspect were perhaps also understandable. "Obama never had the intelligence, the assets to find this excuse for a man," Roth cautiously intoned.

Virginia's eyes narrowed.

"Bullshit" was her retort.

Roth and Stan both showed genuine surprise at her emphatic definitive termination of any empathy toward the ex-president.

"He is the ultimate legacy man." She nearly spat the words.

Looking directly into Roth's eyes, her penetrating gaze left little quarter as to the intensity of her statement. As her gaze shifted toward Stan, she shook her head back and forth, registering disgust, and stated, "His is a frustratingly typical persona of the times. But I am afraid he represents the near timeless repetitive desire embedded deeply within our species justifying self-importance, if not grandeur. Kings put their faces on coinage, erect statues, and hang paintings of themselves in their respective public arenas. Present-day politicians worry more about their so-called place in history and some, identical to this man, attempt to bend the narrative to his self-perceived equal stature among the greats of history. It's actually pathetic when viewed from the peanut gallery so commonplace in the spectrum of personalities. These politicians are so predictable as to be almost frightening in their simplicity. It's almost as though anyone with any shred of decency and humility cannot conceive of becoming president, and thus the field is left for the vain, the narcissists, and those so self-absorbed as to be nearly delusional. I have literally made myself nauseous thinking about it."

"Whoa . . . that's quite a judgment you are entering, Counselor," countered Roth.

Roth had decided to enter the ensuing discussion, believing it to be one of the few times that he might unmask Virginia's lack of maturity toward real-world events, pressures, and conflicting perspectives.

He was wrong.

Her methodological narrative was pure logic, her tone one used in courtrooms across the nation, if not the world, when the legal representative has nailed the other side to the wall. It was emotionless, specific, and devastating.

She rubbed each of her temples, just touching her hairline, with the thumb and opposing fingers of her right hand. She began softly but was careful to enunciate each word clearly.

"So, let's begin with a man who revealed his true nature when awarded the Nobel Peace Prize days into his presidency. Let us not forget that he was being awarded this as a stinging rebuke of George W. Bush by the global elites. Men of honor, maturity, or class who are following another into perhaps the most challenging 'job,' if you can call it that, of the presidency of the United States might hesitate to partake in such a poorly concealed tattooing of his predecessor.

"But not one Barak Hussein Obama. Men of stature and maturity do not need labels assigned or awarded them by others to gauge the value of their contributions. Because as history so often reveals, time and time alone must pass before the true value of one's actions can be assessed. It is seldom in the hot cauldron of real-time events that actions of leaders or leadership can be objectively or optimally evaluated. I will admit that it is tempting to enjoy the warm glow of approval as well as being awarded trinkets for your decisions by those who feel similar. But it is comparable to fame—it seldom lasts and vanishes as does the early morning mist over farmland.

"Mr. Barack revealed an early tell as to his personality and his true nature in accepting this meaningless statement of disapproval toward W. Many in Washington immediately realized that this young man was neither wise to realpolitik nor to the complexity of the issues, probably because he was unable to look away from his own remarkable image in the mirror. I, for one, think it was both!"

Roth was near speechless at the degree of hostility contained in Virginia's rather prescient summary of Obama's level of near self-adulation. He, too, had long felt that this "transformative" politician was average but for the color of his skin. Roth had considered with absolute sincerity that given the color of his skin, even his being average in accomplishment while in office did, in fact, make him noteworthy for his electoral achievement. But then, once an athlete enters the field of play, it is productivity that counts, not the fact that one is from a broken home or has overcome personal demons or has an injury. Substantive value taken in real time but measured within the lineage of history's scales is all that will remain. The rest will be forgotten.

And this same skin pigmentation was used by both his allies and the man himself to deflect nearly any reasonable criticism of his performance. It was not even that he responded with the word or the specific retort of "racism." No, it was that he used the same coded references to the fact that much of America couldn't deal with the fact that he was black. In this, Roth himself found Obama's near reflexive use of the melanin in his skin as a shield for all reasonable criticism appalling. Even reasonable debate regarding his policies was shrouded in the sticky mist of being judged as intolerant of his color, to be labeled a bigot.

Unfortunately, but predictably, the reliance on this cynical utilization of the racism card, this time-proven wedge of identity political divisiveness, yielded a rather bitter harvest for the man and his movement. Middle America, a bastion of support for him—the same people who felt privileged, if not obligated, to provide the opportunity to this man of color—abandoned him. These were the same hardworking individuals, many of Caucasian European, Hispanic, or Oriental ethnicity, who had embraced his lofty rhetoric. But as they came to disagree with his sweeping progressive agenda, a dispute over policy, they who wanted or desired a more gradual change at a slower pace found their views were dismissed. But beyond dismissal, their views and their very persons were labeled ignorant, racist, and bound to an ignoble past that included slavery and codification of a system founded upon inequality.

The foreseeable outcome was that Obama lost these individuals who had once looked upon him as a great source of unification that they themselves felt was long overdue. Roth himself would never forgive Obama, not because of his policies or his view of the future but because of his intolerance to anyone who disagreed with him. In effect, Roth admitted to himself that he was angry with Obama because the leader had squandered the immense opportunity that had been provided him, that he himself had helped create. That he could have been a force of unification within the United States unlike anyone previously. And instead, he would be remembered by many later in history as a divisive, hyperpolarizing political figure.

But what shocked Roth regarding Virginia's near visceral anger was that it unmasked within him similar emotions that had been entombed. He realized that his concerns were similar, if not identical.

Roth then asked a simple question.

"Do you feel he betrayed you personally?"

She had looked directly at Roth and then out over his left shoulder. "I don't know, Jacob, perhaps. But the man is entitled to his beliefs. It's just that I get tired of his lecturing widows of slain police officers during their memorial services about the need for social justice. His proclivity for being amazingly blind to this total impropriety of these, his actions. A man of nearly singular oratory skill for his generation." She slowly shook her head, almost again registering her difficulty in believing it actually happened. "It was if he was blinkered to the impact of his message, and it was a vile message to these grieving widows."

Roth, too, had witnessed portions of these same memorial services and sat openmouthed and shocked at the near indecency of Obama's comments. Knowing that the president could have shared his views on social justice at any other time and the press would have printed every word, but to do so during the grieving process for five families was indecent. It was at this point that Roth knew Obama was unable to exercise mature judgment. The level of emerging narcissism was frightening.

Rather more gently than was required, Roth stated, "Well, you do understand why he received more than 95 percent of the African American vote, don't you?"

"Yes, Jacob, I do. They were entitled to celebrate his meteoric rise and felt privileged to have him assume the highest office in the land. But there is that little thing called 'performance' that inconveniently gets in the way."

And it was at this moment that Roth knew the underpinnings of Virginia's emotional upheaval within this discussion. At least in part.

Virginia was reflecting a parallel emotional state, torn over her role in special operations and whether she would be celebrated as a woman or as a soldier who performed her duty and operational necessities appropriately. Roth knew she wanted the latter.

"Jacob, let's not condemn the man. For all of his faults or perceived shortcomings, his replacement has not by any means been an improvement."

"Sort of the other side of the same coin." Now it was Stan who spoke.

Before Roth could comment, they were interrupted by a young-looking blond, Navy Lt. Commander Mark Gardner. He walked from the sandbag-reinforced doors the short distance to the table occupied by Stan, Virginia, and Roth. All three stood, and Roth saluted as the lieutenant commander smiled tiredly and looked to his side to find a chair. Having found one quickly within reach, he pulled it up and sat down, looking at the file in his hands before suddenly looking back up and motioning for the others to sit with him.

"Sorry to interrupt, folks," Gardner wearily stated. "I have some recent satellite imagery that I was asked to discuss, as Command has inferred that these photos may scrub the mission."

Immediately, Roth tensed as Virginia looked up sharply, her eyes boring into the superior officer.

Gardner laid out three highly classified photos that had been securely digitally transmitted from Middle East Command (CENTCOM) at MacDill AFB in Tampa, Florida, and then reconstructed with classified software. The images had originally been procured from the National Geospatial-Intelligence Agency, the eastern campus located at Ft. Belvoir North Area in Spring Field, Virginia. Appreciated as NGA East, this center happened to be one of the lesser-known monstrosities occupying 2.3 million square feet of office space and facilities, thus being the third largest government building in the Washington, DC, metropolitan area after the Pentagon and the Ronald Reagan Building.

The images were of such remarkable clarity, it had been a long-running joke that pictures from these satellites enabled one to read the headlines of the old Soviet Pravda newspaper being held by Russian citizens in Red Square in Moscow. While actually true, that was in the 1980s, and subsequent clans composed of the scraggly bearded technogeeks that America grew almost as quickly as crabgrass had assiduously upgraded such imagery to nearly unimaginable levels. These refined images had been securely transmitted as an apparent stream of random numbers and keystrokes. Again, such cybersecure transmissions was facilitated by these same odd technology-loving individuals—they who established a deeper love for a flat backlit screen with an attached keyboard than they would ever experience for another human being, including the woman who birthed them.

But it was certain details within these sharp images that gave the people at the table pause. The first photo was an ultracrisp standard black-and-white picture taken near dusk, as revealed by the angulation of sunlight, which incidentally allowed the technicians back at Ft. Belvoir to judge the height of the wall. Further, a figure carrying a Kalashnikov was positioned in the middle of a small but demarcated path running along the border of the wall. But it was the ground immediately bordering this pathway that provided these same technical experts their time-sensitive opportunity.

The next image that the lieutenant commander laid out for Roth and his team was the infrared image using the exact same angle and moment in time. Now, the team could see the heat signature of the figure—a warm living object, the bright left hand draped over the relatively cooler barrel of the automatic weapon. But immediately adjacent to his left shoulder, furthest from the wall, were a series of rounded dark spherical structures spread over the soil. Of interest was the simultaneous black-and-white photo that showed a barren surface of this same patch of soil, empty rock and gravel unoccupied by any physical objects.

The team wholly recognized the differential cooling of the soil and metal canisters that had been buried just under the surface topography of the desert: antipersonnel devices commonly known as land mines. What caused this obvious change in appearance between the two types of photos, one infrared and one regular light-based, were these mines. As if buried tennis balls were creating an uneven quiltlike spicular appearance in the infrared photo, the metal canisters were cooling after being warmed by the day's sun at a differential rate than the soil surrounding them. Undetectable to the naked eye, but Virginia's previous request that drones with infrared technology scout the surroundings had indeed first hinted at these troublemakers. Then the folks at Ft. Belvoir had used the billion-dollar cameras up in space to detail their precise locations.

Gardner looked at each of the team members arrayed in front of him and quietly exhaled before beginning to speak. "So, they are concerned that we could be walking into a bear trap that could get the team killed and result in mission failure. They are considering cancelling the use of your team and simply sending cruise missiles in to demolish the site."

At this point, it was Virginia who spoke up. "So as did Clinton, who uselessly fired some cruise missiles at remote sites in the desert after the bombings of our embassies in Kenya and Tanzania. Bombings which killed two hundred and twenty-four people, twelve Americans among them, and injured over four thousand others. The sites in the desert were supposedly Al-Qaeda basecamps, but were later found to be nearly deserted."

Gardner never looked away. Without emotion, he nodded his head and said, "Yes."

Now Roth spoke. "Perhaps it might be important to underscore to Command that besides actionable intelligence that might be found and invaluable, there might be hostages still present that would be sacrificed in that approach. Every individual on the team understands the risks, and we are ready to go. We are ready NOW."

Gardner smiled. He looked thoughtfully into the eyes of Stan as the grandson of a pure warrior spoke. "Good. I'll recommend we move; we have timely material that will be obsolete in eight hours. I will ask forgiveness for the launching rather than permission. These risk-adverse administrators are going to get cold feet and scrub this if we don't get a move on. They may shit-can me later, but it's time we ended this ISIS guy."

Roth nodded toward his trusted superior and said evenly, "It's only a career, and it's time we brought this prick to justice."

Gardner's smile was restrained and ephemeral. "Good luck, folks. We go . . ." He looked at his watch. "Jacob?"

Roth's response was declarative. "In eighty-seven minutes."

Thirty minutes before boarding the helicopters, Virginia sat with her team members, intently listening and ticking through each section of the final briefing. She was asked two questions since she was at the very tip of the spear and without emotion adroitly addressed each of them, revealing both a depth of comprehension and perhaps even foresight as to what possible scenarios her teammates might encounter. This mission would require their helicopters to land some short but significant distance from the compound supposedly housing al Al Hassan Abbas. The team would have to advance on foot for a short but open distance, different than landing directly in the compound, as was the situation in finding and eliminating bin Laden.

The reasons were twofold. First, aerial photos—initially from satellites, then drones, and then direct visual inspection by a covert scout team—showed that the innermost courtyard and open areas adjacent to the house would not safely allow landing of a mission helicopter. And importantly, one flying machine setting down in the compound, absent expression of immediate overwhelming force, could get everyone in that chopper killed. If there were defensive personnel in place, a near certainty, according to scouts, the ability to overwhelm them required both surprise but also enough firepower to "cleanse" the area.

The other reason was that the bin Laden mission had lost a helicopter during the raid. Fortunately, there had been no casualties—at least no American ones—but there had been a rather significant and dramatic negative impact accompanying the loss of this bird. Apparently, the pilot had grazed the cinderblock perimeter wall surrounding the compound upon approach, causing a hard landing inside of the perimeter. These were not ordinary pilots, but were among the very best America's military could offer. They were composed of both navy and army personnel from the famous 160th Special Operations Aviation Regiment, or SOAR. They were fearless and incredibly talented, but on this night, one of the helicopters crashed.

The highly modified MH-60 Blackhawk was then unflyable and had to be destroyed. This was the destruction of a multimillion-dollar secret stealth helicopter, but more importantly, the remaining or residual material that was left intact revealed important and potentially critical technical developments that had enabled this functional stealth helicopter. The remaining material, highly classified, included a cloth- or fiber-woven coating of the body of the Blackhawk, and this was stripped from the machine along with disc-fiber coverings over the tail rotor that made the machine invisible to radar. But beyond the markedly absent radar signature of the copter was the acoustic-baffling functionality of this disc covering the tail rotor that remarkably reduced ambient noise associated with the actual operation of the MH-60. This had allowed the team to come in fast and land directly in the compound. Senior officials were certain that these valuable remnants had been sent to China, as it was understood they were engaged in developing a completely stealth component to their offensive air operational capabilities.

The upshot of this unpublicized disaster was that the American technological edge had been partially erased and senior military leadership was now balancing the need for troops to approach silently against the potential of losing another, perhaps more intact, version of this advanced weaponry. But Virginia was focused only on the fact that they would have several hundred yards to cross, some out in the open without protective cover, as they approached al Al Hassan Abbas's compound. She would be in the lead on one of the three columns, a distinct honor voted on by her teammates and endorsed by Roth and Hayes. She had no intention of being killed, but rather death than failure in performance of her mission.

At the end of this direct and quite abrupt final briefing, Virginia rose to leave, intending to make a direct line to her barracks to check her gear, her weapons, and perhaps take a potential last look at her room. She thought that perhaps a prayer was to be offered asking that she do her duty well, whatever the outcome.

Four minutes later, Stan, exiting their cramped two-bed barracks room with Broderick, asked his friend if there was anything that could have been forgotten that might be important. Both had also been at the meeting and were heading to the flight line.

"Brod, can you think of anything, anything at all we forgot or overlooked?"

Silent for several moments, Broderick looked up. In front of Stan, his closest friend said, almost whispered, "We forgot to pray."

Stan nodded to his buddy. He then stood, facing Broderick, and slowly lowered himself until his two knees touched the ground. His hands found each other and as his fingers interlaced, he bowed his head in supplication and began a quiet prayer.

"Dear Lord, it is difficult to ask you to endorse the killing of other members of your flock, for each soul who has entered this life is a reflection of your sacred blessing upon us. But I am asking this now, to bless the men and perhaps the single woman who will embark upon this quest to right the scales of decency."

Broderick, sitting and facing his kneeling friend, had initially tensed, but understanding that he was witness to a moment of unguarded, naked privacy, he, too, lowered to his knees.

Broderick Pickney felt the moment, one so sacred that his eyes immediately misted as his head bowed forward. His ears heard the soft but clear articulations from his friend as though it were life's blood carrying meaning and grace. He strained to maintain a semblance of normal composure, as his legs felt funny and his chest suddenly seemed heavy. He knew he was privileged to hear one of the most personal, most intimate acts—that of a prayer being offered, and of one of his closest friends delivering the supplication, asking God for assistance.

"I ask, Lord, that if any of us are not to return that you take me, and me alone. All I ask—and it is a big request, but please—I ask only that I perform my duty and my responsibilities satisfactorily so that my teammates survive and justice for Catherine Morgan is provided. I thank you,

Lord. In the name of the Father, the Son, and the Holly Spirit. Amen."

Stan raised his head, hands still together, palms touching each other, and looked at Broderick. His friend was motionless, his fixed gaze now was staring at him. Both barely were breathing.

Broderick Luther Pickney's eyes were wide. A single tear slipped from his left eye and rolled down his cheek, gently dripping onto his desert-camouflage fatigues. The native South Carolinian slowly but deliberately stood, and still staring at Stan, not four feet from him, Broderick Luther Pickney rendered a salute to his closest friend. A gesture that delivered an unfathomable love between brothers, absent physical passion but with unending, almost infinite poignancy. Pickney stood for a full ten seconds, and Stan's eyes watered slightly. Then Broderick brought his right arm down and an understated smile formed before he exited the room, gently pulling the door closed to their shared quarters. Stan followed, as both were moving purposefully to the helicopters.

For Virginia, she wanted Roth to hold her for just a few seconds and reassure her that she would do her duty, that she would not fail to support her teammates, and that whether she returned or not, she would have been judged satisfactory for the mission. And thus, exiting her room after checking and rechecking her gear now for the twentieth time, she saw Roth moving deliberately toward the debark zone. Virginia approached Roth and he slowed, taking in her face. Her features were serious, her movement deliberate. She asked directly, "Lt. Roth, a word, please?"

Roth slowed even more, his eyes never leaving her, and nodded slightly. Her use of his formal rank and the tone of her request reassured him. She was readying herself for the mission; there would not be any excuse for deviation, and he knew she would never allow any. But though he was prepared to respond to whatever her request might be, he wondered if she felt that her presence somehow might compromise the mission. He knew this was not a realistic concern, but he understood her potential need to raise the subject.

But instead she stated, "I just want reassurance, as much as someone can reasonably provide, that you feel our team is prepared for this mission."

Roth nodded, immediately understanding that every soldier entering combat for the first time worried more about failure to complete their assigned tasks than the likelihood of being killed or injured. It was not that they ever truly ignored or overlooked their potential intimate future, just that they prioritized their tasks as their preeminent focus. All else was secondary. She was asking not really for her welfare, but to ensure that she had not overlooked some critical problem in her preparation that would impact her other team members. Roth read this concern as it surfaced within those pools of thoughtful reflection, her penetrating stare expressing hope that she had done her utmost to ensure success.

"I have been on fourteen of these missions, Petty Officer Mahoney. Our team is as ready now as I have ever experienced." And then he added what he knew she yearned for. "You are ready, Virginia."

It was not gratitude on her face, or even respectful appreciation, but relief paired with her own knowing confirmation. "Thank you."

It was not an embrace or a last kiss, but it would have to do. She saluted him and moved rapidly toward the embarkation zone.

Four helicopters were positioned within an area surrounded by barbed wire, heavily guarded by US security personnel armed with automatic weapons and ordered to kill anyone not authorized to enter the area. There could be no arguments or discussions at the entrance point with any individual who had not been formally authorized, previously cleared, and now recognized by these guards. They could very well kill a three-star general if he or she had the hubris to think they could approach the area without the proper preclearance processing. Excuses for failing to follow this binary decision tree—recognize authorized individual, process them for potential entry; no recognition upon approach, kill them—were not tolerated. Even the humane gesture by one of the guards, attempting to redirect someone approaching the area, could and had resulted in the guard being reprimanded and sent home. Signs were posted clearly, in English, French, Arabic, Kurdish, and even Persian as to the complete intolerance and deadly consequences for any perceived violation involving this highly secure aircraft area.

Two Sikorsky Black Hawks had their tail rotors rotating. The rotors were partially hidden behind a metal disc, almost a smooth symmetrical woklike structure. But it was not just the shape forming a type of hubcap over the backend or tail rotor that was novel; it was also the fiber-ceramic composition of this rotor shield that was both new and highly classified. Both Sikorskys also had their composition ceramic-metal alloy sliding side doors open, each with a helmeted armed crewmember crouched in the doorway, one on bended knee, the other sitting on the nylon seat.

A cursory glance would have suggested that these MH-60 helicopters were without exposed side guns or evidence of weaponry, but that would be incorrect. Fifty-caliber air-cooled machine guns could be rotated from their internal cabin position, rendering them fixed or mobile on metal-jointed pylons, making the Sikorsky a lethal killing machine. Further, depending upon the mission, the MH-60 could undergo a variety of significant weapons configurations to be an advanced attack helicopter. The birds sitting in front of Roth as he approached and returned the salute to the guards were highly modified ultrasecret stealth variants of the Sikorsky MH-60 used in the bin Laden mission.

In the ensuing years, technology had continually advanced, but they were still similar to the machines used that night in Abbottabad. Major changes were not in basic structure, but in the protective coating of the aircraft that had continually been improved to reduce the electronic signature and dampen the acoustic profile of these birds. The result was an almost absent characteristic decibel profile presented to the human ear for these flying metal machines. Someone had casually suggested that a neighbor's lawnmower made more noise than these seven-ton-plus lethal flying machines. An unknowingly prescient observation.

Roth moved closer to the ranking guard and asked, "We ready here?"

"Yes, sir."

"You have been briefed?"

"Of course, sir, thirty-seven minutes ago." The senior sergeant was suddenly worried that he sounded insubordinate, as he had aggressively confirmed Roth's apparent demand, but Roth was already moving on to his concerns.

"Ok, I need no breach of our security as we ready this—none. Any issues, any problems, anybody who looks out of place, get rid of them. Correct?" Roth's tone was uncharacteristically hard, uncompromising, and direct. It was obvious to the senior master sergeant that Roth was under pre-engagement stress. Nerves were becoming taught, emanating his own harmonic signature.

"Yes, sir." The man saluted his superior.

Outside of the seconds before engagement with hostile forces, those last precious few moments before chaos began —this timeframe was the most trying on soldiers. It didn't matter if they were veterans, such as Roth, or rookies to combat, such as Virginia. All felt the steady acceleration of heightened senses, the clarity of purpose and hair-trigger responsiveness.

Their hastening readiness mirrored sand cascading through the hourglass, individual granules picking up speed as the narrow waist approached. The funneled tapering passage accelerating each grain as it hurtled toward the oblivion of being buried with its neighbors. Each member of the team felt the pull toward an unknown outcome, the slow but perceptible quickening of their life while paradoxically each second seemed longer, each minute slowed.

Roth knew that he had an additional four MH-60s coming from Al-Tanf and that the operational format would be to land his four Sikorskys first, then these additional four would be positioned to be onsite outside of al Al Hassan Abbas's compound one minute after his team landed. Together, a force being carried by eight helicopters, almost forty-five highly trained and lethal special operations personnel, would certainly provide overwhelming force. One perhaps not-so-minor footnote is that for the first time, one of these special operations individuals would be an active-duty American female. But this was for the press to glorify, if they would indeed ever have knowledge of it.

Lastly, two additional large Chinooks, each with twenty-two SEALs, would be behind Roth's initial assault team, coming from Al-Asad just in case additional personnel were required or there were other problems. Roth's current base location was closer to the designated target, but each helicopter had challenges negotiating air space crossing though sectors controlled by Russians, their allies, or the still active remnants of ISIS.

Roth carefully reflected on their destination. al Al Hassan Abbas's walled-in structure was on the outskirts of Barisha, Idlib Governorate, Syria. The walls were nine feet high and adjacent to the living quarters, within the walled-in protected area, was a clear zone that satellite imagery noted had be occupied by a truck or some other vehicle during different sweeps of the "eye in the sky." This area was also so small that the military's best covert or special operation pilots, the night stalkers, had repeatedly voiced hesitation on their ability to land within the compound. And with knowledge of what happened in the bin Laden raid, planners had eliminated this now foreseeable potential issue of crashing a MH-60 and decided to land the teams 500–700 yards away.

But this also meant that the advancement toward al Al Hassan Abbas's compound would traverse open areas with variable numbers of trees and shrubs to provide minimal cover for the troops. This exposure would place them in imminent danger, but if done swiftly and under the cover of darkness, the risk would be acceptable, but not negligible. Further, the use of drones equipped with infrared and thermal sensors would provide real-time updates on any unfriendlies in the area, including the use of dogs employed by the ISIS commander.

Their Kurdish allies had warned that even the goats, seemingly wild and wandering randomly in the orchards feeding on the grass, wore sleeves or cloth-fitted saddles as mid-body coverings packed with explosives, nails, and bolts. Suicide vests for God's creatures, detonated by phone. Along with traditional mines, dead or alive, these goats represented a very real threat to ground troops.

Roth had smiled quietly when a young-looking freckled, red-haired, and green-eyed technical expert stationed in Germany had been flown into their remote desert base days before the go date. The twenty-something youngster had provided them with metal shaving-cream-sized canisters and jars of material thick as jelly, seriously instructing them not to open or break the seals. At the requisite briefing, this expert had discussed that both types of containers housed "male wolf scent." Almost everyone sitting in the tightly cramped operational briefing room, weapons casually slung over shoulders, standing upright against their legs, or between them, had nearly exploded in laughter. Virginia had wrinkled her nose while Roth was quiet with a seemingly knowing smile.

Finally, George, a young Navy SEAL team member, said, "You are joking, right? Not only are we going into combat, perhaps to get offed, but now we're going to have every female bitch wolf trying to show us their hairy hindquarters!"

Spontaneous laughter erupted, along with shouting. This was followed by a strange sucking sound as nearly a dozen lips contemporaneously formed a circular shape and pulled in air, along with groups of eyes transiently widening. The eyes and auditory responses were registering the expected latent reaction of their single female teammate being present in the room. At no time in the history of special operations imminent mission preparedness had this been the case. This was followed by a hushed silence with all eyes immediately finding Virginia, but she was already laughing, and her raised right hand immediately waved off any concern over gender sensitivity. The place again erupted in laughter and hoots.

George stood and, looking at Virginia, managed with at least a trace of honest humility and sincerity, "Sorry, ma'am, I didn't mean any disrespect."

Virginia, still smiling, said, "You call me 'ma'am' again and I will kick your young ass. I am not that old! And by the way"—she turned back to the stunned red-haired technical wizard—"if this is male lupine scent, does that make me into a fucking lesbian?"

The chaos that ensued was enough to bring tears of laughter to nearly half the tightly bound group, and Virginia was leading in the hilarity. She had crossed the threshold beyond acceptance. She had become a valued member.

Roth just gently shook his head, immensely proud of his newly found love and thinking that his team was becoming one family.

That had been five days ago. Now, the humor of the group had been replaced by anticipation and readiness.

As Virginia boarded the Sikorsky, the whirling blades created a downward thudding push of air similar to a giant fan. She said a silent prayer that she would not fail in her duty; her own safety was secondary to this request. Roth was in the lead Sikorsky, clipping the communications gear into his helmet so that he could talk with the pilot.

Suddenly her feet were more firmly planted on the machine's metal floor and her bent legs had to counteract the force of it grabbing air identical to a boat's propeller as it cuts through water. They were moving upward, climbing fast, and hurtling toward their collective destiny. They were, in Virginia's eyes, God's avenging angles delivering His final judgment against a brutal tyrant. Her thoughts briefly wandered as she saw the lights of the crowded LZ begin to shrink, their altitude growing.

Roth, too, reflected on the wonderful remarkable irony of flying off into conflict while the scent of his woman's lavender had yet to fade. He was in love, and he had trouble processing this irony. He, too, thought of the rendering of justice for a human being who had put herself at risk to assist others and then was taken and brutalized for her efforts. He found that the human species was capable of the most subtle forms of tenderness mixed with unfathomable cruelty. He hoped that his actions, his personal conduct, would be seen as justice in the eyes of God. Yet he felt an almost unnerving clarity that perhaps he was to pay a special tax in affording righteousness. But he had no choice. Whatever the price, outside of cowardice, he was willing to pay. For he, Jacob Noah Roth, comparable to so many others who had walked these same roads within the world of armed conflict, those who had sought to bring justice for the vulnerable, knew that evil had to be met with force. And that this force was often of the same violent form that had initiated the harm, the hurt, and the destruction. But evil and the tyrants who espoused it would face an unremitting force to hold them accountable for the misery they propagated.

Roth shook his head ever so slightly as he gripped the nylon safety belt, looking out over the now darkened landscape of the Syrian Desert. Would the taking of human lives by him really represent any fundamental difference than what al Al Hassan Abbas's disturbed vision held? Roth hoped so, but he was not naïve.

In the realm of perfidious activity manifest throughout history, Roth understood that there were numerous examples of autocrats who were responsible for untold suffering and the deaths of innocents. He considered the twentieth century and its enhancement in technology, the mechanization of killing that harvested such cruelty on countless souls across the globe. But Jacob knew it was sophomoric to believe that such enormity in depravity was confined to the most recent century. The Napoleonic wars, the American Civil War, the Roman legions, or the barbaric early European tribes were all among the almost countless examples preceding the modernization of war. The legacy of Japanese, Chinese, or South American tribal peoples reflected a similar capacity for taking life on an increasingly grand scale. But such historic episodes perhaps paled in comparison to modern technology, simply because the efficiency of modern weapons produced a much more prolific and perhaps appalling outcome.

Roth understood this only too well, but in discussions with Virginia over coffee, he had explored her perspective that it was not only the "tyrants" who were responsible for such calamitous activity. He was surprised by her nuanced narrative and thoughtful perspective regarding his questions and hypothesis on the darker impulses of their species. They had shared such illuminating discussions as they sipped awful coffee from Styrofoam cups in the open mess. As she held a half-full cup, she had shared her views that often-elected self-declared righteous leaders "enjoyed" outcomes that were remarkably similar. She had mentioned Lincoln and the catastrophic losses of life and property to both sides along with Roosevelt, who had overseen what history viewed as a "just war."

Yet she also reminded Roth that American and British bombers had let loose an aerial carpet-bombing campaign on Dresden over several nights in February 1945 that resulted in over twenty-five thousand civilian deaths. Some at the time had estimated that the number was nearer ninety thousand killed, and the overwhelming majority civilians. Post-bombing aerial reconnaissance photos so shocked Winston Churchill days after the attack that he began to rethink the results of an Allied bombing strategy that tore at the very fabric of civilization, a strategy that could soil any satisfaction among the victors that the war's end-game strategy was necessary or proper. The RAF and American bombers dropped so much incendiary tonnage into the city that only Dante's nightmares might somehow have envisioned the catastrophic thermal carnage that followed. The inferno caused ambient street level temperatures to skyrocket, and ground-level oxygen, the normal concentrations used for breathing, became fuel, and then the fuel was foreseeably consumed. This meant those people, pets, and other living beings attempting to ventilate their lungs could not.

The superheated air annihilated the civilian population of Dresden. Women, children, grandmothers, and toddlers were vaporized or instantly turned into cinder. Even for Nazi Germany, with its perverse reputation of inhumanity, the indiscriminate immolation of Dresden provoked a rethinking of Allied aerial efforts to win that war. Mahoney summarized with rather remarkable clarity, in Roth's eyes, that Winston Churchill in a memo sent to the Air Chief Marshal Arthur Harris, head of the RAF Bomber Command, had compared the raid to an "act of terror." So many civilian lives, including women and children who were not contributing to the war effort, were eliminated in the fires that both American and British strategic planners for the post-war landscape paused to consider the impact and implications.

The fear voiced by Churchill was that the value of harvesting the charred ruins of hollow emptiness, the blackened carbon remnants that were once human beings instead of a defeated populace, might cast doubt as to who had the moral high ground after the war. This legendary British leader was already calculating the longer-term strategic advantages of casting the Allied effort as "goodness over evil," and such indiscriminate killing could not support this perspective. Similar such future actions simply could not be justified.

Roth was mesmerized by Mahoney's trenchant, almost abrupt analytical summary. Her contemporaneous recollection of names and dates revealed her almost perfect eidetic memory. Her careful choice of words within her chronicling of events was nearly that of a university post-graduate seminar. Roth was captivated, for he loved learning and respected realpolitik in anyone, but coming from a beautiful and desirous woman was enough to threaten his iron professionalism. So much so that he found himself staring into her beautiful eyes, losing all sense of appropriate conduct or discretion. To the enlisted men and a few officers passing the table where the two were sitting, the look on Roth's face betrayed respect, but also the telltale signs of enraptured appreciation. It was a telling expression that in essence announced to anyone with a modicum of observational skills that this man was taken by this woman. And of course, he was. By the end of that discussion, Roth had known that he was in trouble, and as to what had followed . . . well, it was a simple, foreseeable outcome.

But he had also known that she shared the same reservations about killing other human beings, and that the perspective on murder or justice was often defined by a boundary on a map or the address of a family. Human beings simply could not escape their darker nature, and it was at times like these, as Roth was speeding toward the fulfillment of his mission, that he understood the enormity of his actions. That within his responsibility, minute, seemingly inconsequential twists could alter the perception between justice and mindless savagery.

Their grouping of acoustically dampened and radar-eluding helicopters, machines labeled in the popular press as "stealth helicopters," were now flying in a preset formation, using a prototype of Raytheon's covert terrain-following radar that enabled them to hide within mountain passes and valleys. This technology was still under low-rate initial production (LRIP) development by this defense supplier but had been tested and deemed suitable for the covert actions of DEVGRU Team #6. Thus, quietly yet moving rapidly through the air, this flying group of trained killers approached a man deemed appropriate for extrajudicial elimination by the beacon of freedom in the world: the United States of America.

Their target was at that very moment sipping his sweetened tea and wondering when his next visit with his favorite son would occur. This son—evoking the memory of his handsome face caused al Al Hassan Abbas to smile inwardly—was even more obsessed with security than al Al Hassan Abbas himself. Although he contemplated that being found was almost unfathomable, given that this new

American president, a man called Trump, was unlike Obama in that he was a wild card, his son had taken time to stress to his father that it was not outside of the realm of possibility that the Americans would try to capture or kill the head of ISIS. But Hudhayfah al-Badri had to agree with his father that this American with the blond hair and orangeish skin was a bit of a "balawhaird" (blowhard).

So much was being said by Trump for its effect on the world's press, but then again, this was the problem for Hudhayfah al-Badri regarding Trump—one never knew when this man was serious. Trump had told the Chinese Premier Xi Jinping, early in the President's four-year term while dessert was being served at a dinner party, that he, Trump, had just ordered missile strikes on positions in Syria during their mutual enjoyment of chocolate cake. Xi was momentarily flummoxed in that he asked the interpreter sitting slightly behind him to relay the message to him again, although it is widely known that Xi speaks fluent English. This was an attempt for Xi to gain several more moments to process what this "cowboy" was telling him—a cowboy with his finger on the world's most technologically advanced and deadly nuclear arsenal.

For anyone watching the premier's reaction, it was a telling moment. Trump had just delivered several messages to the leader of the world's most populous country and a most poignant rival of America. It had been done within the seemingly disarming caricature of a showman wanting to brag about his new toys. But watching Xi's reaction, his iron self-control riveting as his face fought for expressionless restraint, it was a moment of concern mixed with the uncomfortableness of an inability to predict. For the Chinese, this loss of foreseeability is the cultural sword of Damocles. Nothing is more unnerving to them. Trump had blundered into a rare realm of effective brinksmanship with the Chinese, but was it a blunder? The American press were typically harsh as they castigated Trump for such a sophomoric act, oblivious to the enormity of its impact on Xi.

As the helicopters sped north, hugging the terrain of the Syrian Desert, father and son were separated by nearly the entire north-south dimension of Syria.

Chapter 12

"He leadeth me in paths of righteousness, for His name's sake . . ."
—Psalm23

Virginia quickly lowered her binocular nocturnal optics, and as they locked into place on the front of her helmet, she scanned the green-shadowed surroundings of the Syrian countryside. She saw no movement. Then she was already moving toward the second preset location nestled into the base of a gently rising gravel slope nearly six feet in height. The compound would now be one hundred fifty yards in front of her, just over this last natural earthen barrier. But the space between this gravel impediment and the nine-foot walls of the compound were open, denuded of trees or shrubbery. And within these open spaces, in plain view of guards or ISIS fighters, were planted mines and wired charges fixed to scattered debris.

She knew the several selected pathways, curving or semistraight lanes free of harm that led to the wall. But she also knew that at any time in the last eighteen hours, al Al Hassan Abbas's guards and attendants could have planted new mines or moved existing armaments. She thought this latter was unlikely, given that no one wanted to be handling a primed explosive, but there was always the possibility of newer antipersonnel devices having been planted. She carefully examined the topography of the pine-green landscape, her night vision enhanced with computer-generated magnification, and saw no sign of freshly turned earth. Reassuring, but not conclusive.

Jacob was twenty-five yards to the immediate left of her, kneeling and hand-signaling to someone. The figure's profile suggested it was Stan Ostrowski. Virginia could just discern his movement, as the night was very black; the absent lunar glow had been accounted for. She found the emerald hue of the night vision optics almost ethereal, yet she could easily follow Jacob's movement. Very carefully, sliding on his belly and hugging the gentle contour of the earthen barrier, Jacob nearly slithered up to the embankment's apex. There, he began a systematic assessment using his night vision field glasses but soon switched to regular optics, as the compound's inner dwellings were irregularly outlined in high-intensity light.

As he scanned the surroundings, something caught his eye. Now Roth used the throat-hugging microphone to audibly query his colleague. Ostrowski's earpiece, securely in place, carried the metallic voice of his team leader.

"Stan, do you see that door, the recessed area in the wall? Do you see it?" Roth whispered this, but the communication was excellent, amplified and filtered within patented software designed for background noise cancelling.

Ostrowski, who was on his belly next to Roth, whispered, "Let me look," for Stan had not peeked up over the top of the earthen barrier.

Roth's interest was fixated on movement near one of the recessed steel doors in the outer wall that formed the perimeter of the compound. What made this compound different to anyone but the most casual observer were the intermittent powerful lights spaced irregularly along the top of the perimeter wall. While lights atop walls were not in themselves unique, the ability to vary the direction, so called "motion-tracking" lights to enhance illumination, certainly was. The typical lights surrounding the family dwelling compounds that populated the Syrian rural countryside resembled most farms anywhere in the world: situated at doors to barns or sheds or along pathways, as the intent was to assist the property owner when moving or working at night. This walled-in dwelling more closely resembled a citadel. The perimeter walls were thick and topped by concertina wire. And along the top of the wall, intermittently spaced sturdy steel rods supported cameras and lights that were activated and programed to automatically track movement.

This was an unheard of luxury, if not a signature of advanced technological investment for any rural lodging. Both cost and maintenance marked the residence as housing someone important, someone who didn't want to be surprised by the outside world. But the very presence of such technologically advanced hardware identified the owner as someone different. In fact, it was this excessive alignment of security-based technology that triggered a closer look by the Kurdish scouts who had originally been serendipitously in the area for other reasons.

Even a cursory examination of the dwelling's configured security raised eyebrows and elicited an in-depth examination of the compound and its occupants. The motion-tracking lighting was of exceptional quality, and each was professionally attached to miniature cameras equipped with night rendering image detection. All were directed out into the barren countryside every evening, focused on unoccupied regions away from protected curtilages of the walled-in buildings. Someone wanted to be able to see anyone approaching the house, especially at night.

Even if al Al Hassan Abbas was only in the dwelling intermittently, Kurdish fighters had communicated to the Americans that the house must contain high-value targets. They were not wrong. Relatives, wives, and even children were often left within as their paternal leader continued his random security-driven movements. Valuable data was also stored on computers within the structure—treasure for al Al Hassan Abbas's adversaries.

The challenge for the Kurds and their American allies was to identify when al Al Hassan Abbas was in residence. This became almost a game with the Kurds, whom the Americans very quickly understood to be gifted survivors within the ultrahazardous environment of Syria. Monitoring the house became a routine, and trucks and automobiles were systematically counted and studied. Did that Mercedes contain the leader, al Al Hassan Abbas? Was he naïve enough to travel within a luxury automobile? Or was the weathered small Nissan pickup with stacked canvas-covered crates in its rear bed holding more than inert equipment?

A combination of elements went into a complex spreadsheet that was kept by the Kurds. It expanded slowly and provided them with inferences as to the likelihood of al Al Hassan Abbas's presence at the residence. These included the subtle but telling lights in the second-floor bathroom near the master bedroom, as identified by infrared and thermal imaging. It was known that the butcher of young boys and their mothers preferred to shower at night, perhaps twice every seven to ten days. The light in the rear bathroom illuminated between 8:30 to 9:45 p.m. during two- or three-day intervals randomly every six to eight weeks. It was a tell for those who knew to look. The light had appeared thirty-one hours ago. It was now 4:00 a.m.

Roth moved back down the loose-gravel earthen rise, turned his head, and said something more in a hushed voice to the figure that Virginia had identified as Stan.

Jacob moved to again carefully view the area where the recessed door was bathed in shadow as Stan positioned himself slightly to Jacob's right. Stan's silhouette revealed a M24 Remington model 700, a bolt action sniper platform that was modified using a modular accessory rail system designed to accommodate the elongated sound suppressor. This weapon fired a 175-grain round boat-tail projectile effectively up to 1,500 meters, designed to kill with stealth. And as Stan incrementally positioned himself, ever so slowly, the linear shadow of his rifle barrel became visible, horizontal, and then still. What seemed an eternity to Virginia was, in fact, twenty-seven seconds, the elapsed time between Stan's optimal positioning, target selection, and target engagement. Then, the weapon's telltale kick, and the projectile was moving toward its location. Stan's rifle gave a simultaneous pop, but this sound was almost instantly erased in the gentle desert breeze. A faint short hiss as though a tire had briefly released air from its metal stem valve was almost imperceptible.

And less than a second later, there was an incongruent movement near the steel door and the figure of a man, suddenly transformed into a lifeless body of an ISIS guard, moved unnaturally. His head snapped up momentarily, an odd jerking motion, and then he slumped as he fell forward halfway into the gravel path that hugged the perimeter wall. His face now rested in the gravel. Jacob's continual assessment to detect other unfriendlies did not provide evidence of anyone. All was clear, and he gave the hand signal for his team to move rapidly over the embankment and to the wall.

But Jacob was incorrect—he had missed someone. For within the shadow of the recessed door was the slender figure of a woman clad in dark, almost black robes. She had gone unseen, as she had been pressed against the rear of the doorframe, instantly frozen in fear and confusion. She had met the now dead man in hopes of providing him with evidence of her affection, and he had been overwhelmed with happiness at her willingness to chance detection by his comrades by meeting him in secret at the wall when he was on guard duty.

At first she had registered only uncertainty, as he had just stated tenderly how happy he was to see her and that her scented hair, a trace of sandalwood, added to her beauty. She had smiled, slightly turning her face, modestly hiding her joy within her hooded robe. She had not wanted to hide her happiness entirely, as she had intended to please him. But then his head snapped back and his torso fell forward, striking his head on the gravel pathway. She had frozen in fear. Something had happened—something very wrong had transpired. And then she saw the dark liquid beginning to pool under his face where it had contacted the light-colored gravel. And as she stared at the growing black ink spot, processing this odd development, her breathing suddenly accelerated and she tried to scream. But initially, no sound emanated. And then it did, and her scream pierced the night as only primal fear can penetrate the subconscious.

The lights evenly spread along the top of the wall instantly illuminated, but their utility was short-lived. Two members of the team, positioned one hundred yards from the wall and nestled in the rolling desert where Jacob's team had originally viewed the compound, now targeted the lights and their companion cameras with rounds. These expensive surveillance assets were rendered useless within seventy-three seconds along with all but two of the lights that were positioned furthest from the team's corridors of approach.

Roth and his team were thirty-five yards from the wall when the scream pierced the black arid night. The door behind the woman was violently jerked open and a man carrying a Kalashnikov grabbed the screaming woman's robe, about to strike her when he saw his third cousin face down in the gravel. He looked up instantly and caught the streaking shadows of Virginia and Broderick as they closed the distance to the wall. Simultaneously, he pulled the woman to the ground and stepped into the recessed enclosure, now almost standing over the body of this kinsman. He yanked the trigger on his weapon and sprayed lethal 7.62x39mm lead missiles toward the approaching figures.

But he was too late. Both Virginia and Broderick had already seen him and were hugging the ground when his automatic weapon erupted.

Virginia's reflexes and training kicked in, and her weapon was firing almost before she realized that she had aimed it. Two rounds caught the man in the leg and lower abdomen and he spun, falling over his dead cousin and his cousin's would-be paramour. He was clutching his belly, drawn up into the fetal position.

He began to moan and gasped an urgent call for his deceased mother to come help him. The young woman, now face down on the gravel pathway, was wedged in between the two men, trapped and terrified. As she struggled to right herself, she continued screaming, but the door behind her had snapped shut and she heard the heavy steel bar locking it slammed into place. She was now isolated, outside, exposed to those who had killed the man she had come to meet. And she knew she was going to die.

Virginia was first to the door and looked down at the wounded man. Pinning each of his arms perpendicular to his torso, with the assistance of Broderick, she rolled him over, ready to kill him if he concealed a weapon. He did not, and it was clear that his wounds, while not immediately life-threatening, would be if left unattended. The woman's wails suddenly stopped; her eyes widened as she recognized a woman within the uniform of the American elite forces. She barely breathed as she initially failed to believe what her eyes conveyed. The striking beauty of a woman glared back at her and firmly moved her, making the robed woman face the door while Virginia zip-tied her hands behind her. Then

Virginia thoroughly but without unneeded force searched the entirety of the woman's robed body. The stunned woman was without weapons and, more importantly, without lethal charges comprising a suicide vest.

Virginia then rapidly repeated the binding of the man's hands behind him while using hand signals to inform Jacob that the door was secure, at least from the outside. The woman and the man were then blindfolded. The problem for the team was that the wall was reinforced cinderblock with rebar and the doors, including the double door for vehicles, was a reinforced steel plate that had been camouflaged to resemble wood. While the team could penetrate the wall, they had to be careful as to limit the time spent gaining access, as there were numerous suspected tunnel systems and al Al Hassan Abbas was adept in disappearing down any of them.

But Virginia felt that the optimal access was through the very door they stood beside. The guards were apt to position themselves to best defend the major conduit, the double vehicle door fifty yards from Virginia's location, leaving the single door more vulnerable. Further, if needed, they could blow the vehicle doors, creating a diversion while the major elements of the team gained access through this side door.

She quickly communicated her thoughts to Jacob, who had instantly arrived at the same conclusion, and because this was one of several scenarios that the team had discussed, he calmly informed Stan. Within twenty-eight seconds, the charges were expertly positioned along the wall's larger entrance doors, but hostile small arms fire was growing. Waiting longer would pin the team down and impede entry into the compound.

Fortunately, the diversion was somewhat more than the American team had planned in that the detonation actually blew the steel door of the gated entrance from its hinges.

It fell back into the compound.

The ferocity of the subsequent firefight was a surprise for Roth's team, as the focused intensity of automatic weapons fire into the created opening now prevented any advancement.

But it was Virginia's plan with the detonation of the side door, nine seconds after the main entry eruption, that ensured successful access. Her only fleeting concern was that blowing open the recessed door might collapse the surrounding wall on top of her, but while the wall held, the door did not.

In spite of its reinforced frame, the door was blown from its hinges and now askew but still partially adherent to its frame. Almost simultaneously, Virginia tossed three M67 fragmentation grenades through the created rent while rotating to dive back toward the safety of the perimeter path. The almost instantaneous detonation did further dislodge the door, along with the structural integrity of the adjacent wall holding the door's frame.

She and four other team members poured through the created fissure, rapidly gaining access that proved pivotal to the overall success of entry. She was first through, and as she squeezed though the opening, she dove and hit the hard ground rolling once.

Seeking cover behind an empty and heavily damaged fifty-five-gallon barrel of oil sitting near a truck, her weapon had already locked on the nearest ISIS guard. Instantly she took in the remaining dangers and then, refocusing using her

L3 Harris Technologies integrated land systems laser dot scope, she methodically squeezed her trigger and killed four figures within seconds. Concentrating on anyone within the compound aiming a weapon toward the Americans outside, she repeated her lethal routine. Seven men were killed by her before one of them realized that their compound had been breached at another site. As this man turned, now finding Virginia and raising his Kalashnikov to kill her, Broderick emptied the remainder of his clip into him. Two rounds entered and destroyed his face.

Within forty-seven seconds, eighteen ISIS personnel were dead or mortally wounded.

Jacob's team along with Stan were now streaming through the front gate, having avoided the mines thanks to Virginia's infrared and thermal-drone scouting. As the team entered the front, it naturally fanned out and Hansept was near the lead position at the furthest left corner of the expanding moving wedge of men. He was closest to Broderick and Virginia but still twelve yards away when three ISIS fighters stormed out of the door of an accessory brick building directly in front of Hansept. The lead fighter pointed his handgun at the man on Hansept's immediate right shoulder, and Hansept had time to simply cut the man down. His weapon was shouldered and he was crouched, weapon touching his face as he moved forward in the classic aiming position.

But he froze. He didn't move, and he didn't fire. He became immobile, his eyes fixed and wide as the ISIS guard began to accelerate toward the Americans, his right arm raised with a dark metal profile of an Iranian 9mm PC-9.

The handgun spit a plume of yellow-orange flame and a twenty-seven-year-old American two feet from Hansept's shoulder, Jason Sanders, collapsed screaming. The ISIS guard was now even closer to the Americans and beginning to reposition his handgun. And while two other American team members slightly behind Hansept had witnessed this entire episode, they were already returning fire toward the advancing guard. In fact, the first man closest to Hansept had already fired simultaneously with Virginia spewing a deadly fan of projectiles at the same ISIS fighter.

Spinning him reminiscent of a child's top, the precession of his body completed a single revolution before he collapsed, his chest torn. Ragged holes from two separate fields of fire were spilling life's coppery fluid freely into the gravel.

Virginia screamed, "Ostrowski, get him right!" while pointing at Hansept.

Ostrowski had seen the last moments of Hansept's frozen choreography of fear. He, along with the others, knew that Hansept was done; he was no longer viable within the team. Stan nodded and yelled, "Mahoney, tunnels! Too much time!"

Virginia immediately nodded, understanding instantly that al Hassan Abbas

was probably moving toward safety through his tunnel system. They had spent too much time out here.

Still shouldering her weapon, she raced toward the middle of the main building, the two-story whitewashed structure that comprised the main living quarters of al Al Hassan Abbas. Slowing as she approached a slightly recessed solid wooden door with a larger black steel handle and plate, she saw it opened to the side of the house that faced the main driveway. This small roadway led to the car port at the northern boundary of the surrounding wall. This storage area was wide enough for three vehicles and had a makeshift rough timber and tile roof.

Virginia paused by the door and pulled the handle and the door opened out into the street. Virginia's mind was rapidly assessing for threats, instantly processing any variations or strangeness that might conceal lethal force. She momentarily thought that this was a strange way to hang a door!

And then she saw the sliver of a metal plate beneath the crude 5x4-ft thick straw pad serving as an entry mat. She stopped and put up her fist for the team to stop and shelter immediately.

So, this is our welcome! she sarcastically thought. She knew that she had just avoided stepping on; it was a pressure-plate-activated mine in doorway, or perhaps the pressure plate set off several explosives in multiple positions. She pulled out her adhesive plastic image of a skull with two bones crossing at its chin and pulled the adhesive backing off of it before slapping it onto the door's outer surface and closing it gently. It was marked now for explosive ordnance disposal personnel, EOD, to assess, but prohibited from being an active entry.

She then motioned to Broderick to accompany her into the single elongated 3x4-ft window, its sill at collarbone level. He looked at her and understood immediately, hoisting her into a vertically higher state using his powerful arms so that she now sat on his right shoulder. His neck craned to the left, and two team members on each side of him were also actively surveying for threats.

Virginia rapidly examined the window along with the interior views available from her perch. A tap on the window revealed that it was glass, and it was surprisingly expensive: a paneled layer of two sheets with double-pane sealing argon glass to make the window a relatively efficient thermal insulator. Without waiting, she used the butt of her M4A1 carbine and smashed the window.

Fortunately for Broderick and Virginia, most of the glass followed the vector of force and landed inside of the house. Within nineteen seconds, five team members led by Virginia were inside the house and racing toward the basement.

The door to the unpainted wooden stairs was open, and she viewed the short sequence of steps to the basement dirt floor. A bright light source showed that the stairs were free of wiring or plastic wraps or evidence of explosives. Virginia descended deliberately as Broderick's hand just missed grabbing and arresting her shoulder.

Once she reached the basement Virginia stopped, crouching and assessing the room. The illumination from a bright blue-white light occupied the center of a hanging ballast. The room was relatively large by American standards and nearly empty, but it was clear that the bricked walls were without any door or exit. Even careful examination showed no hidden or trap doors.

Suddenly from above there was the sound of an American M-9 Beretta firing two rounds. It just beyond the entrance to the basement stairwell in the main hall of the house. A woman's scream, followed by a thud—a body had hit the floor above.

There were now three members of the team approaching the basement door. They had found and shot an ISIS soldier/guard as he had turned into the hallway filled with Americans. This had resulted in two other inhabitants of the house, one man and one woman, immediately freezing their movement in the hallway. As they instantly they raised their hands in surrender, an ever-suspicious Broderick, who had waited at the head of the stairs, now ordered them to kneel.

Searching them was actually a culturally sensitive task, as the women of Syria, similar to women anywhere, were not used to unfamiliar males groping their bodies in search of weapons or secret enjoyment. The Americans on the team led by Roth had been well trained. These men, and now a single woman, were without any trace of jocular satisfaction from embarrassing a female, even one potentially committed to possessing a suicide vest, an improvised explosive device, or anything else that could be triggered to kill Americans.

Instead, Broderick quickly searched the man who was now face down on the floor and zip-tied his hands behind him. The woman, already lying on her stomach, was searched next, her back and legs carefully manually assessed. But upon rolling her over, the Americans used Conan, a Belgian Malinois, to gently sniff her breasts. Wagging its tail, it declared that no explosive residue was detectable. The woman, wide-eyed with terror, might have been less afraid or upset if Broderick himself had exposed her breasts to the now growing team of five men, as the dog would not take his eyes from her face. She was obviously not a dog lover, and Conan was also well trained and eyed the young woman suspiciously. Broderick secured her hands, and by this time Virginia was up from the basement.

"Blind alley downstairs. No doors, no entry or escape routes detectable." She was frowning as she explained to Roth, who had entered from the outside and was now rapidly assessing the time-sensitive needs of the team.

The area was secure, but al Al Hassan Abbas was nowhere to be seen.

"This is a diversion. We're going to spend fifteen minutes finding the hidden door to a tunnel system, and in that time our quarry will be gone." Roth's tone was ominous, his body tight with the expectation of further combat.

With that, he grabbed the prone ISIS guard, lifted him to his feet, and marched him into the basement. With Virginia starting to follow, Roth turned his head back toward her and stated sharply, "Bring the beauty queen and the other male."

Virginia had never heard the intonation in Roth's command. It was without mercy; it was almost violent. But she willingly complied.

Grabbing the sobbing woman by her left arm above the elbow, who was indeed a beautiful woman of twenty-three years, Virginia pushed her forward while ordering her to the basement.

Roth, Virginia, and Broderick were in the large nearly barren room that Virginia had first entered. Roth immediately agreed with her that there were no hidden exit doors or facades.

Hansept had entered the house and moved to the top of the stairs. Other team members were searching the remaining rooms as per the organized preset protocol. He stood with two other members watching and securing the stairwell and then he descended three steps and crouched, using his right knee to stabilize his position. From there, he could see the room and its occupants clearly. The room itself was expansive, as it continued laterally from the staircase to the left almost six meters and then back under the staircase to the wall, which demarcated the boundary of the room on his right shoulder.

The wall along the right of the stairs was stone and brick and was, for casual appearances, solid without a break. But Roth and Mahoney had immediately sensed the disparity in proportions of this lower room compared with the floor above. At least an additional half of this large surface footprint extended over what was the lower level, rendering the basement area only 50 percent of the area of the larger ground floor above. Mahoney had been in many Midwest basements, and it was typical for the basement to mirror the footprint of the surface structure. To them this meant that there was more, just not visible from their location.

But her suspicion was met with a wall running the length of the staircase, solid with no apparent openings. Hansept also looked down the wall and saw no breaks, no seams that hid an entry, but he watched Mahoney begin to examine the wall facing the stairs as she held the arm of the Syrian woman. Roth had now zip-tied the hands of the ISIS guard and both were standing under a white metal rectangle containing two fluorescent tube lights. The fixture's base hung just six inches from the top of Roth's head, and he was almost three inches taller than his ISIS captive.

Hansept now witnessed Mahoney move, with the woman in tow, back to the foot of the staircase directly below Hansept, stopping in the square patch of rock and dirt at its base. Her eyes examined the irregular stone wall where each step had been securely implanted, the width of each step running to a solid opposing wooden cut stringer, empty of any handrail or balusters. Three feet beyond the last step, a second solid stone surface ran at a right angle to the perimeter wall, its length almost six meters. No windows were present.

Hansept glanced down, and to his left he caught Roth looking at the ISIS guard. Roth's eyes were absent mercy, and as Roth and Hansept refocused on Mahoney, they both paused as she momentarily released the woman, turning on her flashlight even though the ambient light in the underground room was adequate. She then clapped her gloved hands together close to the joining of the two walls at the base of the stairs and immediately held her flashlight at her waist with the cone of intense light directed superiorly. Never losing proximity to the Syrian woman, Mahoney carefully examined the agitated dust and particulate matter she had loosened from her sudden applause.

The ISIS guard started to move toward her, but Roth's M4A carbine suddenly thrust up beneath the guard's mandible, cold steel halting any thought of additional movement.

Roth watched Virginia follow the illuminated motion of the falling particulate and the Brownian motion of dust. Mahoney caught it first—Roth sensed more than he visualized the effect—but streams of almost silent airflow distorted the normal randomness of falling dust and inert matter. The flow was being directed away from the solid wall. It was most notable near the right-angle seam joining the two walls at the foot of the stairs, a clear indication that open space, not earth, was on the other side of the wall. Open space as in tunnels. Roth could not hide his smile.

Mahoney now quickly moved back to join Roth and the ISIS captive. She ushered the young Syrian woman with her back to the generous space of the room, where she stood three feet from Roth. The ISIS guard's eyes now conveyed an element of doubt that had replaced unbridled arrogance. Things for him, he had thought, could have been immeasurably worse. He could have joined his colleagues in their final defense and lay among the dead. Instead, he thought that these Americans were so soft, they would almost certainly move him to Guantanamo and within five to seven years, in his mid-forties, some American president, as a gesture of goodwill or because of political pressure, probably would free them to return to Syria. He would be a hero, celebrated at mosque, provided a bride or two from wealthy benefactors, and he could settle in. His years of captivity would be tolerable; he'd be well-fed, read in his spare time, and exercise as often as he wanted. Their ideas of prisons were more in line with vacations along the Black Sea, not quite the Mediterranean, but in truth, with his limited budget, it was not that far from the reality of his fiscal constraints. He derisively sneered, and that was a mistake—for Mahoney, the woman soldier of the Americans, caught the movement of his wrinkled lip.

The guard, for his part, never considered that this woman was an actual soldier. He had seen the soft eyes of that woman that his leader al Al Hassan Abbas had abused, enjoying her sensual presence despite her terror. He knew that all women were the same as this, including this naïve cousin of his friend standing with the American, whom he had agreed to protect. He had no doubts that underneath that camouflage uniform, this American bitch was representative of all women, literally and symbolically, for these were the teachings of his Iman and the laws that governed his religion. Mahoney, meanwhile, could not quite explain the building rage within her, but she knew she was at the edge of reason, perhaps the boundary of her sanity.

The young captive woman's eyes followed Virginia as she approached Roth and the ISIS guard, who had almost hourly made both subtle and rather overt suggestions to her that she had rebuffed. If only her cousin had understood that this man was not the austere disciplined follower of Allah, but in fact was the same as every other young male she had encountered: quick to see her beauty and interested in exploring the limits of her tolerance. Some were almost comical in their approach; others, like this one, were frightening, as she wondered if he would overpower her resistance and then convince others that she had instigated his lust.

Ostrowski was now also at the foot of the stairs. He looked up at Hansept, frowning slightly in recognition of this individual and the events surrounding him. Ostrowski's eyes conveyed a career-ending summation. Swirling deeply within his globes was their silent judgment. Hansept felt their verdict with an inherent sadness, but the result was as though he had been slapped in the face.

At this moment, Roth motioned to Broderick, who climbed back up the stairs and went to retrieve Ibrahim to address the prisoners in their native Levantine or Mesopotamian Arabic, although Roth strongly suspected that both spoke some English. Ibrahim appeared at the top of the stairs within twenty seconds and descended, joining Roth and Mahoney along with their prisoners. Broderick also hastened to join them. Standing slightly apart from ISIS guard's right shoulder, he was a meter behind him.

Roth, wasting no time, then asked the ISIS guard through Ibrahim if there were entrances to a tunnel system. The guard smiled and said nothing. But the look of utter hatred fouled the air as the ISIS prisoner dismissed the translator as an apostate.

Roth then asked the woman, "What about you? Are you also going to protect the animal who raped Catherine Morgan?"

The ISIS guard sharply growled, "Your voice must be silent." This was said in English.

And at this, Roth slapped him in the teeth with the barrel of an M-9 Beretta handgun.

The guard's head snapped back and his lower lip split and bled freely. The guard was shocked at the sudden violence; he had not expected this from Americans.

He quickly recovered and glared at Roth, conveying his pseudobravery. And then he decided to show this American filth what Syrian men were really made of.

He spit at Roth.

The bolus of liquid spittle bizarrely hit their mark. Roth's right cheek was covered in the red-tinged liquid from the ISIS prisoner's lip, but it was not Roth who registered anger—it was Mahoney.

However, remarkably, ominously, Roth did not move.

There was no reflexive attempt to protect his face. The expectorant responded to gravity's force and slowly slid from Roth's right cheek down to his jawline, where it began to drip onto his uniform.

Still, the American remained motionless, but his eyes communicated a calm building malevolence.

The ISIS guard had not anticipated Roth's lack of response. It was not normal. Instead of evasive action or a protective response, this American stood silently and allowed the spittle to slowly respond to gravity.

But the American's eyes, unwavering, fixed, and exploring those of the guard's, communicated something the guard had never previously seen, and it frightened the Syrian.

But something else had begun.

Within seconds, it was Mahoney's eyes that registered unbridled force that neither Broderick nor Stan had ever previously witnessed. She tensed, coiled almost as a serpent ready to strike.

The musty dampness of the brick-walled basement was suddenly oppressive, its pungent scent almost as a grave.

The guard no longer sneered; a slight grimace linked to uncertainty had replaced the confident scowl of moments before.

Roth politely, almost softly, asked the woman again in near perfect Arabic, "Would you assist us in finding the rapist?"

The request from this man was almost gentle. Both Ibrahim's and the woman's pupils dilated in instant recognition that Roth had a language proficiency not previously recognized. His features were handsome, conveying seigneurial rank, as if untroubled by the insolence of her companion. His head remained entirely motionless; only the bloody spittle continued to drip onto his uniform. He had not moved to wipe it clean.

Her lips trembled, and the ISIS guard again raised his face toward her and hissed, "Shut your stupid mouth."

Now Roth turned to readdress him.

But Virginia stepped up close to the ISIS fighter, interposing herself between Roth and the captive guard. And although four inches shorter and eight inches from his face, she calmly, almost as a prayer, began to carefully deliver her words through Ibrahim. "So, you think it is Allah's intent that men rape women? That they force them to be taken without agreement, without consent? This is what you believe is Allah's will?" Mahoney's voice remained soft, almost tender.

The last vestiges of bloody spittle dripped from Roth's jaw onto his pixilated desert uniform. His demeanor remained almost supernaturally calm, but this was transient.

For it was the eyes of Virginia Mahoney that carried a malignancy, a revulsion as though she was crossing that ephemeral boundary separating the actions of a professional soldier from that of a rabid animal. Those eyes now bored into the guard, conveying dissipating serenity and now scarcely masking a building unquenchable fury. The question hung in the air as the empty silence stretched into infinity.

Broderick was growing uncomfortable. Roth, too, for he sensed but could not quite fathom a predictable outcome to Mahoney's almost placid tonal inquest, coupled with a force in her eyes that he had never previously witnessed.

Roth unknowingly, however, was nearer the truth of what was to follow. He did not fully understand yet, for if he had understood what had already been initiated and that the fuse had already burned beyond its failsafe point, he might have intervened. But then again, perhaps not.

Yet Roth sensed that this ISIS soldier, if one could call these butchers soldiers, had crossed over a line of demarcation that once passed was terminal. Even the guard knew something had changed in this "American whore," but he did not fully realize that he was millimeters away from this point of no return.

While Roth was not absolutely certain that his prescient understanding was correct, it was.

Virginia waited in silence for seemingly minutes, but in actuality it was less than twelve seconds. And then the ISIS guard, beginning to regain his bravado and arrogance, spilled the forbidden knowledge. The language cascaded in near perfect English, no translation or translator needed. And this was the point of no return.

"I was there, and yes, he took her. Our leader took her and used her for his pleasure, as she was a godless whore— she was there for his use and enjoyment! I was there and she screamed and squealed so much, an American pig, and we all laughed, stupid American bitch. She understood too late who was in charge and who really mattered! And he passed her to us when he was done. When he was finished with the harlot, me and my brothers also used her!" The bound man began to laugh derisively.

And then his eyes widened slightly, perhaps imagining further forbidden pleasure that might have been, as he was looking straight into the eyes of this quite beautiful woman in a combat uniform. Another beautiful woman to be taken and used for the pleasure of the true believers.

Mahoney returned his leer with equanimity for a fraction of a second before she turned back toward the woman.

As her head turned, as her face moved, its slow, steady motion silently traversed the space to where Roth stood. His eyes captured Virginia's, and briefly their eyes locked.

Roth almost gasped. He had never seen Virginia absent her veneer of military professionalism, her analytical purpose. Jacob Roth had never seen her near-total self-control falter. But what he saw now unsettled him. For Roth was now witness to naked intimacy, an unguarded hatred—in its purest form, a bloodlust had replaced restraint. He knew the ISIS guard was going to die, and he also knew he was but a moment too late to stop it.

Virginia Mahoney's eyes had become smoldering coals of helical violence. Her face remained expressionless—a false state of calm, a sudden drop in the barometric pressure, a palpable calm before hurricane-force winds erupted.

Her facial muscles actually bunched, tightening as though preparing to be struck by a fist, protruding as they tented, and then subtlety distorted the smooth contour of skin overlying her jaw line. A failed attempt within herself to control a burning building rage.

But her rage was a mist rising off inland water, momentary and fleeting, then gone. Her acceptance of what was to come had instantly locked into place.

Virginia's expression was hard, merciless, and despite her anger she paused, suddenly aware that her life had now arrived at a pivotal turning point. She was barely breathing.

As Mahoney slowly turned from him, she locked eyes with those of the Syrian woman. She in turn froze, trembling in fear. Fear of the unknown, fear of the future, her future and the future actions of this woman, this American warrior who had suddenly become calm, disturbingly serene.

Virginia's movement was an incremental ballet, an ultrasmooth transition of minor adjustment as she again slowly turned her head back toward the ISIS guard. "Men do not speak of women with such disrespect."

And the guard glowered at her, his sneer returned. His upper lip pulled back, his bloody upper teeth exposed, the sneer gaining in style but empty of force.

Virginia looked at Broderick on the other side of the guard. "Brod, please move." It was a pleasant request, a friend asking her buddy for a favor. A request to avoid being in the arc of a golf club's swing on a breezy sunny afternoon.

But the tone contained a finality that Broderick Luther Pickney knew he would never hear on a suburban course on a sunny afternoon, or when smiling relaxed friends were enjoying the bond of friendship.

This was all that Virginia Mahoney asked, this simple request.

And Broderick moved, but his eyes conveyed a worry for his friend who was walking toward an infinite abyss. Broderick's eyes narrowed with concern and his head moved slightly forward, tilting as he tried to read her intentions, a most trusted friend's purpose.

Virginia, again turning back toward the woman, asked, "How do we get to the tunnels?"

The ISIS guard started to move toward the woman to put his face next to hers, but Virginia almost casually placed the end of the barrel of the Beretta on his upper lip, sliding it ever so gently toward the opening of his mouth.

The woman, alarmed, looked around randomly and found Ostrowski, who was looking at her. Their eyes connected.

Ostrowski had tensed; a telltale stillness had appeared in Virginia's eyes.

This was danger. He had seen this before in others when a conclusive decision had replaced the normality of fear or self-preservation. In the seconds, the instant before Roth himself had raced into an open field during a firefight to retrieve a wounded colleague who was at risk of being captured by Taliban fighters.

On that occasion, Roth's eyes had conveyed terminal acceptance, a calmness that communicated a mortal peace. A future left in the hands of his Creator. That look had returned, but now it existed in Virginia Mahoney, and Ostrowski's entire frame was suddenly taut in anticipation of trouble.

The twenty-three-year-old Syrian woman looked back at Virginia, and as the ISIS guard reared his head to denounce the young woman . . .

Virginia Mahoney pulled the trigger.

The guard's brains exploded from the back of his head, a bloody mist erupting and spraying blood and cerebral matter the consistency of ground raw chicken meat over the lower bricks of the wall.

His cheeks instantly expanded before collapsing from the force of the explosion and propulsive gas that erupted from the end of her 9mm M9 Beretta and then ejected out the back of the man's head. A golf ball-sized defect. As his head snapped back, the guard collapsed.

His legs twitched for fourteen seconds. His bladder unflatteringly spilled its remaining contents as he lay crumpled on the ground.

Prone on his back, his right leg folded awkwardly beneath the left. He eyes transitioned to a visionless stare, life's energy gone. Blood seeped along the uneven earthen floor.

The noise was deafening, and the mixed odors of urine, blood, and rotten eggs suddenly permeated the tight basement confines. The smoke from the single shot drifted to fill the area, a blue haze under the florescent light.

Broderick's eyes were wide now, not with fear but with the realization that his friend, a most trusted friend and first of her kind in combat special operations, had just crossed a bridge and could never return.

Virginia Mahoney had just executed a bound and incapacitated prisoner.

Mahoney turned to the woman who herself had emptied the contents of her bladder, soaking the inner thighs of her traditional Syrian coverings. Her legs were shaking and she vomited, retching as her torso flung forward.

Hansept inwardly smiled. The door had closed on Virginia Mahoney.

Hazel liquid poured from the Syrian woman's mouth and nose.

She shuddered, then sputtered and nearly fell, but Mahoney caught her, a gloved hand under the Syrian's left shoulder gently maintaining her balance.

Roth, speechless, had grabbed and supported her other arm. Roth's gaze focused on Virginia.

Through genuine tears of shock and near disbelief, the twenty-three-year-old Syrian woman wailed a primeval, shrill piercing sound, that of a wounded vulnerable animal. A sound so terrible that it caused the hardened combatants standing in the basement of the world's most wanted terrorist to narrow their eyes, an attempt to shelter their souls.

Sinking to her knees, she gasped and motioned with her head toward the wooden stairs.

"Pull them out from the wall!" shouted Virginia.

Stan was already at the foot of the stairs and pulled at the staircase, or more precisely the stringer that held each of the individual planks or tread, and it moved away from the wall. The embedded tread that formed the stepping surface of each individual step remained inserted into the wall, but there was movement.

The last two risers and treads attached to the terminal portion of the stringer opened a three-foot crack in the wall abutting the staircase. It was a tight fit, but adequate. When closed in its normal position, the rough semifinished wall was a perfect blend of shadows and irregular brick and plaster, disguising any opening.

Within fifteen seconds Virginia, Roth, Stan, and Broderick were leading Hansept and two others along with Conan the Belgian Malinois into a much larger musty earthen space behind the bricked wall of the basement. This was the unaccounted-for area under the other half of the house that lay above. The space was patterned similar to half of a Western wagon wheel cut almost exactly in two. The thick axle at the center was where Roth and his team were standing and it extended almost twenty feet beyond the bricked enclosure of the basement, and the "spokes" were four separate tunnel entrances leading away from the open subterranean vault.

While the team moved quickly to follow the opening into the underground concealed escape route, Broderick had difficulty pulling his eyes from his team member. He, along with Roth, was still attempting to process what Virginia Mahoney had done. It was the same for Stan, as each of these dedicated teammates were shocked to their core in response to the savagery that Virginia had displayed. But as much as they were disquieted by this event, it was the future response of Hansept that was to have the greatest lasting impact.

Roth said to Stan, "Let Conan pick up the scent."

And the dog was released.

Sniffing, its head bent sharply down, the dog's nose nearly scraped the dry but musty dirt of a tomb as it moved rapidly, its tail curling up behind it. And then suddenly the canine began wagging its tail and his head came up sharply, looking toward one of the two tunnels to the right of where Roth and his team were standing.

Pausing only briefly, the dog shot down the shaft entrance that was the crudest opening, partially obstructed with discarded lumber and plank remnants. It occupied the farthest opening to the right of the group. Roth was first to move and was crouched, bent at the waist, as he ran to the opening, his night vision goggles lowered over his eyes and his weapon cradled in his right arm, elbow bent.

The rest followed their spacing established during rigorous training, following their commander and hoping to complete their mission. Hoping to render justice to a beautiful young woman who had surrendered her life, a life given in pursuit of assistance for those trapped within the unspeakable brutality of the Syrian civil war.

As Roth silently moved into the tunnel, rapidly following his canine tracker, thoughts flashed into his mind—an almost uncanny vision of his love handcuffed and incarcerated. He vowed he would not allow this. He would lay down his life to prevent it. What he could not have known was this was a prescient vision, a near supernatural insight, but one that would test his character as a man, his commitment to justice, to honor to his very spiritual foundation.

But such is the nature of armed conflict for all who enter its ephemeral violent world. No one escapes.

Chapter 13

"Yea, though I walk through the valley of the shadow of death . . ."
—*Psalm 23*

Roth's training had instilled basic reflexive canons to follow under combat conditions. One such rule was when in pursuit of an enemy, ensure that irregular stops, planned but situationally spontaneous, are made to assess surrounding conditions. A critical habit to be instilled in those who engage in the most demanding of professions: the hunting of humans. Do not run headlong into a preset trap.

Roth also had moved to access his backpack, extracting his optics for thermal recognition. This was a somewhat bulky piece of equipment, some would argue too cumbersome for true combat operations, but he had use of it now in the near total blackness of the tunnel. Different from binoculars used in daylight, the thermal detector differs only in that thermal-infrared wavelengths are passively emitted by the object and are selectively detected by the scope. These specific wavelengths are filtered and instantly gathered by the scope in a scanning process through use of a phased array infrared detector, and the actual wavelength elements from the heat given off by the detected object create a picture called a thermogram. Modern computer microchips attached to the scope itself instantly gather and process nearly an infinite number of these emitted waves to create a complete picture of a person or living object where the radiated heat in real time is the source of detection.

This, in essence, allowed him to see the thermal disparities between the warmth of human beings versus their relatively less hot or cooler inert surroundings, such as the cooler earth of the tunnel walls. In effect, this disparity identified individuals in complete blackout conditions such as existed in these subterranean channels.

Yet importantly, and not as well appreciated, was the ability of this technology to also identify metal objects, if large enough, and if their temperatures were inherently different than their surroundings. Roth was interested in the potential rate of ambient cooling of any explosives planted by al Al Hassan Abbas, as this might enable him to detect their presence before their inherent temperatures matched their surroundings. Once the inert material reached the same temperature as the surrounding earthen walls, thermal detection was impossible.

As Roth raced into the tunnel, he paused after fourteen seconds, crouching to one knee, and surveyed both the distant dark chamber and its imperfectly reinforced walls. His hearing was key, and he also carried a sound amplifier and an earpiece. Activating it, he heard muffled noise above background clatter. Something was out there, and Conan was running toward it.

No metal was identified as he scanned the curving wall to the right. But this did not mean there were no explosives. The problem was Semtex, a stable but highly explosive compound discovered by a Czech chemist during the Viet Nam war. It could be shaped into nearly an infinite array of objects to fit between supporting tunnel wooden beams, similar to the most primitive form used in this tunnel. It could also be remotely detonated, potentially causing a catastrophic collapse of the tunnel and the entrapment of the entire team. Roth knew if the metal encasing the Semtex reached the ambient temperature, or that equal to the earth around it, Roth could not count on detection by his thermal scope.

But he was again up and running deeper into the blackened channel and his team, evenly spaced behind him, followed his lead. Roth had two small reflective adhesive labels, each with a proprietary phosphorus surface coating, stuck on the back of his combat helmet. They were easily seen and followed by the team using their own night vision optics.

Virginia watched him as he in textbook fashion pursued, stopped, assessed, and pursued. Spacing was critical to the team, because if Roth triggered a booby trap, he would die, but the spacing might limit injury to his team from a greater collapse of the tunnel.

Suddenly, Roth skidded to a stop and lay flat on the floor of the darkened vacant tube. He spoke softly into his throat microphone system, and his proximity was so close as to practically be whispering into a collective set of ears.

"Movement twenty-five to thirty yards ahead."

And with that, Conan began to bark.

Virginia hurriedly cautioned, "Suicide vest possible."

Roth stated, "Roger that."

But Roth moved forward. Crouching low to the ground, his senses took in the pungent heavy dampness of the earthen floor. His right knee touched the dirt as he paused just at the beginning of a gentle dogleg bend to the right, then leaned forward, his head now able to see down the black corridor. Two thermal images were seen.

The figures were of disparate height; the colorless pixilated thermogram could not accurately identify facial features. A larger outline—a man. Holding something—a Kalashnikov. A smaller figure holding on to his waist—a child!

Roth cursed to himself as he instantly processed that al Al Hassan Abbas had one of his numerous children, or grandchildren, in front of him, using his offspring as a shield.

Roth would not shoot a child.

But he called out, "So fathers now must sacrifice their children?" And then out of a combination of frustration and anger mixed with an eerie sense of dread, Roth laughed. It was a merciless laugh, a sneer mixed with contempt.

And the sound carried down the blackened corridor to the ears of the terrorist. The rapist and murderer of an American aid volunteer.

Conan was forty-five yards from the ISIS leader, Roth about eighty-five yards. The dog hugged the wall, his belly and chest on the ground, face snug between his outstretched paws. As trained, the dog was limiting his profile when confronting the object of his chase. Roth whistled and the dog turned his massive head, jumped up, and ran back toward the American.

al Al Hassan Abbas heard a dog but could not identify whether it was running away or toward him.

"You will not take me alive. I am not a puppet for your president!"

285

Roth spontaneously chuckled, "No, you are a dead man breathing his last moments of Allah's gift of life. And your child will see you die." Roth felt Virginia's presence alongside of him and whispered, "Just around the corner, he and a child are at the back of the tunnel. I don't see any exit."

Virginia stated slowly, carefully weighing her words, as she was uncertain as to their merit, "Do you think I can get the kid to safety and we can deal with him?"

Roth, processing her suggestion, stated, "I don't know. We can try, but it will be dangerous. He's going to use that kid as a shield or offensively to attack us."

"Roger that. But can we at least give it a go? This is a kid we're dealing with, and this is not going to end well . . . right?"

"You are correct. Ok . . . go ahead."

Virginia nudged a bit closer to the bend of the tunnel and forcefully called to al Al Hassan Abbas, "Let the child come to us. No jacket, nothing to carry . . . let the child slowly walk toward us."

The sound of a woman's voice momentarily confused al Al Hassan Abbas. "Who are you, a woman?!" He laughed derisively. "Another godless American whore? I enjoyed the last American whore. She was begging me to take her!"

Spontaneously, almost before she knew she was responding, Virginia barked in near perfect Arabic, "Allah Yakhthek! May God take your soul." A phrase requesting that God should embark on this task immediately, because the object of the declarative is wanted dead!

Silence greeted the insult as al Al Hassan Abbas confronted a growing realization that his life was to be measured in minutes, if not seconds.

But Roth and Virginia could not know that al Al Hassan Abbas held a small metal cylindrical object in the palm of his left hand. Thicker than a pen, slightly larger than a modern keyless car entry fob, this was a dead-man detonator with a central mobile spring-activated plunger. If its owner let go of the plunger, it sprung up to reposition itself. If left in this configuration for five seconds, once activated, an electronic charge was generated into the grapefruit-sized metal canisters, each positioned in separate pockets of the vest that al Al Hassan Abbas wore. The vest was constructed with a total of five canisters positioned over the upper mid-abdomen and low back, and each canister, slightly larger than a soup can, contained C4 explosive. Each was surrounded by plastic envelopes containing nails and ball bearings. The electronic trigger would detonate all five canisters simultaneously, creating a moderately large fragmentation bomb. Anyone within forty to fifty yards would be cut down from the supersonic "blade" effect of the multiple moving metal nails and bearings.

Roth attempted to move his left hand to pull on Virginia's right shoulder to reposition her safely behind the bend in the tunnel.

But before he had even touched her uniform, she was up on one knee in a firing position, targeting al Al Hassan Abbas. She mockingly yelled a communication that dripped with sarcasm, "You have brought dishonor to Allah, to your family. You are an apostate, and I will rub my feet on your lifeless face. You will be buried with the foxes."

This was among the most inflammatory of statements to a true follower of Islam. Virginia knew it as she deliberately goaded this vile creature.

She had been examining his position, concentrating her view within her M4A1 scope, and attempting to reconfirm his outline in the emerald image separate from the much smaller figure believed to be a child. His large head, with his traditional kaffiyeh, made his silhouette appear even more as a bulb sitting atop a lamp, and Mahoney suddenly could see him adjusting something in his hand.

Roth saw this too.

Both immediately registered that this might be a hand grenade or ordnance that could be hurled toward them, and Mahoney instantly retargeted the thermal image.

As he suddenly moved a step toward their position, she depressed trigger of her M4A1 assault rifle. Her target was the small area of what she believed was al Al Hassan Abbas's head, an even tighter area near his right eye. The gun kicked, its muffled sound immediately followed by Mahoney diving behind the tunnel's bend and lying prone.

She had fired from eighty-seven meters, a single round.

Even in the near ethereal green of the night optics, the small plume of a black cloud could be seen erupting from al Al Hassan Abbas's kaffiyeh, attenuated in its force but still visible. The round had struck its position almost perfectly; Mahoney's assessment of where his right eye was located had been remarkably accurate. The man's head snapped back and both his arms reflexively shot upwards, almost as though he were beholding a vision.

His body fell back and crumpled to the earthen floor of the tunnel.

al Al Hassan Abbas's eyes no longer held any vision, at least not of his earthly surroundings.

The metal projectile had traveled at 2,900 feet per second from Virginia's weapon, disintegrating this predator's surface tissue and carving a large straight cylindrical burr hole though his face, skull, and brain.

And then they heard a child's scream, but it was cut short.

The tunnel instantly glowed with a bright yellow-white light followed simultaneously by the eruption of a thunderous sound, an explosion. Roth rolled over Virginia reflexively, protecting her as she hugged the ground and the dog. His action was immediately followed by a dramatic change in pressure. Virginia was flattened against the dog, and all three were pushed harder into the damp musty tunnel floor.

Stan and Broderick were far enough displaced from the explosion to feel the concussive force of the pressure change, but the metallic objects traversing distances at ultrafast speeds meant to maim, injure, and kill fortunately could not negotiate the curves within the subterranean conduits.

But all felt the sudden howling wind that instantaneously accelerated from the dying light and blew dirt and debris over Virginia, Roth, and their canine companion.

The closest bend in the tunnel's pathway had saved these three from certain death. The metal fragments from al Al Hassan Abbas's suicide vest arced across the open space at a supersonic rate, slamming into and embedding the tunnel's earthen walls and wooden beams.

Conan suddenly yelped. Roth pulled up his night vision optics and Virginia turned on her flashlight. The dog was bleeding from its neck, and Roth yelled back down the tunnel for medical assistance.

Conan had gotten clipped by a metal fragment slicing into his neck, but minutes later, exploration by the team's medic found no vital structures damaged. He would fully recover. al Al Hassan Abbas, or more precisely the remnants of the ISIS leader, would not. Both he and his young companion, perhaps a son or grandson, were scattered along the tunnel's walls. Fragments of clothing and body parts, mostly shredded tissue and torn bones, lined an irregular circle that coincided with the blast trajectory of the vest.

Remarkably, much of the tunnel remained intact with only a couple of support beams damaged and partially collapsed. Someone had engineered and constructed an extraordinary reinforced earthen tunnel, but the blast itself was only meant to kill those around the one robed in this death garment. It was not positioned or designed to disrupt solid structures.

It had served its purpose.

Two hours later, the tunnel system had been thoroughly explored, mapped, and had charges placed within to detonate and destroy the structures for any future use. Prisoners were quickly and superficially interrogated, and computers and other intelligence material were taken from the house.

Perhaps the most unpleasant part of the job was the subsequent collection of the tissues and bone fragments.

Delicately loaded into sealed plastic bags, tagged, and labeled along with screw-top containers to ensure, it would be used to ensure via tissue and genetic analysis that the biological detritus was indeed al Al Hassan Abbas. Unfortunately, portions were also subsequently identified as one of his children.

Reaching the outside courtyard, Virginia looked at Roth and with her right hand gently touched a laceration below Roth's left eye. The wound was almost an inch long and on the extreme right of the open cut, nearest the lateral aspect of his left eye, blood still was moist, the clotted material dripping slightly down his cheek. His face reflected both the blood of a man interrogated and his own.

"Yeah, something nicked me from the blast. I'm fine."

Virginia, ignoring him, called over to Stan, "Ostrowski, can you get the medic? Lt. Roth has an owie."

"Roger, Mahoney!" Stan smiled at her, but he could not hide the troubled frown directed at one of his dearest friends and female team member.

Chapter 14

"Surely goodness and mercy shall follow me . . ."

Catherine Lucille Drake was a bit deflated, if not almost depressed, concerning the prospect of dealing with her client —a client mandatorily assigned to her by Command. As she exited the elevator on the third floor of the TSO office structure, Washington Naval Yard, heading to the initial meeting with Petty Officer Second Class Virginia Mahoney, she let out a deep breath and considered the prospective encounter. Drake had read the files on her but just as importantly had talked to two of her commanders, including a Lt. Roth, as Catherine explicated Mahoney's background and her scholastic performance along with her single combat mission performance. She had even reviewed original summations of interviews conducted when she had first applied to the US military and not only survived but thrived in basic and then in her advanced training. It was an impressive record, and Catherine was uncomfortable in her surprise.

In fact, Catherine had been stunned to see her scholastic aptitude scores and her grades. She had even read two of her written monographs, one abbreviated that was published under a pseudonym in the periodical Shipmate Magazine. Normally, this publication's purpose was to be a well-intentioned if not backdoor fundraiser and "interest maintainer" for all things navy and Naval Academy. Her monograph regarding parallels between the Roman legion and SEAL training and philosophical preparations had been percipient, not to mention provocative. While few initially knew that its author was enlisted, and not an officer candidate or midshipman, its substantive content justified its very appearance as no major deviation from the legacy publication record of Shipmate. The subsequent seeping rumor that this had been penned by a "nonofficer girl" only added to the growing mythology surrounding her and the cold, hard understanding that this woman was different.

The article itself detailed Mahoney's concerns regarding the current administrative trend of emphasizing the correct philosophical indoctrination of SEAL candidates. This consisted of the proper "political speak" and perspectives, versus substantive real-world requisite training for the modern warrior. One might argue that such criticisms were a routine manifestation of the unending dynamic tension between the paper warriors and those within the Pentagon who had truly entered the belly of the beast that is combat. But Mahoney's article was a clarion call to navy leadership demanding they focus on skillsets enabling survival for those asked by their nation to enter the unforgiving cauldron of war. For someone having not yet tasted actual combat, it was a near prophetic view into the requisite tools and perspective for optimizing performance and survival.

Mahoney's premise was that the foreseeable "flavor of the month" curriculum espoused by desk jockeys married to lawyers was irrelevant. When humans are interested in killing other humans, the dispassionate rhetoric of eager intellectual legal adherents has little relevance. In fact, it has as much impact on combat outcomes as the metrics of cow manure has on one's golf handicap. But such legality as to rules allowed during combat is a remarkably often repeated exercise among governments collectively run by bureaucrats, a belief that any of these rhetorical exercises or the legal gospel so carefully constructed truly matter. It is only a mirage offered by those unable to process that war is beyond human comprehension as to its instantaneous horror.

In contrast, Mahoney suggested, even demanded that naval leadership understand the prescient need to protect those asked to wage war. And her view was that this was done by providing them with effective, necessary, essential skills to kill other human beings. This was not a comfortable discussion for historically mixed company during Friday night cocktails or during breakfast table banter. It was, in fact, an uncomfortable discussion for leaders to have with mainstream media personalities who themselves were more interested in feel-good morality than in the world as it really existed.

But Mahoney did not waver in her premise. It was simply that the mental, emotional, and spiritual proficiencies essential to the modern combatant must be linked to expertise in lethality, and vice versa. But her essay's message was not so ham-fisted as to dismiss the need for some protective shield for those asked to engage in the timeless plague of combat. She noted that yes, a requirement to prevent complete degenerative collapse of combatant outcomes is essential to preclude the appearance of unfocused savagery— human beings killing without reason, need, or purpose. Mahoney acknowledged a "bloodlust" that can rise from its germinal origins exists in all and must be prevented, not only to protect the victims but the perpetrators. Unbridled horror stains the souls of those guilty of its commission and may collapse nations, if not civilizations.

This was the critical "vice versa," according to Mahoney. Mahoney demanded that the outcomes of the sanctioned violence labeled "combat" must be understood to impact the victor's soul as well as their physical body. Mahoney went even further in her exposé, aggressively calling on leadership to formulate training that would enable recovery of the emotional and spiritual injury suffered in combat. She underscored that the blending of emotional, spiritual, and physical attributes of the modern warrior are essential for a just and noble outcome in combat, even when often faced with the maniacal mindset of modern adversaries.

The priority of ensuring recovery for those exposed to the otherwise soulless or soul-robbing experience of war must be equal, if not greater than any tactical espoused strategy of battle, she argued. Such are the skills that have been validated over the four millennium of the recorded history of conflict. These skills are immutable, and such are the skills that render a small sliver of post-traumatic equanimity to those who have rendered lethality to others.

Mahoney was aggressive in her stance that technological advances employing either aggressive or defensive weaponry are rendered useless if placed in the hands of those without this articulated preparation, indeed this blended competency. For it is these same skills, values, and considerations, a proficiency within an individual's character, that will make the difference between victory and defeat. The line between the just warrior and the noble loser is fine but must remain a scholarly obsession, not a practical outcome. Winning is the only outcome acceptable. But winning cannot endorse or tolerate unrestrained barbarism.

The elements of character, present or absent, are similar to those espoused within the Roman legions or the ancient Judean warriors. These determine success or failure. The article created a bit of a stir and received unprecedented feedback from readership, with more letters to the editor than any other article previously published in the periodical. Many senior veterans, composed of retired officers, had assumed that the author's name was a pseudonym. They immediately concluded that the author of this well-written, sharply pointed barb directed toward administrative "paper warriors" was just protecting himself. Because the sentiment was nearly uniformly in vocal agreement with Mahoney's assertion, most would have been shocked into silence by the voice coming from a beautiful young woman.

But there was a slightly different response from Command. Their visible consternation was evident but was drowned out by this much more powerful response of seasoned veterans: those who had been exposed to the ageless beast, the recurrent nightmare called combat, for they lit up the editorial offices of Shipmate Magazine. They, members of the battle-scarred and aging collegium, demanded adherence, understanding, and support for the realpolitik of Mahoney's thesis. Many also demanded that the author not be punished, but rewarded!

Her combat performance on the al Al Hassan Abbas mission had been remarkable, as authored by Roth and others on the team in after-action summaries. The tightly written, still classified reports had been heavily redacted, but

Catherine had argued aggressively for access if she was to provide any semblance of a credible defense. Remarkably, the evidence supported that her bullet had killed this ISIS filth. A single shot in a lightless tunnel had completed the mission, but Catherine was involved because someone had reported criminal activity leading to the isolation of the ISIS commander.

Catherine had previously seen the often unbelievable efforts of other young warriors, all men, committed to both mission and teammates. But still, when she studied Virginia's efforts on behalf of her subordinates and her country, Catherine was uncomfortable. This woman was not a Neanderthal, some steroid-enhanced muscled bodybuilder who loved war and the adrenaline-filled episodes accompanying its violence. The background on this woman, Virginia Mahoney, was different, as was her position in the armed forces. The lawyer still had to remind herself that Catherine was dealing with a fellow female, one who was the first of her kind on a special operations team and now stood accused of a crime. What a mess!

Yet still, Catherine had previously seen the arguably misleading narrative of superior officers who had painted a picture of a most pure warrior spirit in others, only then to find a drunken substance-abusing lunatic. Someone who enjoyed the adrenaline rush of combat and the hero worship of unknowing civilians back home in their small rural towns and villages. She considered that meeting this woman might have some wrinkles in comparison to the typical knuckle-dragging types, but she could not be certain. Was this woman a man wannabe? Was she so enamored with the label of "warrior" and "lethality of purpose" that she had passed into a nebulous psychiatric state?

But the first hint that she might have been wrong was when she encountered the two marine guards standing outside the interview room. Normally, these men were for show. The accused was unlikely to run, reflecting on how far one could get in the heavily fortified and secure environment of the Washington Naval Yard. This habitually led to the guards being relaxed, leaning against the wall or sitting in one of two chairs positioned just beyond the door to the conference room. But these two were nearly board-stiff in their military posture and bearing. Their bearing suggested inspection by an admiral, not observation of a secure and often shackled prisoner.

Are they waiting for her? Unlikely.

The marines hated the officers from Naval JAG, and one could only imagine their smoldering distaste for a female. She briefly imagined their eye rolls if ever they were informed that said officer, a JAG officer and lawyer, was also a woman who was intimate with another woman. But she dismissed this vagrant thought almost before it materialized in her mind.

Fuck 'em. This is my territory—I am the force to be feared. The weapons that I carry are unknown and unmatched by these grunts.

She silently raised her eyebrows at the absurdity of her ongoing self-directed monologue, and as she reached the first of the two guards, their demeanor was maintained.

Why the formality? she thought. Ah. She immediately concluded that there must have been another officer inside already, but no there was no one in the immediate vicinity. No one besides a sitting female was in the room. Who are they performing for? Ok, let's test the water . . .

She slowed and spoke carefully, "You gentleman look sharp . . . are we expecting someone from Command?"

"No, ma'am."

And nothing else? No banter, no familiarity, just textbook formality? Odd . . .

"Any issues, problems with Petty Officer Mahoney?"

"None, ma'am." Again, the more senior-ranking guard spoke only those two words. Nothing else was offered, and no other sounds emanated from their mouths.

Something has ruffled these guys . . .

Then it happened.

"Captain, do you know who this woman is?" It was asked in a respectful tone, but the implication was that the prisoner was someone important, someone they respected.

"Sergeant, as you must realize, I wouldn't be here unless I knew the circumstances surrounding her conduct. That is public record."

The guard turned his face away from Catherine and spoke as if in basic training with cold formality, "I apologize, Captain." Again, nothing else was offered, and he continued, along with his companion, to stare straight ahead.

And Catherine began to have a cold apprehension tickle the back of her scalp.

What is going on?

"Sergeant, is there something . . . something special I need to consider here before I enter the room?"

The younger guard spoke for the first time, "Mahoney is someone, someone special. At least to us."

And the cold uncomfortable tickle began to intensify on her scalp.

These guys are in awe of this woman, she suddenly realized.

Almost simultaneously and barely audible, the senior guard whispered, "We call her Icarus."

She paused, not quite believing what was just uttered. She deliberately and somewhat forcefully engaged the other marine guard. "Excuse me, what? You called her . . . what's that?

"Icarus, ma'am."

Normally, hearing this type of moniker, she would have reasoned that it represented some form of derogatory label. Yet she sensed respect, almost veneration, that these two men directed toward Mahoney. All of her premature judgment suddenly collapsed. She also did not allow her usual courtroom theatrics of manufactured sarcasm to surface. In fact, she found herself disconcerted.

Her troubled perplexity must have registered, and the younger guard looked at her. He hesitated but now, nearly rolling his eyes, he stated, "She is a perfect warrior . . . ma'am. Except for her one fatal flaw, and it may have allowed them to destroy her." It was stated softly, but its clarity of diction connoted a deliberate intensity, coupled with locked eyes registered upon Catherine's own startled reaction.

Without being asked, he simply stated in the same soft, almost whispered tone, "She . . . she is a true believer. Yes, meaningless or important, but always dangerous missions."

She stepped forward. "And now, those water walkers, those who hurt us more than the Taliban or anyone—they will destroy her. But we will be watching . . . ma'am."

"Corporal! That is enough, Jenkins."

The senior guard's admonishment was genuine, but Catherine sensed that it was really for his younger companion's protection.

She sensed that she had just been threatened by a corporal in the United States Marines. It was subtle, but clear, and she also sensed it contained real gravity, a real mass of pent-up frustration and anger.

She frowned, her mind racing to consider the ever-shifting landscape of tribal alliances within the military governed by the sophistry of professional partisan politicians.

Catherine had entered the convoluted byzantine court of Elizabeth the First, and she suddenly realized that she was uncertain as to her abilities or understanding of the forces arrayed against her.

As she walked into the room, she saw that Mahoney was standing but unable to salute, as she was in shackles. Both ankles and hands were restrained with a spacing chain holding both her arms and legs so that she could not raise her hands above her waist.

"Gentlemen." Catherine turned back to the guards. "I think the petty officer can be trusted. Let's remove these, please."

But remarkably, the older guard stated softly, "I have been requested not to remove them, ma'am. I apologize, but I must decline to do so."

"Who told you to leave them on?" Catherine demanded.

The guard's eyes moved from Drake to Mahoney, and he nodded toward the woman in chains. He then turned back to lock eyes with Drake before gently closing the door, leaving Mahoney and Drake alone in the room.

What the hell? What kind of game is this Mahoney playing? Catherine's mind raced. And why would a marine-enlisted guard basically respond to my request with a polite but affirmative "Sorry, but no way, Captain!"?

"Listen, Petty Officer. I know you may enjoy the show, but I have a job to do. Perhaps we need to understand that I am not one for theatrics, so let's leave the over-the-top incarceration victimization for another time, ok?"

Mahoney stared straight ahead and was silent.

Catherine waited and then sighed before saying, "Ok, have it your way. It will be fairly hard to defend you if you aren't going to speak with me."

Mahoney turned her head slowly and stated quietly, almost so soft as to be unintelligible, "I know this is a burden for you, as you are normally the high and mighty legendary prosecutor, and I know that you enjoy picking apart the lives of knuckle-draggers, as I am, to achieve your personal goals, so I will make this simple for you. I am guilty. I shot that ISIS guard in the forehead at point-blank range. He had his hands tied behind his back, he was unable to move, and I judged his life was to be sacrificed . . . ended to gain critical information.

"I needed the entry points to the tunnel system, and his life was the simplest way to procure them in a timely manner. Otherwise, our mission would fail and would have to be repeated, perhaps in far more unfriendly environs, with teammates now in greater harm's way. It was a gamble that I had to take to convince our captive, a young Syrian woman, to acknowledge where the entry point or points were, and it worked. I was—we were able to gain access to the tunnel and complete the mission, which was authorized by the president of the United States. That mission was to kill al Al Hassan Abbas and bring closure for Mr. and Mrs. Mueller in the loss of their daughter at the hands of that abomination. It was not to capture him; it was not to bring him to a US courtroom. It was to kill, murder, execute him without trial or due process. He was not to survive the mission.

"I don't expect you care one way or another about either al Al Hassan Abbas, the guard, the woman he repeatedly raped and murdered, or the mission. And I am quite certain you care little for or about me, so if you don't mind, take my statement and we can be done. I will appear before the court absent your presence so as not to stain your stellar reputation. I will plead guilty, and then you can get on with your important and influential life." Mahoney had turned her face away from Catherine again and remained motionless, staring into empty space in front of her.

Catherine Drake simply looked at her and had to remind herself to close her mouth; she was perplexed, if not nonplussed. She was also becoming irate. Who the hell does this girl think she is?

Seconds passed, although it seemed hours, and Catherine looked down at her stack of documents and reports as her mind continued its rapid considerations. Should I just turn around and walk out? She was offended, or perhaps she was both surprised and offended.

What Mahoney stated was closer to the truth than perhaps she wanted to admit, even to herself. She had fought with her superiors against representing Mahoney, afraid she would perform poorly in pursuit of justice for this "gorilla" of a killer. Her heart and head would not be committed to this Neanderthal, and her defense would take time away from her prosecution of other malignant personalities within the military. Overall, the experience would be irritating. Her other prosecutorial activities highlighted her professional expertise, her stature. They were things that she was good at, and things that had begun to form the foundation of her growing reputation. She would have normally jumped at the chance to prosecute this girl. Another notch on her legal weapon, another scalp on her legal belt.

But then she had been ordered to defend her, then forced to read about her to examine who this woman was, and the more Catherine read, the more she worried. She was seeing within Mahoney qualities that she normally respected, if not outright admired. And this troubled her.

She worried because the more she read about Mahoney, the more she saw brilliance linked to resolve. Catherine was discovering an unbending personality possessing characteristics that allowed her to easily accept her mission and its parameters, even though some of these were absurd and would almost certainly result in innocent Americans being injured or killed in response to a political agenda that was ill-conceived and untimely. Yes, even though they were idiotic and she, Mahoney, knew they were potentially idiotic. Virginia Mahoney accepted these preset conditions, all of them. She was also successful in competing in the rarefied air of a totally male domain. She had never offered excuses, but Mahoney was perceptive, even subtle in her understanding of the rapidly shifting political currents always present within her profession and those who governed her profession.

And now, she sat in fetters and had provided an insuperable logic regarding her motivations and actions. Mahoney had just expressed a decisive conclusion, and her summation was that of irrefutable reason. Catherine was unable to penetrate its veracity.

"Petty Officer Mahoney, you have not even heard a word from me regarding our approach before the court. So, if you don't mind, could I at least discuss this with you first? And then I will fill out whatever plea you desire. You are the boss of your destiny. And in spite or perhaps separate from what I may think is appropriate, I will respect your decision."

The smile that formed in Virginia's eyes was blended understanding and empathy. Not sympathy, not anger, not arrogance.

Catherine decided to try a different tactic.

"Sometimes these things look rather bad, bleak, if you will. But if we start by reviewing events and discussing the situation, there are often items that may assist me in assisting you, perhaps even changing the narrative of the event."

A gentle nod of Mahoney's head with a slightly furrowed brow indicated she was contemplating these comments, reluctantly judging and then eliminating them from further consideration.

Still no verbal response. So, Catherine thought one last stimulus was worth the risk, although her legal judgement rather doubted it would be effective. Catherine hesitated as she wondered if such was polemical, even appropriate. Would her Northwestern professor of courtroom tactics and professional standards embrace such a question in similar circumstances, or judge Catherine's potential action sophistic?

"Mahoney, is this the way you want your loved ones to view you? As a silent victim to a crime that, without explanation or context, renders you almost the same as those you were sent to bring to justice?"

Turning her face toward Catherine, locking eyes with her, Mahoney now asked, "Do you love someone, Captain?" Mahoney's voice again was almost inaudible.

"Do I . . . ? What does . . . well, Petty Officer, listen. I am not on trial, Mahoney, and my 'loved ones' are both private and irrelevant at this moment, ok?"

"I think your answer, at least to me, is entirely relevant, Captain Drake. You have my life in your hands. I want to know if I can respect and trust you as an individual. Do you understand, possess the same emotions and values that I do? Can you represent me and my beliefs, my life? Or are you . . . do you find my actions my values so execrable as to represent a form of fancy subterfuge? My values being naïve bullshit to be dismissed as matinee dialogue in an old Western—a John Wayne film? Because, Captain, some of us still aspire to those bullshit values. You know . . . right and wrong. So, do you love someone?" Mahoney asked quietly.

Catherine watched the prisoner carefully; her body language was a mixture of conflicting expression. She was shackled, but her bearing was nearly seigneurial, a leader of leaders. Her eyes were absent of any vapor of star-crossed delusion, of rah-rah peroration. Virginia Mahoney intrinsically knew she had looked into the pit and understood the viper's home. But she was still willing to enter, to crawl into the darkness.

Catherine Drake had seen this conflict expressed in the eyes and silent expressive communication before, and her realization was now unsettling. She had once seen the tough but thoughtful conflict within a fighter ace of WWII. A man who had loved her, who had been so great an influence on her moral grounding of right and wrong. The likeness between Mahoney and this man was disquieting. She attempted to push the thought from her mind.

"Before I answer that, Mahoney, your life is not at risk. The charge is manslaughter, although yes, I agree that if what you just said to me is accurate, murder as a charge against you might seem possible. But so far, we have no indication that is on the horizon."

"My life, Captain—my life, my value as a woman, as an individual a human being, is in your hands, Captain. Depending on what you say, what argument you use, my life either has meaning or not . . . my actions in Syria have value or not. I think it entirely appropriate to say you have my life, legacy, value, even my soul in your hands, Captain."

"I am not a spiritual counselor, Mahoney. I do not deal in souls." And Catherine suddenly realized that she had committed a sophomoric error: don't speak, don't ask questions, and don't conjecture unless you know the response, the correctness of it, and the gravity of its implication beforehand. She waited, uncertain of Mahoney's reply.

"Really, I would think that defending innocents of a crime, one that may render their lives meaningless or labeled as criminal or evil, is entirely about souls."

"It is rendering a person's life as to have meaning, substance or not. You are very much dealing with the soul of that person. And unlike the priest, rabbi, imam, or minister, you actually get timely feedback as to how you fared. I believe it is called a verdict!"

Catherine Drake had actually never considered this quasireligious connection to her work. In fact, she had always taken pride in her secular view of the law, as its intent was to have it applied equally to all. She was far too experienced to dismiss the reality that money, celebrity, politics, and power frequently polluted the pure application of the law, but the intent was entirely secular. The law was to be applied equally to all. After all, that was the bedrock in the formation of the very nation that both Mahoney and she represented, the nation that gave rise to the American experiment. Kings had fought for this separation between church and state—just ask Henry II and his motivation against two systems of justice. It was American bedrock: "All men are created equal . . ."

But here was a young combat special operations warrior, a hero to many, a woman, the first of her kind, willing to risk her life—her soul, as she put it—to carry out orders, the often politically tainted whims of a nation, and she was asking Catherine if she understood that she dealt in souls. Catherine knew she was in trouble.

For she not only was interested in continuing this dialogue with Mahoney, but she was reminded of past warmth and excitement in discussing similarly weighted questions with that former WWII fighter pilot, her long-deceased grandfather. This realization frightened her—the thoughts connecting these two individuals had seeped back into her mind.

Mahoney was not her grandfather; she had no connection to him, and she had just admitted to murdering or at least executing a bound prisoner.

But so had her grandfather. Through ordnance, as the Army Air Force of WWII had called it. Her grandfather had explained, while shaking his head in sad recollection, that the word "ordnance" was an attempt to sterilize their WWII activities.

Simple comments uttered during dreamy early summer mornings. His chipped white mug of coffee, him sitting in the old Adirondack chair while she sat on the swing, thinking that she was starved and waiting for breakfast. The stillness of the air. The dampness of the thick green grass, the mist still visible as it floated upwards to be burned off by the heat of the early morning sun. Flowers in bloom and the smell of lilacs were wonderful but incongruent memories when matched up with her grandfather's narrative.

The actual horror of what the murderous explosives accomplished when dropped from his P-51 Mustang late in the war required language to minimize the reality of what they did. They were indiscriminate in their killing. Women, children, infants, old men, and young girls were all killed by ordnance dropped by her grandfather. His actions had been celebrated. But the deaths of these innocents were real and never left his dreams . . . ever. They had haunted her grandfather's often sleepless nights fifty years later.

Mahoney was charged with manslaughter, a death, but her actions were not indiscriminate. She had intended to kill that particular ISIS guard, probably looked him in the eyes and pulled the trigger. The more appropriate charge was murder. But who was more a murderer? Mahoney, or her beloved grandfather?

Who was more likely to have sacrificed their soul? She knew that her grandfather would have liked Mahoney. Catherine pushed away the absurd picture in her mind of the two of them sitting, talking. Mahoney in the rope swing and her grandfather sitting nearby in the peeling wooden Adirondack chair. Both were at ease in the other's presence. She blinked to ensure the mental image disappeared.

"To your question, Mahoney, yes. I do love someone, but this is really not about me."

"Mother, father, husband, man, woman, lover . . . ?" she trailed off softly.

"Besides irrelevant, your question is a bit personal, Petty Officer Mahoney." But Catherine did not snap back at her; she simply stated the obvious, as she would have to Jenna in the kitchen about the need to pick up groceries. She actually was comfortable with this young woman.

"I could care less if you're gay or lesbian or whatever the proper word is this month, Captain. I would like to know if you actually have opened your soul to another human being. Are you vulnerable?"

The shock of her words caught Catherine off guard, and she stiffened. She also knew Mahoney had seen her response, the tell that confirmed her suspicion. Catherine's face hardened, but she also blushed. She cursed herself for her moment of inadvertent confirmation and glared at the younger woman. But Mahoney's face was now turned toward Catherine. Her eyes, ever vigilant, were absorbing a response, but without judgment or predation. Mahoney's eyes communicated peace and acceptance.

Catherine's potential fury was gone before it even surfaced. And realizing that Mahoney was ready to make a point, Catherine hesitated before ripping into her client using her considerable prosecutorial demeanor to attack her. She waited, thinking, How the hell does she know I'm gay?

But her anger rapidly dissipated as somehow, she absorbed that Mahoney was communicating a respectful acceptance.

And as Catherine was thinking about Virginia's response and the fact that she, Catherine, was indeed vulnerable, her head tilted as her mind considered the unforeseen depth of this young warrior. Was she for real? Was the character, the humility, and the concept of honor that her grandfather possessed also inherent in this young woman?

The two of them, the prosecutor and the warrior, were rotating planets orbiting each other as they examined the personal topography of their respective new worlds. For each, the new world was strikingly different than first imagined.

Finally, Catherine admitted in an almost exasperated tone, "Ok, yes. I love someone, Petty Officer Mahoney, and I am vulnerable. Your point?"

"Would it bother you to know that she is being raped, brutalized, and then murdered by a savage monster who thinks it's fun to hear your lover scream in pain and fear? Would it stir revenge in your soul, Captain?"

Mahoney had used "she." Catherine knew Mahoney knew, yet there was no triumph, no snarky smile. She only respectfully waited for Catherine's answer.

Catherine sighed and drew a deep breath. For some reason her tone, her quiet, thoughtful concern, was so different than what Catherine had expected. There was no defiance, no bravado, no anger. She was, Catherine realized, at peace.

And thus, the lawyer in love and bound to another woman felt that there was no need to hide her relationship, her proclivities, her sexual orientation, or whatever the woke idiots were calling it this month!

Then she stated, "I would want to kill that person, to destroy them and to set the scales in their proper place, yes, Petty Officer. Yes, Virginia, I would."

Now Virginia again looked at her and Catherine at Virginia. Tears were in Virginia's eyes, and Catherine Drake's widened in stunned silence. Their gazes were frozen. She said quietly, "I rendered justice, Captain. I am neither ashamed nor regretful. I will stand before my God and ask

Him if I was right, but you and your system—our system has little credibility left for me. Frankly, it has little importance."

Moments passed. Catherine's heart was pounding slightly. "Virginia Mahoney, we live in a world where the laws are all we have, and we have to live within those laws or there is chaos. If we do not follow those laws, we become . . . we become them. Unfortunately, that is reality."

"I know, Captain. The same laws that allow the president of the United States to order me to pursue a man with prejudice, to kill him, to exterminate him and everyone protecting him within combat operations. But he doesn't have to get his hands dirty, and I am left to deal with the realities, as you call them, to accomplish that order. I was ordered to kill this man for what he did to that beautiful soul who was in Syria simply trying to assist others within the tragedy of that country's civil war.

"Respectfully, Captain Drake, I submit that those who enter the horror and insanity of war, those who have to kill to survive . . . your concept of law, of the potential consequences of losing those legal boundaries or structures governing human behavior, they are washed away the moment one enters combat. The very second one steps foot in the arena. There is no overarching restraint in the need to kill enemy combatants, no matter what you folks philosophically argue. Killing another human being scars the soul, Captain. Laws that make that ok, or argue that one type of killing is acceptable and others are not . . . I'm not sure even you believe that."

"Would the chaos and horror be even worse without legal elements checking the most extreme behavior? Undoubtedly."

"But ask anyone as they kill an individual attempting to kill them if the law makes this act better, easier, somehow more palatable."

As Catherine was listening to her, the images of her grandfather would not leave. The vision in her mind resurfaced of the two of these individuals sharing the strong black coffee that her grandfather loved, sitting in the backyard, and she frowned. Yep, Grandpa would have liked her . . . Catherine was certain of that.

But a flicker of light illuminated Catherine's mind. What did she say? "To exterminate him and everyone protecting him within combat operations"? Yes, that is something that is true . . .

She asked Mahoney, "You said something important about your orders that perhaps will be of use to us—"

But Virginia cut her off.

"I will not allow you to use the law or the lawyer's tactics to save me, Counselor. I will stand before my peers and simply tell the truth. Do you think for a moment you get to splice the hairs so fine as to always have pure outcomes in combat? You don't seem like a naïve individual. I would actually think you are rather brilliant, or at least very bright.

"Combat is unlike anything you have ever experienced. I have only entered that insanity once, but I would wager that anyone surviving Utah Beach on June 6, 1944, never has to wonder ever again what has changed for them. Five seconds of combat changes a human being for eternity. And sitting behind your desk thinking of how to bend shape and carve the legal definitions into a persuasive dictum will never enable you to understand that fact, Captain. Let it go. I did what I did, and I would do it immediately right now if faced with the same circumstances."

Catherine's gaze was directed toward the window of the office, her body tense as Virginia relived the events.

"Catherine Morgan may never know, but her parents now know that monster al Al Hassan Abbas is dead. I shot him as well, in the eye. I killed him. I am not happy or excited or pleased with myself. I killed another human being, a father, a husband, a brother. I killed him. And if I had to kill fifteen bound ISIS guards to get to al Al Hassan Abbas to simply kill him too, then I would. It is that simple. Those were my orders: kill al Al Hassan Abbas. Am I a monster myself? Perhaps I am, but I was sent to do a job, and I needed to get it done. Let's call it an expiation, an effort to save my soul. I needed to get it done."

And again, Mahoney surprised Catherine with her frank but brutally intimate admission. An act of atonement. To save her soul? Why?

But of course, the lawyer knew why. Virginia had regrets over in effect murdering the ISIS guard. But then she said as a matter of fact, without emotion, that she in effect had come to terms with this event. Normally Catherine would have scoffed at the bravado of such a statement or the self-convincing exercise of "being ok" with one's conduct. But Mahoney did not appear to be in this group of self-justifiers who insist they are ok because they have to defend their actions to the outside world.

315

She spoke again, softly but clearly enunciating her thoughts, "Would I have killed fifteen or even one innocent civilian? NO. Children? Before God, I would answer NO. But an ISIS guard who reveled in his delight over sharing Catherine Morgan's abused and traumatized body with his colleagues, the 'American whore,' as he called her? Yes, Counselor, I would have killed, eliminated, or murdered fifteen of those animals, without question. So, let's make this easy and you can consider yourself relieved as my legal representative, go home, and sleep well. I will."

Normally, when Catherine ran into an uncooperative client at odds with her legal expertise, she would have both dismissed their logic and almost certainly stood up and walked out of the room. But for reasons that were grounded in her client's thoughtful articulation and her bedrock values, the legal practitioner remained seated. Thinking over Mahoney's comments, she was no longer just wondering about how to manipulate the events to her advantage.

"Are you willing to make a statement, Virginia?"

"Not if it is in conflict with what I believe or for expediency to reduce a charge. I know what I did."

"You are willing to go to jail for thirty years to adhere to your personal beliefs?"

"Would you ask Nelson Mandela that question, Counselor? Would you ask Gandhi?"

In spite of herself, Catherine smiled. "Someone has the makings of a trial lawyer," she intoned.

It was said softly, a compliment to Mahoney, as she was again caught off guard by her capacious grasp of logic and history.

"And just so you know, both those guys are dead." Catherine smiled as she stated the obvious.

Both of them chuckled and Catherine felt Virginia's response was a gift worth waiting for, a reward in itself.

"Petty Officer Mahoney—Virginia, I am going to ask a personal favor." Catherine looked directly at her, their gazes locked as Virginia sat slightly bent forward, the chain tethering her ankle fetters to her wrist cuffs, not quite adequate in length. "Would you wait on your decision to fire me or relieve me as your legal representative until the morning? If you still are of the opinion that I will not be of help, let me know and I will disappear, or simply file the request you have outlined as to your culpability. If you feel differently, then let's meet in two days. I have some people I need to talk to, including other members of your team."

"Please don't harm them." Virginia said this slightly more forcefully than any other statement, and Catherine recognized it as an emotional plea.

Catherine looked at her directly. Somehow it became a promise, a covenant, and one that lawyers are taught to never make. The twists and turns of legal procedural journeys are legendary in their unpredictability—Don't promise what you can't guarantee, Counselor. But Catherine knew it was too late for the typical sterile rules of an attorney-client relationship. "I will not." Catherine had sealed the covenant.

And as she said this, Catherine felt the lock of a true promise click shut—that first "I love you" to the person you suddenly understand is, and accept as, your soulmate. That individual you want in your life. And Catherine Drake, the military prosecutor with the reputation of a sharpened cold steel knife, suddenly felt vulnerable. She realized she wanted this woman's approval, her respect, and perhaps even her friendship as an equal.

And Catherine almost shivered

With that, she stood up, scooped up her papers, and walked to the door, where she used her right hand to knock on the door.

As it opened, she turned back to look at Virginia Mahoney. She was standing at attention as best she could, for her shackled feet and hands prevented her full erect posture.

Catherine nodded toward her and stated evenly, "It was . . . it was a pleasure to meet you." She then turned and left the room.

Both guards looked at each other as the overheard words uttered by this Captain struck their ears. They were surprised at the conciliatory tone, at the seemingly apparent display of respect from this aggressive—some even might argue reputationally formidable—lawyer who had actually enjoyed meeting a client! That is weird in itself.

As Drake walked back down the hall, she turned toward the elevator. Both guards watched her before the senior guard pivoted and looked into the room where Mahoney was still standing.

He stated, "Petty Officer, ma'am, is there anything we can do for you, ma'am?"

"No, I'm fine. We are good here. But thank you." Virginia's half smile was genuine, as was the guard's query.

"Yes, ma'am." And all three individuals waited for the order to escort Virginia back to her cell.

At that very moment, the source of the legal case against Virginia Mahoney sat silently, alone in the annex reserved for NCOs, and contemplated his near total isolation. He had been abandoned, without friends, reviled, despised.

Such direct hostility might destroy a man trained to value a team, but not this man. Only his hatred for a single individual allowed him sustenance, and as he sat with an empty thick white and chipped coffee cup before him, he was seeing it again, almost as a looping film clip played over and over. He was reliving the events of the al Al Hassan Abbas mission and seeing the object of his antipathy: one Virginia Lois Mahoney.

Chapter 15

". . . and I shall dwell in the House of the Lord, forever."
—Psalm23

The military courtroom was spotless but crowded, with both civilians and military personnel squeezed into its very limited gallery. The warm, rich auburn cherrywood molding running the length of the capacious room had been waxed and buffed to nearly a mirror's reflective power. Formal demarcation of the spectator's gallery from the actual litigation arena was also imposed by a beautiful thirty-six-inch-high wall of Virginia white oak, indigenous American hardwood, its subtle grain dancing in rivulets.

The existing floor had been the bitter struggle of those wanting to preserve heritage versus those demanding upgrades to reasonable maintenance. The polished pine planking sealed with multiple coats of varnish gave testament to those of the former mindset having won the day. It, too, glistened, lovingly dry-mopped each day. Distinct from modern courtrooms where tiles made of acoustic-absorbing material reduced ambient noise, this room amplified whispers. And thus, a low murmur as spectators in the modest gallery communicated in hushed verbiage, looking around seeking familiar faces, produced a measurable tenor.

The opposing legal teams sat at the front of the room, separated by a central aisle. Each three-person team comfortably installed behind two long rectangular wooden slabs of solid American cherry. Styled in a Colonial American design, these unyielding tables comfortably accommodated three chairs, ergonomically designed and riding on an unbreakable glass barrier to protect the ancient pine floor. Comfortable but simple, denoting the unbending authority emanating from the impressive wooden structures in front of them. There was a respective table for each team, both facing the witness stand and this imposing judge's bench.

The room itself had been modified, as normally it was an appellate courtroom and was distinct in both the content of arguments and the judicial protocols governing professional activity from the current participants. But the nature of the case, the trial, and the fact that the subject of the trial was who she was—an individual of growing public interest—caused Navy Command to rethink and determine the optimal site for trial was to be within the Washington Naval Yard. The yard itself was a ceremonial and bureaucratic center for US naval operations. It represented the oldest shore location for the water-based forces of the United States of America, and it was the nerve center of US naval operations. Enclosed within a walled perimeter, monitored and patrolled at all times, it afforded the impression of a secure location. Later events would ultimately challenge this formal notion.

The perch of the judicial referee rose from the floor, facing the legal representatives and the gallery. It was an impressive dark-brown wall of American oak, the center and largest section composed of three rectangular wooden panels, each polished as to allow reflection of the wood's beautiful but subtle grain caught by the ambient lightning above. Half of a Greek column formed the boarder of each panel, its raised grooved surface interrupting the silken polished oak forming the front of the magisterial judge's roost. From this center, it extended laterally to provide the witness stand on the judge's immediate left and the clerk's desk to the right.

Each of these latter structures was smaller in stature than the massive center, and although their panels facing the courtroom were recessed compared to the judge's imposing citadel, the witness actually sat slightly in front of the judge. On the left, the witness box contained a chair but no desk or writing surface. It was also lower by almost eighteen inches, as the judge literally climbed up to a raised platform, a lifeguard's chair. This navy captain served as the legal umpire, using two stairs to ascend to a platform secured on two sides by paneled oak walls. The style was unchanged from the 1920s and was intended to intimidate, to overwhelm, to communicate the power that arose from the chair.

Catherine Drake occupied the solid wooden table on the right, situated in front of the witness stand, with the jury seated on her right shoulder. Nine feet separated her from the juror's box, wherein two rows of solid captain's chairs, each separated by eleven inches, housed the triers of fact: military active-duty personnel. The jury selection had been routine. They were officers and to a person had understood the gravity of their role, the power of their collective finding. They sat quietly, with some minor fidgeting with hands, pulling on sleeves of uniforms, and looking toward the gallery, perhaps in hope or fear of seeing someone they knew. The prosecution was also seated, Drake's colleagues, two men and a woman. A seasoned captain, he had been assigned the lead for prosecution and was to Catherine's immediate left. Only the judge and the defendant were absent.

And then, on the left wall at the rear boundary of the room, a large door was pulled open. Silently entering, a huge man wearing a sidearm firmly attached to his belt, a naval officer of the law and court bailiff, carefully scanned the room for nearly twelve seconds before motioning to a strikingly beautiful young woman. A woman who had been transformed.

His communication was respectful, almost servient as he pulled the door open, expanding the entry to the courtroom further, then led a woman dressed in a naval uniform, crisply pressed and adorned with specific combat and unit citations aligned along her left front jacket. Despite the attempted gender sterility of the uniform, the deliberate elimination or de-emphasis of any provocative curves inherent to the female form, she carried herself almost as a statue but was very much a woman. There was no doubt this was a woman, and a beauty. All eyes were riveted on her, the regal stature and her stunning face and robin's-egg-blue eyes. Blue, but with a hint of purple that made men refocus on them after almost magnetically falling under their alluring spell. Her hairline and smooth, defined lips along with sharp-angled cheekbones rode high on her face. Her slightly Romanesque nose, not large. Her chin, squared but softened slightly by the gentle curve of her jaw as it followed a fluent feminine line toward her neck. Her sand-washed hair was pulled tight, pinned in back. There was no makeup, only a touch of clear gloss present on her lips, as the woman had been concerned about her mouth and lips being too dry and rendering her unable to enunciate clearly in the court. No other embellishment was permitted, sought, and as everyone now understood, none was needed—absolutely none.

The bailiff led the accused to the seat next to Catherine and stepped away. Virginia Lois Mahoney stood next to Catherine as a second female bailiff came forward and removed her handcuffs and leg fetters attached to her ankles. This individual was also respectful and smiled warmly to Virginia, who returned the communication with a half smile and a nod.

The defendant then turned and warmly but silently acknowledged Catherine. Much had occurred since their first meeting, and Catherine found that she herself had begun to travel a road or pathway she had never considered possible. Her former life, with its high-powered legal battles and adrenaline-rushed exchanges within the adversarial context of a system of laws, had brought her to the pinnacle. Her inherent cynical disdain shielded her from the nuances of inconsistencies found in judgements brought against the accused that she had facilitated and enabled by her aggressive, if not sometimes over-the-top prosecutions. The sentences handed down often mirroring her demands of the court became surprisingly common, as both judges and opposing counsel found her logic and trenchant insights irrebuttable. Respect had mushroomed from her colleagues, perhaps grudgingly given, but the snarky comments had withered under the immense talent shown by this naval officer who had brought her version of prosecutorial fever to bear against those who violated the law of the United States of America and its military culture.

She had ignored the outside world and the calls for reining in the near limitless resources the government could foster against an accused. The growing chorus, once perceived as a tiny minority of outspoken ultraconservative defense attorneys, now had been supplanted as legislators from both parties openly and privately worried that the weaponization of prosecutorial action had become all too common. Catherine had smirked at such notions, as she willfully dismissed such cautionary warnings as "sour grapes" from losers and those found guilty or liable for improper actions. "Get a better defense counsel", was her internal soundbite. And she had continued never missing a beat or a rung in the ladder of her self-perceived importance.

But then the stumble occurred. The prosecutor was now a defending attorney, one of those! And despite her unsuccessful attempts to convince Command that she was ill-suited to this role, she had been ordered. She had considered, quietly thought that perhaps Command had not wanted her talent to be marshalled against this particular individual, this woman, and thus had conveniently removed her from consideration as the prosecutor by placing her in the role of defense. Perhaps. But she had also realized that her opposite, one Isaiah James Wallace, whom she had known for nine years, was her equal. He also was without mercy.

But her unfamiliar role was only the initial change that had quickly cascaded into a freefall of ambiguity and insecurity for Catherine, for she had then encountered the accused, this Virginia Lois Mahoney, and the well-lit path of certainty, long ago illuminated for Drake, somehow had been extinguished. Catherine wanted and had attempted to dismiss this woman as a brazen, ego-driven Amazon void of intelligence, of any comprehension except the mantra of word salad so embedded in the culture of special operations. Drake had expected the routine of "just following orders" linked to "the mission comes first" as the tag lines of a gorilla wannabe, a woman who aspired to be a man. One of those oddballs who craved the excitement of danger, a woman in a man's world. One who coveted being different, to have this define who she was, as despite being a woman, she could kill just like a man.

Catherine Drake, cynical, self-important, and wise beyond her years, thus had been unprepared for Virginia. Slowly at first, the young defendant spoke truth to power and used examples within history and philosophy to underscore her understated brilliance. Her biblical knowledge stunned Catherine, and it was not the stereotypic allegorical use so common among the born-again crowd. Indeed, this young lady had read and analyzed and was then able to articulate within the arguments of rabbinical scholarship and papal legality the foundations of the Western culture. Virginia's beliefs, if not actual argumentative commentaries in long unprecedented discussions with Catherine, were nuanced and original. The senior legal expert was captivated and almost— yes, almost—eager to resume discussions with her client.

But as always, there was a barrier that Catherine could not overcome. And this was that where Catherine wanted legal relevance and expediency to enable her to plant seeds of doubt within the near certain foreseeable pending prosecution, Virginia would not allow it. As Catherine strove to underscore weaknesses within the legal record, the pending testimony from the slate of prosecution witnesses, Virginia simply had said no.

For Virginia was willing to be found guilty and incarcerated for her actions and she offered no excuses, only factual events that had caused her to kill a bound prisoner as her team hunted for al Al Hassan Abbas in a time-sensitive environment. Virginia had no fear of the legal findings, for she alone would stand before her God; then and only then would she answer for her actions. Normally, Catherine would have scoffed at the stupidity and the naïveté that adherence to such rigid religious or spiritual ideology would harvest. For she knew that Isaiah Wallace would smile and simply use Virginia's words against her, and the court-martial proceedings would be over. Over before and despite any effort that Catherine could mount in Virginia's defense. Catherine typically would have requested permission to resign as her attorney, citing irreconcilable differences if not the defendant's refusal to cooperate. But the more Catherine listened to Virginia's perspectives, the more deeply she knew Virginia not only believed but had mounted some of the most remarkable examples to place her actions within the proper real-world context. And Catherine knew she was also growing to love this woman, not in a carnal sense, but as an older sister to a cherished younger sibling.

Catherine had fallen from her self-made pedestal. Cascading through self-enamored conceptual, ego-absorbed myths, her fall had been composed of a disorienting fear. She had realized that her self-imposed importance was a sham. She questioned her very purpose suddenly as well as the reality that it was not in keeping with values she respected.

She fell and she landed. But she was uninjured, as apparently she had touched back down to bedrock. Somehow, the landscape now visible was unusually clear. A fresh moist but drying breeze had cleansed the view after an early morning spring rain. She was no longer convinced that nearly all of her previously held certainties, in fact, were real. The earth had shifted, the tectonic plates had moved, and although the air was clear and her vision better, so was her understanding of an uncomfortable realization: her prior hubris was palpable.

She not only would not abandon Virginia, but she would argue her case using Virginia's own logic. Winning or losing suddenly was not her focus as a personal notch of legal victory; her overarching concern was to protect her client. It was to articulate Virginia's voice and those who shared Virginia's burden, undertaken for their nation—Catherine's great nation who threw into harm's way young volunteers, demanding that they accomplish often monumental geopolitical moves on a chess board only to abandon them if the mechanics of the move were somehow imperfect. If the result or the process did not comport with the lofty expectations of men in flannel suits eating at the best restaurants in DC. These young warriors were fodder for the press and the self-righteous politicians who appeared for weekend televised soundbites, expressing self-adorned gravitas, their wisdom deemed omnipotent. Never a hair out of place, teeth whitened to a near fluorescent intensity.

And the young warriors, those asked to descend into the life-sucking horror, the arena of physical violence, were left to wither on the administrative state's vine of sanctimony.

Catherine had walked into her office one morning and realized she was done. Her former life and its comfortable delusion as to her importance and purpose were done. And she felt a sense of liberating freedom that somehow, she had lost her concern over what her colleagues would say, whether her precious reputation would suffer. Once again, she thought that her grandfather, that P51 fighter pilot, might just have begun to regain his pride in his granddaughter. She was going to defend this woman in a manner that shook the pillars of the republic's temple and make them peer into the cauldron of reality.

These thoughts briefly flashed before Catherine's eyes as the judge, a senior captain in the US Navy, now entered from a separate door embedded within the back wall of the room. Wearing his uniform, bedecked with medals, awards, and citations, he was a rarity in the naval legal community whose reputation carried its own weight, for this man had seen combat during Operation Just Cause, the invasion of Panama in 1989–1990. Reportedly to protect the lives of American citizens and bring the then-head of Panama, General Noriega, to justice, President George Herbert Walker Bush had authorized the invasion.

The judge, then a young Navy SEAL officer, had led his team to Rio Hato, where the Panamanian strongman maintained a residence and private jet. During operations, his team destroyed the aircraft but was ambushed by forces loyal to Noriega, and four SEALs were killed. The man who would go on to become a respected judge and now sat in front of Drake had piloted his men to safety after destroying those who had ambushed his men. His actions were judged beyond normal expediency by his superiors, and he was awarded the Navy Cross. As Drake took in the seigniorial figure as he slowly climbed and then seated himself in his chair, her thoughts wandered briefly again to those who possessed this special brand of courage.

For she now understood, in her numerous conversations with Virginia, that courage was common in the arena of combat, where men and now women representing the American experiment with both remarkable gestures and infinitely minor acts of valor protected their fellow combatants. It was the brand of courage previously misunderstood by Catherine, who had found the actions of Martin Luther King Jr. or Gandhi had better fit her definition of heroic, but she now understood, truly realized, that this ephemeral human trait came in many shapes and sizes. For someone as intelligent and well-read as Catherine, she had been almost embarrassed at her lack of understanding and acceptance. These warriors were not the steroid-filled maniacs who liberal lecturers in law school had described, and despite her intuitive intellectual editorial abilities, she had stumbled upon her personal realization, and only recently, that she had indeed unwittingly assimilated much of the noise spewed by activists parading as law professors.

Catherine respectfully stood and waited for the theatrics of the court's tradition to unfold: the pronouncement of the clerk as to the presiding officer, the judge, and those involved, the Navy of the United States of America versus her client. As she sat, she quickly reviewed the probable strategies of her opposing counsel and her responses and the elemental points that she would bring to the front of the argument to place Virginia Lois Mahoney in the position of an honorable combatant who had made decisions in pursuit of the president's orders. The jury would be told the truth, and the onus of guilt or innocence would fall upon their shoulders.

Within this context, she would have to hear testimony from Hansept, who would tell the world that Virginia had executed a captured, incapacitated, nonthreatening combatant. Her actions had been taken without trial or permission but extrajudicially; Virginia had murdered a prisoner. To that end, Catherine Drake had been told by her client, the actual individual accused of that murder, that these facts were true. She, Virginia Lois Mahoney, had pulled the trigger that killed al Al Hassan Abbas's guard, a co-felon who had also raped, perhaps multiple times, and brutalized the captured American woman, one Catherine Morgan. Subsequent evidence supported that Catherine had then been murdered, but that al Al Hassan Abbas blamed the American or Jordanian air raids on ISIS camps for the American woman's death.

Those in the American intelligence community knew this was a lie; al Al Hassan Abbas had personally or through his orders had her murdered. In effect, he had enjoyed her young, soft, beautiful body and held her down, her hands bound and tied, as he licked her face, taking without invitation or permission and repeatedly slapping and then beating her physically as he ripped her clothes off. He had grown excited as he tore her underwear off, rendering her naked, squeezing her breasts and watching her cry out in pain and embarrassment. Then, as he forced himself on top of her and into her, he reveled in her tears and whimpered appeals for mercy. He had repeatedly stripped her of any dignity and laughed at her vulnerability. And when he had grown bored with her, he gave her to his guards, and they were repetitious in their actions as their leader had been. And then, damaged and broken, beaten with her face swollen and no longer beautiful, al Al Hassan Abbas had ended her life.

And Virginia, a woman raised by parents to respect life, to honor other individuals for the talents held within, had placed a gun to the head of one of these men—one of al Al Hassan Abbas's fellow perpetrators who had boasted of his participation in the harm to Catherine—and killed him in cold blood. She had executed this animal not in a fit of rage, but to enable her team to find al Al Hassan Abbas, where Virginia herself, it turned out, had killed this human filth as well. Not only did she feel no remorse, but she had told Catherine that when she looked in the mirror, she saw only the face of a professional who had been asked to do something distasteful, unpleasant but necessary to right a wrong. And she had willingly accepted her role and the fate that followed her actions.

Virginia had prohibited Catherine from finding loopholes in the law, soft spots in the testimony, or practicing the lawyerly tactics of focusing on the character of the witness to effectively denigrate their value or worth, thus obliterating their merit to in effect nullify or impeach and discredit their testimony. The outcome was to lessen any impact of facts being offered. No—Virginia would not hear of it, and she would not allow it. She would stand before her peers and acknowledge her actions. Actions taken that had enabled the finding of the perpetrator of horrific actions against a young and perhaps, some would argue, naïve woman who only wanted to bring assistance to those trapped within the nightmare of the Syrian civil war. Virginia was not proud of her actions, but she was satisfied they were necessary; the mission had been successful in large part because of her actions. She was not proud, nor was she ashamed.

She had told Catherine, "Let them hear what I was ordered to do, what we were all ordered to do, and that we brought justice for Catherine and be done with it. Prison will not be so difficult. I will survive." And Catherine had willingly complied. Against every element of her professional training, she had jettisoned her hard-fought expertise in rendering opposing testimony hollow in impeaching the credibility of hostile witnesses or those tossed into the theater of the court to undermine her client's purpose, value, or credibility. And strangely, in the early morning hours as Catherine peered into the mirror, she, too, found acceptance and enduring curiosity as to the woman who stared back at her.

As these realizations briefly populated her thoughts she shifted slightly to her left and found Isaiah Wallace watching her. His face was unreadable, not hostile but studious, his eyes hazel globes of deep still water, purposefully calm but with fast-moving undercurrents belying their unruffled surface. He himself had established a reputation closest to a legal predator, sniffing the air as though on the Serengeti Plain, a jackal sensing missteps by opposing counsel. Sensing who was a vulnerable straggler. He had impressed those around him, including Catherine, as he was unrelenting in his preparation and willingness to examine the language of statutes long thought devoid of any novel interpretive holdings. He was creative but driven, and this latter contained almost a sense of desperation, as if his actions contained some requisite variable that validated his very being.

Few knew that Isaiah was a throwaway, the adopted child of a typical lower-middle-class couple without money or a college education, but grounded in the residual values of 1950s postwar America. Prayers still were said in the morning at breakfast, the stars and stripes acknowledged along with the Pledge of Allegiance before the school day's lessons began. Their America had all but disappeared, yet their son had flourished. Isaiah had demonstrated remarkable intelligence, surprising if not almost intimidating his astonished parents. His ability to memorize self-demonstrable readings from the US Constitution and even short installments of the Federalist Papers had moved them to worry. His shocked parents had to ask a close friend, a neighbor and community lawyer, what their son had exposed himself to by reading these papers. From that moment, their friend, the community attorney, realized that this child was different, special, and gifted. Their neighbor reassured Isaiah's parents that his readings were not demonic or part of a cult of satanic worshippers, but essays that had formed the republic in which they lived. They were simultaneously relieved and then aware that their cherished son, taken from a chaotic and unforgiving environment, a social cauldron labeling him "unwanted," had potential gifts beyond their humble imaginings.

Isaiah, who had pushed himself in high school, reading and studying almost to the detriment of outside friendships or athletic participation, had been awarded by acceptance into Yale. There, his academic record was remarkable, and three years after graduation he found himself admitted into Yale's legendary law school. His parents were proud of their son—an understatement—yet they never quite understood his hollowed-out core of absent identity, a paucity of knowing where he belonged. Indeed, his diminished self-worth, known only to a few who carefully looked within, was at odds with his practiced performance of self-effacing confidence. Few might have imagined that Isaiah was a desperate captive within the imposter syndrome variable in its intensity, but common in those adopted. Those who had grown up intuitively knowing that they were different, that those surrounding them were not similar. Often, this inculcated a sense of not truly belonging. Not really being a member of the tribe, whether without or often in spite of loving parents, if fortunate. But for many less so, if reality was examined, there nonetheless was the inherent status of an outsider. Of never finding balance because the environment was not their own, n'appartient pas. To not belong.

Isaiah had thus also exhausted himself at Yale Law. Emotionally unable to find serenity or security in his status within one of the world's most prestigious centers of learning, his frenetic pace surprised and occasionally annoyed his classmates, who found his efforts beyond necessary. Yet often surpassing the collective, Isaiah James Wallace had contributed to the Yale Law Journal, and in fact several of his professors found his arguments regarding the tension within the federal bench apropos the separation of powers extremely perceptive. Several had discussed his predictable early appointment to the bench.

Perhaps in a telling understatement, Isaiah had shocked these same legal dons and classmates, but most of all his father when, upon graduation, he entered the US Navy as a member of the Judge Advocate General's Corps. Yet his mother, who had long sensed his need for reinforced acceptance, found his choice not so peculiar, even strangely predictable. She bathed in the warm compliments regarding her son from girlfriends as she sat weekly for discussions within their Bible study group, and Isaiah flourished in the navy. The structure, the forthright atmosphere, and the need to support a greater mission somehow fit within his personal quest to belong, and for the first time in his life, he began to sense that he finally had found somewhere he "fit."

And then Command had ordered him to be the lead prosecutor in the case against one Virginia Lois Mahoney. Isaiah knew this case was radioactive. Being the voice of condemnation against the first female within special operations—a woman who had earned her place within rarefied air, a covert warrior for the United States of America —was now being paraded as the newest pariah by those who "knew more and knew best." Isaiah knew he was in unfamiliar but treacherous surroundings.

He understood the tasteless gruel he was being asked to consume and validate. Those demanding adherence to codes of conduct best described as fanciful salsas populating Hollywood cartoons and written by sanctimonious legal scholars, those absent any experience within or even any understanding of the bloody chalice of combat. These individuals populated a group wherein self-awareness of inherent limitations was simply absent. Isaiah knew that Mahoney had entered the land of quicksand and he, by default, had joined her. His name, his career, and his future could very well be at risk. Institutions have long memories. Those known for their traditions, commitment to ancient codes of conduct, and a near obsessive defiance to ideological fads retain everything.

Thus, Isaiah had instructed his team to play by the rules. Their conduct as prosecutors would be hermetically sealed. An appellate review by the United States Court of Appeals for the Armed Forces would find no objectional prosecutorial behavior. There would be no comportment that raised collegial eyebrows. Wallace also was very aware of growing anger among segments of the US population regarding the perception of government-sanctioned prosecutorial conduct. Such perceptions had noted that specific personalities, politically aligned and emboldened, had usurped the imprimatur mantle of government legitimacy. They had become rouge participants in conduct outside the norm, if not patently unethical. Even at times arguably illegal behavior, as seen when reviewing acts by one Andrew Weissmann during the proceedings against Enron. Such behavior, while not professional, was nonetheless despicable. It needed to be reined in, and it required courage or fortitude to stand up to such pernicious behavior and the growing storm brewing within the former hallowed halls of justice. But lawyers are not known for courage.

Wallace recognized that within the American adversarial-based legal system, there were at least two sides to every story, and thus many of stature within the legal system paused before raising hard objections to alleged collegial misconduct. Yet when viewed with the emolument of time, actions by prosecutors such as Andrew Weissmann injured the very underpinnings of a system they espoused to revere, found in the comments supporting tacit violation of the law by prominent scholars of jurisprudence, such as Erwin Chemerinsky. Quietly admitting a need to pursue his personal vision of racial diversity while ignoring the Supreme Court's mandate that favored status based on race was, indeed, illegal only weakened the law, debased those who practiced it and, in the eyes of many, the need to follow it.

Isaiah James Wallace was not going to be a member of this club. He accepted the roughened edges and the imperfect reality that all lawyers inhabit and thus tolerate. But boundaries exist that are firm, solid, and their crossing is prohibited. At least they should be regarded as such, and for generations, those within the legal profession found comfort in such collective discernment. But now Isaiah and, he knew, Catherine shared a mutual concern, for these tacit yet enduring demarcations had been breached and left to erode. This troubled Isaiah, as he appreciated that winning was not everything. It often was not even the enduring endpoint. Victors in the present might represent ultimate losers within the unforgiving crucible of history's gavel. A most famous victory for slave owners, Scott v. Sandford, reinforced the narrative that human beings were property and without rights. It was a short-lived triumph.

But only those with exceptional perspicacity understood how hollow the flawed judgment was. The victory proved elusive. Through force of argument, each opposing counsel operated within a preordained meticulously articulated process. Violation of the rules and destruction of this process brought humanity closer to anarchy, to solutions achieved via force and violence applied by the strong against the weak.

This is the enduring vertebral column that makes law unique. It is the clash of elegant cerebral energy, the bringing force of logic, emotion, and evidence to underpin and support a system of elegant human synthesis. The construction of emotive and thematic narratives to achieve just outcomes. But perhaps more importantly, it is a countering means to the tribal violence haunting mankind since first walking upright among the arid hills of the Olduvai Gorge. Thus, the rules mattered. They were sacrosanct. They, in fact, were the law.

Wallace was comfortable with this, as he was with the knowledge that his opposite, Catherine Drake, was also aware and respectful of the rules. Not just the written perimeters, but the intent and thus the permissible behavior. For this, he acknowledged Catherine as a professional. In fact, he secretly admired her, but was careful to hide behind their respective titles and positions to render interaction between the two of them sterile.

As the intervals of allowed time for presenting evidence and hearing testimony during the trial were tightly controlled, each side had met its schedule with appropriate preparation. Their collective goals were to inhibit the court from denying or trimming its presentation of evidence. Yet even with their habitual precision characteristic of military preparation, each side did its best to object to or impede the court's acceptance of material evidence that would possibly be difficult to rebut.

As a result, in a meeting before the trial with both lawyers present in the judge's chambers, a detailed and humorless discussion addressed the possibility of infrequent but serious objections being raised. Two issues were in play for both parties, and during this sixty-five-minute meeting, the court, as represented by the judge, chose to pause as he considered objections that Catherine raised regarding hearsay and prejudicial evidence that would taint the proceedings against her client.

The first was overruled in favor of the prosecution, as Hansept's testimony regarding what had been uttered by the bound prisoner moments before he was shot was felt to be within the exceptions, allowing such testimony to be admissible as evidence. The second was the preemptive foundation or discussion by Wallace as to Virginia's gender, perhaps placing greater stress on her to prove her merits or value to the team, and thus she had gone too far in showing how aggressive she could be.

Catherine had no difficulty in having the judge side with her as to the prejudicial content of such comments. But each of the three parties sitting in the judge's chambers knew that Wallace was seeking a deeper, if not broader unmasking of the role that gender was to have, if any, in the trial of the accused. He had brought this to the forefront in a rather harmless discussion of whether gender posed a possible source of stress by way of an explanation for the crime of murdering an unarmed noncombatant.

But all parties also understood that this argument of gender's influence on events could be used in various, some rather unflattering, perspectives to undermine Virginia's role within the special operations team. The judge, immediately grasping both the contents of the stated query but also the tacit inherent derivative contents of its potential, set firm boundaries. Gender was off-limits unless factual or evidentiary concerns were at issue.

The meeting ended with Catherine knowing that she was in the fight of her life, a career-defining challenge that pitted her intelligence, her values, and her will against a force that, while not evil, sought to destroy her client.

But her client had become the embodiment of Catherine's own self-worth.

The trial would not only define Catherine's career but, to a greater extent than she secretly wanted to admit, her own inherent significance and value as a person seeking justice. And thus, the agreed upon schedule of the trial and the roadmap that the judge had agreed to was one of a straightforward discussion of Virginia's actions. These would be remembered and entered into evidence by witnesses present for the events, the mission that eliminated al Al Hassan Abbas. And for the first time, Catherine began to appreciate how empty such words and their conceptual implications were to the stresses of those who had lived moments of combat, now to be arguably challenged by individuals sitting in comfortable isolation, wholly separate from the whirlwind violence experienced. A vehemence demonstrating the limitless capacity of human brutality and cruelty. Such an attempting to overlay legal order was akin to bringing form to a natural vacuum.

As Catherine rose from the compact solid round table where all three had been seated in the judge's chambers, she intuitively grasped her role and the potential consequences found within her efforts. From deep within, a calming breeze touched her, and she deliberately turned to Wallace. In front of the judge, she extended her hand and stated, "Whatever happens, I want you to understand that I have always respected you and your talent."

Wallace was so astonished that while he extended his hand, this adroit polished wordsmith with practiced skills successful in melting a jury's resistance to his persuasion, could only belatedly smile before finding his voice and uttering, "Thank you."

The judge, less than seven feet from the exchange, stood silently looking at Catherine and secretly wondered if he understood the gravity of events that were about to unfold.

It was to be a simple fact: he did not.

Wallace extended his arm toward the door, the graceful gesture of ages past inviting the woman to precede him. She smiled and walked to the door, allowing him to open it, and both silently exited.

That had been one month prior to the trial beginning.

Isaiah now stood and held her gaze for almost three seconds. His eyes then closed, and he instead looked down to his papers neatly arranged in front of him. Catherine, although not unnerved, was intrigued by his somber yet deliberate silent contact, but she was at a loss as to what

Isaiah was telling her. The thought as to what it might be lingered for just seconds before returning to the present.

The formalities of opening the trial process, the court-martial, had now finished. The judge had been introduced, and the interval of respectful standing concluded. Catherine turned slightly as she pulled her chair to a more comfortable position, her eyes sweeping the gallery of visitors. Civilian, military, and as her view began to close, her eyes caught Hansept. He, too, was looking at her, but his face was readable. It was, in fact, a neon sign transmitting loathing and bitterness. He was the wounded animal, injured, trapped, and ready to expend any and all remaining energy to defend his territory. More than a predator, he had been backed into a psychological corner, unable to escape. And he harbored anger, irrational levels of pure hatred directed toward the focus of his emotive visceral energy.

Catherine instantly was aware that she had become the surrogate target for this man, this failed warrior. And despite her training, despite her distance from Hansept, she involuntarily shivered. The game was on.

Chapter 16

"A man must not accept his fate, or he will be destroyed by it."
—Spartacus

The opening statements were now to be presented to the court. Isaiah had carefully picked through the various approaches to be used and in the end decided that a simple statement of the facts, void of drama or insinuation regarding Virginia Lois Mahoney, was his preferred approach. He was not going to demonize her; he was going to present the facts and let the past events and current perspectives provide their own inertia.

Isaiah stood, pushing his chair back as he rose. Instantly, the hush in the large room was profound. He looked down at his papers, as he had blocked out the specific points he felt necessary to articulate. The formal reading of the case, its numerical identifier, the parties involved, and the charges brought by the government now were part of the historic record.

"Ladies and gentleman." Turning slightly to his left, he then acknowledged the judge, "Your Honor, and all present." And with that, he began.

"Rule 156 in Definition of War Crimes Volume II, chapter 44, from the International Committee of the Red Cross provides a summation of customary international law and incorporates the Geneva Convention Accords. The United States of America both endorses these accords and holds our nation's defenders to the allowable, if not essential conduct articulated within. In Section A, Summary of State, practice establishes this rule as a norm of customary international law applicable in both international and noninternational armed conflicts."

Isaiah paused, allowing the jury to absorb the rather lengthy introduction, but this was a deliberate break to ensure appropriate gravitas for his citations. Isaiah strove to ensure that the court and its members, especially those of the jury, fully understood that they were now guardians of principles. Protectors of standards that represented the enduring moral clarity of the civilized world. This was the philosophical, often religious distillation of the human species' attempt to pull itself back from the brink of descent into behavior equivalent to that of rabid animals. Without adherence to such, levels of savagery between belligerents would descend into unspeakable horrors. And although history would provide repetitive evidence that this indeed was not uncommon, if almost frequent, his words represented the last barrier between humanity and unspeakable evil.

He resumed a quiet but almost cautionary articulated volume, looking up from his reading and pausing intermittently to establish eye-contact with different members of the men and women sitting in the jury box. "Section I under Related Practice notes 'grave breaches of the Geneva Conventions' and includes, in the case of an international armed conflict, any of the following acts committed against persons or property protected under the provisions of the relevant Geneva Convention. This includes willful killing; torture or inhuman treatment, including biological experiments; willfully causing great suffering or serious injury to body or health; and willfully depriving a prisoner of war or other protected person of the rights of a fair and regular trial."

Isaiah stopped.

The declaration was now made; the charge had now been uttered in public.

That the defendant, a strikingly beautiful woman sitting with another woman, had murdered a bound and incapacitated prisoner. Willful killing. Willfully causing great suffering or serious injury to body.

She had executed him.

"We are unfortunately assembled to review the actions taken by one Virginia Lois Mahoney, who stands charged with manslaughter for the killing of an unarmed bound prisoner during operations to capture al Al Hassan Abbas, an international fugitive. We will hear testimony from members of that special operations team present during the actions on that specific day, witness to the events that transpired, that will identify the individual who pulled the trigger, killing a captured, bound, and incapacitated prisoner of war.

"We will hear those same members carefully recreate the exact circumstances that resulted in this same bound and incapacitated prisoner, his hands immobilized behind his back, his mouth filling with blood after being struck by another member of the team, having the barrel of Petty Officer Mahoney's Berretta sidearm deliberately placed by her on his face. She then calmly pulled the trigger of her sidearm, and this same prisoner was instantly killed. He was murdered, but the government of the United States has charged her with a lesser crime, that of voluntary manslaughter. It was an intentional act, done without haste and without competing priorities of having to protect other team members. Such an act is not only illegal—it is immoral and stands in contrast to conduct that is permitted by the international community during operations, even during operations when engaged in the sanctioned armed conflict of war."

Isaiah paused briefly and let his eyes again deliberately connect with each member of the jury sitting in the first row. He did not stare, he did not glower, but simply briefly attempted to lock his eyes onto theirs, and it was of interest to him that each replied by engaging his visual communication. Within sixteen seconds, his silent query had passed through the last member of the first row. Every individual had responded. Already aware of the total silence, he contemplated the second half of his opening statement that reviewed the need for accountability for actions taken, even in the theater of war and armed conflict. But he chose to eliminate this, as simplicity was often confirmative. He finished, acknowledged this to the judge, and looked toward his seat.

Virginia had sat silently watching him, aware that he was simply, almost verbatim, reciting the Uniform Code of Conduct and its regulations for tolerated activity during combat operations. Her eyes followed his every facial mannerism, his body language, and his underperformance of gestures made even more powerful by their parsed appearance. Her eyes reflected deep pools of clarity, ultraclean yet not stagnant. For their depth did not hide the slow but continuous spiraling of intelligence, the ongoing processing of her surroundings, and while she felt serenity as to her actions as summarized by Wallace, it was Catherine who internally quivered with energy, as she wanted to blast this remarkably effective strategy by her opposing council. But she did not, and externally one could not find evidence of such energy—only the mask of feigned near indifference to the words uttered by Wallace framing the actions of her client and the consequences he believed now relevant to the violation of international law.

Virginia could feel the energy emanating from her lawyer; the ambient heat generated was almost palpable. Yet Virginia was among those, almost alone, in the capacious room who were at peace. She had understood from the moment she felt the solid metal weapon in her hand, as she stood in the small underground cramped space, almost a crypt within the Syrian plains, that her fate was accelerating; it was moving forward at the speed of light. She had foreseen that her actions would alter her life, Jacob's life, and perhaps all the lives of those touched by the events of that specific mission. Even the trajectory of her nation might sense and then bend to the force of its conclusions as it was exposed to a choice between moral clarity and expediency of purpose, of purity of intent versus necessary resolve.

Wallace's intent in itself was an understated but poignant conceptual distinction. The necessity of conduct within armed conflict that must protect the innocent, the vulnerable, those who were not combatants, those longer able or willing to fight. They must be moved to zones of safety, whether physically or emotionally and psychologically. They were thus rendered noncombatants, and further targeting of them was immoral and, by our nation's participation in the Geneva Accords, unlawful. The defendant sitting in front of the jury, despite her obvious beauty and the striking lines of her near regal profile, had executed a bound prisoner.

Virginia Lois Mahoney was the first woman, the first female to earn her place within a special operations team considered by most to be among the very best at a most dangerous occupation. She was not a token; she had justified her presence by being not only physically capable, but intellectually superior to most in the instantaneous integrating data and choosing immediately and correctly. Her status was legitimate, unadulterated, and lethal. She was, in fact, a warrior. But in an instant, Mahoney had forfeited her status as immune from prosecution for killing other human beings, as they are within the theater of war; they were armed combatants. She had killed an incapacitated prisoner unable to partake in combat, someone removed from the arena of war.

Wallace pivoted slightly. He began his short journey to his seat adjacent to the center aisle, not eight feet from Virginia's chair. As he passed the corner of the prosecution's table, his gaze met Virginia's. For a brief moment, as though through piercing illuminating tunnels of light forming conduit passageways, their eyes, bodies, and beings connected and communication transpired. Wallace's message was one of understanding, empathy, and reluctant participation; Virginia's was forgiveness. She understood his role and accepted his efforts, even silently complimenting his narrative. In that instant, both found knowledge in their roles as but players on the preset stage that had been set in motion.

Both understood that they were moving without control to an unmarked endpoint, unable to slow or deviate from its outcome.

And Catherine, sitting next to Virginia, somehow sensed this communication and briefly looked to her client, seeking to understand, to share, or to object. Catherine's eyes left Virginia and looked toward Wallace, her interest briefly showing, and then she frowned, as she intuitively knew she had missed the message between him and Virginia. She gently pushed her chair back and walked toward the jury, almost brushing shoulders with Wallace as he had turned to take his seat. He was looking at his hands.

Catherine had decided to address the jury with facts and then end with questions to allow the seeds of doubt to grow, to bubble up from the events being discussed and then serve as the overlying fog of uncertainty. Her manner was formal and her face expressed a frown of discomfort, yet also one of need. There was a concern that existed deep within her, and she intended to share this with the men and women now seated in front of her.

"Ladies and gentlemen, the events that will be discussed are in large part agreed upon by both parties in attendance here. One party, an individual tasked to accomplish a goal, an order, but perhaps even something more, as she was asked to render righteousness for a victim who had suffered a crime so vile that even discussing it now will open wounds among those touched by this menace, wounds that may never truly heal. The other party, the faceless but titanic power demanding this action, one having nearly unlimited resources to initiate such a just retribution for this crime, now wants to destroy the very instrument it demanded complete the task."

As Catherine spoke, there was no sound. Having exceptional hearing, Catherine understood that perhaps only once or twice before in her career had there been such gravity assigned to her words, so much consequence to what she was able to communicate to others. And paradoxically, she did not feel fear or trepidation within her sudden realization—no, she was strengthened to the point of heroic sacrifice. She would make her stand with Virginia; she would offer her career and all that was dear to her in her attempt to influence and shape the ultimate result reached by these men and women in front of her, the jury. Her focus was now complete, almost superhuman, and she understood that this is what men in combat have communicated, that instant of immutable total concentration.

"I will not demean the process nor insult the intelligence of the men and women chosen to render judgment as to the guilt or innocence of my client, but I am going to ask some difficult questions. I am going to place you collectively into the belly of this beast, this superheated cauldron we blithely label as 'combat.' I must do so for you collectively to understand what was demanded of my client, the variables, the roadblocks, the life-threatening impediments that she had to overcome to achieve what this nation—her nation, your nation—demanded of her. And then, in consideration of such, your judgment will be appropriate to render a verdict that not only she will live with, but also each of you.

"For make no mistake on this fact, my colleagues, ladies, and gentlemen of the jury: you may one day also be placed in circumstances that demand the same split-second action and prioritization of mission success. And your action will then be subjected to analysis in the cold light of a courtroom, thousands of miles from that spot, without the time constraints or need of instant action. And you will think back to this courtroom and wonder, 'How can they understand what I experienced, the circumstances of what occurred?'

"The president of the United States of America had issued an order to kill this man. It was an order that did not allow, condone, or provide incentive to capture and return him to trial. The order was couched in the verbal requirements to ensure that it was enforceable and would be viewed as defendable. It was, as they say, a legal order. But all knew, from the occupant of the Oval Office who issued it to those who articulated its content and those who would carry the burden of completing its intent, that it was a demand for the extrajudicial execution of a human being. There was to be no trial, no hearing of evidence, no allowance of any explanation; the subject of the executive order was to be eliminated.

"So, as we contemplate the guilt or innocence of my client, let us perhaps first query as to what system allows such an order to be issued. Let us ask: What system demands its military members effectively kill a man who has been deemed unworthy of existence by the leader of this same system? How do we hold this individual responsible for orders that are held valid and the execution of which requires exposure to harm, danger, injury, and death? Where do we draw the line?

"Ladies and gentleman, you will find in paragraph 347 of the *Rules of Land Warfare* the following statement: 'Individuals of the armed forces will not be punished for these offenses [*violations of the customs and laws of war*] in case they are committed under the orders or sanction of their government or commanders. The commanders ordering the commission of such acts, or under whose authority they are committed by their troops, may be punished by the belligerent into whose hands they may fall.' As such, we may now propose that my client's actions, her summation of actions, were committed under orders of her government and her ultimate commander, the president of the United States of America.

"As such, she is not guilty, but should be decorated as an honorable member of the team that was tasked to carry out the order. When you, ladies and gentlemen, answer these questions truthfully, looking at your own reflections in the mirror of your soul, you will arrive at a place that is different than that of the sterile opinion just issued by my respectful opposing counsel."

As Catherine finished, she looked down toward her feet, then up as she sought the several sets of eyes within the jury box. Pausing, she connected briefly with each of them and then turned and walked back to her chair. Virginia looked into the distance, her face betraying nothing, her gaze impenetrable. But it was Wallace who next found Catherine's eyes, and his connection was immediate and telling. He was communicating something odd, as Catherine had never seen this from Wallace, and yet it was as unmistakable as it was peculiar—it was pride.

Several others in the courtroom also absorbed the opening statements, but the impact of each was predictably different. Sitting near the back along the far wall behind the defendant's table was a handsome young man who appeared to be relaxed to anyone viewing him. But he hid his reactions much the same way he had learned to conceal his fear before missions and the reality that he might not live to return.

Jacob Noah Roth listened to the words of Catherine, and as the precious drops of blood within a tourniquet are prevented from escaping, held within to protect if not portend recovery, Jacob absorbed her words. Instantly, he knew Catherine was laying down her career and her future to protect Virginia, to allow recovery, and slowly equanimity replaced his taut nerves. Jacob had not wanted Virginia to know that he was to attend, but he was not so foolish as to think she hadn't known he would come. He knew she now felt his presence in the courtroom. She had always known he would come. And as Jacob looked toward the heavens, he asked only that God would reassure his beloved that Jacob would do whatever was necessary to protect her. Oaths of allegiance, formal orders, or past promises uttered toward a nation had been replaced, disintegrating as melting ice becomes water and then vapor. Her protection was all he found noble; it was the reason he found breath. He was her vehicle, her protector, and God would tell him what was required.

What Jacob wanted more than anything was to switch places with Virginia, to be the individual facing these most serious charges. It was the least he could have done, as he was her commander, and he also was in love with this woman. But there he sat, feeling alone and helpless as the one soul in the universe that he wanted to share life with was being accused of intentional manslaughter—close, but not quite murder. He blamed himself that he had not lied and told the investigators that it was him, his actions, who had directly caused the death of the prisoner. Or that the prisoner had managed to wiggle free, and that her response was instantaneous and justified.

But he had not, and now he was left with the tasteless ashes of his failure to bend the events to benefit Virginia. His despair was nearly palpable, but he held out hope that his prayers would be answered. How stunned he would have been to understand what awaited them, for there were others in the courtroom also to become players within a drama yet to unfold.

Hansept had been told that he was to be called as the prosecution's first witness. He thus sat in the second row, near the end of the isle, with ready access to the witness box. His response during the opening statements was perhaps the most interesting to the outsider. He had looked down at his hands, tightly clasped with knuckles white from pressure and eyes slowly but deliberately closing, forcefully shutting. He also reviewed his actions, his bitter comments regarding one Virginia Louis Mahoney. The tiny snippets of editorial commentary made against her but, in truth, against the empty vessel of courage and strength that occupied his innermost being.

For deep within him, hidden from all and only rarely visited, Hansept craved the respectful recognition that came easily and without effort to Virginia. She who apparently answered to something, some purpose higher than herself, and was thus able to shut out the noise. That cacophony in life that so often disrupts purity of intent or motivation that is righteous. In his eyes, Virginia floated above this disruptive energy, so ever-present yet without grounding or reason. To Hansept, Mahoney glided as though an enabled spirit dedicated to decency and justice. He fought to keep his lips above the surface mud, being swallowed by life's amorphous waste, sucking in the soiled ugliness.

His repetitive dream always ended with him falling into blackness and asking without his lips moving, "Why?" But there was never an answer as he awoke, frequently drenched in sweat, eyes wide open and reflecting momentary terror. He supplanted his inadequate uncertainty with hatred of the one he wanted to be.

And thus, the process had begun. The legal methodology that would determine the fate of the only female thus far admitted into the ranks of America's special operations. But what was unknown to Virginia, to Hansept, to Isaiah, or the presiding judge was that the initiation of these verbal and cerebral official activities would match the start of a much more physical process. One physical and deadly. These uniformed participants of the adversarial legal process could not have imagined the contemporaneous but hidden inertia that had begun. And thus, while these military judicial teams focused on ensuring fairness based on overwhelming responsibilities given to Virginia and her special operations teammates, others had also begun to act.

One such individual sat within the courtroom and studied the prosecutor's nuanced movements, foreseeing the outcomes. This individual waited within the flock of onlookers to understand when intervention was possible, when vulnerability was exposed. She was the conduit of information providing a select group of others with the optimal timing for when to strike their prey.

And remarkably, she was ignorant of this last point: that their prey was Virginia Lois Mahoney, and that they intended to kill her.

Chapter 17

"Tantum religio potuit suadere malorum."
"So potent was religion in persuading to do wrong."
—Lucretius (98–55 BC), Roman poet

The Enemy Within

This young woman gazed at the events of the courtroom, ever thoughtful, while sitting next to the center aisle of the gallery, in the third row of five behind Wallace's rectangular table. Comfortably positioned in what was almost a church's pew, her gaze would have betrayed her if anyone had been interested. For she did not share the contemplative vulnerabilities of those who might have known the participants or were enveloped by the gravity of the coming proceedings, nor was she in awe of the formal surroundings similar to those who felt intimidated by the consequential traditions of the legal system or those who had waited in line to see and record the proceedings.

Rather, she was there to find the illicit sophistry within the ideals forming the very pageantry of the American dream. To study how these men and women could parade as loyal devotees of a system that embraced the subjugation of Palestinians, the continued economic suppression of Iranians who themselves simply wanted a better existence. She was there to record and expose the rot within the system, or so she thought.

She was actually there to assist in planning an attack, yet even she did not know her real purpose. But thus, to anyone of knowledge and prescient understanding, her penetrating observation was subtlety distinct from that of the gaggle.

Susan Donall had grown up in a small town northeast of Atlanta, Georgia. Her childhood had been protected by a doting father who labored honorably in a sawmill, a man who saw the world as it was but was unable to convey his life's observations due to a limited education and the reluctant belief that his thoughtful surveillances were without merit. His daughter was a carbon copy of her mother, not quite beautiful, but strikingly attractive as she blossomed early in her youth. And Susan was aware of this, as she fell in love with the reflection in the bathroom mirror that often elicited an odd, almost hungry stare from men, even those old as her father, when she passed them in the small commercial area of their town.

She was also, however, blessed with a first-rate mind that stunned her father and mother in that mathematics came easily and carried an internal logic that pleased Susan almost as much as it spoke to her. By the time she was a graduating middle schooler, she had scored in the top 0.3 percent of the nation's youth in mathematical aptitude testing. But it was her full, expansive breasts on her medium frame and her shapely legs that Susan was most enamored with, for she found that her slightly thin-lipped smile and staged raising of her eyebrows as she returned an interested gaze from a male classmate consistently led to her being approached. And as she became more adventurous, the transition from classmates her own age to older men, occasionally much older, had identical responses.

Her mother immediately saw danger lurking within her only child, but she was unable to penetrate the brazen hubris in her daughter during stolen moments in their home's small but tidy kitchen or while alone together in their single used family automobile. Susan grew to tolerate her father, if only because she used him as the metric beyond which she would measure her deliberate journey in leaving her upbringing and surroundings. As to her mother, she despised her as exactly the cow she both feared and yet had pledged not to become.

Both parents were elevated to special status within their select Baptist congregation as Susan was awarded numerous scholarships after graduation from high school, but she chose the University of Pennsylvania in Philadelphia, an Ivy League school close to the military-industrial-political complex of the American colossus: Washington, DC. It was Annapolis, the Pentagon, but especially the growing web of dedicated resources involved in our nation's protective espionage leviathan that exerted an almost magnetic drawing force on Susan. UPenn, or Penn, as the students often called their home, was a natural fit for Susan, and she did her best to completely shed her rural Georgia roots. As so often transpires, seeking to belong unbalances an individual's inherent decency, their learned familial, societal, and cultural values, as they instead adopt "correctness" and the mantra of the group.

And thus, Susan exemplified this rather mundane but so predictable counterfeit transformation. Unfortunately, Susan had little of the solid goodness instilled from her parents who themselves were genuine, if not giving people adherent to the Christian values espoused each Sunday within their small red-bricked Baptist church. She had never aspired to or valued such communal tenets, and thus she rapidly became a living caricature of the self-absorbed elitist. Traversing Penn's tree-lined concrete walkways, contemplating her interests within the shadows of the institution's buildings, she enjoyed her sense of unique purpose. What that was remained nebulous, and if her father had asked her to explain her thoughts, like so many of her classmates, she would have scoffed at his inability to grasp her edified perspectives, shamefully unaware of her vacuous content.

And identical to Penn's excessively ornate building edifices, structures reflecting architecture of the Second Empire, Susan could not understand that within the penetralia of her soul was the germinal source, the embryo of a future that would harbor evil. Whereas the buildings of the campus detailed iron cresting on the roof, heavily bracketed cornices, quoins, and balustrades, her thoughts—self-directed, grandiose, and gilded with empty ornamentation—were without gravity. She had absorbed the rhetoric of the mob, the robotic intonations of necessary class warfare against imaginary oppressors.

Sealed tightly within her indecorous but talented mind were the nascent foundations of such a growing malignant perspective. And thus Susan began to summate that her surroundings, the grounds of the university itself, were the ornate legacy of one class of men: white men. And their harsh, often violent subjugation of people of color and women was too frequently glossed over by the "progress" of this land called the United States. That their gains were illegitimate and their progress was born of the blood and uncompensated labors of others went ignored. In between the remarkable inherent beauty of a mind that allowed her rapid fluency within mathematical constructs found impassible by many, Susan read and absorbed the literature of the oppressed. And similar to many of those with young, impressionable minds, a broader and more objective view of history's nuanced travel of a skeptical questioning of repetitive claims of wholesale bigotry and hatred became a mathematical genius buried within an emotional rage fed by unhinged voices of similar sentiment.

At the end of her first semester in her junior year, she changed majors from mathematics to journalism, as she found the gnawing resentment growing within her overwhelming any desire to study complex mathematical relationships, no matter how quickly or efficiently her mind could process such constructs compared to her classmates. Her science and engineering guidance professor was deeply disappointed that someone who possessed such a gift for the abstract world of mathematics had decided against pursuing further study within this arcane world, although he tacitly wondered if Susan might be one of those "crossovers" who eventually found success in journalism, exploring and explaining the often mind-numbing mathematical theories to those less endowed with her innate gifts.

But Susan was not lazy, nor was she without discipline, and she immersed herself into her new chosen field with a heightened sense of coming late to the party with much to catch up on. Her new journalism guidance counselor, a female herself still searching for the subject to ignite her interest, found Susan's devotion and energy refreshing, if not a bit intimidating. But Susan rapidly distinguished herself within her classes, as she was assertive and able to process complex arguments rapidly but almost always enveloped her responses within the paradigm of heartless oppressors versus indigenous victims. For the most part, her ultraliberal professors found the woke-centered ideas of colonial masters abusing populations of native peoples not only acceptable, but in agreement with their almost robotic-minded ideologies. The fact that these same Caucasian male professors spewed such simplistic overviews of history, tracing such lineage to current global strife, ignored other equally valid and perhaps more relevant contributing variables. But within these academic circles, these elite purveyors of history were remarkably uniform, if not almost void of dissonance when it came to who was responsible for many of the world's most intractable difficulties. Almost as though within a catchy Madison Avenue commercial jingle, the perpetrator was repetitively obvious: the white heterosexual Christian conservative male.

Tightly compartmentalized, this eye-catching feminine figure with shapely legs and abundant breasts found these same white men universal in their gravitation to her, and she despised them. And as Susan rapidly matriculated through her studies, she began two habits that would have lasting toxic legacies. First, she initiated weekend nocturnal journeys to the watering holes serving many of those same males, those who worked within or near the beltway's power centers. Those locations on the tourist maps were demarcated as restricted to any visitation, unapproachable even if within a vetted group adherent to an ultrastrict and/or an approved itinerary. These were the locations of several of the lesser-known Washington establishment centers of surveillance, collections of unknown yet breathtaking technology focused on the identification of anti-American geopolitical threats.

At the same time, she indulged in online chat rooms, searching for the proper echo chamber reflective of her sordid one-sided philosophical mindset. A perspective that now had been stained by jargon and jingo aimed at "freeing the masses from their oppressors," the young woman unable to realize that her descent into the opaque world of identity victimhood, a surprisingly well-heeled political agitation of "us against them," demanded adherence and even total commitment to force-fed subjectivity. Objective discussion was anathema to the masters of class warfare.

What she did not know, and perhaps emotionally refused to consider, was that the interest generated by one such young man of similar historic perspectives to Susan was a plant—part of an Iranian cyberwarfare unit whose sole purpose was to entrap, undress, or "fleece" naïve Westerners and mine their personal histories.

His background had been a tightly woven tapestry of shifting alliances within Tehran's hypermobile tribal landscape, a panorama that focused on a single endgame: survival. And Ehsan Karimi had survived. In fact, he had flourished within Tehran's byzantine court environment of competing influences. Popular one month, suspected the next —the mistake that Western intelligence agencies made was assuming that personalities exemplified by Ali Ibrhim Arjang

Ali Ibrhim Arjangwere universally embraced, if not respected, within Iran's cultural landscape. Such was simply not true. As in any institutional setting, personalities often are in conflict, and past slights, perceived disrespect, and, to those in charge, the very template of history registering these emotional barometers enabled a manipulative control of their minions.

But Ehsan had survived such childish games of ascendance, as he focused on the Great Satan, America. It was Ehsan who had originated the kidnapping of Catherine Morgan, understanding her sacrifice was but a conduit to harm the Americans. And although Ehsan secretly despised the idiots at the apex of Iranian power, the mullahs who clung to power as burrowed parasites penetrating the hide of equine thoroughbreds, he truly hated the Americans. Ehsan had lost his brother to America's ham-fisted efforts to harm his country and thus loathed these naïve yet ultrapowerful Western ideologues, lecturing the world as to what was best while harming those it thought threatening. Iran had suffered, and its people had been harmed. But Ehsan had risen and now oversaw critical elements of the Iranian efforts to play the game.

Playing the long game reflective of their allies in the People's Republic of China, Iran had constructed a unit whose directed mission was to extend its tentacles into the very essence of their enemies. Tehran's military was not configured to extend kinetic harm to those outside of Iran; its sole purpose was to preserve power for the mullahs. Thus, the mullahs used this to incite hatred of the Americans as to solidify their tenuous grip on power. The military was their insurance that countless Iranians who themselves despised these ossified blinkered religious zealots would not have the tools to overthrow them. The mullahs were now experts at balancing the use of anti-American populism to buttress their hold on power, yet Tehran now wanted to supplant the American's influence within the Persian Gulf. They ultimately wanted to become the new regional power.

Consolidation of the theocracy allowed expansion of their goals, and the mullahs had blessed Ehsan's novel yet prudent strategic plans. Reaching into the very fabric of the American cultural itself was now a possibility. The weaponization of the internet had an almost unlimited potential, and Ehsan's brilliance served as nectar for the avarice of the theocracy. Susan's participation within ideological chatrooms exposed her to those hoping to gain entry and influence over naïve mindless American "children," those suffused within a cultural ennui wrapped within a cocoon of unprecedented comfort gained through the blood and sacrifice of parents and grandparents hoping to provide a better life for their offspring. Affluence without purpose is a shapeless toxicity seeking meaningless justification. The Iranians viewed large segments of the American landscape as yet another in a long historical line of useful yet expendable fodder—unthinking, self-absorbed, and lacking fundamental appreciation of those wishing to dethrone the American hegemony.

The long-assimilated and inherent articulated predicate of the American Constitution was the concept of an individual's God-given rights. Included among these were the obvious First Amendment rights of free speech, freedom of association, and freedom of worship. But to these clueless Americans, such gifts had become so assimilated within their culture as to generate no understanding that for many within the repressive, if not predatory governments of other countries, such "rights" were unimaginable.

And this included not just the most flagrant of the abusive suppressive governments on the planet, but also "enlightened" governments found in Switzerland, where speech that voiced disagreement with the herd mentality could result in arrest or fines, as the definition of "disruptive or hate speech" was used to muzzle disagreement via three legal provisions: article 261 of the Criminal Code forbids racist and antireligious statements; article 173 outlaws attacks against "personal honour"; and article 28 of the Civil Code guarantees "personality rights."

Under these regulations, cases with specific racist or antireligious elements, including Holocaust denial, are directly punishable by up to three years in prison or a fine. Other instances—such as attacks on nonmentioned minorities, such as LGBT people—are similarly punishable, but the need to fight their case might be found under the broader umbrellas of personal honor or personality rights. It is obvious that the line between hate speech, articulated by the US Supreme Court and in the laws enacted in other "civilized" democracies, are perilously close to censorship, if not actually bleeding over the line.

But the Iranian effort was insensitive to the finer points of a nuanced legal argument of variables influencing or constituting free speech. They were digging for and mining data within the vast universe of the internet. Algorithms that had been strengthened by Google's wizards, knowing that they were working with Iranian sources, had assisted the

Persian effort to monitor and surveil its own citizens. Such efforts were strikingly similar to those used by Alphabet, Google's parent company, working with Communist China and Beijing's efforts to enable tighter control of and identification of "threats" to Beijing's total control over a restless population.

It was not difficult to foresee that this same technology would be employed against Iran's adversaries, and chief among this group was the Great Satan. So, in summation, the corporation that enjoyed the American legal protections against copyright infringement or violation of personal property was working with a country, or several nations, whose sole goal was to supplant the American notion of individual liberties. The ability to ignore or willfully disregard the consequential impact of personal decisions is one of the more peculiar traits found within the human species. Nowhere was this psychological or perhaps moral phenotype more evident than among policymakers of both the American government and its closely aligned corporate ruling class.

And thus, as Susan began her wireless entry into collective opinions regarding "systemic racism," identifying the historic injustices propagated by white males against their victims, she slowly but carefully was vetted by those searching for individuals using such verbiage in the ether. Ehsan's subordinates began to execute his plan using the subtle fidelity within his remarkable manipulative insights. Her chosen verbiage triggered algorithmic prompts and were numerically matched and then quantitated with the identification of her internet address. With relatively few of the younger generation using encrypted message or blinded personal addresses, this was a relatively easy task similar to what Google and others used to target specific advertisements toward users. It surprised naïve consumers within the vast wireless environment when discussing camping plans or tentative schedules with relatives to suddenly have camping companies preferentially display numerous items in their ads that conformed to the user's camping proposals. The idea of selling personal information on the internet was now well-known, but remarkably few consumers took steps to shield themselves from the data brokers engaged in wanton misappropriation of their personal information or use patterns.

In similar fashion but with nefarious intent, Iran was replicating Google's algorithmic screening, surveilling their own population and mining Americans of interest. Susan had thus identified herself as someone of potential consequence, but the quantity of those in America using such language was several magnitudes beyond Iran's capability of individual or human review. Thus, ongoing sifting refinement of persons of interest were initiated and continued by the use of algorithmic formats. Displayed in a user-friendly layout, Iranian cyber experts reviewed this data daily with the next step of pulling Susan's address into a group of similar responders, those in this particular chatroom or one similar, with the next phase of the Iranian screening process now activated.

This third phase of algorithmic involvement was to generate ever-more specific questions from bots that plumbed the responses, effectively funneling them into targeted groupings of American students on the other end. Those that were particularly hostile to these questions were identified, and those holding supportive views were also harvested. In such a manner, Iranians and their illegal teams of Tehran-paid cells could and did target young men that were perhaps descendants of holdovers to the Shah's regime, children of those having fled when Mohammad Reza Pahlavi was ousted. Within the past decade, Tehran had found that eliminating them on American soil, if deemed necessary, was surprisingly uncomplicated. These were often masked as unfortunate events brought on by gun-loving Americans, linked to inner-city violence.

The thought of targeted assassinations of young Americans of Iranian heritage hostile to the Tehran mullahs was simply unthinkable to Washington's bureaucratic elite. Unthinkable, yet it was a reality carefully but prudently accomplished. Tehran, via Ehsan's arguments, had thus successfully replicated Jerusalem's assassination, in the suburbs of Tehran, of leading Iranian physicists in charge of Iran's quest for an atomic bomb. But no such wet operations were necessary with Susan, for as they generated a number of questions and electronically reaped her responses, thus began the last comprehensive phase of Susan's introduction to the Iranian intelligence teams. Depending on the subject and the bot-generated questions, Iranian intelligence supervisors could adjust the parameters of sensitivity to ensure or gamble that the recipients were of value to the Persian regime.

At a preset metric deemed favorable by the Iranian intelligence cyber team, Susan's responses to a pleasant and "victimized" Palestinian man of twenty-two years living in

Gaza, named Ahmed, had transitioned her into the rarefied group of actual Iranian human agents who now took over for the electronic bots and began to carefully construct an online relationship with Susan. Within the discussions were grainy, somewhat unfocused pictures of Ahmed standing in front of a concrete shell of a bombed and largely destroyed "hospital" in Gaza as he bemoaned his frustrated dreams of becoming a physician dedicated to the care of all people in need. He also made the comment that while he understood the European mindset of enslaving people of color, he nevertheless could not accept this fate as his future. Such pure intent along with his apologies for being so typical a man, dedicated to his mother and somewhat less religious than his parents, intrigued Susan.

The fact that the "bombed hospital" was the remnant of a commercial building in Syria—used for storing ISIS weaponry, destroyed by Russian precision rockets—and the inconvenient fact that no such young man existed—hence a grainy, out-of-focus image—were judged not to be limiting factors by the Iranians, as they wanted to know if their young woman was an American plant. Both sides played the game, but the Americans were in some ways late to the party, as they were slow to recognize that their revolutionary technology introduced by a dropout at Harvard and two Stanford classmates did not guarantee American dominance in the use or application of information-based skills. The Americans were learning quickly that many from nations who themselves had never conceptualized or dreamed of an internet were now the masters in its use for predatory activities.

Susan was enamored with this man, his tightly clipped jet-black hair, and his muscled torso, ill-defined within the grainy photo that was supplied to her personal email along with his self-effacing comments on his broken iPhone. She was beyond his need for apologies and over the next several weeks uncritically, if not sympathetically, accepted his "so correct" views on American capitalism, inherent institutional racism, and the need for Palestinian freedom outside of Israeli influence. The absence of comments about the true tyrants of Gaza and the Palestinians, Hamas, or the barbarism that this so-called political group would sponsor in their murder of over 1,200 innocent noncombatant Israelis, including women, children, and babies, didn't register with Susan. She was in love—in love with a concept, a figment of the ether constructed by clever Iranian intelligence officers dedicated to the destruction of Susan, her homeland, her parents, her culture, and her history. She was in love, blind to this or any other reality.

For the Iranians, the hard part had now begun: separating Susan, or whom she appeared to be, from the possible CIA plant that she might be. Within the arena of international espionage was the unspoken acceptance that success was predicated on engagement of a worthy adversary. "Giants do not celebrate victories over midgets" were the harsh utterings of a former CIA station chief during the height of the Cold War. For Iran, duping Americans to harm the Great Satan was cause for national celebration; for the Americans, foiling such efforts were the subject of a yawn. And this underscored the inherent, almost fatal misstep by the Americans: even a mouse can harm an elephant. The

American intelligence community had not yet registered its guard to full alert concerning the Iranians, and this was to prove nearly catastrophic.

The Iranians now led Susan through several weeks of mindless chatter with carefully ladled pretexts, set within messages, suggestive of the normal developing sexual tension that might simmer between a young man who was interested in a receptive young woman. Always respectful, but with an increasing granular probing as to Susan's ideas. Frequently, but not overcomplimentary, they would selectively challenging her with factual Middle Eastern historical political movements, names of important but lesser-known Persian philosophers. Susan was smitten. Here was a young man, one her age, who wanted to discuss important issues and left out the self-promoting feathering of his ersatz grandiose accomplishments.

Yet Susan could not know, and probably would have rejected any suggestion of such, that the electronic chatter between the two were the cumulative insights of hard reality-based combatants of the Iranian Ministry of Intelligence and Security, known as MOIS. With the input of dedicated female resources, the back and forth that was seemingly so casual between two individuals, but of increasing interest to Susan, was in reality the distillation of focused MOIS dialogue. Often generated as summations after sometimes bitter arguments among staff, these seemingly wandering but pleasant electronic communications were not banter; they were the agreed-upon preset, manipulated, and in fact rehearsed dialogues from two or three factions of Iranian MOIS operatives. Determined to plant the hook in this naïve

American's mouth, little was left to chance. But the long game for them was similar to that of the Chinese, who knew that within twenty years, such a find just might be harvested into a valuable or even a generational talent serving her masters in Tehran.

When Susan offhandedly complained to Ahmed that she found her weekend interactions lacking with men similar to him in age but so full of themselves, the fine mist of gold flakes floated down on the MOIS listeners. They had indeed struck a vein of precious metal—metal that might be malleable into information or action that could harm the Great Satan. Thus, the game continued as she shared that her weekends were "wasted" parading herself among members of the elite American intelligence services. She carefully explained that she felt she was continually being undressed by these overpaid and coddled American "soldier wannabes" who "just knew" they were "soooo smart" compared to any and all of their adversaries. These men didn't take her seriously but nearly universally ended up staring at her protruding chest, or as she communicated to her Tehran operatives, her "feminine features tastefully covered" within her blouse.

Even the humorless female MOIS agents, upon hearing this, sputtered sarcastic snorting laughs, then shook their heads while collectively raising their eyebrows at Susan's lack of self-awareness. These Persian women secretly conveyed among each other the new moniker for her: the American slut. But Susan went even further to complain to her imaginary electronic boyfriend Ahmed that "nature had overendowed her," as she hoped this would not be offensive to him. Upon reading this, the youngest MOIS female team member became momentarily slack-jawed as she rolled her eyes and, in hushed tones to her female superior, uttered a rather uncompromising slur in Farsi: "You are filthy!" The inability of this American slut to grasp that it was she who freely visited these establishments while parading herself as though she were one of the Victoria's Secret models strutting the Parisian runway, clad only in cutaway underwear that revealed every wrinkle of the female form. And while the Iranian MOIS female asset might also secretly harbor interest in how feminine she herself would look in similar undergarments, she found the American's lack of insight appalling, if not insulting to all women.

Susan, unable to receive any of this criticism, continued her dialogue with the imaginary Ahmed. She had a special respect for his beliefs, and given that those of the Islamic faith could not drink alcohol, she reflected upon the pious humility of this individual. That he and his colleagues were less likely to be emboldened and boorish due to the inebriating effect of ethanol and that they might just be different from her fellow countrymen, who became more aggressively suggestive of their inherent primal interests the higher their blood alcohol levels became, was a boon.

Of course, the collective MOIS agents were absent any moral interest in the compliments to their faith, as they were absorbed by those whom Susan bumped into. The real prize might not be Susan, or at least not entirely, but rather those she engaged on weekend gatherings. And thus, slowly, the web of intersecting interest grew in Tehran. The result was the beginning of careful monitoring of Susan in real time by real Iranian MOIS agents in America. The fact that there were such agents in the homeland of America might surprise, if not shock the typical American. For most citizens, the ability to grasp that the very nature of their culture, the result of enshrined Constitutional rights along with a specific Bill of Rights, created a very special challenge in ensuring the safety for her people. The passing of the outsider Donald Trump, loved by many and despised by even more, resulted in a chief executive who, through petulance and misguided policy, created a very dangerous if not cataclysmic problem for his nation: a porous southern border with Mexico.

Those in the know, both friend and foe, understood immediately upon the change in Oval Office tenants that the ability to pass illegal undocumented agents into the land of liberty had just become much easier. And thus, groups with ties to Mexico's drug cartels, Iran's revolutionary guard, and Palestinian terrorists within Hamas and Lebanon's Hezbollah began their coordinated movement of assets into the United States of America. And while the knowledge of silent terrorist entry was hidden to most Americans, the general knowledge of the porous border was not. It was both as obvious as it was harmful. The flood of fentanyl, a powerful synthetic opioid, transited into the US via this open conduit left its indelible stain in the American heartland. Almost as a septic tank's putrid malfunction, fentanyl and its purulent stain killed hundreds if not thousands of young Americans.

Sadly, teens often experimenting for the first time with illicit street drugs also encountered their last time. And as the bodies piled up, this crisis was also to serve as the template outcome for a nation growing increasingly insecure as to their collective safety and their leader's failure to enforce existing laws ironically put in place for the very purpose of their protection. But it was more than failure—for a growing segment of the populace came the awareness that the Southern Border Crisis, as it came to be known, was a product of the petulant directives of a man suffering from ever-increasing age-related cognitive decline. Joseph Biden, the deeply flawed and fabulously incompetent chief executive of the American nation, wanted the opposite of his predecessor. No matter how reasonable the prior directives or outcomes had been, Biden wanted to be seen as overturning his predecessor's "hateful" actions. Further, Biden's goal was the demographic replacement of a white increasingly conservative populace with those of color, beholden to the Democrat party and ensuring their permanent hold on power. The collateral damage of dead Americans or raped and abused children sold into sexual slavery within the corporate workings of the Mexican drug cartels was apparently acceptable if the ultimate goal of holding on to power was achieved. The American people watched with growing realization as to the building horror.

The border was open, and the frightening underbelly of the fentanyl crisis gave evidence to young women and girls, as young as eleven, being raped by "coyotes" before being transporting to the border and then sold or delivered into sexual slavery within the growing presence of the Mexican narcotics cartels operating in the US. The brutal irony was soon to become evident to any who cared to look: that the son of the very same individual whose policies permitted this calamity, the president's drug-addicted son, spent his ill-gotten gains on the subjects of this trafficking. These women who grew up in a caged, brutally violent environment physically serviced those who paid their keepers and lived while being subjected day-to-day to the predations of those who used them as disposable rags. Many who viewed this horror began to understand that the president ultimately bore responsibility for the largest wave of sexual trafficking of children ever witnessed.

But to the Iranians, the chaos at the Southern border was an effective diversion as they successfully but silently imported their proxies into America. Iranian intentions had long been feared by those living within her neighborhood including the Saudis, Egypt, Jordan, and Iraq, but the mindset of the early nineteenth century still prevailed among many in Washington, DC. They looked at the vast expanses of two bodies of water, two oceans, somehow knowing that these would protect the North American homeland. Lost in their delusional comfort was the reality that the enemy was now within, brought in through porous borders and influential misinformation pumped each twenty-four-hour news cycle into the impressionable minds of coddled youth with empty values, absent commitment or allegiance, and walking within vacant lives predicated on video games and envy over the latest tattoos seen on classmates.

The youth of America, now receiving its news from TikTok and other mediums with direct ties to the Chinese Communist Party, were unaware and unwilling to argue as to the possibility of false information they had been continuously fed. But the realization that the US-Mexican border was open still did not prepare adversaries in Tehran,

Gaza City, or Caracas for the ease with which nearly anything could be flushed into the American heartland. And thus, four of these "illegals"—two men and two women—began their careful surveillance of Susan. One of the men was selected to represent Ahmed's cousin, and he would approach Susan when the timing was correct. Then the real data transfer and planning could begin.

And within the mist of this diversion was the reappearance of Hudhayfah, the surviving son of a distorted zealot who had raped and murdered an innocent American aid worker. Hudhayfah knew of his father's proclivities and had frowned at the senseless abuse of an "American whore" but apparently his father had been physically attracted to this woman, most certainly a primeval lust Hudhayfah had concluded. And now his team had also entered through the leaky Arizona border to ultimately join in a plan from an Iranian superior, a young man like himself. Hudhayfah was to support a separate Iranian team, but Hudhayfah knew very little of his Iranian handler's plan. For Ehsan Karim's plan was opaque and rigidly compartmentalized to ensure security.

For Hudhayfah's men, dedicated ISIS soldiers, were actually a suicide team, similar to those from Saudi Arabia who took down the World Trade Center on September 11, 2001. Their mission facilitated and planed by the Iranians was to join efforts to strike at those who had destroyed ISIS ensuring their joyous participation. For Hudhayfah, the prize was the elimination of the woman who had killed his father. But even more important to Ehsan Karim sitting in Teheran, this was the first move within his complex game of deadly chess. It was the beginning of the execution of his true goal.

The Iranians viewed Hudhayfah's team as expendable fodder and used them as proxies replicating their successes in the Middle East employing the same strategies. Teheran's precious and real payback was the assassination the orange-skinned president of the United States for his termination of Ali Ibrhim Arjang

Chapter 18

"The world is a dangerous place to live; not because of the people who are evil, but because of the people who don't do anything about it."
—Albert Einstein

The team had largely been assembled in Lashkarak Takavar Training Centre, Iran, with four of the members of the team being regular members of the special operations team. Two others were primarily sniper-trained at Manjil Takavar Training Centre and were expertly qualified. Three were naval demolition experts. All but two had entered via the porous southern border during the first twenty months of Joseph Robinette Biden's presidency. They had escaped detection by US Border Patrol, as they were hidden within groups of illegal immigrants seeking entry into the US, but they quietly separated when all were close to the border. Border Patrol estimated that there were probably in excess of 1.6 million individuals who were "got-aways" since January 2021, the beginning of Biden's presidency, and official records thus had no idea who these individuals were.

Iran, with tacit approval from Mexico's federal government, simmering with hostility toward the Americans, outlined strategic areas of low probability of capture. While there was no formal agreement between these two nations, there did not have to be. A majority of representatives in Mexico's narco-corrupted bureaucracy were only too eager to bring harm to their northern neighbor. Considered a superpower insensitive to the legality of Mexico's territorial sovereignty—willing to enter and conduct raids, arrests, and interdictions, as Washington called it, at any time of their choosing—Mexican authorities shared no illusions about the projection of power by American officials. Mexico had a long history of antipathy toward its very powerful northern titan. More recently, this was made even worse by the hypocrisy emanating from those in the US, who demanded that Mexico "clean up its 'drug-infested' political landscape." Mexico's pithy response was to remind is neighboring behemoth that products don't sell unless there is demand.

But conversations between Iranian and Mexican stakeholders explored the optimal routes of entry for Iranian persons of value. The fact that the Mexicans didn't share these interesting conversations with their American counterparts was yet another indication of how damaged the relationship between these two bordering nations really had become. Mexican authorities used their ample ties to the formalized drug cartels operating along the Mexican-American border to confirm what routes were less prone to being fraught with apprehension. As it happened, these were often remote regions of Southern Arizona, and the strategy was as simple as it was effective. Taking groups of two to four individuals and walking though these remote areas, US Border Patrol would allocate teams to catch each small group but be overwhelmed when a critical number of such groups was intercepted, usually seven to ten. Remaining groups, up to twenty in total with small numbers in each, would simply walk until out of sight, never being apprehended. Vehicles with drivers aware of transit and arrival windows would be waiting at remote desert or mountain roads. Forged identification and clothing suggesting they were hikers or campers would also be waiting so that any random surveillance or stopping of a particular automobile, either a SUV or truck pulling a camper, would invariably be cleared by border agents as legitimate US citizens out for recreation.

Iran had forfeited fourteen trained commandos captured over twenty months, and these were instructed to claim asylum and cooperate fully with authorities. They eventually returned home, as Tehran wanted American efforts to have no ability to tie these illegals to their most valuable assets operating within the American landscape, but they were among the thousands of individuals entering the southern border and being inefficiently processed for later court dates. Some of these court dates were ten years after entry into the US, and this was only if they actually chose to appear for their assigned legal hearing. But for these fourteen individuals detected; 106 highly trained individuals had successfully entered without detection. They were now in the US, illegal teams of highly trained saboteurs setting up their own teams and refining plans to attack and destroy critical infrastructure within the US when instructed to strike by Tehran.

Team #3, as designated by Tehran, running parallel to Hudhayfah's team, thus had come together in the last fourteen months, composed of its highly trained and talented members. Their mission was inherently unique, as they had been assigned to electrical grids outside of Charleston Air Force Base. They were joined by Hudhayfah's remnant ISIS soldiers. There, these joint commandos were to complicate the operational ease by which its inhabitants, air force transport and fighter wings, could conduct normal duties in a crisis. It was not to ensure that these USAF assets were destroyed—the team had little illusion as to their impact—but to render the base less effective or slowed during a need for critical response time. This was enough, as judged by Iran. Thus, they set about identifying electrical infrastructure and grids that were critical to supply the base with functional power. The team also identified two hangars close to the perimeter fences that could be attacked with its sheltered fighters damaged or even destroyed. This alone would shock the Americans and certainly sow confusion for the necessary interval. Iran would be able to tell the Americans that there was no safe zone within the US that Iran could not touch.

Their other assignment was much less popular, but composed of a very talented cell separate from this operational team tasked to hit the American base in Charleston. This quite accomplished tightly integrated group was actually composed of the most gifted of the personnel and were judged to be critical by Ehsan in Tehran. They were to contact and establish a relationship through Iranian assets in Northern Virginia, using one of their team members, with certain individuals thought potentially valuable in Washington, DC. One of these individuals was Susan Donall. They would work with Iranian intelligence assets in DC to gain her trust and use her as a conduit to provide a highly valued time-sensitive payback for the past elimination of their asset in Syria and the highly publicized killing of their beloved General, Ali Ibrhim Arjang, considered at the time to be the second most powerful person in Iran. The current Iranian leader and his servants in intelligence had stated publicly that there would be payback for the Trump administration's murder of Arjang.

Yet these Americans had also sought out and killed their proxy, the useful zealot al Al Hassan Abbas. There must be retribution, they seethed, or the "cowboys" in Washington would continue to prance around as though they owned the Middle East. Discussions in Tehran held privately with Ali Khamenei, with Ehsan honored to be asked to briefly attend one gathering, centered on the fact that the Americans needed to experience a setback that stunned the world. Firing missiles into their camps that dotted the Syrian and Iraqi landscape no longer seemed to be effective. They must regret the targeted assassination of Khamenei's friend and political ally. The vehicle to facilitate such action was one woman: Susan Donall.

One hundred and eighty days—six months—before Virginia Lois Mahoney's trial began, the team had received orders to prioritize the operational contact in Washington, DC. The game was officially on. The first move in the complex geopolitical execution of the "big prize" was now moving forward. Ehsan wondered deep in his being as to the wisdom of his orchestrated intent, whether the killing of an American President, the ultimate act of retribution would pay dividends for his country or ensure its destruction.

Chapter 19

"Non semper ea sunt quae videntur."
"Things are seldom what they seem."

Susan found the very handsome well-dressed man, somewhere in his mid-thirties, sitting comfortably at the bar. She had seen him previously, perhaps twice in the last four Fridays. There was a hint that he was a bit out of place, given that he still wore a three-piece suit and his clothes looked freshly pressed, almost runway perfect. His demeanor did not suggest fatigue at the end of a busy week, being upset with his colleagues, or harboring resentment regarding his supervisor's illogical decisions. His posture was comfortable, nearly regal—obviously he came from money or wanted everyone to believe this fact. But he looked up from his phone resting on the solid mahogany surface of the ancient bar, adjacent to a folded edition of The Washington Post, and smiled. A tentative but seemingly preoccupied greeting, and then he looked back to his phone, or perhaps it was the paper. Susan thought it was the sort of smile that was neither threatening nor unwelcoming. It was filled with humility, an invitation to ask about the weather. He was ok. He looked safe.

As such, it communicated exactly what Ahmed had practiced, receiving direct and penetrating feedback from female team members as he strove to hit the optimal nonverbal statement. Susan knew that she had seen him and that he had been paired with a beautiful raven-haired beauty and another man, both near his age, all well-mannered and expensively dressed. Nothing gaudy, but clean lines within classic clothes that communicated money and understated prestige. She had watched them out of the corner of her eye. They had stayed at the bar consuming perhaps one drink, but not even finishing the glass of wine or the tumbler of Chivas as the two cubes of frozen water gradually melted. They had spoken in hushed tones, this man gently placing his hand on the other's shoulder as a clear statement of support and agreement. He seemed different; he just didn't fit the typical ego-driven government worker so often a tenant of the establishment. And this interested her.

"Ahmed" waited about fifteen seconds and then looked up again directly at her. Each allowed their eyes to lock, however briefly. He smiled again, and Susan contemplated whether he actually lifted his eyebrows slightly—and invitation to join him? The next move was the most dangerous for him, as it might accelerate or destroy any hope of a relationship with his target. He frowned and then looked in her direction again, raised his glass toward her, and this time his eyebrows did elevate as his lips formed a slight pensive gesture, his upper body turned toward her. She had his attention.

Susan laughed despite her nervousness and walked over, sitting down with an empty bar stool between them. She then looked at him, saying nothing, waiting for and ready to assess his first response. Was it to be a pleasant "Oh, I apologize, I'm meeting someone later," or something more definitive?

"I have seen you here previously but was too apprehensive to invite you to join me with my cousin and her husband a couple of weeks ago. I hope you will forgive me?"

He smiled, attentive to her response, and she was pleased by this humble yet direct statement.

"Well, you three looked complete. I would have considered myself an outsider."

"No, not at all. You would have been and are welcome to join us! We have a difficult time making friends here in the States."

"Why is that?" she bit hard at the bait that had been so carefully placed in front of her.

He looked at her carefully and then said, "We are from Palestine, or what we refer to as Palestine—it is now Israel. It is hard to meet folks here who do not prejudge us."

The hook had been implanted, but he had to be careful to let it sink deep into her, not allowing her even a momentary doubt as to his authenticity.

Susan looked at him, her eyes sweeping over his person, his clothes, his presence. "You don't look like the typical Palestinian displaced individual, if I may be so direct. I hope I am not offending you?"

He smiled, attempting to convey painful memories along with a disarming warmth. "No, not at all. We are not all basket makers or shop owners. Some of us ran businesses, and my family is composed of numerous physicians. I am the black sheep, as I chose computer science and engineering instead of cardiac surgery as my father and brother practice."

Susan nearly inhaled audibly, as she was stunned despite her practiced insouciance. She managed to smile weakly before bending toward Ahmed and whispering, "Americans only hear one side of the story and they are lazy, so don't expect empathy from them."

Again, Ahmed smiled and artfully looked down at the paper before raising his eyes and locking with Susan's now inviting gaze. "Sometimes it takes special individuals who are not part of the crowd to understand what really exists or has existed in history. But perhaps I have said too much?"

"No, you have said the truth, and unfortunately this is often lacking in our press and popular news."

For almost two hours they sat, Susan sipping her wine that Ahmed had insisted he purchase for her and him barely touching a Chivas. In fact, he took only one sip, and it was barely enough to wet his lower lip. By the time he told her he needed to get home, as he had work early in the morning, she was captivated and wanted to see him again but was careful not to push too hard, not wanting to become the typical American whore.

He asked if she needed him to walk her to her car or to public transportation—he did not offer to drive her—and she said if he would be so kind as to escort her to her car, she would be very appreciative. The night ended with a handshake and his statement that he was truly surprised to have met someone with her obvious depth of "understanding and intelligence" but was both surprised and happy. She returned the compliment, and the night ended with her quickly scribbling her phone number down and inviting him to call her if he desired.

He feigned surprise and gratitude, smiling with his eyes as he pressed her hand slightly more deliberately and turned and walked away. The pieces were now set on the board, and over the ensuing four months the relationship would enter the typical phases of attentiveness and exploration with limited but highly choreographed physical intimacy. He "discovered" her interest in journalism, something that was known to the Iranians from her emails and texts. Over the ensuing month the two talked extensively, or rather he asked many questions and she discussed, pontificated, lectured . . .

They rarely held hands but talked while sitting at restaurants, sipping coffee outside of bistros, resting after long strolls as they drank bottled water, and walking within the National Zoological Park, commonly called the National Zoo. And this facilitated a distinctly uncommon component to these conversations, as Susan later reflected. Ahmed was the first man she had met who was genuinely focused on her and not telling her about himself, his talents, or his accomplishments. This enthralled her. Her vanity, if not sanctimony and ego, had yet to discriminate between interest and directed manipulation. Almost resembling an individual dehydrated, incapacitated, and weak now provided with cool fresh water, Susan gulped without insight or thought as to other potentially nefarious motivations for the offer.

Ahmed "guided" this nescient journalistic fever slowly and incrementally toward the mission directive. He feigned hope in the need for objectivity in the upcoming trial of a woman accused of killing an unarmed prisoner during a special operations raid of al Al Hassan Abbas's compound in Syria. He asked her what she felt regarding the reported events and gradually complimented her insights, but asked her if she had ever thought about viewing the proceedings. Perhaps there was more to the story than she or the public was aware.

He then provided a remarkable "confession" to her that he felt the entire process was based on hypocrisy and he was convinced that the woman was just a pawn to allow the government of the United States to wash their hands clean of their culpability in killing, extrajudicially, the ISIS leader. He worried, as Susan slowed during their walk by the great cat enclosure at the National Zoo, that he had overplayed his hand. She was quiet for several seconds—something that, he later related to his team, was laughably rare! But he had struck his mark. She considered and then enthusiastically agreed to the suggestion. To Susan, Ahmed's spontaneous suggestion highlighted his belief in her talents and prescient views. She would go to the trial and evaluate the circumstances. Then perhaps, as he humbly noted, the two of them could collaborate with others in setting the truth for the masses to understand. She smiled, inwardly believing him to have validated her inherent talent.

However, he also hinted that if Susan thought that indeed this Virginia woman was guilty, perhaps it was appropriate for Susan and Ahmed to call for action to render a just sentence beyond the show or mock trial that was occurring. Susan didn't fully query as to his meaning, but she felt that to please him, she would attend the trial and discuss the proceedings with him. Not only was there no harm in doing so, she thought, but she also felt that indeed she might learn something about the empty justice spewed forth by the government of the United States of America. She would have a remarkable project to submit at the end of the semester, as she was required to provide a final paper to receive her journalism credentials from the university. This, of course, paired with the fact that her actions would solidify their relationship.

And so, it was Susan's own idea to attend the trial—or at least this was the conclusion in her own highly malleable panorama of moral surety. She was there to ensure her presence in the limited seating of the spectator's gallery to acquire evidence of the hypocrisy of Virginia's own testimony and the fallacy of American justice.

However, she was actually there to gather information for Ahmed's team, critical in planning a breach of security and allowing, if not facilitating, the killing of all in the room. She couldn't see past her own ego-centered sightlessness as to why this strikingly handsome and accomplished man was so interested in her. She couldn't process his feeble background stories and logic he gave her as to why she needed to be at the trial, or to be taking detailed notes as to the security arrangements, carefully quantifying the numbers of armed guards and the entrances and physical impediments to reach the courtroom. If she had heard the conversations that she had engaged in played back within a classroom or analytical format, she would have immediately realized their insincerity linked to a cloud of darkened emptiness. For to anyone eavesdropping, the conversations would always have sounded directed—both focused and with practiced skill—toward obtaining detailed information about those guarding and those within the courtroom.

And deep within MOIS, the simmering anger over the loss of an older brother remained the catalyst for a mission to murder everyone in a courtroom in America. Ehsan's palpable hostility for the Americans had only grown in the years since US policy had facilitated weapons procurement for Saddam Hussein's Iraq during the nearly eight-year conflict with Tehran's government, Ehsan's employer. He had lost his older brother, a man Ehsan had idolized and loved, from the direct result of Hussein having access to advanced weaponry. The remnant injury had never healed, and the pernicious fury coupled with genuine talent had since elevated Ehsan to his senior position within MOIS. All knew his story, although he never discussed it publicly. But all were aware of his seemingly unnatural enmity directed toward the American culture and government.

Ehsan was setting up the chessboard to strike within the very heart of the American experience, the long-held pinnacle of self-government and liberty. But this was a nation recently so self-absorbed within the amorphous concepts of what was "proper" as to become a laughingstock among nations wondering if the American experiment of citizen-led government had finally run its course. Ehsan wanted to hasten what he hoped would be its ignoble end. He could not let go of the personal loss of a beloved sibling, failing to understand that his own ossified leadership had contributed, if not were largely responsible, for the events leading to his brother's death. His brother, along with nearly half a million others on each side of this neighborhood bloodbath, had been lost due to a prolonged conflict whose genesis lay within opposing views of Islamic religious practice that morphed into intractable political differences and suspicions. But these were arguments that would never see light within Tehran or Baghdad, as objective reflection is anathema to idolatry, and on each side, the cognoscente could not see past their "golden calf."

But Susan would not or perhaps could not realize that she was being used. Thus, she had embellished and told the naval security office in charge of courtroom protection that she was a University of Pennsylvania senior working on her graduating thesis and was incidentally from Virginia's hometown. She had confidentially discussed her plans with her Penn advisor, who thought the project "interesting and proper"—translated as "woke"—as it highlighted her own misgivings about the military and the US government's duplicity. The hometown element was fictitious, but both her advisor and Susan suffered no concern as to their fabrication, as the ends justify the means within their collective philosophical and moral landscapes. The letter, with an official University of Pennsylvania seal, provided the imprimatur, and foreseeably a clerk within naval security thought it "reasonable" and provided Susan with clearance to attend. But not before demanding signatures on numerous forms that articulated her attire, conduct, and Susan's endorsement of naval decisions to exclude her or anyone thought troublesome. The forms also articulated that every individual entering the courtroom would be subjected to detailed body searching by a member of the same gender.

The female sergeant had looked at her directly and after searching her small knapsack—finding only writing material, as no computers, cameras, or voice recorders were allowed—subjected her to a very thorough, if not intimate, searching of her person.

But over the first days of the trial, Susan was remarkably talented in providing Ahmed and the intelligence officers within Iran's collegium with intel. The wheels had been set in motion, and the various Iranian members of four distinct teams now were beginning the end phase of their extensive preparations. With Ehsan orchestrating their integrated actions, their conduct would forever change the American public's view of their homeland, the safety of their nation, and the government's ability in providing its citizens with basic security.

Chapter 20

"It ain't no murder killing beasts like that."
—H. G. Wells, The War of the Worlds

Hansept had not been one of Jacob's closest teammates, as there were aspects of Hansept's character and his conduct that appeared to be walled off to the outsider. Within the tightly knit teams of special operations, hidden agendas or unreachable dimensions within a man were often markings of cautionary problems, and they stood out to observant commanders as brightly as the 1950s Las Vegas billboards on the strip. Jacob inherently found such a desire to hide one's unfathomable qualities or characteristics from others on the team as loose planks near the end of a narrow rail-less wooden dock. Common in the clear water lakes of the Northern Midwest, in the dense deciduous forests of Wisconsin or Minnesota, these structures were as fingers protruding into the lake but were often pulled out of the water each winter, as the thick ice that formed would shift and crush their timber moorings as matchsticks. Their moorings would shift, placing stress on the symmetry of the dock, and the planks might loosen.

And thus, walking on these docks after the first freeze, when ice had formed but was still thin on the lake's surface, could render steps on wooden planks tricky. One was aware that the beauty of the lake was to be viewed and enjoyed after careful inspection of where one put their feet. Individuals unable to find calm within themselves, to be comfortable in their own skin, identified an individual that, under stress, might have planks that, while perhaps not rickety, were insecure. Jacob realized he was not a trained psychiatrist or psychologist, but in truth his ability to read men had so often proven correct in the violent cauldron of combat that his prescient observations needed no formalized degrees or wall-adorning certifications.

But Roth had watched Hansept closely during the endless training drills and mock scenarios, and Hansept had performed extremely well—in fact, almost perfectly. This was not uncharacteristic for such a person with clandestine sepulchers of vulnerability. And while every individual possessed a unique array, some were able to accept their inadequacies while yearning for improvement, and some could not. Hansept was of the latter. And yet Roth was still surprised witnessing this man's "freeze" during their mission —surprised, but in truth, not entirely. Some plank had been dislodged.

Now, Hansept rose slowly from his preassigned seat. His uniform had been pressed, its creases razor-sharp. The prosecution had indeed called their star witness, the spectator to the killing, one who observed in real time the unauthorized murder of a bound prisoner. He now was in the center aisle and walked the short distance to the hinged gate, the only entrance allowing access from the gallery to the functional legal arena, the witness stand, the jury box, and the well. The polished three-foot-high Virginia white oak divider, composed of evenly spaced glistening pickets. Each vertical picket, separated by six inches, hinted of a subtle natural grain. The surface of each four-inch barrel was comprised of meticulously carved wood forming a gentle twist, a candy cane effect that revealed a subtle luster in the ambient light thrown down from hanging ornamental art deco pendant lamps. The beauty of the divider was so obvious that those in the front row of the gallery took care to avoid inadvertent contact, and although armed security would have removed any items immediately, most never considered draping clothing over the beauty of the wood.

Each of the eight suspended lights composed two rows of four separate ornate bronze structures equally spaced, creating two parallel paths and dividing the large courtroom into three long sections from the entrance to the wall behind the judge's perch. Each emanated radiant energy through frosted art deco half globes, brightly illuminating the ceiling but also producing a cone of dappled softer luminosity projecting to the floor and benches below. Such decorative bronze structures were no longer in fashion, a vestigial reminder of days when the symbolic gravity assigned to proceedings were held to be a remnant expression of American legal independence distinct but equal to the country of her origin, Great Britain. American laws were hers alone, and though they descended from English common law, they were reflective of the pioneering spirit of the peoples who left the rigid social and cultural captivity of the king's land. Over two and a half centuries later, again it was to be another reminder to those same pioneering people that liberty, freedom, and justice may be inherent providential gifts, but accepted and enjoyed only at the cost of very real plebian blood, sweat, and tears.

Hansept pushed through the gate but stopped as he reached the end of the prosecution's table. The court bailiff approached him to escort him to the witness box, and Roth watched and saw the nearly hidden tells of a man in conflict with himself. His stride was restricted; it had lost whatever fluidity of motion was previously displayed. His head was off-angle, tilted slightly, suggesting uncertainty not only as to his testimony but also his place within the drama of the proceedings. Hansept was, to those who knew him well, walking in a foreign land, familiarity completely gone. He was at war with himself.

He was seated, sworn in, and asked to tell only the truth. The rehearsed narrative began with Wallace initiating a series of questions to establish who Hansept was and why he was the lead prosecution witness. Brief background information or foundation was laid for context, allowing the jury and members of the public to understand who this man was and why he was present as the prosecution's first and star witness.

Minutes into the interrogation, Isaiah Wallace established that Hansept alone was willing to testify to the truth of events in the mission that killed al Al Hassan Abbas. He then posed the critical question: "Was the prisoner incapacitated and unable to participate any further in offensive capabilities?" Movement was instantaneous from the defense table.

Catherine had nearly jumped to her feet, rising quickly before she assertively delivered, "Objection, Your Honor! Calls for speculation by witness."

The judge looked at her and then to the prosecution. "Sustained."

The senior captain sitting in the judge's perch frowned a bit. "Please limit your questions to factual evidence,

Counselor, or lay foundation as to opinion being expressed. But remember, this individual has not been called as an expert witness."

"Yes, Your Honor. Petty Officer Hansept, from your location that we have established at the head of the stairs, perhaps three and a half to four yards from Petty Officer Mahoney, directly visualizing events at that time, was the prisoner incapacitated? Meaning were his hands bound, hands and arms immobile via regulation-dictated actions specifying disarming and rendering a captive enemy combatant unable to continue offensive actions against American forces?"

Catherine again rose, but now more slowly. "Your Honor, again, calls for speculation."

"No, Counselor, now it is a simple question as to whether the witness saw that the prisoner's hands were bound and whether this met with legal definitions found in regulations dictating that the prisoner was unable to continue offensive kinetic activity against American forces. Our personnel are educated as to the priority of knowing these rules and their impact even in the chaotic field of ongoing combat operations. Overruled."

Virginia had been looking directly at Hansept, and at this moment he turned his head slightly and locked eyes with her. It was only for a moment, but it was noticed by all who were watching Hansept as the events unfolded.

He then he spoke directly to her, and not in response to Wallace's question, "In situations that are as fluid as what we experienced, I cannot say with certainty that the prisoner was incapacitated or not still able to initiate offensive kinetic actions against American forces."

There was a hushed silence in the room. Seconds seemed to turn into hours before Wallace stumbled as he sought to understand and process what he had just heard. Virginia's outward expression remained as if in stone, but her eyes narrowed and her heart accelerated. What is Hansept doing?

Catherine, who had been glancing down at her notes, responded as though shocked by electricity. Her face whipped up as she jerked her eyes both to Hansept and then immediately to Virginia. Stunned into silence, Catherine quickly recovered and tried to vocalize some rejoinder. Virginia looked directly at her and the attorney froze; even her breathing momentarily halted. Silence descended, and both women understood words were unnecessary. The Earth had moved; the tectonic plates of a legal process characterized by predictability had shifted. All parties had suddenly entered uncharted territory.

Wallace, among the quickest to react to adversity, partially recovered and said perhaps in a slightly more aggressive tone than he intended, "Petty Officer Hansept, you have previously testified that the prisoner was bound and totally unable to render any offensive threat to the special operations team, American forces, or the individuals in that room. This was said under oath. It was delivered without coercion or pressure, but was volunteered. Are you changing your testimony, Petty Officer Hansept?"

Hansept again looked at Virginia and she at him. The two could have been anywhere, as the exchange was eerily similar to their past wordless communications in Iraq, Syria, and within undocumented incursions into Lebanon. The exchange was a statement between souls absent defenses or protections, a linking of two individuals that needed to communicate, to share and support one another. This in itself was unprecedented, but it now was reality.

"I cannot say with certainty that the prisoner was incapacitated or unable to initiate offensive actions against American forces."

His eyes never left Virginia's, and her returned penetrating look communicated empathy and support. Only Hansept could feel and process what Virginia was providing him, but it was an accurate reflection of her "statement" to him. His head then bowed, and his body relaxed.

Wallace saw this and rapidly tried to chart a path to manage the building wreckage of his case.

"Your Honor, with the court's permission, I would like to ask for a recess, as this testimony is at odds with what has previously been freely offered and in detailed fashion. Before I notify the court as to the change in the witness's status as hostile or in opposition to our case, I would like to review my records and notes, ensure that I have accurately understood this witness's prior testimony under oath, and then proceed. I apologize to the court for this unanticipated delay, but I think it is obvious that his response is not one anticipated from his prior statements."

The judge, despite his reputation for iron discipline, smiled. Not without empathy for the prosecution's perilous situation, he nodded before uttering, "I think that a brief recess is appropriate. Let us recommence our activities the day after tomorrow, at nine o'clock sharp. Counselor, that should give you time to re-examine your material and perhaps consult with your witness, who will remain under oath and available for direct, cross, and redirect if needed. " He recognized both the gravity of the issues before the court and the unforeseen change in Hansept's admission to Wallace.

And with this, the senior captain, a decorated combat veteran acting as the judge, gently tapped his gavel on its solid wooden block and declared, "The court is in recess until nine a.m. the day after tomorrow." He rose and exited through the door on the wall behind his perch.

Wallace was already placing his paperwork into his lawyer's square rolling briefcase. He was frowning, and the insertion of his notes and court documents was perhaps more aggressive than he realized. He was both frustrated and angry that he hadn't planned for this outcome. Unforeseeability during a proceeding is a nightmare for all attorneys.

He glanced up again, looking at Catherine to find her slowly shuffling her paperwork. He pushed his chair back and rounded the table, briskly walking toward to exit on the side wall of the courtroom. This was an exit reserved for the legal participants. His stride was purposeful, but if care had been rendered in observation, a thoughtful observer could have identified an unnatural wafting. Not quite but close to rudderless sudden unmooring, reflecting an uncertainty that had now crept into his movement. Isaiah Wallace knew he was adrift, uncertain and without a map as to his destination within this proceeding. This very public proceeding.

As Susan filed out with the small group of spectators, even she, without formal legal training, knew the prosecution had stumbled and that their first star witness had not delivered the anticipated evidentiary testimony. Hansept had not been in the witness box for more than four minutes when the recess, more accurately a delay, had been requested. Everyone in the courtroom was in shock. She could not wait to tell Ahmed.

Roth, too, had been shocked, motionless. He frowned slightly as he immediately began processing the possible motives for Hansept's change of testimony and what it might mean for Virginia or for Hansept himself. As he rose, he paused to allow others to file past him, as his seating position was closest to the far wall. There was a single large door for those merely in attendance, slightly off-center, as it allowed the spectators to exit from the aisle on the right side of the courtroom if one was standing looking toward the judge's perch. It was a choke point for security, guarded at all times. Roth instinctively examined the room and as he had countless times in his life, processing vulnerabilities to defense or attack.

There were five other doors: the judge's, one designated for the accused to enter, one for legal teams on the opposite wall facing this door and a yard beyond the jury box toward the gallery, and the jury entrance was in the opposite corner of the same wall as the judge's entrance. The final door, marked "Emergency Only," was off Roth's shoulder on the same wall as where Virginia had entered, but this exit was within the spectator's area. This door was sealed but accessible during an emergency.

Somewhere deep within his psyche, Roth felt the growing awareness that this room would become pivotal to his survival. But more than that, this room might just influence Virginia's life, his nation's awareness, and its concept of the price required to ensure the durable legacy of the American experiment. Roth sensed a percolating zeitgeist of unease. He was suddenly pensive, almost uncertain in his belief that a "government of the people, by the people, and for the people" as a central hallowed principle of his nation's founders would endure. And somehow, oddly, he suddenly sensed it might be decided within the walls of this very room.

Susan had exited the room before Roth was anywhere near the back public double doors guarded by court bailiffs and armed military guards. A female bailiff had respectfully stood by Virginia and replaced the fetters on her ankles and around her waist before locking her wrists. The young military guard demonstrated extreme deference toward Mahoney, knowing her past exploits and her remarkable skill, and even whispered to Virginia, "You ok? Lean on me if you lose your balance."

Virginia, sensing the near awe of her junior military escort, smiled and softly stated, "I weigh too much for you to catch me." Both young women shared a genuine chuckle.

She escorted Virginia back through the assigned exit, deliberately walking through the cinderblock and reinforced poured concrete or rebar-constructed halls to her cell. No pictures hung on these walls. Their surfaces were a pallid military gray, and only smoke detectors and emergency lighting fixtures intermittently spaced according to federal code served as adornments. The whole time, the young guard carefully scanned the environment for any possible threat, looking back over her right and then left shoulder every twelve to fifteen seconds to assess potential violation of protocols dictating no unauthorized loiters. Only a guard five yards in front of them and two additional soldiers seven yards behind them were allowed in the hall when Virginia was being escorted back to or from her cell.

Virginia, recognizing her excellent training, had to smile inwardly as to the near impossibility of such a threat materializing from the near impenetrable halls of the secure structure.

Virginia Lois Mahoney could not have known how wrong her easy dismissal would prove to be. But she did not have long to wait.

Chapter 21

"There is a time for war, and a time for peace."
—Ecclesiastes

As she left the courtroom, Susan ruminated on the events and began to form a summary for her anticipated meeting with Ahmed later that evening. She was excited but in truth equally anxious. Within her recent meetings, or what her mother would call "dates," Ahmed had become more interested in her opinions, a behavior welcomed by a woman dating a man. But in one of these exchanges, an intensity that bordered on fanaticism had surfaced in their dialogue. He had been asking her about her ability if not her willingness to describe in detail all aspects of the courtroom, its geography and positioning of those during pretrial proceedings. Susan had visited the naval courtroom several times in the two weeks prior to the trial's beginning and had to register with security. She was allowed to see the room, and she had spoken with security personnel.

As the conversation had continued, intensity had supplanted the pleasant dialogue between the two. His dark-brown eyes had become almost black as he pressed her to understand how important her observations of seemingly irrelevant variables were. These included how many guards were in the room at the beginning of proceedings, where they were positioned in reference to the defendant, and most emphatically, if the exits were populated by armed soldiers.

If she had been honest with herself, she would have sensed that these exchanges were interrogations and not conversations. But she couldn't admit that something else was afoot. And thus, as he engaged in an examination of her potential courtroom observations, he had peppered her with queries regarding the environment and the specific locations of courtroom personnel. He went so far as to demanding that she identify their weapons, and how well she thought these courtroom guards were trained. Were they obese, old men graying and only present for show? She had laughed nervously during this tense exchange and objected that she, of all people, was ill-equipped to offer such insights.

The harsh intensity of his immediate response had almost frightened Susan. His handsome face had instantly become almost lupine as his lips pulled back, his teeth shown, a predator unmasked. But as though suddenly self-aware, Ahmed instantly transitioned back into the erudite sophisticate. Through flattering comments spoken with charm, a softened response, he offered that her insights might be more accurate than the so-called experts'. But the remnant energy of his reaction had unsettled her. Deep within her subconscious, she wondered if and even began to sense that Ahmed might be someone else.

The intensity of these mannerisms seemed abnormal, if not portending possession of an unquenchable inherent rage. She had seen its force in that single moment of unguarded clarity. The curtains had been pulled back if only for that instant, but an explosive fury had been witnessed, deeply buried but slowly surfacing as if flotsam from a sunken vessel. The depths could no longer contain it, and within Ahmed's being, now even a tiny spark seemed ready to ignite a deadly inferno.

Yet only briefly did her consciousness flash a red light of warning as she briefly considered her role as to what history described. Was she the "useful idiot"? Was she becoming a tool to enable something terrible to succeed? But the warning had dimmed as Ahmed reasserted his alluring charisma.

He had playfully quizzed her on the architecture, on the placement of the lighting. Within the exchange, he suggested that her knowledge was broader as to eclectic subjects than she realized, and he chuckled that he needed to begin more disciplined study to keep up. To an observer, his efforts were deliberate, a recreation of the desired ambiance momentarily pierced and unsettled. Inwardly, Susan saw him become pensive, his handsome face thoughtful and, as an aside, quite striking. He was cursing himself for his previous lapse; his emotions almost gave the game away. But that evening had passed, and now, nearly two weeks later, the trial had begun and she had all but forgotten that ugly momentary crack in his porcelain surface. Almost.

That night, Susan met Ahmad in one of the more expensive restaurants in Old Georgetown. He was elegantly dressed in a deep-blue Kiton suit—very conservative, understated, costing $12,000 or even more—and a blood-red tie with a tiny pattern of fleur-de-lis throughout the material. Deep brown-black tasseled loafers were visible but slightly hidden as the cuffs of his trousers appropriately touched his shoes when he stood. He looked more the model in a men's magazine advertising expensive chronometers or yachts. The only item missing was the cosmetically enhanced bottle blonde clad in a silk blouse, her top buttons open, hinting at cleavage and oversized mammary glands, clutching his arm and pushing her face into his shoulder. There was no such woman, but Susan found herself wondering if she was to be the one inserted into such a façade.

He brightened when he saw her and encircled her waist, pulling her a bit tighter than she expected with his arm. To any outsider, this was a power couple. Ahmed's plain white Charvet shirt adorned with gold and onyx cufflinks, his suit, and his coifed but short-cut hair spoke to understated wealth, if not influence.

"Hey, I thought you were going to stand me up!" He smiled, and his almost perfect white teeth produced a glowing, entrancing welcome for Susan.

If only she could have known how many times he had practiced this in front of his mirror and that the brightness of his enamel had been demanded by a MOIS female asset. "Americans are obsessed with white teeth," she had told him.

Ahmed led her to a small table, and the waiter was already pulling a chair back and, with his right arm, inviting her to sit. Ahmed waved him off, and he seated Susan himself. She sensed something had transpired and he was waiting to share news with her, but she also had news to tell him regarding the trial.

As he settled in the chair across from Susan, his eyes nearly caressed her figure as she sat opposite him. A small vintage Tiffany & Co. centerpiece of genuine sterling silver formed a delicate bowl that separated the two. She wore a simple silk cream-colored blouse with a delicate necklace of 18-carat yellow gold, amplifying the gentle curve of her neck. An expensive but classic long deep-blue skirt reached her knees, her navy-blue stockings softening her feminine but muscular legs. A gray blazer with a subtle checkered pattern hugged her shoulders, open in the front.

The centerpiece held a short candle, its flickering creating a bouncing light that enhanced the intimacy, as the room's ambient lighting was low. The dining room itself was remarkably quiet, given the eleven additional settings that were almost identical to Susan's. Waiters were instructed to speak in hushed tones and to listen carefully to customers, all in an attempt to hold the sound to a minimum. Additionally, perforated fabric-wrapped tiles along the walls were designed to absorb the background sound, acoustically dampening their impact.

Ahmed smiled and carefully stated, "Well, I have some things to discuss."

In spite of her self-imposed discipline, she nearly blurted out, "I also have some things to share!"

Always the gentleman, he nodded. "You go first. Women have a special place in our culture, so please, I insist that you begin."

The irony of his statement was lost on Susan, as she accepted this compliment without thinking. Not twelve months from their dinner, Hamas terrorists would invade Southern Israel and systematically murder over 1,200 innocent civilians. Their barbarism would mark a watershed of human decency within the twenty-first century. It would also mark the end of any reasonable discussion of Palestinian autonomy for longer than the elite socialists populating the halls of the US Department of State could have imagined.

Chapter 22

"Veritas patet."
"Truth becomes obvious."

The final verdict of the dinner ultimately suffused Susan with a primordial fear. A chill grew in her being, slowly replacing the warmth of expectant intimacy. As the first mountain winds of winter cool the land for months of cyclic sleep, Susan was aware the relationship had been altered. Ahmed had become remarkably silent, at times seemingly fighting for self-control as she recounted the blundering prosecution of the first witness, a man called Hansept. He remained silent for almost a full five minutes after she had begun to describe events, a frozen ersatz attempted smile fixed in place. But his eyes spoke truth, and they betrayed him. They were locked on Susan, predatory, his head fixed in place, absorbing every word. And then he began to slowly, methodically question her on familiar subjects. The number of bailiffs, the positioning of additional guards along with the specific armaments that each of these individuals carried. She had taken notes, and as she checked her memory against her courtroom observations this seemed to please him, although he asked if anyone had noted this activity.

She had responded that she was careful to be discrete but not suspicious in her documentation of events during the proceedings. He had again smiled, but his was not one communicating warmth, nor was it shared with her. It was as if he was sitting alone. He looked out into the distance, his eyes flickering slightly as he frowned, his lips flattened thoughtfully. He had become detached from her, his mind hovering in some distant land, one inhabited by ghosts. He slowly came back and looked directly at her. His penetrating focus was unfamiliar to her; it was filled with purpose, a summation of decisions long in the planning.

Susan could not have known, and even if her closest friend had shown her irrefutable proof, she would have dismissed such as "conspiracy propositions." She simply could not fathom that sitting in Tehran, a younger sibling of a long-dead older brother had greenlit an operation to harvest American naïveté, the sophomoric belief that the homeland of the American landscape was untouchable. Events would soon unfold demonstrating how very incorrect such assumptions were and how much Susan lived within a fantasy world, the bitter summation of hubris and unfettered sanctimony.

Susan was momentarily important to Ehsan, but she, too, would soon be discarded. Another intermediary within a complex series of chess moves all intended to deliver a message to Washington, DC: "You are no more untouchable that anyone else, and every bit as vulnerable." They had promised retribution for the killing of Ali Ibrhim Arjang, and indeed Tehran was keeping their word. Ehsan was keeping his long-held silent promise to his older brother. This was the first move to the ultimate payback. The outcomes were to be identical.

Now, sitting in the upscale restaurant, Ahmed queried Susan as to their ages, heights, and again her subjective assessment of their skill, touching on whether she thought that each person she recalled was going to be a difficult adversary.

And the light blinked.

Suddenly, a tiny warning light began to glow within Susan's being. As she leaned back into her chair, absorbing the intensity of his interrogation, uneasiness grew. Finally, in that moment she understood what she had become. What she always had been.

She was a conduit of information for some larger operation.

Her heart skipped, and her face suddenly flushed. She felt betrayed, used, as though she had been undressed and physically entered without her consent, her very being violated. And the act, while not a physical assault, was in fact more brutal, for her trust, her desire for his approval and admiration, had all been but a requisite pretense to his unfolding theatrical production. She was being used, and she instantly transitioned in that moment of understanding.

Maturation often comes within hardship or failure, the unsettling of foundations once thought secure. Susan's immutable bedrock now was rolling as waves crashing onto a shore. Her grounded, "so correct" beliefs were suddenly wavering indecisive. Such moments of brief self-awareness percolate to the surface and can be viewed, if only for seconds, as glistening snowflakes radiant in the sunlight, but quickly returning to elemental shapeless moisture.

She looked down at her hands, now clasped, her knuckles now white. She nodded slowly as her carefully chosen evening presentation suddenly collapsed. Her minimum use of eyeshadow, her most expensive clothes, the touch of her overpriced Creed perfume, and even her undergarments had all been selected with utmost care. She felt ashamed, used, and then building within her was rage. But maturation comes in spurts and swirls, identical to tiny eddies of a brook along its banks. Her conduct would be professional, her response cold, sterile, hermetic. She smiled at Ahmed, a cold dismissal, and immediately he was alert, leaning in toward her. But it was too late; he had lost her. She had already left, just not physically.

She pushed back her chair, quickly scanning her side of the table to ensure she had her small clutch, and stood, not even extending her hand as she quietly uttered a malevolent departure.

"Thank you for a wonderful evening, sir. My best wishes in your future success, whatever you are up to, but I have an unfortunate conflict. My cat misses me, and I must attend her." Her last comment dripped with sarcasm, a fiery slap to his clean-shaven face.

And with that, she pulled her arms tight up and into her chest and marched deliberately to the front of the spacious dining area. The maître d' was not at his highly polished greeting station, and as Susan turned toward the glass doors, she was met by an affluent elderly couple having just entered. Slowing carefully as she approached them, Susan forced a tight smile and allowed the man in his mid-seventies to hold open the first of two glass doors for her. As their gaze momentarily connected, his eyes held a trace of empathy as to why a beautiful young woman was deliberately and quite rapidly exiting alone. She briefly held up her hand, motioning for him not to bother with the outside door, as she was already leaning her shoulder into it, a bit more aggressively than was required, and then she was almost outside. As the door was nearly fully open, a beautiful raven-haired woman smelling of lavender side-stepped her and entered, ducking under her arm. Susan instantly recognized that despite her face being veiled in a Paris silken shawl or a hijab, there was an air of familiarity to her; her radiant olive-toned complexion mirrored Ahmed's.

As Susan felt the cool air of the Georgetown evening, she said a silent thanks as to her foresight; she had driven her roommate's Subaru to meet Ahmed. The Forrester, a compact SUV marketed as ecofriendly, was a favorite of the au courant UPenn crowd.

Inside, Ahmed had just finished his third text using an encrypted phone, purchased in America but modified by MOIS, loaded with programs that prevented even the most advanced CIA eavesdropping, or so they believed. His first text, sent as Susan was only halfway to the front of the dining room, was simply one word: "leaving." This had activated the team waiting in a parked black Mercedes sedan fifty feet from the entrance to the restaurant. The female member of the team had quickly arranged her hijab and exited the car, briskly walking to the front of the dining establishment and nearly crashing into Susan as she pushed through the outer glass doors of the establishment. Simultaneously, a handsome, powerfully built man, registered as a diplomat to the Pakistani embassy but an asset of Iran's MOIS, exited the other back door of the Mercedes on the street side and looked both ways for police or any form of law enforcement.

His right hand smoothed his finely tailored navy-blue Brioni suit jacket, and his palm felt the handle of the Sig Sauer tucked at his belted waist. The weapon, fitted for a 22 long rifle caliber, had been modified with an acoustic suppressor. He crossed the street and moved toward the now silent storefronts of expensive antique shops and a Ghurka leather goods store. The Mercedes had been circling earlier and parked in three different locations all close to the restaurant, each location selected as allowed by customers coming and going in the earlier evening traffic. But now it was near 8:45 p.m., and the shortened foot traffic of the autumn days had mostly cleared.

The MOIS agent walked deliberately as though traversing a familiar pathway that led him to one of the ultraexpensive townhouses lining the tree-shaded street just beyond the corner businesses. He slowed, his form becoming difficult to outline in his dark suit. Night had descended, and although the streetlamps gave attractive cones of soft white light every eight to ten yards, their intensity and illumination had been deliberately decreased. Such was the objective as a nod to "the woke" concern expressed by rabid environmentally focused DC bureaucrats. Trees and foliage needed to understand day from night, and bright lights confused their biological rhythms.

Ahmed's second text was to a backup team located two blocks away, its four-member team sitting in a van with markings identical to a FedEx delivery vehicle. But this vehicle was not owned by the American corporation. This text was also a single word: "Cancellation." The vehicle, carefully modified with tightly fitting but removable magnetically attached thick canvas rectangular coverings, had two per side that adorned the flat windowless panels of the midsized van, hiding the FedEx markings. The team had assembled, packed their weapons, and made their way from an isolated garage in the western suburbs of Arlington, Virginia. They sat with a man and an older woman in the front seats and two men behind them, the van idling in an open-air public parking garage, carefully situated to avoid fixed camera surveillance. These were highly trained operatives from carefully selected Iranian MOIS assets. Their specialty was rapid penetration of "secure" locations and elimination of specific targets with removal of evidence.

All within the van knew that unforeseen obstacles could foil their objectives, but they were hardened to challenges encountered, having successfully murdered several Iranian dissidents who had relocated in Europe and the United States. They had even attempted, twice, to eliminate the late Shah's son, now in his early sixties, during his travels to Europe but had failed, as one arm of their integrated team had been exposed within a London suburb, with the present Georgetown team having to think quickly to escape undetected from their location near Parliament. To date, the Iranians had no real understanding of what had gone wrong, but their superiors considered the range of possibilities from luck to a traitor within one of the teams or their tightly held diplomatic corps with knowledge of the plan. The team had scurried back to their London embassy and hid out until each of the four members were assiduously siphoned back through Switzerland to Greece and then to Iran before being reconstituted into their current integrated crew.

They had a critical window to accomplish their objective and they were already moving rapidly, but within the posted limits of Georgetown's streets. The last thing they wanted was to attract the attention of law enforcement and be pulled over for breaking the speed limit. They had chosen their location with care, rejecting an underground parking facility. While offering greater privacy, it could not reliably receive texts within the massive concrete structures. Thus, sitting in the rear of the open asphalt parking facility, as the electronic message appeared, they immediately responded by exiting through the automated gate and were moving quickly toward their destination. Traffic was light, again a planned but unreliable variable, and their progress was swift.

The team was within one block and one parallel street from the target of MOIS's interest within eighty-seven seconds. As they rounded the corner, entering the side street harboring the dining establishment, they saw parking was allowed on only one side, as the old Georgetown streets were notorious for their narrow confines—a remnant of early colonial life, one without trucks and mechanization. Susan had to traverse this street and then enter a sheltered walkway opposite the establishment she had just exited. This led to two short flights of stairs and a three-story parking garage situated immediately behind the antique shops and boutique Gurkha store.

Someone might have told her that walking alone into a sheltered, somewhat isolated corridor was ill-advised for a single female at that time of night, but the structure was illuminated, and she could readily observe an absence of any other human traffic. She also had her right hand on a small

419

aerosol can of Mace pepper spray. What she could not have known, however, was that the well-dressed MOIS asset with the Sig Sauer was already kneeling in front of an adjacent Porsche 911 out of camera view, having carefully but rapidly picked his way along the walls of the parking facility to reach his destination. He also carried a powerful transmitter the size of a package of cigarettes that emitted a rapidly oscillating frequency of electromagnetic energy designed to disrupt and distort the most common commercially available visual surveillance equipment. Its range was limited, but as he approached wall-mounted cameras that monitored the parking deck, he toggled the switch and passed underneath the camera, certain that a momentary static disrupted the continuous filming. He was not invisible, just unidentifiable.

The asset chose his position based on his training, as he remained hidden from camera view and yet close enough that when he toggled the transmitting switch, he would again briefly disrupt image quality, degrading surveillance. There was a specific activity that had to be blurred to any subsequent review, and the powerfully built MOIS agent knew that future review would be a certainty.

The second team in the ersatz FedEx van slowed and perchance, an empty space was found, allowing them to park and wait less than half a residential block from the garage. Their wait was not to be long. Upon receipt of Ahmed's second text, the teams were moving expeditiously but cautiously, always scanning the environment for law enforcement. Additionally, the team had been trained to attempt to time activities to intervals when pedestrian traffic was low or absent. This was not a requisite element, but one that simply reduced potential collateral damage.

Susan traversed the walkway rapidly and exited through a windowless steel door that swung open with a grunt of grinding rusty hinges. She took in her surroundings, confirming an almost packed parking floor, but her rapid inspection demonstrated no human forms. Her steps were audible as her heels clicked along the cement. The MOIS agent flicked the tiny switch of the plastic transmitter and the oscillating electromagnetic pulses began. The transmitter lay on the hood of the Porsche, within his immediate reach, to ensure transmission to the camera feed. He unconsciously massaged the sound suppressor, ensuring it was firmly tightened to the end of the weapon. He had chambered the first round as he had initially taken up his position and subsequently rechecked his weapon three additional times.

Sometimes luck or providence, good or bad, presents itself at critical moments of an individual's life, and just as often there is a plaintive heavenly query as to why. The MOIS agent, his real name Ahura Lankarani, realized that he and his target were momentarily alone in the parking garage. And while this hardened humorless tool of Iranian foreign policy did not view this as a sign of Allah's favor, he nevertheless understood good fortune. Inwardly, he smiled.

Susan's pace was brisk as she rounded the left rear bumper of her roommate's car, her key fob in hand, the small can of concentrated repellent in the other. She suddenly sensed she was not alone and raised her chin quickly, turning slightly and glancing toward the front of the adjoining

421

parking space. But it was too late to alter her location, run, or even scream.

The explosive acceleration of two lead .22 long rifle rounds sounded as if compressed gas suddenly was released from a punctured tire; the range was less than three yards. Striking her in the left chest above the shapely contour of her breast, their effect was immediate. Designed to inflict maximum injury, the hollow-point construction of the lead projectiles entered her body with the width of a lead pencil, but meeting the resistance of soft tissue and bone in her torso, they expanded into a lethal cutting funnel of kinetic energy.

Susan's flight or fight response kicked in as surging adrenaline levels responded to her sudden recognized peril, but she couldn't move. The traumatic impact of the Iranian's two rounds had mortally damaged Susan's heart, tearing through her delicate cardiac wall, each tiny fragment of lead from the disintegrating bullets tumbling and twisting and slicing as tiny blades. Her heart responded to the adrenaline surge, increasing both its rate and contractile force, but it was useless; the life-giving, sustaining fluid was now without direction or purpose. Blood flooded into her thoracic cavity, gushing through shredded cardiac tissue. In contrast, a delicate tiny crimson blossom appeared above her breast, slowly enlarging as it discolored her silken blouse. Astonished, her dying eyes wide with questioning, searing fear continued to hold Ahura's gaze for nearly 3.4 seconds, an explanation sought. But his empty soul offered no response.

As she began to collapse, Ahura moved rapidly toward her, closing the already short distance. A third round fired from three feet, his extended arm steady, hit her squarely in her left eye. The accelerating force of this deadly projectile converted her once beautiful and agile mind, one of such promise, into a liquid-protein paste.

Susan's head hit the cement with the sound of a pumpkin being dropped onto a rock. The dull, almost hollow acoustic signature of her plummeting onto the hard surface was confirmative. Her life was gone.

The agent bent down and immediately grabbed the back of her coat collar forcefully but without violence, repositioning her so that she lay parallel to the parked automobile. He reached for her left shoe that had slipped off her foot, its jerky spasm now motionless, and pushed it into the side pocket of her attractive gray blazer. His text, already formed, had been sent at the same time he had stood to fire the last round into her face.

A single word and number, "Ready-2," and the FedEx van parked less than a half block from the garage pulled out into the street and entered the facility. As they approached the parking facility's entrance cameras, they also activated their oscillating frequencies, a larger and farther-reaching mobile device than Ahura's, in effect jamming and distorting the images of the vehicle.

The van slid though the opening gates of the garage and within twenty seconds was turning into the sloping connector that carried them up to their teammate's second floor. As they stopped midway behind the Subaru and Porsche, the panel door opened and the two agents along with Ahura rapidly loaded Susan's earthly remains into the van, placing her almost gently onto a thick plastic body bag spread on the van's metal floor.

The sliding door was shut, and the two agents in the back of the van pulled the edges of the bag around her form and zippered it shut. The van was already moving, the magnetically adherent coverings on the FedEx logo now in place, and the van exited via the automated gate before turning slowly into the near empty side street. They paused at the stop sign and then again turned, now traveling on a four-lane boulevard heading toward the Key Bridge and George Washington Memorial Parkway.

Their destination was a three-car commercial garage previously owned by a successful first-generation mechanic from Egypt who had trouble believing his good fortune when an apparent father and son had offered him an overly generous amount to purchase his business three years ago. They had paid in cash, the value nearly 70% more than what the actual market would bear, but they winked at him and suggested that perhaps he should just report that he had been offered far less. The mechanic's wife of forty-four years was suspicious, but when the money was delivered—in ten separate cashier's checks delivered over five weeks to four banks—she found that she and her husband were suddenly comfortable, if not affluent. She couldn't ignore these peculiar aspects of the transaction or that it had been recorded as a loan payback, allowing acceptance of the money outside of IRS rules for taxable income. In fact, she was surprised that the name of her husband's garage and business had been left unaltered after the sale.

She did ask him how these two "family members" were going to financially survive; she knew enough about running the business to doubt these buyers would be able to efficiently price their services, having so grossly overpaid for their purchase. But she secretly wondered if the final cost was even applicable to the purchase of her husband's legitimate business. She also whispered to him as to why the checks had been deposited through seven different banks in smaller sums, each of a different amount, yet in summation totaling the agreed upon value by the transacting parties. To her, it looked as though this father and son wanted to avoid attention, IRS taxable income, or bank auditor interest. She, always the one more aware of hidden potential problems than her husband, smelled duplicity, as though these men were laundering money. But the reality that her husband no longer had to rise at 4:30 to ensure that he was at work by 6:15, often returning at 8:00 p.m. exhausted, or that her partner of nearly half a century was now smiling and talking about their future was an unanticipated wonderful change. A change that enabled her concerns to fade.

The magnitude of his transformation continued, as she was shocked by her husband's suggestion that they relocate to enjoy their retirement. And with more than a warm smile, she supported his idea, and the couple sold their tiny bungalow—again for a reasonable profit—and within two months had moved to South Carolina, where their money and lifestyle would be enhanced by the lower cost of living. Their American dream had been fulfilled and her disquiet, while cogent, slowly faded as the deep green of freshly cut grass sitting for hours in the sun.

Her stunned visualization of events transpiring in Washington, DC, and streaming live over the internet fourteen months later would have been even more intense had she connected the sale of their business to a global chess game, one whose consequences set in motion countermoves and retaliations decades in the future.

Chapter 23

"A sword never kills anybody; it is a tool in the killer's hand."
—*Lucius Annaeus Seneca*

It was almost as if water seeking its pathway in responding to the Earth's gravity selected an optimal course —irreversible, unalterable, as it flowed down an embankment into the sea. Predictable in its relentless course, beautiful, a pathway streaming into culverts and around embedded impediments to pour its energy into a greater body and disappear. And thus, when over, those wanting to understand how such an orchestrated terror attack could possibly occur would be able to connect and reconstruct its temporal signature. To almost admire, if not respect the obligatory dedication to its deadly methodology, an inertia sacrificing existence to principle, delivering a final message to American culture and its beautiful landscape.

They would be able to observe and marvel at the inherent logical symmetry found in the operational tactics taken by the Iranian cell. From entry at the Arizona border, fostered by a feckless American president ignoring his sworn lawful duty to both uphold the laws of the nation that empowered him to protect the citizens that elected him, to law enforcement agencies of among the world's most advanced, composed of those most talented, but distracted by the political whims of an aging corrupt, cognitively impaired leader. A president who, unable to appreciate the folly of his obsession with his rival for office, prosecuted his fellow citizens for trespass, seeking for them decades of imprisonment and thus critically undermining, indeed diverting the resources sworn to protect our nation as was their moral, legal, their fundamental purpose. It was the perfect storm, a nation divided, distracted, and misled by a legacy press that had become a shell of its prior commitment to objective truth. Not two decades after terror had destroyed landmark structures in our most populous city and murdered thousands of our fellow citizens, the nation again slept while all around it, silent shadows slithered into positions of harm.

For the Iranian team, its commitment had been as though in preparation for an Olympic sporting event. Months had elapsed during which contacts had been established, plans made, revised, discarded, and remade. Days had become weeks, months, and then a year, their research and formulation magnificent made easier by a sleeping giant at war with itself. As the noose tightened around one target, a courtroom on a military installation in the nation's federal capital, those participants in the actions within this legal arena identical to the nation they loved were sleepwalking into unimagined carnage.

Yet not all were drinking from this soporific brew. His name was Adam Daniels, and his probationary interval within the coveted section of analytics was drawing to an end, as was his enthusiasm for making a career out of the CIA. He had spent nearly six years at the preeminent American symbol of clandestine activities and had begun to understand why his nation's intelligence service and their product were being degraded. A foreseeable combination of administrative turf battles linked to bloated civil servant mentalities had crippled a once-proud agile agency. Their product had slowly, methodically become a tasteless diluted rinse, their summations of adversarial intent and purpose framed in nearly opaque guarded legalese. Narratives wrapped in wet tissue ambiguity, purposeful only in avoiding risk or the assignment of any future responsibility. Accuracy or actionable conclusions had been supplanted by a timid bureaucratic void. The herd tightly gathered around the most visible watering hole, all drinking together with their eyes open but unseeing.

But Adam had entered the halls of Langley wanting to use his intellectual gifts to safeguard his nation and the countless innocents who toiled within her boundaries. He intuitively grasped the disparities between those who wished America evil and harm and the parents, grandparents, and relatives who focused each morning on herding children onto yellow buses into schools. He found a near oppressive environment of conformity within the CIA. Infrequent but requisite meetings within sensitive compartmented information facilities (SCIFs) routinely manifested a programmed monotone of adversarial intent, objectives, and goals. On display was a Kabuki theater of tribal bureaucratic alliances rather than trenchant discussions of any value. And thus, the product was a foreseeable intonation of unifocal drivel void of actionable usefulness or insight. But Adam had a restless soul, and he found himself careful but needful to discuss germinating worries within the analytics he oversaw.

For Adam had been one of the CIA's younger computer whizzes, originally tasked to extract and collate meaning from the near infinite number of electronic signals that populated the communication ether due to the ubiquitous use of cellphones. The program had immersed Adam within a world containing parallel conflicts of dystopian personalities and ingenious theoretical purpose. His immediate supervisor was slow to unmask her true intent, which had little to do with safeguarding the nation against another 9/11 surprise attack but was instead a desire to spend every nickel allocated to her projects and thus secure her advancement within a dysfunctional beehive. But in a rather bizarre mutation of the CIA's oppressive, if not banal, sterility as to creative potential, Adam was given near free hand to develop and execute focused programs using the world's most powerful and elite supercomputers. He had spent his first four years in near technological nirvana. But as the programs began to show their remarkable capabilities, the culture of the CIA came knocking, and government lawyers sounded increasingly nervous regarding the potential for violations of the Fourth Amendment, the appearance of illegal search and seizure.

But what was really in play was the need to bury Adam's remarkable success within an opaque bureaucratic catacomb, allowing its resurrection when the original players were gone and those of political appointment, void of moral or legal conscience, arrived: analysists who served the en vogue ideology. Adam had deliberately built in guardrails and purposefully focused upon cohorts within the illegal border crossings of individuals wherein harmful intent was beyond possible—it was probable. The lawyers, with a wink and nod from executives within the collegium, were pausing his efforts to provide their political allies with future surveillance tools against their political foes. This was domestic spying, a misuse of Adam's genius, and an illegal use of his intellect. A use so far removed from the founding charter of the CIA as to be a jaw-dropping abuse of its power and position.

But Adam took an almost perverse joy in convincing the lawyers of his boyish naïveté, of compliance with their demands, while immediately and accurately seeing through their sophistry. And as the access of his programs became increasingly difficult, or at least should have been due to requisite approval from exploding levels of review and denied approval from supervisors, Adam's remarkable talent manifested. The CIA would have been proud of his ability and should have been alert to his hidden backdoor use of his own creation. But they were too arrogant in their own conclusions as to the "boy genius's" inability to wander outside their preset appraisal of his talent or his personality of robotic compliance with their demands. Adam had become, in many ways, the perfect spy.

The sad reality, but distinctly fortunate, was that Adam was spying for the America he loved and had sworn to protect, not the bureaucracy of self-created ideologues. Adam continued to use, develop, and refine his creations beyond any foreseeable understanding of the self-absorbed, absurdly grandiose administrators of the palace guard.

His program took simple concepts and goals and then he applied his uncanny integration of mathematical insight into statistical models, blending them with symphonic beauty into the language of the machines. A rather simplistic explanation was to identify certain words or groups of words within cellphone texts and verbal statements and then move them through a series of statistical platforms to allow potential grouping and association. This permitted outliers to pop out and then be sifted through the next layer, separating with increasing delicacy the aberrations sought.

He used several languages with a proprietary template formed using a modified variant of the Wind Talkers, the unbreakable Navajo code used during the US Marine island-hopping campaign of WWII. He then examined actual words in several languages that could be used but were unusual in their single-word appearance. Then he did the same for common groupings of these words, then expanded this to groupings of expressions, looking at frequency of use in each culture or ethnicity.

His goal was to find phrases or forms of expression that indicated a contact or alert and then focus on where the signals originated from. In other words, where was the cell phone being activated? Then he began the most arduous process of processing the encrypted messages coming out of the desert in Arizona, Southern Texas, California, or New Mexico. Each effort was a combination of collecting signals, collating them, and then displaying them in a format that was able to identify odd appearance. Finally, Adam's real genius was to identify and combine temporal appearance, location, oddity of use, and language origin (English, Spanish, or Farsi). The last variable, and perhaps the most interesting to Adam, was that he then mechanistically linked this to the degree of encrypted sophistication.

His premise was to ask why migrants crossing the southern American border would need advanced technical sub-rosa forms of communication. But he then also hooked a tail onto each cell phone and examined its signature and then its time of disappearance, suggesting a "burner phone" or simply a phone used by an individual crossing into the US and then replaced as they were provided another phone. But remarkably, Adam's program looked at the temporal disappearance of phone use and a new phone being utilized matched to an area, expanding its radius and the use of encryption or odd choices of language. While this might identify innocents, the program also immediately matched the new signal to the major carrier's lists of customers, with both time and demographic data. So, a new phone signal instantly matched to a young woman of college age without previous contact was of little interest, but archived for future use if needed. A new number matched to a migrant, or an odd name, or one too frequently in use—the proverbial John Doe —was identified, as was the use of single encrypted messages from the desert or other areas of focused interest. The more the computers processed and collated data, the more accurate the eavesdropping became, and Adam was then able to shift from the focus on the southern border of the American West and trace the migration of signals to larger US cities.

He took pleasure in his efforts, as he found correlations beyond his preset statistical values of chance and was able to identify neighborhood drug dealers and human traffickers of prostitution. Technically, such monitoring was illegal unless linked to both court approval and the CIA's charter allowing for use to protect the nation from foreign adversaries. But Adam noted that his superiors were less worried about his program's near incendiary power and more of being exposed to the public or congressional authorities by some whistle-blower. Twice, he anonymously provided Washington, DC, police with numerical data tied to names of street drug distributors that allowed local law enforcement to identify the higher-ups and arrest them for other actionable violations of the law. These individuals were convinced of a snitch being in their crew and never considered that the supercomputers at Langley were tracking their terse one-word "conversations" or encrypted communications, as such CIA cooperation was in itself a violation of the law.

But in the last months, Adam had begun to discover evidence of coordinated communications between small groups whose signatures often changed, taking his program minutes or even longer intervals to reconfirm their identities. The movement was seemingly random, but closer inspection showed patterns of movement and interaction suggesting cooperative intent. And Adam could not hide his interest; it had become obsessive. He felt more than knew that something poisonous lurked within the shadows of this data. And thus, almost as if he were that dusty graying professor fixated on romantic medieval ballads, with wire-rimmed glasses, tan pants, and a fraying tweed blazer, he gently but continuously probed the metrics spewed out by his creative genius. Langley's supercomputers had become Adam, and he them. Adam's subtle variations in examination of the groupings were as if he had repeatedly but deliberately used a delicate artist's brush to unearth buried evidence of human activity. He altered the program's variables, and each time he asked the humming machines to assess these variations in his hunches.

The data went from troubling to alarming. The past two months had been enough to cause Adam to suffer sleepless nights as he reviewed the findings in his conscious and then his unconscious brain, each toiling with permutations that all suggested harm would follow. Harm and damage to innocents, specifically, and Adam knew he would get no traction to his concerns from his superiors. They would immediately understand that he was still using his creation freely, something they had administratively forbidden. But even if these "woke" ideologues accepted Adam's conclusions, which was highly improbable, Adam's deductions drawn from meticulous assessments were beyond their interests. It was the chance of exposure of Adam's programming capabilities, their rather amazing potential and unparalleled power, that must remain hidden from all but the self-anointed elites. And thus, to anyone able to transform such data into action, the clandestine community could not risk exposure to outside authorities capable of actual oversight or regulation. But Adam was troubled beyond a decision to remain inactive, yet he had no formal outlet for constructive discussion or query.

As he sat in his apartment, a gutted warehouse refurbished into several large dwellings, he pondered the issue during the early morning hours as the city slept, or was at least briefly calm. It was 2:30 a.m. Rain tapped gently against his windows, gathering into puddles as it reached the antiquated stone sills. It was in these dreamless morning hours when Adam often did his most imaginative thinking, a probing of his nimble mind. And he knew that now was such a time. The ambient streetlight cast long shadows into the main room. Its diffuse yellow light touched the bare brick wall and partially illuminated his floor-to-ceiling bookshelf, its polished standards with fluted front casings. The bookshelf held Adam's sparse but valued life's treasures, pictures and ceremonial plaques engraved with two citations of excellence. His ruminations continued, his mind in hyperdrive.

Running over the paucity of options, he let his mind wander and found himself looking across the expanse of the room to the bookshelf and the brick wall. Its rough, dry cement, decades old. The random powder-gray smudges staining the pocked auburn surface of rough bricks. A framed picture of a man taller than Adam but his age, smiling, his arm slung around Adam's shoulder, sat prominently on the bookshelf. Adam looked happy, perhaps slightly embarrassed, as if caught in a moment of unguarded delight but reacting to being the object of humor with lifelong friends. The picture itself was over a decade old, a five-year high school reunion, taken by another former classmate who commented that the taller man's probability of attending future events was "unlikely."

Adam suddenly sat up and his heart rate accelerated, thinking Why not? and creatively exploring options. The quiet of the night helped. The gentle rain continued, the streetlight sparkled creating its own prism, a spectrum of separating colors. Yes, I might ask him. He had texted Adam some eleven months previously and the two had met for dinner, or rather a beer and a sandwich at a sports bar. The man in this picture had been a boy filling into a man's frame; the individual who met Adam at the bar, shook his hand, and warmly embraced him was not that man. He had aged ten years, a permeating wisdom, and yet sadness hung on his frame. He looked incredibly fit, strong, his eyes alert, taking in every motion of those around him. But the eyes were within a face that betrayed events seen and experiences encountered that, in truth, no human being should encounter. The expressed warmth was genuine, but so was the fatigue showing unguarded for Adam, a lifelong friend.

Adam had almost gasped upon seeing him up close. His face fell only a bit, and briefly, but this man, whose friendship meant the world to Adam, had understood immediately and smiled. A crinkled, almost tender pulling of his lips revealed his dimples, barely visible, and he raised his eyebrows as if confirming Adam's response. A warm sincerity of acceptance that yes, his soul had been scared, his nights seldom free from the screams of colleagues shattered during missions undertaken to safeguard the American homeland—or at least that was how these missions were framed.

And Adam had instantly lost his ego, his humorous but cutting humor, and his defenses. He reached in again, hugged his friend, and whispered in his ear, "Anything that you need, anything, and I will deliver or die trying." As they pulled apart, their eyes locked. Each man knew that a covenant had been made, unbreakable eternal. The man nodded slightly and squeezed Adam's arms with his powerful hands, a gesture confirming the promise, its acceptance, its magnitude of emotive force.

The recipient was Jacob Noah Roth.

Chapter 24

Die Judicii
Day of Judgment

Adam had met with Jacob Noah Roth three separate times and explained as much as he could without violating the most sacred levels of security clearance. But his commentaries and explanations were detailed, and only absent innocent names of individuals caught in the web of the CIA's systemic duplicity toward the government it served and the public it allegedly protected. Everything else was on the table, and knowing that Jacob's security clearance probably matched his, at least as missions evolved and actionable outcomes became reality, he had little to fear from his dearest friend. A soldier's soldier, a man of integrity, and a man whom Adam admired and had at times envied. But both men were now deep within a bond, a covenant to each other and the ethereal concept of patriotism directed to a nation tearing itself apart, unable to mitigate its differences or tolerate diversity of thought.

Ironically, the last meeting had taken place walking along the pathway adjacent to the great cat exhibit at the National Zoo, three weeks before the trial was scheduled to begin. Adam and Jacob could not know, as they shuffled between gawking children delightfully squealing as the animals paced or suddenly looked toward their human spectators, that Susan and Ahmed had traversed these same paths. Nor was it considered that the very object of their discussions was of the same content and remarkably, to effect, the same tactical object as the couple that preceded them. But one was to unleash terror, the other to prevent it.

As Adam and Jacob walked, stopping frequently and observing the predators, they rounded the trisectioned habitats of female lions, a male lion, and the Sumatran tiger, interweaving discussions of the Yankees and Cubs and quickly using these as substitute names for either sensitive or classified nouns or managerial decisions. Jacob frequently made Adam laugh with witty jokes or self-deprecating statements, yet it was upon later reflection, when Adam needed to fight back tears as he grasped the horror his friend concealed, that he realized he hid such events behind humorous dismissive masks. And then the stunning comment from Adam triggered the slow curl of a powerful wave.

"Interest has been shown in some trial or some legal proceeding at the Naval Yard, my friend. Probably a lot like this guy here . . ." Adam pointed to the tiger, who was slowly moving toward the crowd of onlookers, his rippled body of muscle and tendons showing through his magnificent striped burnt-orange-brown coat.

"Trial!" Jacob, astonished, swung his head around and momentarily lost the ambiance of a casual interaction.

Adam, looking at Jacob and then beyond him, instinctively checking for any interest in random strangers, spoke with a smile, "Yeah, but I think that struck a nerve somehow. Tell me . . ."

And Jacob, recovering, deliberately slowed his movement, pulled at his right ear as in thought, and smiled. Jacob then related the long-delayed trial of Virginia Mahoney, who had killed a Syrian accomplice of al Al

Hassan Abbas in order to gain time-sensitive knowledge about the escape tunnels al Al Hassan Abbas was using.

Adam instantly understood, as whispers of Virginia's trial, the political as well as legal themes and concerns, had suffused the DC landscape. It had been a raging river of internal commentary within both the intelligence and armed forces communities. But he had not been told, nor had the general public been informed, exactly when the trial would begin nor the details of the case. The more Jacob commented, using either animal names or baseball metaphors, the more focused Adam's body language became. He could not hide the deep concentration that enveloped him.

"Adam, see that cat." Jacob pointed at the aging male lion as they had now circled into the lion's habitat display. "He will actually attend this proposed habitat and may, in fact, be called as star participant in the animal show."

Now it was Adam whose head momentarily whipped up to face Jacob, but he immediately smiled and pointed at the lion. "That guy, really?" And he laughed, but even Adam knew his performance was substandard. The laugh was forced, a poor demonstration of humor, but it would pass among strangers.

And thus, both understood that indeed, the electronic traffic that Adam was monitoring and collating had originally possibly suggested but now almost certainly confirmed the targeting of the very trial that Jacob was to attend.

"Ok, so tell me how the Cubs are going to defend against the Yankees' starting lineup?" It was Adam who now began the planning of how Jacob could defend himself and his people if there was a concentrated attack on the court within the Naval Yard.

As they talked, Jacob thought through the myriad of possibilities that Adam had raised—including that Adam's data was wrong, that his deductions, conclusions, and fears were misplaced or just incorrect. But deep inside, Jacob sensed that his high school friend was not only correct, but that his summations were prescient, his worries exactly correct regarding the potential for an attack on the court.

The cell phone buzzed at 5:01. The message was short, encrypted, and confirmative. Adam had again emphasized that the location was the appellate court room, known now as the location of Mahoney's trial, and strangely, rather early this morning. Adam underscored the time and placed appropriate question marks by it, as he thought it odd that such a kinetic force would be planned for so early in the day. Jacob knew that this morning, different from most, the participants were to gather early to address the snarled testimony of Rich Hansept. The judge, a decorated combat admiral, had summoned the legal teams and was convening court just after 8:30 a.m. with the public phase beginning at 9:00.

Jacob immediately put his coffee cup down and walked the short distance to his bedroom, placing his thumb on the black oval glass surface on a steel box bolted to the floor of his refurbished brick townhouse. His apartment was expensive, but the military had become rather interested in special operations personnel being located close to operational bases and senior combatants being able to afford the steadily rising prices for rent. Response times were essential and maintaining teams took foresight, as excessive turnover could be lethal. The audible click was almost immediate. As he pulled open the door, he gripped the Hellcat, a Springfield Armory micro-compact 9mm semiautomatic handgun. Its weight felt reassuringly heavy in his hand. Thirteen rounds and one in the chamber, no safety. The firepower was significant, rather substantial for such a small platform.

He picked up the weapon, ejected the clip, and pulled back the slide. The single round popped up and he grabbed it in mid-flight. He rechecked the weapon; it was now empty. His eyes moved rapidly to examine the weapon's specific parts, ensuring later performance if needed. The single round was reinserted, the clip assertively pushed into place with the locking click audible. Jacob would have a fighting chance, if needed. He felt saddened but alert, an increasingly common emotion he now experienced before missions. The realization that he would perform to his utmost and that this almost certainly meant he would kill or harm the Creator's miracle of existence: human beings.

He reviewed his operational plans. Both Adam and Jacob had been very careful to meticulously cover each aspect of the possible appropriate responses. And when the courtroom's location had become known, they had met one last time in Adam's residence to share coffee and analyze the geography of any potential armed assault.

Both men knew that attacking a federal installation, especially the Naval Yard in Washington, DC, was clearly a suicide mission. Destruction would be significant, and mercy or reasonable expectations from combat absent. They also knew that once inside the gates, resistance might actually be minimal. This was not a primary marine base with a huge armory daily dispensing weapons to men and women in training, parading in fields or on designated streets as they honed skills needed for lethality and the timeless theater of war. This was a naval base whose role had transitioned over the years to become almost exclusively administrative.

Uniformed clerks, secretaries, and bureaucrats of every flavor burrowed into concrete and steel hives of activity, ensuring that the machinery needed to run a country's water-based warriors continued. They, the base managers, the senior captains, and admirals, had been warned of the vulnerability of this vital nerve center becoming an increasingly ripe target. But responses had been on paper; they needed assets to respond, outlined to be drawn from Quantico, the police, or the National Guard from units in DC. All of these were other operating centers where those with weapons worked and lived. The problem was, of course, that any hostile intervention would have accomplished 98 percent of its mission before any troops arrived—traffic permitting—in the busy metropolitan area of DC.

Jacob knew this and surmised that a small but trained foreign special operations team had been directed to destroy the woman who killed one of their most prominent proxy personalities. He understood that such action had a higher likelihood of success than the paper warriors defending the naval base could imagine. Their mindset was not to provide real defense, but to satisfy those cognoscente within the reflecting pool herd that the problem was taken care of, that it had been addressed. Pearl Harbor had peacefully slept one

Sunday morning decades ago, just as America now slumbered. Jacob worried that only Adam had understood the parallels in lethal hubris and its potential for similar outcomes.

As Jacob exited his apartment at 7:10 a.m., his sense of foreboding was almost palpable. He knew that any sophisticated group of adversarial special operations understood that the trial had hit an unanticipated bump. Virginia might just have her lawyer successfully move to dismiss charges or to delay the trial for months, as the behind-the-scenes wrangling over an unexpected conflicting testimony had almost assuredly derailed the prosecutions primary witness.

And thus, at 7:20 a.m. that same morning, Jacob texted his colleague, a member of senior Naval Support Activity (NSA) Annapolis. This man was in effect a police officer with numerous security duties, one of which was safeguarding the Washington Naval Yard Appellate courtroom. It had been temporarily transformed into the functioning judicial theater for one Virginia Lois Mahoney. The text was simple and yet caused an immediate response: "Jacob Noah Roth here. Call me please."

Jacob answered on his car speakers via Bluetooth at a low volume and greeted the almost immediate response from his friend and colleague, "Hey, Matt, you good?"

"I was until five seconds ago. There a problem?" came the slow rural North Carolina drawl, calm but cautious.

"Identifier Alpha 23-56: Need to inform you I have and will have today. Not I say again, not 'Uncle Stewart's' favorite. Gate five in fifteen."

And with that, Jacob had just used an old authenticating code and numeric tag that immediately alerted his former colleague of two things: that there was a serious issue, and that he was in possession of a loaded weapon without imprimatur authorization.

Despite his training and automated response to combat-related authenticators, Matt nearly sputtered, "Damn it, Jacob!" but then instantly added, "Ok, tell Uncle Stew all will be ready." And the line went dead.

Matt Darlin had seen Jacob's dedication to team members, mission parameters, and the amorphous concept of honor up close in two clandestine interdictions in Syria. He had trained with Roth for months, knew him almost as a brother, and had even been pulled from certain death by him after being seriously wounded, bleeding from his right thigh after a mortar attack. Jacob had carried him on his back—no small task, as Matt Darlin was 206 pounds of solid Tar Heel muscle and bone. Roth had tightly wound his AR-15's sling around Matt's upper leg to stem an otherwise fatal hemorrhage. Matt now walked with a limp and had subsequently been routed for discharge as "medically unfit" for duty.

But one particularly incensed naval commander—himself wearing the special warfare insignia of an eagle clutching a US Navy anchor, trident, and flintlock-style pistol —had terrified the mindless bureaucrats, nearly liquefying their colonic contents, during a Wednesday morning meeting that adjudicated such decisions. Turning red-faced, this lean combat veteran had heard what Roth had done and the object of Roth's heroic actions. He had stood, pushing up from the large table with stacks of files ready for medical termination from the US Navy active-duty roster, and carefully leaned forward, placing both of his hands flat on the table before him.

He started speaking, softly at first, interrupting the mindless gossip between two Department of Defense employees who were recalling the Philadelphia Eagles loss to the NY Giants on Monday Night Football. The commander, a native of Idaho, tall, lean, but muscular, had penetrating nearly gray eyes. They smoldered, showing a cold, deeply entrenched fire as he stared at his hands. A thin minimally puckered white line slightly distorted the smooth contour of his otherwise very handsome face. A scar running vertically from his left maxilla turning slightly toward the gonial angle, or the external inflection point of his mandible, detailed a previous injury. Despite the plastic surgeon's remarkable skill, the reconstructive efforts could not hide the footprint of the IED, a fragment that, an inch higher, would have taken his eye and perhaps entered his brain.

Commander Wagner slowly, methodically recited the action report filed summarizing Roth's activities to pull Darlin from the flaming ruins of a vehicle that had just been struck by mortar fire, killing three members of the special operations team and seriously injuring Matt Darlin. Racing toward the residual of a Toyota Tundra, engulfed in flames and split in two, Darlin's team had been unlucky, but Roth saw that Darlin was alive. Ducking between other vehicles in an abandoned Syrian hospital's parking lot, Roth dodged ISIS automatic weapon rounds that tore into the remaining trucks and old Mercedes sedans, shattering windows and punching dime-size holes in their metal skins. Reaching Matt, Roth immediately reached into the flames and, feeling the heat begin to painfully cook his hands, did not hesitate as he forcefully grabbed his teammate's vest and pulled Matt from the behind the wheel. Seeing his leg gushing thick red liquid, Roth pulled a sterile gauze package from his backpack and clamped it onto the hemorrhaging leg. Two rounds zipped through Roth's uniform, grazing his shoulder, and were to leave telltale scars mirroring train tracks, but Roth held his ground as he attended Darlin. The adjustable strap for Roth's M4A1 carbine was removed from the stock and looping it around Matt's leg, Roth tightened the strap, pushing the gauze packing deeply into the wound.

Roth was known among his subordinate teammates as a man who had taken countless online courses and attended numerous EMS courses and carried a small compartmentalized backpack stuffed with medical materials. The other compartment carried additional clips for his M4A1. Not required as the team leader to be a medic, he nevertheless took pride in attending his teammates upon completion of missions to ensure that their physical health and conditions were examined. All of this was within the AARs (after-action reviews), including the fact that Roth had carried Darlin on his back for one mile to a designated rendezvous point for extraction. This was also commented upon, as the author of the AAR did not skimp on the fact that Darlin was a "big dude" and Roth, drenched in sweat, categorically refused to share the weight of his teammate.

At the completion of Commander Wagner's near perfect recitation of the AAR regarding the mission that had nearly cost Matthew Darlin his leg, if not his life, and had rewarded Jacob Roth with two additional linear dermal keepsakes, the naval officer looked up. His voice was almost imperceptible, as though speaking to his lover in sharing a moment of intimacy. But it was the understated order or demand that brokered no dissent.

"I would encourage this august body to carefully examine Matthew Darlin's record and ensure that the United States Navy continues to enjoy the contributions from this individual. I will accept NO other outcome."

And with that, Wagner straightened, turned, and pausing at the front of the room as he walked toward the door, he pivoted and provided a near perfect demonstration of a salute to the flag of the United States that hung proudly next to the room's exit.

Darlin had been reassigned to Naval Yard Security but remained on active duty.

The commander was promoted to navy captain.

Matt was transferred from special operations, a SEAL, into law enforcement. Relationships are often established within transient intervals in the armed forces, but their seemingly short duration does not mean they are without emotive permanence. Matt trusted Jacob, his life having been saved by this man. Matt was fond of him, a brother different than the one who now worked in the IT sector in Durham. Jacob, whose face revealed deeply carved, prematurely distinct wrinkles, making him look older, perhaps wiser, and ever worried. To many, including women who met Jacob, these sharply cut lines in an otherwise handsome face were startling, eye-catching, causing them to stop and admire and then immediately sense sadness. They had no idea how close they were to truth, as Jacob's expressions were indeed a compilation of history, savagery and kindness, hatred and love. A face telling anyone interested, and many women were, that opening this book was not going to be a light read. But it might just be transformative.

And thus, Matt was immediately alarmed at his former team member's communication. Roth did not play games. Something was concerning—something important.

Standing just inside the reinforced concrete and sepia-colored brick guard station at the 9th Street entrance, Matt carefully observed the approach of his most respected colleague. An ancient black-rimmed, white-faced twelve-inch clock positioned on the station's pale gray wall showed 8:07 as Jacob slowly pulled his automobile into a demarcated space and killed the engine. The sign read "Official Vehicles ONLY." The next line, in smaller but legible block print, read "Risk Towing and Damage." Roth put both his hands clearly on the wheel at the ten and two positions—a habit, and to dissuade a newbie from any idea that he was a problem.

But Matt was already ambulating to him, the limp noticeable but only just. It was a matter of pride to the man, as it was only when he was home at the end of his day, his wife's head buried in his shoulder, that he allowed his full disability to slow him. Even then, he fought to reduce the limp.

Jacob exited the car and stood in plain view—again, habit—completely visible to camera surveillance and Matt's underlings.

"So, what's on the menu today?" was the cryptic inquiry.

"Colleague's interest. Very detailed" was Jacob's response.

"Where?"

"Iranian team, perhaps crossing remote Arizona, sector 6. No confirmation, but somehow, electronically with colleague-friend's supercomputers at Langley, he is bothered." Perhaps only Jacob could sense Matt tense ever so slightly. "Already noticed?" Jacob probed his friend.

"Yeah, perhaps. Van with no markings, but weird side coverings noted by my puke-newbie."

"Going to have to consider buying him a beer, my friend."

"Her, and she has seen it four times in last time days. She, Petty Officer Vivian Brewer demanded that she extend her shift and saw the VOI the fourth time just before six p.m. yesterday. Single driver, packages in front, passenger seat, too close to the window, and didn't move or jostle. You know our wonderful DC roads mirror Syria's best, or close—lots of bumps and potholes. She thinks packages had a camera within a box or package, attached or locked into the window. Filming us, the gates."

"But which gate, Matt?"

"That is the conundrum, isn't it?" Matt responded.

Matt looked back at Jacob's car. "Grey 2009 Porsche 911-S. Didn't think they paid us that much." This was said with a smile, mixed with genuine warmth for his friend.

"Present, Matt. Divorce finalized and I didn't have to pay alimony. Judge was a woman and was pretty observant as to the other party's habits."

For perhaps the first time, Matt heard Jacob joke regarding the painful separation from a woman he had loved, but who had discarded the honor and affections of this man as a clump of used toilet paper. Matt broke into a big grin and said without hesitation, "About time, my friend. I need it to be seen for Jenny. Kind of give her a hint, ok?"

Now it was Jacob who smiled. "Sure, good luck with that!"

And both men chuckled.

"The question again. What gate, Matt?"

"We have no idea of where or when—?"

Jacob cut him off. "'When' is like soon, now, according to my source, friend, colleague, and totally trust him, if you are interested."

"Good, I assumed so. But what gate would you want?"

"Least fortified, and here, let's think. These folks are not stupid. Least fortified can apply to person, power, or structure. If it were me, I would take structure over person power, because of Maginot."

Matt smiled, "Always the student Jacob, I love it. Structure offers poor resistance if it is empty of personnel."

"Then let's focus on the probable object of their mission, one Virginia Lois Mahoney, being tried in the special courtroom, the appellate facility that is being used for this high-profile case. It's one block over from this gate, from this very spot, and it uses a smaller back street, really a lane in this tightly consolidated 'yard.' So, if I were them, I would be driving a van filled with six to eight personnel, with a dump truck or garbage truck filled with weight or mass as the lead, and blow through the iron and brick gated entrance. First vehicle, the massive brunt to penetrate, followed closely by agents to eliminate any resistance. Two remain behind, four, five, or six go to the designation and hit the target or targets."

"Thus, we are actually really thinking this, here—gate five. And what do you think the total time is?" Matt asked.

"From the moment they turn into the short access here . . ." Jacob pivoted slightly and with his left arm swept in an arc, outlining the fifty-seven feet from the main road to their position. "And with the gate seventy feet from the edge of M Street SE, under two minutes to eliminate resistance, ninety seconds to reach the courtroom."

"Suggestions?" Matt was surveying the tightly compacted buildings within the brick perimeter wall that separated this portion of the Naval Yard from the civilian world.

"Two problems," Jacob spoke softly. "You will be on your own here. No one will allow you to formally request assets, resources, or material to prepare for an incident that is within the domain of 'nonexistent.' Second, those very assets must be liquid and silent. Capable of rapid redeployment and quiet, answering only to you. Next to impossible."

"Difficult, but not impossible" was Matt's laconic reply. "Jacob, let me ask one very simple question. Why? Why are they doing this? What is the real message? I think I get it, but your insight is always valuable." And then to lighten the darkening clouds of worry, he added, "Can't believe I am saying that!"

Both men laughed.

"Ali Ibrhim Arjang and al Al Hassan Abbas. They are telling us that they, like us, can strike anywhere at any time to finish business. While they don't have predator drones above our sky, at least not yet, they will accomplish exactly the same outcome using human assets, expendable but to be glorified."

Matt nodded. "Yeah, agree, but getting those bastards . . . we delivered a message, at least for a brief moment."

"Well, until we had a new administration composed of self-deluded naïve people. No idea of how the world works, what the Iranians respect, or the Chinese or Russians."

Matt's drawl was almost imperceptible. "You forgot the North Koreans."

"I did, indeed" was Jacob's reply. "Matt, I am concerned that we may have something within the next twelve hours, as there is a very high chance that Virginia's charges may be dropped, suspended, the trial paused, and that could be for an indefinite interval. Thus, decisions already made, they may be setting in motion in real time something that is already coming our way."

"Jacob, you mind? How about the keys, and leave it parked here? Less maneuverability in the lane, and we don't use this gate except for deliveries. Ck?"

Jacob smiled and tossed Matt the key fob. "Full disclosure, M4 with three clips in the trunk. That's at the front of the car, Matt." Both men smiled.

"You have permission to bring that on the yard?"

"What do you think?"

"Of course!" Matt shook his head. "Well, full disclosure, it could get a bit nicked up if there's any excitement today."

Jacob turned, waved to his friend, and began walking the short distance to the courthouse. Almost out of earshot, in the heavy background noise of car traffic and tightly compacted buildings, Matt's voice came as an order, without explanation or warmth. "Roth, back here now!"

Jacob turned and was running.

Matt had already popped the front trunk of the Porsche and had reached inside to grab the stock of the M4 and the banded clips containing thirty rounds each of its standard 5.56x45mm munitions. But he did this in a manner that partially, if not totally obscured his actions from those on the street, using the car's hood and body to block his extraction of the weapon.

As Jacob approached, Vivian was partially hidden inside the brick guard house holding standard binoculars, leaning with her shoulder to steady her view.

Matt quickly traversed the short interval between the Porsche and the brick structure.

"Viv here spotted a little potential convoy two blocks from here, just turning now into M."

"I see it, Viv—garbage truck, followed by two vans. Ok, get Rogers and tell him to bring Mayfield and Busk. They need their M4s and sidearms. Then alert the other gates. Do it now!"

But the slight statured very attractive woman, with a tight blond ponytail emanating from the back of her baseball cap, was already on her private cell and speaking assertively with a distinct, if not appealing, Tennessee twang.

"Chief Darlin orders you and the boys to gate five, immediate, no drill. Grab as much firepower as you can on the run—need you here in ninety seconds." And she killed the connection.

"Folks, there are now four of us, and I can't believe this, but we may be in for a fun morning. Jacob, pull the vest on. You too, Viv and Jason."

But the slender woman, with clear but uncommonly almost iridescent blue-green eyes, had already tossed a bulletproof vest to Roth and slipped one over her head while handing one to her boss. Her coworker, Jason Pierce, was already wearing his, and the M4 was casually looped over his right shoulder. He was stuffing two additional loaded clips into the tight pockets of the vest.

With that, Matthew Darlin stepped out, his M4 visible and his limp less so, as he entered the entrance lane in front of the guard house. Vivian took up a position, crouching behind a cement block positioned to funnel traffic into a narrowing gauntlet. The block was seven feet from the most distant wall of the guardhouse, closest to the door and the perimeter wall of the Naval Yard. A second block stood at the other corner of the structure, closest to the public street, M. The other male guard, previously deployed in Afghanistan, tucked himself into the guard house door, also partially shielded.

Jacob had disappeared around the back of the structure, anchored his left foot up on the wall-attached rectangular metal box containing the central heating elements, and quickly lifted himself onto the low roof. He was partially hidden, as there was an ornate trim almost fourteen inches high that ran along the entire street exposed sides. A combination of foot-long linear spear-shaped metal rods capped with a triangular metal emblem of the naval security force's insignia, with woven rope in the spacing. At the two respective front corners of the roof, two of the rods were six inches higher and served as lightning rods with metal cables running to a grounding connector in the back of the building.

Jacob's position was perhaps the best view of events to unfold as he lay on his belly and positioned his M4 weapon, his cell phone already dialing his teammates Ostrowski and Pickney. As Jacob scanned the busy street, he, too, saw the lumbering orange-and-green garbage truck slowly turn onto the street paralleling the Naval Yard, allowing cars to speed by. This created an empty space in front of this laboring giant, yet two white vans appeared to linger behind it before they then pulled out into the adjoining lane but did not pass the truck. This maneuver, however, did impede traffic, allowing this larger member of the threesome to suddenly accelerate beyond any reasonable speed on a city street.

Now, as the three-member convoy continued to pick up speed, Jacob strained to see the occupant of the front seat. A darkened windshield prevented any visual inspection of either driver or additional passengers, but the truck's speed was now almost sixty-two miles per hour as its proximity to the side lane entrance to the Naval Yard rapidly approached. Jacob suddenly noted that the front of the garbage-collecting vehicle had been modified. He could not fully appreciate the details, but eighteen-inch-thick steel extensions, five of them, were evenly spaced and welded to the truck's solid frame. And unlike spacing bumpers, with flat ends allowing a truck to properly position itself as it moved to hoist a large metal container filled with refuse, these tips were sharp spearheads made of dense heavy metal, piercing triangles for ramming or shattering objects such as brick walls.

The street entrance to gate five had opposing corner concrete barriers positioned at the beginning of the much smaller lane. Jacob could see that these impediments were not going to stop this vehicle, whose speed was now unlawful. Matt was again on his cell, calling for reinforcements while also alerting other gates as to the developing hostile event and warning them. And then it happened.

The truck suddenly lurched to the right and clipped the corner of the concrete block closest to the main thoroughfare. Twenty tons of steel with lethal momentum sent chips of melded calcium, limestone, sand, and gravel exploding into the air, and the barrier lifted and toppled harmlessly out of the truck's path. The truck's speed was unaffected, and as it barreled into the guardhouse, the remaining concrete barriers positioned to avoid such an outcome were ineffective as they were lifted and hurtled back into the air, killer chunks of supersonic cement. The foundation of the building shook, the truck stopped its movement, and the flat front began steaming and smoking, partially filling the guardhouse with noxious gas.

But Jacob, from his perch, did not wait for the rapidly approaching vehicle to hit these last structures before unloading nearly two full clips into the front of the truck, shattering and imploding the large plexiglass window. He then immediately rolled to his right and retargeted on the two white vans, concentrating his remaining firepower while steadying his body. He felt the building move under him as the massive garbage truck finally hit the front wall and destroyed the structural underpinnings. As the roof's far left corner suddenly began to collapse, he repeatedly fired into the first of these vans. Trailing behind and to the side of the larger vehicle, it suddenly changed course before almost simultaneously swerving and screeching to a sudden stop. Jacob realized that he had eliminated the driver, whose lifeless body had lost control.

The side door instantly flew open, and three individuals clothed in black wearing facial coverings with only eyes, nose, and mouth openings jumped out and immediately began running in an attempt to position themselves behind the far rear of the much larger garbage truck. All had Kalashnikov weapons, their banana-shaped clips distinctive and polished wooden stocks indicative of the Siberian forests sacrificed for these Soviet-era weapons. The second individual, a large man, was already bleeding from his left shoulder. Jacob aimed and pulled the M4's trigger, feeling the kick as though the weapon was irritated at being pinched. The two rounds hit the moving figure almost exactly where Jacob had positioned the laser attached to the M4's rail, and the moving figure screamed as liquid and tissue erupted from the base of his neck. His arms reflexively pulled up with his hands balling into fists and his body instantly violently rotated, his weapon being almost ejected from his grip and spinning before it clattered to the cement. Almost tripping his trailing partner, the man's legs twitched in spasm, but his eyes were already without life and he, too, hit the pockmarked cement.

Viv had moved from behind the barrier as the truck accelerated toward her, narrowly escaping the impact of the vehicle and the fragmented concrete block as it partially disintegrated upon impact. As she rounded the right front of the now motionless, but hissing and steaming garbage truck, she saw the first man who had exited the van, now crouching as he unloaded his Kalashnikov at Matt. But even with a limp, Darlin had anticipated this and dove behind Jacob's highly polished pristine 911 Porsche. As the last rounds from the reliable Soviet-made weapon tore into Roth's sports car, Matt held his fire, afraid he might hit Vivian. But Vivian, with a distinct firing line, pulled the trigger of her M4 as she fell to the cement to reduce her profile.

Two of her rounds ripped into the crouching figure and he suddenly stood, arching his back as his arms flung outward as though embracing the sky. A third round hit the back of his head, but this might have remained unnoticed if not for the sudden explosion of his right eye. Vivian's other five rounds missed their target but shattered Roth's side window, disfiguring the smooth tapered lines of his beloved "chick magnet."

The third Iranian had exited the van, already firing his weapon and scrambling, bent over, directly toward the partially collapsed guardhouse. Without aiming, he fired repeatedly in small bursts, causing Vivian and Jason to seek cover. A ricochet caught Jason in the right shoulder and he reflexively rose up as he began turning to re-enter the guard house to hide. Unfortunately, this was enough for a member of the second van to concentrate automatic fire on his position, and he was struck by multiple lead missiles from a barrage that tore into the wall of the guardhouse. His M4 fell from his hand and struck the ground with a telltale finality that Vivian, upon hearing the clang of metal, instantly knew was a bad sign.

Matt was at the rear of the Porsche and began firing into front passenger's side of the second van. He had missed the opening of the door, not seeing a burly darkly clothed occupant who had just seconds previously flung open the door and raced toward the guardhouse as he crouched and fired at Jason and Vivian.

Jacob, on the sagging roof of the damaged building, popped his head up and without taking aim fired six round bursts into the region of the last man exiting the first van. He then caught sight of the large man running the short distance between the first van and the garbage truck. Now it was Jacob who stood erect and precisely aimed and emptied his last clip into the area between the two vehicles as the man running ducked. A muffled scream, and then nothing.

Vivian now was up and fired into this same space but from the ground level. She watched carefully for movement of any kind. There was none.

Matt screamed, "Get back, seek cover!"

The driver of the second van was dead, hit by multiple rounds from Matt. He lay slouched over the wheel, the passenger door open, the door's glass marred by delicate spiderweb patterns surrounding each hole forming near radiant circles.

461

As if by some miracle, Matt would later speak earnestly of divine providence, as none of his rounds had entered the back of the van.

It was packed with TNT to be triggered by a remote detonator.

Matt was on the phone. "Probable IED, truck. Need you now, full equipment! No drill, NOW! Gate five, Matt here, code 535."

With that and the immediate coded identifier, the recipient on the call raced out of his office and nearly broke the door open to the room housing their equipment. His colleagues saw his face and yelled at him, "Real or drill?"

"Real, gate five! Bring everything now you can get, don't wait! Open the armory!"

Matt's words had been spoken hurriedly to one of his best friends, Mike Forester, a former Nebraska football player, offensive line, who at his peak weighed 270 pounds and stood just under six feet three inches. Mike had left the university upon graduation and enlisted in the navy, testing in the upper 0.2 percent, and he was interested in and approved to join the navy Explosive Ordnance Disposal (EOD). Mike had the misfortune to become nearly legendary in Iraq, as his affectionate moniker as assigned by the troops was Pointer, after the English hunting dogs bred to detect hidden game. Mike could almost pick up the scent of IEDs hidden in the road and spent his deployment identifying explosive devices meant to injure or kill American soldiers. He was embarrassed by the near "rock star" status he grew to enjoy among his fellow combatants.

But Iraqi insurgents had also grown to understand his abilities and placed a sub-rosa bounty on this man. They had almost succeeded in their mission to eliminate him but for the heroic actions of a colleague who sensed that an old woman in a market was not, in fact, what she appeared to be. As the "woman" clothed in a blue burka saw them, walking with a bent shuffling gait and an old gnarled wooden branch serving as a cane, she slowly but circuitously approached a group of three soldiers. Mike, among a group of three, was suddenly pushed to the side as his colleague Isaac drew his weapon and with one loping motion bear-hugged this approaching "woman." He had seen Nike sneakers transiently appear under her robes, the shuffling gait meant to hide such exposure, and had immediately acted upon the ruse. As he wrestled "her" to the ground, she struggled to raise her left arm, then a Makarov semiautomatic pistol appeared and she squeezed its trigger.

The distinctive sound of the Makarov, made deafening in the cloistered market stalls and closed ancient venue, was immediately followed by Isaac screaming. Struck in the thigh and lower abdomen, he doubled up, losing his grip on the assailant, but Mike had drawn his Beretta M9 and nearly emptied the entire clip into the woman. The robed figure snapped back as a round hit the underside of her chin and the top of her head popped, reddish liquid and matter the consistency of ground chicken spattering an actual woman standing in front of her stall. She started screaming as the dying insurgent's arms underwent an instant jerking spasm, extended fully, and then he collapsed. The Makarov flew, arcing up and landing in an adjacent stall within a basket of stacked samoon, a delicious flatbread.

The now dead "woman" was a twenty-nine-year-old male Iraqi insurgent whose family had received payment and special treatment by Iranian-backed insurgents, as all knew the young man's life was certainly to be sacrificed. Remarkably, he wore no suicide vest. The discussion by his commanders worried that he might detonate himself in his nervousness or that chance might prematurely announce his intentions, harming many others and creating a backlash that was becoming unwelcomed among the forces opposed to American-Iraqi occupation.

The man's death had indeed occurred, but not Isaac's. Rushed to an American army hospital within the green zone, the allegedly safe-protected area, Isaac's life was saved but he now had use of a colostomy, as his colon had been partially destroyed by the bullet and its fragments.

Mike now raced out of his office with his helmet in hand, a bulky space astronaut-looking globe of dense bulletproof patented plexiglass composition allowing even armor piercing rounds to shatter but not traverse its clear dense structure. He had four short blocks to make before and two of his buddies were bringing up the rear with the bulk of his EOD equipment and customized attire. He had run past his Ford F-250 truck and, electronically unlocking its rear cabin doors, grabbed a heavy canvas bag containing the remainder of his personalized vestments, swinging them onto his shoulder while holding his M4 weapon in his right arm.

Various clerks, DOD civilians, and other active-duty navy personnel exiting their cars or walking between office locations in the Naval Yard were suddenly alert as to something serious taking place. The strange noise coming from gate five heard by the civilians, representing the signature of automatic weapon fire to those who had tasted combat, had many already crashing their secure mini-armories housed in each location. The focused immediacy in the appearance of men and women racing to these locked enclosures within several buildings brokered no resistance from those guarding the weapons. Within seconds, buildings were being secured by armed Americans ready to defend their various locations. The vaulted sense of urgency was universal among those having taken up arms to defend their nation.

But this was to be unnecessary. A total of eleven Iranian-trained special operations combatants had been killed. One American lay dead, his torso wedged in between a half-closed guardhouse door, the door itself partially crushed from the weight of the roof collapsing after being rammed by the modified garbage truck. Vivian had been slightly wounded, Matt had suffered several bruises acquired via a hard, ignoble cement surface of the road, and his damaged leg throbbed as if objecting to his rejoining active combat. Jacob's body was untouched, but his thoughts and mind were afire. He realized their actions and the results of this day were fortuitous in the extreme.

A later AAR with extensive interviews with men and women who actually had tasted the bitterness of combat published a summation that was among the most highly classified of reports issued by any Washington effort. In it, they documented the heroic actions of a very small group of outsiders, people within a chain of command, but with no clear responsibility for the investigative interest, the remarkable conclusive aggregates, nor the near unbelievable final activities that defended and held a supposedly secure US military installation in the heart of the country's administrative powered elite.

Their findings temporarily sent shockwaves through the administrative state, the deep waters of the bureaucratic fossilized landscape compiled over generations of transformational rule. Reflective of many before, powerful ruling empires that had fortuitously awakened to a reality that found them unscathed after calamitous and destructive conflict, they had misunderstood the tides of history and the transient nature of their occupation at the apex of influence and power. Their misreading of the past ensured repetitive mistakes so often discussed regarding their predecessors but that somehow felt irrelevant to their present exalted position. And once again, those within this ruling class misidentified and glibly accepted that a "divine force" was responsible for their nation's lofty position and status.

Sadly, this inherent sanctimony espoused their total ignorance of those precedent kings and ancient rulers who had also cited an eerily similar divine right of royalty, unbeholden to earthly restraint, believing their influence and position was eternal—and then finding it was not.

And remarkably, this same AAR might have shunned as ridiculous any acceptance that a young special operations veteran might have been contemplating these very thoughts as he viewed the wreckage of those who had intended to kill Americans.

Jacob's eyes viewed their bodies and the still-steaming engine of the now immobile behemoth green-and-orange refuse truck. Blood was still seeping onto the concrete surface from several of these combatants, including one whose involuntary leg spasms was still brushing the side of his boot against the street's hard surface. Other security personnel were arriving and Mike, adorned in the regalia of his blast suit, seemed to reenact the original moon walk. Designed for maximal protection for its occupant, the suit attempted to deflect or completely inhibit supersonic projectiles that originated from an explosive device as well as reduce the concussive blast wave. With patented layers of Kevlar, now with ceramic plates strategically located to reduce explosive lethality, the suit was state-of-the-art. Mike deliberately strode toward the second van after consulting with Matt, his thoughts recalibrating to those he knew were requisite for survival in disarming what appeared to be the back of a consumer van filled with professional military-grade explosives. He briefly found irony in his need to perform his skills within the city landscape of his nation's capital, but these thoughts vanished as he refocused on the needs at hand.

His protective helmet appeared as a smooth globe. Its surface was a dull green, but the clear plexiglass window allowing visual inspection caught and reflected the morning's growing sunlight. It was cool enough that he didn't have to worry about heat-related stress, as the suit could grow increasingly uncomfortable when surrounding temperatures rose, as in Baghdad's afternoons.

Matt was now securing the area. Others within the navy's police units were arriving, and local law enforcement had redirected traffic closing the road leading into gate five. Matt's rapid assessment of the environment provided for a rather wide circular space of empty. He was taking no chances, as his concern had not lessened. So frequently in Iraq and Afghanistan, American forces had condescendingly dismissed the acuity of their enemy. They had chuckled at the caveman, almost neolithic mentality of a culture that did not want to emerge from the 1200s. But within this arrogant disdain of the Americans was the failure to understand that these same Afghanistan warriors and their ancestors had successfully thwarted all attempts by successive global powers to conquer them. Ancient Persians and those from the subcontinent of India, the British, the Russians, and now the Americans were to form a long, near continuous line of those smirking as to their superiority while dying in futile attempts to subjugate these peoples.

Matt had taken a personal near-intimate oath with his fellow teammates to prohibit such group or collective egotism, instead looking at his enemy through the eyes of one who sees distinct, if not remarkably different, goals than those in the "advanced West," but with the instincts of a predator. And thus, now he was thinking of something that was making his stomach rebel, and a wave of nausea begin.

Remarkably, another man standing not seven yards from him was also considering these same variables as he contemplated what might now be waiting for the Naval Yard. Jacob Noah Roth had tasted the success of surgical precision strikes against adversaries caught unprepared and unaware of

America's lethal potential. But Jacob had also suffered the near-despondent awareness of his nation's naïve foolishness. So much could have been done to prevent the need to rally young men, and now women, for interventions in hostile high-risk environments. Jacob was not gullible; he did not see the world through prisms of artificial beauty. He saw what was, and yet he hoped for the best based on prudent, trenchant considerations of the worst that might just happen. And now he was thinking, similar to one of his closest of friends, that there was a small chance that something else was still afoot.

Special warriors, those celebrated by their respective nations throughout history's expanse, if interviewed, would share that something ill-defined, something amorphous but powerful had suddenly pushed them into action that later was judged heroic, remarkable, anticipatory, or simply unexplainable. The result was often their demise, their last breaths being taken as they successfully finished their sudden "assigned task" or demonstrated via their actions what was necessary for those within the collegium. But more often than not, if such interviews could have been provided or records unearthed, the constancy of being propelled into action by inexplicable forces was the thread of commonality between these individuals who based their lives on action, if not anticipation.

At this moment, 8:37 a.m., Jacob was himself inexplicably being propelled and yelling to Matt as he turned and raced toward the building holding the trial that had been temporarily paused forty-eight hours ago.

"Matt, need to check—possible distraction!" Jacob had already turned and was running at full speed toward the court.

And just as remarkably, Matt understood what was happening and in turn shouted at Vivian, who was dabbing blood away from several superficial forehead lacerations related to exploding fragments of concrete.

"Viv, Jacob—courtroom now!"

She instantly looked up at Matt as he was frantically waving his arm toward Jacob's rapidly diminishing silhouette. Without questioning, she was running before she was aware that she had grabbed her weapon, unconscious of the fact that she had also grabbed two full unused clips of ammunition.

As Jacob's legs churned beneath his torso, his mind raced, considering his options. He rounded the narrow pathway between buildings separating the headquarters of the Naval Judge Advocate's operational center, the navy's legal department, with the special courthouse assigned to hear this most special of issues. He had hoped to find the court facility guarded but absent a need for assistance.

He would be wrong on both accounts; no guards were present. At least none still alive.

Chapter 25

Summarium Judicium
Summary Judgment

Of Jacob's favorite historical military deceptions, the ruse involving the human construction of a horse outside the gates of Troy was a singular preference. For Jacob had actually studied the Trojan War, discussed it for hours with teammates, and lifted military tactics from the events, knowing that much of the "factual basis" is appreciated within the lore of a legendary allegory. But it is precisely because of the symbolic nature of this deception that the story holds lessons for those willing to absorb its subtleties.

Do not underestimate your enemy. Do not assign ossified tactics or inelastic command to their side reflecting the state of talent or culture that surrounds you. Remain vigilant to pure genius and attempt to continually manipulate the chess pieces to their advantage and your vulnerability. Perhaps 3,300 years after Troy made the lethal mistake of opening its gates to the seemingly harmless symbol of their city, allegedly left as a peace offering, a sleeping America awoke to a similar surprise. Who would have thought that the belligerence of Japan and its previous Rape of Nanking would next manifest on a Sunday morning surprise attack, destroying significant assets of the US Navy while Japanese and American diplomats were still discussing delicate issues in Washington, DC?

Jacob had long considered and discussed that the tactical plan to attack Pearl Harbor was audacious, risky, and remarkably atypical for the historic approach of or the Japanese mentality to conduct war—and brilliant. Strategically, its results were a disaster, for Yamamoto, the plans architect, horribly misjudged the impact that their raid would have on the American populace. Pearl Harbor's intent was to force the Americans to sue for peace, a reasonable outcome reflective of a divided and isolationist populace. A populace, generally thought by this Japanese mindset, to be a group of high-living, self-absorbed people unwilling to sacrifice the party life, the comforts, or indulgencies of peace. But within hours, on December 8, 1941, the instantaneous superheated annealing of near-uniform American rage resulted in a declaration of war against the Japanese.

In fact, this misjudgment was to turn the shining luster in the brilliance of their attack on Pearl to ash. Historians later gave much credit to the Japanese in saving Europe from Hitler's remarkable war machine. Without Pearl Harbor, the divisions within America would have been significant; the populace did not want to involve itself in yet another war in Europe after having participated in one less than a quarter of a century earlier! Pearl Harbor fundamentally, instantly, and dramatically changed the calculus.

Now, Jacob was thinking about the Trojan horse planted at gate five and the real goal of the Iranian leadership. They wanted Virginia Mahoney dead. She had killed their leader and was celebrated as the woman who had slain al Al Hassan Abbas. Most intelligence reports noted that American and Iranian interests had experienced a rare single point of alignment regarding both powers desire to degrade and destroy ISIS in 2014, but the endgame was viewed as very different between the two nations. Iranian interests wanted to fill the vacuum created by ISIS, and of course, America wanted to maintain her position as the dominant influencer of Middle East events.

Through 2014–2017, when al Al Hassan Abbas's forces were degraded by American resources linked to Kurdish, democratic Syrian, and Iraqi ground forces, his position as a power player in the politics of the Levant ended. His influence via ISIS (ISIL), corresponding to modern-day Jordan, Lebanon, Syria, and Israel along with other bordering areas, had been dramatically reduced. And thus, to regroup and to maintain his own position, al Al Hassan Abbas had been in talks with Iranian representatives. Iranian concerns are and always have been intended to reduce the presence of American influence in the area, and they will use whomever they can to achieve these goals. Whether it be those who Tehran would not invite to their dinner table or those whom they might have ultimate respect for, it did not matter; the need to reduce American influence in the area, their backyard, was their true primary goal.

Their various conduits for military kinetics to harass Americans have been Hamas, Hezbollah, the Houthis, and remnants of the loosely recoalesced ISIS terror organization. It did not matter that months before, the Sunni ISIS brigades that laid waste to large elements of Northern Iraq and Southern Syria had also butchered and murdered Shi'i Muslims. Iran would harness such distasteful Sunni forces to combat a common enemy: the Americans. And thus, as al Al Hassan Abbas was in the process of changing his position and realigning with Tehran's interests, he was killed by an

American—and an American woman, no less! And just as importantly, their president, the one they called the Orange Man, had subsequently called for the murder one of Tehran's most exalted figures: Ali Ibrhim Arjang. Both variables had been setbacks for Tehran, but the latter was shockingly unacceptable, and the Iranians had long memories.

Thus, the solution to both embarrass the Americans and show the Islamic world who really represented the future of power in the Levant and the Greater Middle East was to murder one Virginia Mahoney. And not just eliminate her, but to do so by Iranian special operatives, succeeding in the most fortified city within the "safest," most "technologically advanced" installations in the "most powerful" country in the world. Social media would be set afire. How delicious, the irony of the toothless tiger being exposed for what it was— unable to protect its own even in the very heart of the country that espoused to be the leader of the world's liberal order. Did the Americans really believe that they could be led by a cognitively impaired, historically corrupt grifter and maintain preeminence throughout the globe? The mullahs in Tehran waited with barely concealed delight.

There was only one small, almost infinitesimally tiny problem. His name was Jacob Noah Roth, and his commitment to his nation superseded any nebulous loyalty to a demented eighty-one-year-old parasite who, even when his cognition had been allegedly intact, found so much comfort in the perpetual repetition of lies as to believe, if not author, a fantasy existence. For this man, whether copying speeches from other leaders or lying about past accomplishments, seemed unable or unwilling to communicate truth, fact, or accurate history. But none of this mattered to Roth. He was a warrior, committed to the concept instilled in him by parents who believed in the uniqueness of the American dream, the governance of the nation by its citizens through honestly elected officials.

Roth was now racing to the front door of the building, and he knew instantly there was trouble. Unknown to him, however, were the targets of his concerns, for even his analytical cognition might not have grasped the inherent duplicity of two individuals responsible for the first body he encountered.

These were two Virginia suburbanites who, by all accounts, had found their version of the American dream. Neighbors would subsequently express shock and near uniform disbelief at the possibility that these two individuals would have the capacity to do evil in the form of deliberate organized murder, within a military unit, no less, and one aligned with Tehran. But these fellow members of the suburban class would be wrong. The "husband" of this pair was an illegal who had found work in an Iranian-owned export business itself owned by individuals in Belgium. The business surprisingly made rather handsome profits and was carefully compliant with US tax laws, as capricious if not arbitrary as they were, but the true owners were Tehran intelligence. They had started a custom carpet and rug company nearly fifteen years earlier in the belief that their agents could use this business as a portal to come and go within the American landscape almost undetected, and they had been correct.

The company catered to the higher-end clientele, placing Asian or Middle Eastern handwoven wool, silk, or blended carpets within the townhouses of Georgetown or the sprawling estates that dotted the Virginia countryside. And thus, the company almost by default was invited into the homes and lives of the powered elites in the DC environment. These very moneyed clients purchasing carpets were also frequently those within critical interfaces of government or civilian-government roles. For each location, pictures were taken, many clandestinely, of irrelevant spaces or sections of the home off-limits to strangers. Silent partners of those arranging delivery or the laying of the carpet slipped into rooms, and papers, postage, and even official documents brought home but carelessly left on the surface of a magnificent rosewood desk in wood-paneled scholarly studies were photographed. These trained MOIS agents, upon encountering security cameras in homes, used their pocket-sized jamming devices to transiently corrupt the images being obtained, hiding their silent movement and activities. But remarkably, more often than not, the security cameras were on the exterior or in the doorways of the main entrance, not within the interiors of these magnificent homes.

Once the photos were obtained, they were itemized and sent back through encrypted messages to MOIS. The alleged husband did not run the business, as his primary job was to gather and categorize the intelligence obtained through the company's legitimate activities, but he was paid a handsome salary skimmed off the top and supplemented by MOIS. The woman was his partner, and by almost any reasonable definition she fit the definition of his wife, but they were never intimate and had never been married. Her role had been assigned by MOIS, and she had been trained as an assassin. As a typical well-off couple, both cohabitated a plush Alexandria home, yet closer inspection of their activities would find that she traveled extensively. Her trips were allegedly for the inspection and purchase of carpets in Europe and the Middle East, but she had taken five trips to support or be the primary kinetic force in eliminating known Iranian dissidents living in Europe. Objectively, she was well trained; the objects of her missions, those targeted by Tehran, were no longer breathing.

The mullahs in Tehran had decided that these two had lived their Western lifestyles long enough and now payment was due to their masters. Each had reluctantly and somewhat bitterly accepted the fact that their lives were to be sacrificed, but each had families and relatives still within Iran subject to imprimatur influence, if not violent reprisal, and thus conceptually, objecting to their mission was not an option. The woman's closest "friend," yet another MOIS asset, worked at the Naval Yard legal division as a highly competent computer engineer, updating and modifying patches for the military's obsolete software systems that in effect ran the day-to-day human resource functions of the naval legal division itself. Her friend had been employed for seven years and received outstanding semiannual reviews, never arguing about compensation, always working overtime when required, and even coming in on holidays to finish or complete tasks. Eventual review by naval investigators examining the web of infiltration by MOIS assets would comment that these characteristics alone, of "never complaining and just working," were so odd as to raise a red flag as to the potential loyalties of the individual—a sad testament to the degrading values found in the American workforce. Sadder still was the degree of vetting absent in the hiring and examination of employees brought into one of the most significant military locations in the United States of America.

This female "friend" employed at the Naval Yard was an attractive forty-three-year-old woman, herself a MOIS agent but void of lethal skills or training. This small missing variable ultimately did not matter. Her task was to transport the Iranian "couple," assets reluctantly sacrificing their spurious roles as owners of a successful exclusive carpet importer and now unveiling their true mission as expendable actors in Tehran's geopolitical play. Ehsan's script: a suicide mission at the Washington Naval Yard. Thus, earlier that same morning at gate six, entering from a side street perpendicular the major artery that faced Matt's gate five, she pulled up to the guardhouse and presented her identification through the open driver's side window.

She waited patiently, seemingly distracted by papers sitting on the center console of her car, as the familiar naval security individual scanned the official Naval Yard entrance permit barcode adherent to the inside of her windshield. The handheld laser scanner connected by Bluetooth to the computer highlighted the barcode and registered "Entrance Allowed." A visual inspection by the guard of the familiar face of the woman driving the car completed the entrance examination. The newly installed steel-reinforced gating structure smoothly rose from its horizontal position parallel to the ground, becoming completely vertical. Additionally, three eight-inch steel concrete-filled pipes positioned directly in front of her automobile, at a height of three feet, descended into the Earth, now even with the pavement, allowing her to drive slowly onto the Naval Yard. Briefly turning to her head to the left and looking up into the man's face while simultaneously offering a single wave of her delicate left hand and smiling, she nudged her automobile forward.

Unrecognized by security, or by any cursory inspection of the automobile, was the slight uneven distribution of the automobile's weight, a suggestion that significant mass was bunched in the rear of the Chevy Malibu. If examined closely, a side view of the car would have demonstrated a slight imbalance; the nose of the car was slightly but definitively elevated. This, however, was not appreciated, nor were the three individuals, the apparent "owners" of the carpet business and an additional MOIS agent: one woman and two men. Each possessed modified Heckler and Koch MP5 automatic weapons and body armor. Nearly seven hundred pounds pulled the car's rear closer to the cement, all hidden in the trunk. Anyone opening the trunk without the rapid tapped sequence, a simple expressed code of striking the metal trunk with their finger, would be met with automatic weapon fire form the occupants within.

As this attractive forty-three-year-old driver so easily facilitated entry into the Naval Yard, she maneuvered within its tightly car-lined streets to the reserved parking for the legal personnel. Wedged alongside the massive building was a row of signs positioned prominently but elegantly just inside the bordering curb of parking. The first denoted the

"Judge Advocate General," followed by six other prominent ranking officers. The woman, Darya's, space was one of the unmarked rear slots, and this was perfect for her. As she pulled in between two parallel white lines at the far end of the assigned row of spaces, she nosed the automobile to a stop. She now faced the back of building. Large rectangular windows framed in gray metal were only now beginning to reflect the morning's light. A large white oak, claimed among Virginia's most stunning, had been left alone to grow and now partially obscured the back of the gray edifice of her office building. She fought her anxiety but managed to kill the engine and text a single word, "Ready," before opening the gray side door of the Malibu and pushing herself out to step the short distance to the rear of the car.

The three individuals each possessed a key fob that would automatically open the trunk, but they waited for her to provide the specific tapped sequence: two, followed by three gentle audible taps. She had scanned the back narrow parking area, and she was momentarily alone within the beehive of activity surrounding the designated center for naval legal affairs. Inside of this building, a large courtroom used for appellate hearings had now been modified for a trial of a woman accused of murdering an ISIS guard protecting al Al Hassan Abbas. Darya secretly had applauded this brave woman and her actions in killing this depraved excuse for a man, his heinous actions linked to an internet presence that he himself had cultivated. She found his very physical appearance disgusting, at times unkept, unclean, obese, and entitled, the very epitome of those quasi-self-anointed religious figures within her culture who thought themselves superior, above all Iranians. And, of course, clearly superior to all females.

She had quietly grown accustomed to her assigned role in America and even celebrated her independence, her daily options allowing, if not demanding, self-directed management of her life's mundane choices. For many, such enjoyment would have been dismissed as pedestrian, but Darya knew what awaited her back in Iran and the daily burdens that Iranian women experienced. Many in her beautiful country had long whispered that if revolution was truly to come, it would be the women who both ignited it and pushed it through to consequence. If her people were to be freed from the whims of blinkered, crusty old men, self-adorned in costumes of religious purity, who viewed women as a necessary evil within the biological perpetuation of their species, it would be those of her gender that would end their glacial age of intolerance.

But she had been ordered to assist this three-person team, and her family still resided in Neyshabur. Her brothers and father were proud of her ascent within MOIS. Proud and a bit stunned, as she had tested far superior to her siblings, the disappointment registering in her father that his daughter and not one of his three sons possessed their mother's intelligence and his cunning. But such was the will of Allah. But she could not declare herself a political refugee and seek asylum in America; if she did, her family would be imprisoned, her brothers and father certainly executed. And thus, although she had grown to enjoy the Western respect for her gender and found humor and growing interest in the games played by these American males who made it clear they wanted to enjoy her company, and her body, her fate was sealed.

As she stood by the trunk of her Malibu, her delicate fingers tapped the code. And while opening the trunk, looking both ways, she continued to find no other individuals within the cloistered area. Immediately, three people, all wearing the outerwear of sports coats loosely fitting covering their blunt MP5 automatic weapon, slithered from the trunk and stood closely packed beside her. Each had similar dark pants, including the female, that covered kneepads strapped to their legs, as they wanted a superficial appearance betraying business attire. The open hood of the car's trunk shielded them from any cursory inspection from onlookers peering through the back windows of the gray building.

They walked briskly but in pairs, again relying on the superficial deceit that two professional couples were reporting to the legal center for work. But as they rounded the front corner of the gray stoned building, the first of two uniformed naval police guards, positioned at the front entrance, turned to face them. The sidewalk just wide enough to accommodate two paired adults, the woman employee slightly in front of the man at her side. The uniformed guard immediately sensed that one half of this "couple" did not belong and approached them, raising his left hand—the universal stop signal—with his palm facing out. Within a second, the Iranian male swung his strapped Heckler up and pulled the trigger. The muffled sound of gas escaping from a punctured tire along with an altered popping emanated from the sound suppressor.

The uniformed security officer was hit four times in the chest and neck, spinning and then collapsing with blood pumping vigorously onto the manicured lawn. He died quickly.

The other guard, halfway through the double doors, immediately spun and tried to get back inside, but the second Iranian male, well trained, had already targeted him and let loose a similar burst from his automatic weapon, penetrating his upper posterior thigh on the left before climbing in an arc to land three rounds in his back. This man staggered into the building and collapsed. The first Iranian was already holding the door open with his left hand and scanning the hallway leading into the modified court room. A female clerk rounding the corner from the side hallway heard the flopping clatter of the security officer's fall, and as she looked up, she dropped her paperwork as her hand reached to cover her mouth and scream. This sound was truncated by another hissing of escaping gas accompanied by the popping as seven rounds exited at supersonic velocity from the Heckler. The woman caught the burst in the abdomen through the front of her pale-green silk blouse. Her arms lunged outward as her thorax doubled over, her neck extended and her face momentarily looking toward the ceiling before her body crumpled to the polished tessellated stone and concrete floor's surface.

Inside of the functionally modified but beautifully paneled appellate courtroom, Virginia knew exactly what the sound was. She wheeled to one of the guards and authoritatively commanded him to give her his handgun and at the same time shouted for everyone in the room to get to the floor. Members of the active-duty jury, almost all combat veterans, had already begun to push people to the floor and look for weapons. The foreman, himself a naval captain, had pulled the Beretta from the closest guard's holster before the young man even felt his presence. The captain, in full uniform, ordered the guard to race to procure more weapons. The guard knew authority and experience when he encountered it and immediately ran out the rear exit used by members of the jury.

And then the double back doors, made of exquisite white oak, polished to an almost perfect reflective surface, burst open, and the superior training of the Iranians was in display as they formed a tiered composition of three. The single woman was resting on her knee, her partner on his, and the final armed member positioned above them, forming a wall of automatic weapon's lethality, spraying the room as the doors reached their terminal opening position. Two civilians who had been slow to understand the orders being shouted at them were immediately struck by 9x19mm Parabellum rounds, and their bursting wounds triggered screams by terrified gallery occupants unprepared for the early morning carnage.

Virginia Mahoney, unshackled for her courtroom appearance and now with her hands uncuffed, had been tossed the guard's M11 Sig Sauer P-228 sidearm, as he understood that she had a plan and he did not. He also had a second weapon, a Glock that he had already pulled and checked to ensure the round was chambered. He instinctively pulled her attorney to the floor, and their survival would allow them to share the somewhat humorous recollection that his face had nearly smashed her nose and lips as though in a semiviolent first kiss. Catherine, the legendary prosecutor turned defender of one Virginia Mahoney, and the twenty-eight-year-old guard wearing the US Navy emblem were on the floor in a near lover's embrace. But that was only his first move, as he immediately was up, positioned on bended knee, and aiming at the back double doors now being flung open.

In the seconds Virginia had before the double doors flew open, she raced to the back of the courtroom and now was hugging the wall, her weapon extended in front of her, ready to fire. The doors exploded in movement, opening violently, and Virginia saw the terminal ends of the barrels of the Hecklers were visible, but their owners were not. Not yet. But as the three-person assassination team instantly viewed the room, they realized that the front of the large room had almost no standing people and their target was thus hidden. Their orders were to eliminate her, but as they instantly took in the contents of the room, they also took fire from Catherine's guard and a naval captain who had grabbed the other guard's weapon.

One of the Iranians hit in the neck, just above his protective body armor, reacted with his legs undergoing spasmodic jerking. He suddenly lurched and jammed his much larger body into the woman at his side. Pushed into the courtroom, temporarily fighting for balance, she now was in full view of Virginia, who took aim and rapidly fired three rounds at her left supraclavicular area from twelve yards.

The Iranian woman's head snapped back, caught just below the ear by Mahoney's second round, which alone was lethal. Her hands flew upward as if in prayer, the brain discharging and commanding her arms to raise but without purpose as blood sprayed from the ragged gash of the bullet's entry.

The woman's Heckler crashed to the floor, metal clattering announcing the end of its role in the planned horror. The sound was followed by a hollow thud as if a melon had been dropped on a rural cabin's wooden floor.

Her head ungraciously bounced a single time as it struck the polished pine surface, then as her legs spasmodically discharged, her once attractive face rammed into the oak gallery chairs, her eyes still open but no longer seeing.

Virginia was still kneeling, both arms extended. The clean dull black surface of the borrowed sidearm still held, aiming, but her eyes had followed the dying woman's last movement.

She failed to anticipate the near simultaneous actions of the only remaining member of the three, this last man sensing the direction of the lethal fire that took his colleague. As he spun through the door, his Heckler beginning its lethal burst, the trajectory of the lead missiles made a near perfect line, arcing while almost evenly spaced as they first punctured the highly polished cherrywood molding at the juncture of the ceiling and the side wall. Bullets cascaded toward Virginia's position, a near flawless contour, ready to intercept her and kill her.

The joining of that line and the young woman at its intersection meant Virginia would die. The mullahs in Tehran would be satisfied as to the team's success, their family's rewarded with cash and prestige.

But in the ever-accelerating moments of kinetic force between those who intended to harm and those tasked to defend, two things happened at the same moment, one foreseeable, one not. One was Jacob Noah Roth, and the other was Rich Hansept.

One lived as a hero, his legacy unchanged. One existed as an angry coward, but his memoir would be forever transformed.

One would continue to live and receive the respect, if not awe of a legendary combatant, and one would die, no longer ireful, no longer a poltroon.

It is said that all men have at least one chance at redemption. Perhaps, but for Rich Hansept, his pent-up hatred for the talents so evident in Virginia Mahoney had been his pernicious disease, weakening the very fabric of his being. And then in seconds, as if God tapped him on the shoulder and directed him, giving him one last chance . . .

He took it.

It was to be his final act as a man of honor—an epitaph craved now earned, now rewarded.

As the connecting dots of lethal purpose sped toward Virginia, their final locus of intent took mere seconds to arrive. But in that brief interval, Hansept had already traversed the court's distance and suddenly was flying over Mahoney's left shoulder. She turned her head slightly as the black-uniformed figure flew by, blocking her view and, for the seconds that were needed, shielding her. And then it was over.

Two rounds struck Hansept. One at the base of his skull, killing him instantly, and one in the center of his spine. He was unaware of his surroundings as his body's momentum continued forward, crashing into the wooden-paneled wall. The angle of his neck was suddenly awkward, his mouth ajar, his eyes open but sightless. Blood poured from his partially severed cervical connection to his head.

And again, as those vital seconds passed, Virginia now could see the Iranian in front of her—but he, too, was in motion.

Jacob had entered the unsecured front of the building, and with his M4A1 held firmly in his extended arms, he immediately visualized only a sliver of a black figure moving from a kneeling position to a crouched but deliberate advance. This was the position of one who was firing, one who was killing, and this shadowed figure did not belong.

In less than a second, Jacob took in the court's entrance and the spent cartridges. The figure was the man intent on killing the woman he loved. Although he could not have articulated this thought, he nevertheless instinctively knew it as fact.

And thus, without consideration, he pulled the trigger of his weapon as he moved closer at the angle that exposed the figure to his line of fire. He did not stop until his entire clip was emptied, two quick bursts of nine remaining rounds.

The figure, clad in a loosely fitting sports coat and yet wearing black tactical clothing and protective body armor, was hit seven times by Roth's supersonic projectiles. His exposed left arm was nearly torn off as three rounds hit his shoulder, pulling his weapon down and to the left as he stood up, exposing himself. Two more rounds, traveling slightly less than 2,800 feet per second, harnessed their kinetic force as the first deformed the top of his body armor, eliciting intense discomfort in his left front thoracic area but not penetrating his body. The second round four centimeters above and slightly to the right tore into the base of his neck, its lead missile immediately flattening slightly as it met the resistance of muscle and turned into a vicious oval scythe cutting deeply into his spine. As his head snapped involuntarily forward, as though bowing to Jacob, the top of his skull was exposed. And thus, the last of Jacob's rounds plowed into the top of his head, penetrating and disintegrating into small pellet-sized leaden spheres. Their force vaporized the contents, creating a literal cone of superheated tissue, the remnants of his brain's frontal lobe instantly obliterated. The man crumpled to the floor, and a strange silence descended as though a vacuum had been created.

The aroma of sulfur dioxide like spoiled eggs filled the air. Whimpers now became audible, and then a few screams.

Roth yelled, "All quiet, please, now! Mahoney, check in."

Virginia, knowing that her teammate was assessing injuries, called back, "All good. No damage!" Then Mahoney herself yelled, "Jeremy, check in!"

And the guard who had tossed Virginia his gun called out, "All good, no harm!"

"Captain, you guys ok?"

"Anyone else?" The captain who had selectively removed the sidearm from his nearby guard before ordering him to acquire more spoke quietly, but distinctly, "No injuries personally. Have two wounded, one looks critical . . . calling EMS."

As he uttered these words, he was moving to check on people as they lay on the floor.

In a similar fashion, Mahoney and Roth moved to investigate, the latter standing over the three bodies and systematically searching them for IEDs, or suicide vests. No delayed timers, no explosives, and no life was left within the three dead Iranians.

As Vivian appeared, she silently surveyed the carnage. She was accompanied by the terrorist's driver, the slack-jawed attractive forty-three-year-old Iranian HR employee, now slumped at the door. Her face registered horror, her eyes wide in stunned silence and her hands pulled behind her and zip-tied as Vivian's M4A1 barrel rested at the base of her neck.

As Jacob stood, he found Mahoney standing looking down at Hansept, still awkwardly positioned as he was partially jammed into the wall, his neck bent at an unnatural angle, his mouth partially open. A small amount of blood seeped from his mouth and the back of his finely pressed and dry-cleaned livery, from the collar to the midback, was wet. A viscous deep-red jelly material that revealed its ruby color upon dripping onto the floor had soaked his dress uniform.

An individual who had despised Mahoney because of her talents, her beauty, and had deeply secretly desired her almost more than the oxygen needed to maintain his life. Hansept had wanted her destroyed after his failure in the mission that had killed al Al Hassan Abbas. He had been the prosecution's star witness, pointing to her role in killing an unarmed, bound, and securely detained ISIS guard. Her presence reminded him daily of his lack of courage and her abundance of the same. And he hated Roth almost more than Mahoney, as Hansept knew that Virginia loved Roth and Roth had returned the emotive force, establishing a couple of legendary influence and dignity. He had, at the most elemental level, simply wanted her to love him, and in truth he craved Roth's respect, if not his nonphysical love, too.

His last act had been to prove that they had been wrong about him, that he, too, was of their rare breed. An individual more selfless than even them, as he had tossed his life away knowing he would die but did so joyously to protect the woman he secretly loved. The woman who would never render even the slightest romantic notion concerning him, but he, too, was worthy of her, as worthy as Roth.

And Hansept had been successful in that. As she stood looking down at him, the tears flowed from her eyes. She bent to hold his uninjured shoulder and simply kneeled, looking down at the battered remnants of this young warrior who had sacrificed his life for hers. And in that moment, Roth understood that Hansept had procured in death that which he was not able to acquire in life.

Roth climbed over the last of the Iranians and stood on the opposite side of Hansept. Suddenly, his body altered, and as Virginia looked up, sensing the change in the man she loved, she saw sadness, if not sorrow.

But also she saw in Roth a communicated honor, bestowed to one who had given all he had to offer.

For Roth had rendered the final military acknowledgment of respect.

Roth was standing, his rifle held in his left hand, the fingers of his right against his forehead.

A salute, the final statement of heartfelt remembrance now present.

Virginia in turn stood and also assumed this last customary act of respect. Both stood there, unaware that the guards in the front of the courtroom, then the captain, and then slowly all of the active-duty military personnel and several of the former military members had also stood. Seeing these two at the back of the room standing over their fallen comrade, each also rendered their respectful acknowledgments.

And thus, for seven seconds, anyone who viewed the now-silent courtroom, beautifully lined with highly polished cherry and Virginia white oak, would have witnessed all members of the armed forces standing in dutiful silence, providing traditional recognition to a man, a colleague, a fellow soldier lost in combat.

How does one gather a receipt for the value of another's soul? A soul vibrant and promising only seconds before, now extinguished, asked instantly to sleep forever? One cannot. But surviving warriors—battered, weary, if not exhausted—standing within countless scarred and blood-soaked fields have understood there must be a greater, a more deserving purpose. Throughout the near infinite motion of this planet's repetitive journey through the Creator's void, countless eyes and hearts have sought such understanding, seeking a shred of equanimity as a balance for the loss of those held dear. In the end, it is remembrance, the ancient currency of respectful acknowledgment to those who have given their everything.

Epilogue

Standing in front of the senior captain, her eyes locked with his, the judge's expression was unreadable. It was nine days after the events that had captivated the world, that had put the nation on war footing, with political opportunists demanding indiscriminate bombing of Iranian cities and towns, sinking of their naval vessels, and even some suggesting it was time to use tactical nuclear weapons against the mullahs. But for Virginia, it was time to accept the court's verdict. There she stood, relaxed but focused. The decorated captain held her eyes carefully, then almost rhythmically articulated the findings of the court. And slowly, as though priceless scented oil seeping through delicate cloth, his professionalism gave way to evident personal satisfaction.

Virginia Lois Mahoney had served her nation. She had completed a mission authorized by her president, and she had been uniquely responsible for the success of the mission to eliminate a rabid parasite who had butchered young boys, girls, and grandmothers solely because of their altered beliefs in the Creator. He had also harmed a single American, a woman who was dedicated to serve, to assist, and to comfort those caught within the carnage of Syria. And for this latter act, this religious fraud was terminated, and Virginia had actually been the person responsible for his ignoble end.

She was to remain on active duty, to remain within the special operations theater of activity, and to be released immediately without discipline, forfeiture of pay, and loss of rank or status. The case was dismissed with prejudice.

Catherine turned to her and stated in almost a sad, reminiscent tone, "It's almost as though they want this entire effort to vanish . . ."

And Virginia, turning to her legal representative and now dear friend, responded, "They are embarrassed, ashamed, and frightened as to being found out. Thus, warriors have decided."

Catherine nodded, accepting the wisdom and the understated veracity of her client's comment.

The large courtroom was superficially unchanged, the beauty of its architecture denoted by the inviting auburn cherrywood molding, still gleaming its soft luster in the artificial light. Hanging bronze and iron fixtures representing a style from the 1920s with frosted globes still reflected light to both the ceiling and the polished smoothed pine plank wooden floor. The gate and wooden barrier of Virginia white oak, found throughout the eastern foothills, remained as a boundary between the gallery and the working space of the legal participants. Its subtle grain interposed within the solid wood, and both remained polished to a near perfect reflection.

And yet, the room had been irrevocably altered. A memorial had transformed the previously sterile legal environment. As though in mourning, a somber wisdom permeated within the four walls, a sobriety of loss distinct and embracing anyone who entered. A human being had died protecting those within this room. Human beings had killed those trying to harm innocents and tear at the very fabric of the nation assembled within this same space. And human beings representing evil had been turned back, unable to shake the foundations or beliefs of those assembled within its space. And thus, the room, its contents, its subtle energy would never be the same.

Closer inspection of the left wall upon entering, near the elegant cherrywood molding, revealed two small holes separated by nearly four feet. The delicate perimeters of each defect were uneven, slightly chipped if not somewhat ragged —footprints of bullets left as a reminder. The senior admiral overseeing naval legal affairs had forbidden their erasure. There would be no expurgation of what they symbolized.

On the ancient pine planking, close inspection would now reveal remnants of darkened stain, again a testament to the sacrifice of one who had stood firm and was unbending in the face of evil, willing to spill his life's energy and sacrifice his future to ensure victory. Maintenance found that the stains could not be readily removed, and again the admiral demanded—and all had instantly agreed—that this precious discoloration would remain.

Unwitnessed during the latter hours of each shift, a quiet older man in charge of cleaning the floors of this room would stop each day, examine the altered pine, and, ensuring he was alone, would bend and pat the stain twice. A gesture of his respect, veneration. Moving a single solid wooden chair to stand over the stain, slightly displaced from the last row of the gallery, he ensured this "damaged" pine would not be touched by anyone's shoes. This was now hallowed ground, and identical to the rolling fields of Gettysburg where souls populated those hills, one also occupied this courtroom.

Evil must be met with force, must be eliminated. All entering this now sacred ground would immediately search out these two remnant small defects within the smooth surface of the wall. And as they looked to the pine's discolored planks, they would now, too, acknowledge the burden of justice.

Hansept had been buried two days earlier, his family present, his larger military family also in attendance. All paid their final respects. Virginia and Roth stood side by side. Pickney and Ostrowski as well as their entire special operations team attended and rendered their collective tribute to one who had died with principle, with meaning. His life's purpose had been realized.

Four days after the unpleasantness of being held as a prisoner by her own government, Virginia Lois Mahoney sat with the man she loved and tried to pace the energy coming from him, as his devotion and commitment were remarkably intense. He was in love with her, and it was as powerful as it was pure, visible to all who looked. Broderick Pickney had asked to buy the couple a drink, knowing that it would be a cup of coffee or turn into dinner, as neither consumed alcohol. He also had simply stopped imbibing long ago. Not out of fear, ideology, or purpose, but simply because he felt it dulled his senses, and he would never underestimate when they would be needed for survival. Such warriors lived by their senses.

Stan Ostrowski was also present, and between him and his closest friend, Pickney, was a beautiful blonde-haired nurse, a supervisor at Georgetown Hospital. His companions assembled at the table could readily observe that Stan was rapidly coming to terms with the fact that he, too, was in love, and the object of this powerful emotive force was the blue-eyed small-town Wisconsin native sitting next to him. Roth had never seen Stan fumble for words, and Broderick, twice in the five-minute interval, puckered his lips, attempting to control a smile that would flash his brilliant white teeth as he listened to the garbled words emanating from his closest male friend.

Stan, somewhat exasperated by his inability to smoothly discuss his views, thought he must sound the fool. But Jaclyn, born with a nurse's transparent compassion, had spent years comforting grieving families. Those having witnessed the last moments of loved ones surrendering to cancer had received angelic consolation from this small Wisconsin town's former varsity football cheerleader. Thus, she immediately sensed Stan's hesitant demeanor. Able to communicate hope and provide support to strangers encountering pivotal moments within life's kaleidoscope of shared experiences, Jaclyn understood Stan's jumbled yet wonderful sincerity. She knew he was nervous, and she was deeply touched, complimented, and warmed as she recognized it was because of her presence and his need to impress and perhaps connect with her.

Jaclyn suddenly reached out and gently closed her hand around Stan's large powerful left paw. "You don't mind, do you? They're holding hands under the table . . ." she said, gesturing to Roth and Virginia.

Stan visibly flushed, but not from embarrassment— simply from joy and the realization that this lady was perhaps the one.

Virginia's eyes caught Jaclyn's, and Mahoney smiled but also delivered that protective message that Stan was her brother, that he was special and NOT to be harmed. Jaclyn's focus sharpened momentarily, her response given. Virginia immediately relaxed.

No need to worry. Jaclyn, in fact, was serious about the man whose large hand now encircled hers.

Broderick stood as a stunningly attractive woman with perfect chocolate-colored skin and a regal stature was escorted to their table by the maître d'. The older man, wearing a black short-cut jacket, gently held her elbow as he approached the table. The woman's lithe, almost willowy figure seemed to glide as she walked, her slender hips floating, her shoulders moving in unison. And then she smiled, her teeth perfect and brilliantly white. The older man, as though practiced to perfection, bequeathed her arm to Broderick as he pulled out the chair for her. Broderick assisted this statuesque beauty as she took her seat at the table.

He turned to his friends with a very slight inclination to Stan—his most trusted friend, a man who had saved Broderick from death—and as though intoning the appearance of royalty, he said, "Folks, this is Amaka . . . means 'beautiful' in Hausa in Nigeria."

The woman lowered her eyes in humility, perhaps embarrassed by this powerful man so easily telling strangers the origin of her name.

But Stan Ostrowski and Roth, both standing, smiled and said in unison, "Welcome!"

Stan added, "We are honored that you would join us. We are so glad to meet you. This man is my best friend, my brother. I live in awe of him." Stan's smile was genuine, but not missed was Broderick's momentary flash of surprise and profound humility in response to his candor.

Broderick then stated, "This man is Jacob Roth, our leader and our older brother. He is who we aspire to be." Roth's mouth fell open slightly, not missed by Amaka nor Jaclyn. Virginia looked down, hiding her eyes that had suddenly grown moist.

Roth tilted his head as if to object, but his face suddenly grew serious. The enormity of the statement unsettled him. Not because of flattery or false praise, but because of a profound responsibility to those he took into harm's way. He loved these men. These men were his family, and he would suffer their defeats, setbacks, and injuries as though he himself had been touched by harm.

But it was Virginia who now stood. Speaking to Jaclyn and then to Amaka, she raised her glass and said quietly, "May I offer a tribute to one who is not here, unable to join us tonight, but who will always be close to our hearts? An individual who put herself in danger to assist those suffering in the most ancient form of harm, war. May we offer a solemn remembrance to a special lady, one who was taken too young. Catherine Morgan, we salute you. You are not forgotten."

Note from the Author

Thank you for reading my book. It is a work of fiction, and there are likely numerous military and legal errors due to my lack of experience in evolving military weaponry and CIA technical abilities to surveil. I write from the heart, and was moved to write this to ensure that the world did not forget Kayla Mueller. I am a nobody and warrant little interest, but my heart ached for the loss of this innocent soul.

www.ingramcontent.com/pod-product-compliance
Lightning Source LLC
Chambersburg PA
CBHW051056030726
47504CB00006B/1647